Tilling Time Telling Time

Karen Lorene

Cover design by Madeline Courtney.

ISBN: 0-9618302-7-1
ISBN-13: 978-0-9618302-7-4

To the strong women in my life:

Grandma Laing
Grandma Geiss
Mom: Mildred Geiss

Inspiration crew:

Don, Sammy and Helga, of course

To the women I work with everyday:

Madeline Courtney, Gallery Manager
Nancy Mēgan Corwin
Trudee Hill
Nadine Kariya
Dana Shaw
Lorraine Vagner
Susan Welch

To the women I write with:

Claudia Bach
Harriet Cannon
Kristina Danilchik
Sharon Goldberg
Netter Hansen
Susan Jostrom
Susan Landgraf
(and two great guys: James Stark and Vlado Vulovic)

And a special thank you to my editor:

Susan Jostrom

And one final reader:

Merrill Ringold

"We tell ourselves stories in order to live."
-Joan Didion

CHAPTER ONE

MY PART-TIME JOB IN THE ADMINISTRATION BUILDING AT THE UNIVERSITY OF WASHINGTON

Friday, March 24, 1967

From my desk I can see all of Red Square. Hand in hand, couples cross the brick expanse. I swear the entire campus is nothing but couples. Everyone's a twosome. Makes my head hurt. Sixteen more minutes and I'm finished for the day—I won't have to look at them.

But, I'm hopeful. Maybe, just maybe, a miracle will happen. If a giant miracle doesn't happen, it'll be another Friday night alone. Entirely.

Even in this bad mood, all day I've worked at being nice to all those get-up-and-go irritating students who apply for early fall registration, loans, scholarships. And if it hadn't been for Grandma Millie's words, "Good manners are a mirror," I swear I would let loose with a slew of spikey, demanding, pointedly-specific directions to every idiot presenting an incomplete, unsigned, unreadable, undated application. Well, sure, sometimes I roll my eyes. But, I don't yell, "You over-anxious dim-wit!"

But today hasn't ended. And perhaps, just maybe, someone nice, intelligent, good-looking, available, will walk through that door. And? We'll fall in love.

I call across the room, "Dorothy, is that too much to ask?"

"What?"

"Is it too much to ask for love? Even a little love?"

She keeps right on typing.

For the moment, waiting for the clock to finish off the day, I close my eyes and there I am: home alone, curled up with *Glamour* magazine, eating peanut butter from the jar—dateless.

The door bangs open and in walks some guy. My desk is closest to the door, so Dorothy keeps on typing and I get the crazies who walk in at the very end of the day expecting the world.

"Excuse me?" he says.

Why is that a question for crying out loud? So irritating. I sit up. I move the pencil holder from the left side of the desk to the right side of the desk. Decisively. In case he thinks I was sleeping.

"Yes?" I answer his question with a question.

What about this guy? He's certainly not 'the one.' He stands in front of me out of breath, collar crooked, leather jacket open, shirt label sticking up the back of his neck, with this ridiculous brown hemp bag where a bumper sticker goes from corner to corner: IMPEACH THE F…ER. It's not that I disagree; it's just so old. And his shoes with little dots on the toes like my dad's shoes. Strangest of all, his jeans are pressed. With a crease of all things! Who wears pressed jeans? And then there's this ivory scarf inside his jacket—with fringe. Who does he think he is? Errol Flynn?

The guy hands me an envelope.

I extract his application. Small, precise writing. I examine it. "It's not typed." (I tell him this knowing full well it does not have to be typed.) I can play this question game: "Andrew Althaus? You're transferring from South Seattle Community College?"

He doesn't answer. His eyes narrow and he smiles with his mouth shut, so in effect, he looks a little mean. Why? Why is he looking mean at me? It's the chatty kind of thing I often ask—something to say while I check if he's filled in all the spaces.

I can't help myself. I spit out the words, "Your transcripts?"

He nods at the envelope and in that nod, seems to imply it's *me* that has some kind of a problem. I re-check the envelope. Find his transcripts. Pull back my shoulders and I enunciate precisely, "Okeydokey, Mr. Althaus! That will do."

"When will I hear?"

"Two weeks. Maybe three. Sometime soon." With a single whack I staple the pages together and I slap them in the "IN" box. Without making eye contact, I continue, "Depends on if you qualify for assistance." I could have been *bitchier.* I could have said, "Don't you realize not everybody qualifies?"

Then I do something I know I'm not supposed to do. I pick up his papers; flip through them until I find his grades. I run a bright red fingernail under each line. I'm preparing to tell him not to get his hopes up. Except? His grades? 4.0, 4.0, 4.0!

"Amazing!" I look at him, all astonished, and I say, "You could qualify for a scholarship!"

"I'm here for a loan," he spits out the words, "I don't believe in scholarships."

"What do you mean you don't believe in scholarships? How does one not *believe* in scholarships? They exist!"

He steps forward, puts both hands on my desk, and leans into my space. "I meant, for me," he answers and each word is as sour as a slice of lemon. "Someone who doesn't actually *need* scholarship money, someone who can work, someone who isn't below the poverty level—that someone should *not* apply for scholarships." He steps back and pulls at the cuffs of his shirt, stares at me and says like a bully, "So, if it's okay with you, I'm applying for a loan."

"I was just trying to be helpful."

He doesn't let up, "It is not helpful when you condescend to someone who just drove through an hour's traffic to get this god-damned paper here on time!" The anger in his voice grows. "So, unless there's something else I need to do…"

I return the papers to the "IN" box. "That's all then," I say and I pick up the spread of papers that cover my desk. I tap them into perfect alignment. "That will do!" my words fill the room and I can see that Dorothy isn't typing. She's staring at the two of us, totally immersed in this little interchange.

I stand. I look right at him. I can't believe someone has spoken to me like that. In this office. He doesn't get it. I might just be a summer worker, but for the summer I am, as they told me in my interview, a "keeper" of the University's money. A competent, good gate-keeper.

"Thank you," I snap. He gets the message. He pulls the bag over his shoulder to reveal another bumper sticker: TODAY IS THE FIRST DAY OF THE REST OF YOUR LIFE. How corny is that?

He doesn't say goodbye. He doesn't say thank you. He pushes the door out of his way. I can hear the clip of his wing-tips down the hall.

Dorothy giggles, "Well, you handled that with finesse!"

"Don't laugh. He was awful. What's wrong with this world?"

I hold the carriage of the typewriter as if to control something in the room. Dorothy answers as if she hasn't heard every word. "What do you mean what? I think you mean who?"

"You're right. It's me. Is there something wrong with me? Eric dumps me…"

And even though I've only known Dorothy for two weeks, she says, "You promised you wouldn't say his name again."

"I know, I know. What is it then?"

"Nothing. You're just between times."

"Maybe it's because I cut my hair. Men like long hair. Lots of long hair. Why did I ever cut it? Well, to spite Eric. He wanted me to look like

Joan Baez. Sing like Joan Baez. Now I look like nobody. And I can't even sing."

"Your hair's great. You're fine. The minute you quit looking, someone will appear. Believe me. Brad and I met and married the minute I gave up the search."

"Dorothy, how do you do that?"

"What?"

"Be sure. I'm so not sure. Of anything." I slump down into my chair, close my eyes. Why is life like this? Dorothy isn't that pretty. Dorothy isn't that smart. But there she is: married, settled, complete, identified, secure.

"You didn't notice, but he was interesting," Dorothy says as she slides the cover over her typewriter, pulls her coat from the coat rack, and waits for me at the door.

"Interesting? You've got to be kidding! If looks could kill, I'd be vaporized. He was an ass."

"Maybe so, but you upped the ante," Dorothy says. "First, I think he's going to ask you for coffee, and then I think he might turn the desk over. On top of you."

"He hated me and I didn't even do anything."

"You checked his transcripts. That's why they put everything in envelopes, so people can't see them."

"I *peeked* at his transcripts." I retrieve my purse and books from the bottom desk drawer. "Hard to believe he had such good grades."

"Let me quote you as of yesterday: 'Some students take easy courses and go to the dumbest school to get good grades.'"

"I said that? In haste. Forget I ever said it." I pull at my mini-skirt. Button my jean jacket. This morning I thought I looked cool. Now I just feel stupid. Doubly stupid. And I do say dumb things. In defense of my stupidity, I say, "Who knows. But someone irons his jeans. He's probably not even available."

"Maybe *he* irons his jeans."

"What kind of guy irons his jeans?"

"Well, maybe a nice, smart, good-looking guy irons his jeans. You blew it."

I feel terrible. I wasn't nice. No wonder Eric left me for a petite sorority pledge. Six months already, and Eric still shows up in my dreams. Two years of going steady. Now I'm twenty-one and everyone I know has a guy. I'll grow old and be a spinster. I'll never fall in love again. I probably won't even have the chance. But? Maybe love isn't worth the pain and depression.

Dorothy waits for me as we push through the heavy oak doors of the Administration Building. From the top of the stairs Red Square glows. Across the expanse of cinnamon colored bricks, a slight breeze pushes pink petals from the Yoshina cherry trees that line the Quad.

"I'd love to invite you for dinner to meet Brad, but we have our couples' night tonight."

Just the word, "couples" makes me sad. Sadder.

In silence, we walk to the center of the Quad where the paths converge. Below Denny Hall where we go different ways, Dorothy spreads her arms and says, "Spring is the most magical time, isn't it? Like we live in a big bowl of pink popcorn."

I can barely answer, "Spring? Magical? Maybe for you."

"Think of it this way. He didn't really speak to you. And you were his match. At least you weren't boring. Maybe he'll return. Just to figure you out."

"Like, who's that girl who was truly horrible?"

"Why not?"

Dorothy stands in front of me and raises a finger as if she's about to teach me something: "Quit trying! Consider this—what doesn't kill you, makes you strong!"

"Oh, sure. Nothing like being strong. On a Friday night!"

She calls as she walks away, "Got to run! See you Monday." She waves her hand in a shooing motion, "Go see a movie! *Barefoot in the Park* is at the Neptune."

I don't answer. No way am I going to see a ridiculous romantic movie. Romance doesn't exist. And if it does, it sure doesn't feel like it does.

CHAPTER TWO

A TAPED CONVERSATION

Sunday, March 26, 1967

My life isn't all for nothing. Some things are interesting—my Creative Writing class and my Russian Literature class.

Here's how: take Dr. Zhivago. Lara and Yuri separately walk across this huge Russian tundra. They meet. Coincidence! Something like that happened to me. Mom finds a tape recorder at a neighbor's garage sale. Grandma Millie is intrigued. They play with the tape recorder. They sing songs into the tape recorder. Mom writes to say how much fun they are having. I write back. I ask if they might want to send tapes back and forth. And that very day, I find a tape recorder in the window of Bartell Drugs. On sale. $15.88. I walk into the drug store and buy it. Maybe it's not Russian tundra, but it is a coincidence. Like Dr. Zhivago—Mom's recorder, my recorder and then the best: Grandma Millie takes over the tape recorder—the week I start to write a novel for the writing class.

I tell Professor Hillman I'll be writing about my family. Like a memoir, but I'll make up a bunch of stuff, so it's fiction-ish. He looks doubtful, says I might not finish a novel in a quarter, but I explain I have written a poem and a short story and I already have a book idea. Well, it isn't really my idea. This is a family idea—a secret. With a recorder in Spokane and my recorder in Seattle, I will introduce the subject that I have mulled over since I was ten. The secret? The secret about which we never speak? *Grandpa ran away with the neighbor lady.*

And so begins the first tape I mail home to Spokane:

Sunday, March 26, 1967
Hello, Mom and Grandma Millie.

How goes Dad's potato patch? Have the two of you finished yet with your latest quilt? I think you said the pattern is "log-cabin." What does that mean? Can hardly wait to see it.

You can see how I'm being casual, not starting out right away with "the secret."

I'm going to read you the poem I wrote for my first assignment. Only got a B. My professor commented that it was rather short. He suggested I push a bit harder. He was pleasantly surprised when I told him I would do just that. I'll write a novel. For now, here's the poem. Hope you like it.

My novel is going to be about a woman with a secret. I'll tell you more as I figure it out. Remember, it is fiction! For now, here is my poem. Please Grandma Millie don't think this is about you. It's made up. Mostly.

WE SHARE BONES

In the chapel I touch your forehead
Flat under thin skin a granite plain holds
a mid-west mom. Alone.
She cared for and accepted
demands of children. Alone.
The husband/father disappeared
Or so it was said.

In the chapel I touch your cheek

Your desire not to be rounded
granted. Your eye sockets sculpted.
Your final face reflects
the lineage of Tabatha, Mary Clare,
Jocyln, Martha Ann
Women strong and gone. Alone.

All for now. Love you two! Love to Dad. Love to Uncle Oscar, Love to that crazy brother if he's anywhere around.

Wednesday, April 5, 1967

Ten days later I receive a package from Spokane and in it is the response to my tape. First, Mom catches me up on the garden, her quilt, the weather, and then I hear Grandma Millie's voice:

Sunday, April 2, 1967

Hello sweet Sarah,

I understand you want to write something longer than your poem, and I must say that was a very interesting poem about my death. Very nice. How about a novel? I always wanted to write a novel about my life. Might I interest you? I think my life is full of lessons, or at least some guiding ideas. You are welcome to use any bit of what I say if it fits, or especially, if you find it interesting. I'm not sure how much I might remember, but I'd give it a good try. Let me know!

Love you, Grandma Millie.

I am so pleased at Grandma Millie's response. Maybe she's ready to share the secret about that grandfather I never knew, never saw. About him, I only know the "running-away" thing.

But here's another secret: I was maybe twelve or thirteen. In the attic I dug through a pile of *National Geographic Magazines* looking for an article about whales for an extra-credit report.

Instead, I found a photo. It was *him*—the grandfather. As if the photo had been hidden. Wrapped in tissue. Mom's writing across the upper left-hand corner of the cream-colored folder: "My dad."

The man in the photo was stern. Strong. Handsome in an old-fashioned way. In the photo he wears a stiff white collar. A vested suit. A tie knotted high, held by a gold knot of a stick-pin. His hair—slick and parted on the right is toupee-ish. At the bottom of the folder, in an image of a spread-winged eagle, are the words, Dorian Studios, Gaitsberg, Washington.

And even at that age, I wondered where is everybody? Why are Grandma and my mom and her twin brother Oscar, and their crazy brother, Gabe, not in the photo? My first thought after that was: the man in the photograph looks like a man who *would* run away with the neighbor lady.

As I studied the photo, I missed hearing Mom's steps coming up to the attic. She found me with the photo in my hand. She demanded I give it to her. She demanded I go dry the dishes. I never saw the photo again.

The mystery continues.

And now, here in Seattle, I receive a second tape.

April 12, 1967

Hello Sweetheart,

I'm going to follow your lead and try to remember to date each tape. Might help you keep track (might help your Grandma Millie keep track). You see, she has her moments. Sometimes she doesn't do so well. When I told her she should make another tape, she asked, "Why?" But, the minute I reminded her about your writing class, she was all clear again. She responded, "Oh, my. Turn on that tape recorder!" As I readied it for her she said, "We're going to write a novel!" I'm so pleased with this project. The taping has unlocked her heart—words I never thought I would hear.

"Mom, I'm ready. Come tell your stories!"

On the tape I hear a chair scrape. Then there are sounds of Grandma moving papers around, sipping her tea, and Mom's words of encouragement:

"Talk directly into the microphone. Pretend Sarah is sitting across from you."

And she does. Grandma Millie's voice is loud and clear.

Hello, dear Sarah,

This will be a surprise. I've decided it's time to tell my story. You will be my scribe! We can share credit. Or, if you are concerned about too many of the words being mine, just tell the professor you wrote everything.

There are stories I'd like to share before I forget. True stories. Stories to break your heart.

For one brief moment I wonder, after all these years, if I am ready to hear the story. But, I have a feeling that there is no stopping Grandma Millie. I pull the hood off of my IBM Selectric and as I listen to her words, I type.

My name is Mildred Birnham, and then my name became Millie Lane. I married Luke Lane in 1915. The beginning of our story isn't that unusual. We had a prosperous farm. We produced three wonderful children. Life has its way. Life changed. This is what I remember: well into our marriage, fifteen years or so, Luke started coming home late from his part-time job at the dairy. He always had an excuse. Like: "Daisy's calf didn't come easy. Sorry I missed dinner. They needed me."

It was one of the first times I'd heard the word, "needed." It registered peculiar. I remember thinking, "I needed you."

I let such moments slip by. And I began to believe he was not the husband to be called on anything. Those were the days I didn't have time or energy to even consider excuses, the children's or his. I had ironing, cooking, cleaning, gardening, and children to bring up.

Until he came home late three Fridays in a row. No excuses. Smelled of whiskey. Smelled of something else. I kept quiet—already had the children tucked in bed. Said their prayers. Didn't answer their question, "Where's Pa?"

Then the day came when Luke came home at dawn. Fell into bed. Slept until noon. The children stayed out of his way. They knew a bad mood would be followed by a belt. I wasn't strong enough (or hadn't the will) to confront him. And as for my dear children? I tried but I wasn't always able to protect them.

I remember those days as hard. Gabe didn't do so well in school. The twins were a package of two. Had each other. Gabe slipped away into sleep or books. We were not much of a family any more. Everything turned and Luke wasn't the man I married. I stayed out of his reach. I learned to see a slap, a push, or a punch coming.

Then one Sunday, we were dressed for church. We waited. Without the Model T we wouldn't walk two miles in Sunday clothes. We missed church. We ate dinner in silence. Changed out of our clothes. Did all the chores and I waited.

He didn't come home.

This is a single tape that covers months of my not being strong, not being the one to leave, not demanding loyalty. I didn't know what to do. Something like this had never, ever happened in Gaitsberg. No man left his wife. No man left a farm that was fading, drying up, dying.

It takes a long time to let go of a marriage. Over the months I secretly began to pack our stuff. I kept the family Bible. I was so angry, distraught and confused that I even considered taking off my gold wedding band, but luckily I kept it because later I'd sell it.

Hard as it was, I held on. But Gabe's problems grew and he had to have doctor's care. The twins became more and more removed. I kept a hidden box of egg money. Enough money to get three of us on the train to Spokane and pay for a few month's boarding.

Once we were in Spokane, we walked from the train station down Main Street to the western edge of the town next to Spokane Falls. A large falling-down house sported a sign: Boarder's Wanted. A short distance before the boarding house I had seen another sign: Help Wanted - Laundress needed.

We settled into two rooms and I offered the boarding house owner, Mrs. Swenson, to cook for part of the rent. She agreed. Then I interviewed at Sorbee's Laundry and got that job. No question, I knew about laundry.

A half-mile from where we lived was a high school. Lewis and Clark. The twins did okay. I think they worked at forgetting their father. I did. As for Gabe, his medical problems kept him at Medical Lake. But at least that was closer than Gaitsberg. Best, was being away from gossip and mean words. With Luke gone, away went fear, the doubt, the crush to my spirit. It wasn't easy. But we got by and over the years life got better.

All these years later, I can pull back and remember the good times. But, I must admit—Luke was a hard man to forget."

A sob. On the recorder, words of Grandma Millie stop. My mother's voice catches and I hear her soothing words, *"Mom, it's okay, jus…"*

The tape recorder stops and there is silence.

CHAPTER THREE

MIRACLES DO HAPPEN

Friday, April 21, 1967

Another uneventful week. I take the path south of the Burke Museum and counter my aloneness by breathing in the sunshine warmth of the late afternoon. Long shadows from the madrona trees cut across the western side of campus. I love this path, even when life isn't perfect. One more year and I'll graduate. I'll be this brilliant teacher and I'll create brilliant students.

Then I notice my shadow. It's lean and long. It stretches behind me. It gives me hope. I *will* be strong! Healthy! Athletic! Maybe tonight I will go to a movie alone. *Blow Up* is at the Varsity. Supposedly it has no plot and no point, but it is very, very good. Maybe sitting in a theater by myself won't be all that bad.

At Forty-third I wait for the light and as I wait, I notice this poor shlub kneeling beside a copper-colored Dodge. With a flat tire. When he stands—a lug wrench in one hand, scratching his head with the other, I realize it's *that* guy. Andrew Althaus. He looks around as if he were looking for someone to help him. And then? Our eyes meet.

The light changes to WALK and I can't pretend I haven't seen him. I step into the crosswalk and wave. Just barely. As I approach his car, I do the unexpected. I decide to be charming. No matter what. "Last Friday wasn't such a good day, huh?"

"Ah, the keeper of the funds!" he responds.

"Yeah, well, I did put your application on the top of the pile. You should hear in a week. Maybe two." I nod at his car and can't resist saying, "God's punishing you."

Andrew laughs, "Right. I was a bit of a pisser in your office."

"Well, yes, one might say that."

"This must be karmic retribution," he says with a chuckle and I notice his eyes near-close as if by narrowing his focus he has, and this is the strangest thought, almost reached out and touched me.

"I was thinking I might drop by your office. Say hello. Now it's too late because of this," he points with the wrench.

"At least you know how to change a tire."

Andrew, blinks, that confused blinking look, and says, "What would make you think I couldn't change a tire?"

"Sorry, that was stupid. Didn't mean to insult you. Honest."

"Well, good." Andrew kneels to put the wrench to one of the lug nuts. He strains.

"Left," I say.

"What?" he looks up, shielding his eyes.

"Left-hand threads."

"Huh?"

"Here, like this." I put my books and my purse on the parkway and extend my hand. "Let me have the wrench," I say, and wave him away. "Scoot." I slip the wrench over the nut and the nut loosens and falls into my hand. Two minutes later, all of the nuts lay inside the turned over hubcap.

I stand, pleased. Slap my hands to remove the dust. "Need any more help?"

Andrew laughs, "Yes, I do."

I follow him and we wrestle the spare tire out of the trunk.

When the hubcap is securely fitted, the jack removed, we step back and admire our success. Then, for the second time today, I do something I ordinarily don't do—I hold out my hand and I shake his with a firm, strong grip. "Hope that makes up for my being snippy."

"We're even," he says and gives my hand another squeeze.

Nice—his hand engulfing mine.

"Let me know if you ever have another tire to change."

He lets go and retrieves my books.

"Who do I call?" he asks.

"Call?" I ask, astounded at the question.

"Your name. If I need you to change a tire, I'll need to know your name. Your phone number."

"Oh! Sure. It's Sarah."

"Sarah. Nice name." And he does that squinty-eyed look thing as if he's thinking some deep, deep thought and he asks, "What about dinner? Right now?"

And for once I do the right thing. I answer, "Fine."

We cross the street and walk toward the Coffee Corral. As we cross Forty-second, I'm slightly aware that Andrew is checking me out.

"How'd you know that? The left-turn thread thing?" he asks.

"My dad. Not only did I get tire-changing-lessons, but I got the entire history of the lug wrench and the amount of torque required and why air pressure is important and exactly what air pressure is. But in case I'm not around to help you next time, look at the end of the lug nut. There's an L on it. Stands for 'left'."

"Amazing."

Inside the Coffee Corral, over hamburgers, we start to know each other. I explain I'm getting a minor in English Lit and a major in education.

"*My* major is English Lit."

"So it said. On your application."

By the end of the evening, we've come a long way. We agree that our favorite authors are Vonnegut, Hesse, and Barth. Oh, and Tolstoy, of course.

The next night, we eat bratwurst sandwiches at Werner's European Pastry Shop. Andrew tells me he hopes to take a senior study class on Hemingway and Fitzgerald. If he has time before he graduates, he will take an elective in creative writing.

Then it's my turn. I tell him I plan to teach. Hopefully go on for a doctorate. In something. My lit minor is just because I love reading. For some reason, I don't mention the Creative Writing class. Something in his words, his tone, makes me stay silent. I'm just not ready to share my novel with anyone but Grandma Millie.

While I hesitate, I learn my silence has served me well. Andrew says he will write the great American novel.

I do share my secret hope of teaching somewhere like Summerhill or the University of Chicago Laboratory School.

Next night I cook lemon chicken at my apartment.

Andrew checks the books on my brick-and-board bookshelf. "Interesting," he says. "Good taste in books. What'd you think of *Sotweed Factor*?"

"Loved it. I really like long books I can disappear into."

"Can't believe you aren't a Lit major."

"Well, Dad said, not only should I be able to change tires, but if he and Mom were going to put me through school, I better be able to get a job. Mom works. Dad works. I've worked all through school. It was teaching or nursing. I can't stand blood. I chose teaching."

At dinner we finish the Chianti from the raffia-wrapped bottle he brought. He leans forward with that intense, squinty look. He reaches for my hand. Perfect. I grow warm—from the wine, from the touch, from the way he looks at me.

"You have the blackest eyes I have ever seen. Like coal," he says. "Don't turn your head away. Look at me. It's true. I've never seen such eyes. Like the space between stars."

Sadly, he lets go of my hand.

"Let me show you something." He reaches for his cloth bag. He removes a small black leather-bound book. He flips the pages, so that I can see each title: *Swaggerer, Gourmet Girl, Hippy, Fat Man, My Mother, Crip, Breasts, The Largest Nose.* "It's my portrait book. I try to capture singular characteristics of singular people. Like building a library, but this is for when I write." He writes, *Coal Black Eyes.* 'Collecting words for when I start my novel."

I hold back the question, "What are you waiting for?" I'm trying not to be abrupt and critical, but Mom would have said in a second, "No time like the present," or "Good intentions pave the way to hell." She has learned all these great aphorisms from Grandma Millie. And she uses them.

"What are you thinking?" he asks.

At that moment I quit thinking about Mom and Grandma. Instead, I think if I put one hand back on the table, maybe he will take it. I think I shouldn't have drunk so much wine. I think he has gray-green eyes. I think that my parent's won't understand someone majoring in literature. I think about the small leather book of portraits. I think that one of the words in that portrait book is *Breasts.* And then I worry. I worry that mine are not large enough.

I quit thinking and say, "I've never known a writer."

"To be," Andrew answers and smiles and his eyes hold mine.

I can feel I'm blushing. I'm nervous. I need to do something, anything. I clear the table.

Andrew carries his dishes to the sink and I know it isn't just the small size of the kitchen that makes us sweetly bump each other. And then? He leans over. He kisses me. I memorize that kiss—soft, gentle, full of promise, with the sweet-sour taste of lemon chicken.

And, then, I'm glad I'm not wearing a bra, because what always happens next, happens next, and an hour or so later I think my breasts are just fine.

The next afternoon, after Andrew has left for a tutorial (whatever that is), I sit at the typewriter. I write and I write. I feel like a spy writing about my own life.

I've decided, with the professor's suggestion, to write the whole novel in the present tense. He says it gives a novel more energy. But it makes it difficult because some things happened before and some things are happening now and then there's the future. Whatever I'm doing, it is fun, but it is, really, really difficult.

CHAPTER FOUR

CALLS AND RESPONSE

Wednesday, May 3, 1967

Hi Mom,

Sorry, I've been negligent about getting tapes back to you. I've finals and assignments due, and it's been a bit crazy.

Here's a surprise! I've had a few dates lately! Nothing for you to get excited about (or worried about). I'll tell you more later. For now it's school, school, school!

The recorder works perfectly. I'm planning that most of the summer I'll be sending tapes every week. If I get disciplined about my writing, maybe I'll have this done before school starts in the fall.

Do you remember this? Sometime, somewhere, in my childhood I heard, "Grandpa ran away with the neighbor lady," and I knew I was not supposed to have heard that and I doubly knew I was never to ask about him.

And now, I hope Grandma Millie tells me everything. I want the novel/memoir to be from her point of view. Mostly. I might introduce a bit about my life. All made-up for sure, since there isn't that much excitement, but I'd like the book to be a conversation between the two of us. The professor agrees. 'Interesting structure' is what he called it. I'm on my way to a good grade, I think. I've asked that he grade me chapter by chapter. And he agreed! Someday I'll send him the whole book. I've promised him that.

For now, I have so much to learn. Our assignment this week is to write about death. I got out that poem I read to you on the first tape, and I finished it. I turn it in tomorrow. Thought you would like to hear the final lines:

In the chapel, I touch your hand
Fingers fold, conch like, into themselves.
Crab hands of a diligent cook

no longer bake Sunday pies,
roast beef, stir hambone and lima bean soup.
Resting are your hand bones
with croissant skin.
Were those knuckles loose, like jacks,
I'd cast them and know my future.

In the chapel your shoulder feels familiar.
How did they do that? Lay your rounded body
Flat.
This transformation demands a litany, grace at table, thanks
for joy at birthday parties
for excuses not made
for a life given.

In the chapel your bones
are stone.
Your hair
an ocean spray.
Your gown
Hospital given.
A dress halved.
Tied.

Your bones echo my bones
Your shoulders and mine
Grew close over time.
Each year I carry less of me and more of you.
My inheritance is sure,
revealed,
Your bones are my bones.

It's a mystery to me, these words. Although Grandma seemed to take the first half of the poem nicely. I'm not sure how she'll take this second half. You know how everyone says Grandma Millie and me are so alike? If this is a poem about someone in a coffin, which it is, and I was Grandma's age, it might not please me much. Again, share it as you wish. I'm hoping for an 'A'.

So the writing goes on. When my book is finished you'll be the first to read it. For now, I'm not going to worry about getting it published. Professor Hillman says just keep writing. His first book took him five years. Can you believe that? Five years is forever. Work to do. Got to go. Love you all.

I've been busy, what with Andrew and everything. Then I receive this tape, with a note from Mom.

Saturday, June 17, 1967
Dear Sarah,
This was strange. Your grandma was playing with the tape recorder and I didn't realize we were being recorded. It's a sad recording. You'll see how she is when she's not lucid. Just wanted you to be prepared for the next time you call, or when you come home next. Labor Day? Thanksgiving? Hope it will be soon. It's been awhile since we heard from you.
Love you,
Mom

Nothing prepares me for this tape. By the end, I'm in tears.

"Now, I forget who's sending us these tapes?"
"Your grand-daughter, Sarah."
"Are you sure?"
"Sure she's your granddaughter? Of course she's your granddaughter."
"No, I'm too young to have a granddaughter? Look at me. I'm not old enough to be a grandmother."
"Now, Mom, you are and she is. When she visits us this fall, you'll remember her."
"What if I don't?"
"You will."
"And tell me again, what is this thing?"
"A tape-recorder."
"And why do I talk to it?"
"So you can tell your stories. For Sarah. She wants to know your history."
"Oh, I don't have a history, do I?"
"We all do, Mom, and you do, and Sarah does. We already sent Sarah tapes with your wonderful, interesting words."
"My words? What could I possibly tell her? Someone I can't remember?"
"Yes, she wants you to make a recording about Luke, my dad. He was your husband. I'm your daughter. Your history..."
"That's right, that's who you are. Oh, and I remember Luke. Yes, indeed, I remember Luke. But I can't remember…"
"You will when you tell your stories and we play them back and when Sarah comes to visit you'll have more time to add to your history. She is looking forward to spending time with you…"
"Sarah?"
"Yes, Sarah, your granddaughter. Wait until she gets here. Not that long. When she arrives it will all be clear…I promise…"

And, who are you again?"

"Your daughter."

"Yes, my daughter…"

She chuckles, as if it were a joke. Except it isn't funny.

An hour later, tears under control, I call Mom. She assures me that Grandma Millie has more good days than not-so-good days.

Then she says, "Besides worrying about Mom, I've been worrying about you. No tapes. No letters. What's up?"

"Well, you'll be glad to hear I've had a few more dates."

"A few? So many you can't call home?"

"Well, he's a writer and I'm a writer and we just spend a lot of time working. Working on writing."

"Hopefully you will keep us informed. At least we got to meet that last beau. Not our choice. But, I'm sure this latest one is better. What's his name?"

"Andrew. Andrew Althaus. He's brilliant.".

"If he stays around long enough, perhaps you will bring him for Thanksgiving."

"That's a long way off. I'll see how it goes."

"You might ask him to make a tape."

"Mommmm, he doesn't know about the tapes. Yet. Maybe later. Way, way later."

"You know we worry about you. And now with Grandma having her days, I worry about the two of you. Please, sweetheart, keep us informed."

"I already promised."

"So you did. Grandma's calling. Got to run. Love you, Sarah. We both love, miss, and worry about you. Here's a hug."

The call ends and now I wonder, a month from now, when Mom gets it in her head to call and Andrew answers the phone. How do I tell him to not ever, ever answer the phone? Mom and Dad have strict rules about marriage. They aren't going to understand this 'living together' arrangement. And Andrew? Andrew will never understand my parents.

CHAPTER FIVE

TIME TO TELL

Saturday, August 19, 1967

Andrew and I see each other every day and, I must say, every night…wonderful, wonderful nights. Then Andrew receives word that he has been accepted into the Exploratory Senior Writing Program in the English Lit Department. He is also very decisive about "us." He signs the lease for the apartment above Bartell Drugs. Another week and I'll move in with him. We don't tell his mother or my parents (obviously).

We don't tell, because, as we know full well, what matters is that we love each other. Getting married, as we know from all the statistics—is the path to failure. We are absolutely sure that it is better that we live together and see how it goes. We can get married later if for some reason we change our minds. In the meantime, thank God for birth control pills. We split the rent fifty/fifty.

Andrew is so unique. For instance, Eric (that ex-boyfriend), my dad, and my brother, all know how to change spark plugs, pound nails, roof houses, re-build engines. They all watch sports.

Andrew is not handy and he never watches sports. Not even the Mariners. He spends hours reading. He reads authors I've never read. He reads authors I've never heard of: Schopenhauer, Euripides, Gogol, Plato, Pirandello, Thucydides. When he isn't reading, he writes. When he isn't writing, we talk. And then we stop talking and have a little fun.

Sundays we sleep late wrapped in sheets pulled loose by all that rolling around. We discuss the nature of truth, free will, whether there is a God, and if so, who created Him. I'm ecstatic. It's the year for having it all: love, ideas, sex, and in three more quarters—a degree.

We have long dinners and talk and talk and then we slip under the sheets.

Sometimes, we spend the entire day in bed. And then we talk.

Between times, I've been on a small mission. I'm convincing Andrew to buy a pair of Frye boots. At Goodwill I even found him an old leather briefcase for his books and I've thrown out his cloth bag. I suggest he get his eyes checked and guess what? The squinting and blinking have been erased with a good prescription. I suggest he quit leaving his laundry at his mother's house. And he has! And now I do his laundry and he isn't gone for hours and hours visiting his mom.

The white scarf stays. He convinces me it is a *power scarf*—it helps him write.

And then I receive this letter from Mom:

8-29-67

Dear Sarah,

I didn't want to record this in front of your grandmother and so I'm writing you a letter. Such a forgotten way of communication, don't you think?

I'm so looking forward to Thanksgiving. You've not mentioned it so I'm assuming the Andrew thing might have blown over.

So, I'm saving the making of the mincemeat until you arrive. Grandma will join us, but she is doing poorly. Perhaps she will get by this bit of slowing down, but should she not, she won't be spending much time in the kitchen.

However, I've planned on two things: making the mincemeat and you spending time with Grandma Millie. I reminded her that you are writing a book and she'll be in it. I assured her that you wouldn't forget her or mix up her stories. She mentioned how she looks forward to your visit, but don't be surprised if she repeats herself or mixes up names and places. She has her moments. As you will see.

Love you,

Mom

P.S. Grandma Millie is finishing up another tape (maybe two) and I will mail them soon. She has some incredible moments of lucidity, but afterwards she tends to slide back into confusion and she needs to sleep.

Sunday, September 10, 1967

Andrew is gone for some kind of an intro session in preparation for his advanced class (although you, dear reader, should know that I've finally mentioned my tapes and my writing, but I assured Andrew that it's nothing that important and certainly not as important as the writing he will be doing for his class).

While I wait for the next tapes to arrive, and have some time alone, I'm going to write one more incident that came back to me out of the blue. It's about the secret sentence. Sorry about that cliché, 'out of the blue'.

Sometimes clichés just sneak in and when I do re-writes, I'll certainly remove them. Or, I'll use the ones from my family, because they are crazy and fresh, like, 'out of the black and blue,' or 'pizza paves the way to hell'.

Back to the secret sentence. I knew I wasn't supposed to hear it, when I came into the kitchen with Trigger to get some dog treats, and my mom was patting Grandma Millie's arm. She said in the most soothing voice, "Time to erase that, Mom. You're surrounded by everyone who loves you. That's over and done with." I probably wouldn't have paid attention, but Grandma took the handkerchief she always kept tucked in her sleeve and wiped away her tears.

Being ten, with absolutely no sense of propriety, I demanded, "What's wrong, Grandma?"

"Your Grandpa ran away with the neighbor lady," and then she bawled.

Mom shushed me out of the kitchen, and said, "You, little Missy, did not hear that. Out. Take the dog and we'll see you when dinner's ready."

So Trigger and I went for a long walk, and as you can guess, I never, ever forgot that sentence, and never ever learned an answer. But, maybe, just maybe, come the next two tapes, I will begin to learn. Come Thanksgiving I'll spend as much time with Grandma Millie as possible and maybe, just maybe the story will unfold.

CHAPTER SIX

THE COUNTY FAIR

Saturday, October 7, 1967

After Andrew leaves for his part-time pizza delivery job. I get out my tape recorder and I listen for the second time. It isn't that I don't want Andrew to know about Luke Lane, but I don't want Andrew to know that the two of them, Luke and Andrew, are going to be in this book. Not yet, anyway.

Here is the latest tape:

Hi Sweetie,

Another tape from Grandma Millie. She swears this story begins exactly on Saturday, June 6, 1914. It is so strange what she does and does not remember.

And, I notice that the more Grandma Millie remembers the lighter and younger her voice becomes.

Hello Sarah,

Start typing!

I tied the red-velvet ribbon around my waist, cinching the white cotton dress with eyelet trim. I pinched my cheeks, ran a little finger over my eyebrows. It amazed me. Sometime between the age of fifteen and seventeen, I changed. I was no longer scrawny, elbow-y, and awkward. It was as if God had reached down his finger and said "presto-chango" and the girl I used to be, became someone I was still getting used to. I was afraid I'd be punished for being so pleased with myself. I turned away from the mirror and grabbed my straw bag. I was off to the fair!

Before the screen door slammed, my mother called, "You be good now!" She meant—be a good Baptist girl—no fortune teller, no dance pavilion, no staring at the poor freaks, no flirting—and particularly, no to anything that might be a temptation.

Like Luke Lane.

I walked the half-mile to the fair and by the edge of town I could see the fair banner flap its greeting: WELCOME TO THE GAITSBERG COUNTY FAIR.

Last night's misty rain had washed the world clean. A soft breeze full of morning sun felt as if the world was drying on the line. No question, it was an "anything-can-happen" kind of day! I touched the nickels in my pocket. I touched them again.

The ticket line was three-deep and twenty people long. The carousel's mirrors flashed and the chirpy notes of the calliope bounced over the fair grounds and the sky was full of spun-sugar clouds. I could hardly wait. And then I saw Milt Wiseman. He was ten people ahead of me in line.

Let me tell you. Milt was not my kind of guy. He was short and stocky, with chestnut colored hair, and a sturdy way of standing. His broad face was suntanned the color of a rusty nail. The way his Levi's rested on his hips made him dowdy. Since we graduated from high school Milt had become a dresser—but today wasn't one of those days. Working for his dad at The Gaitsberg Daily News required he dress in suits, vests, and ties during working hours. Today, you would have never guessed that someday he would inherit the local paper. Dress-up days, you could almost say he was a dandy.

In my opinion, he looked silly no matter how he dressed. There was just something about Milt that was unappealing. On my Saturday errands, Milt would stand around waiting for me to walk by the newspaper office, all ready to say hello, and I'd just keep walking. No way was I going to notice him. I had no room in my head (not to mention my heart), for the likes of Milt Wiseman. Milt's only saving grace was that his best friend was Luke Lane.

And then as I stood there in line for my ticket, Luke walked right past me and joined Milt. They traded friendly punches. Bounced on their toes. Dodged like boxers. It probably should have bothered me that he cut in line, but the truth was, I was pleased he was there.

Luke was taller than Milt by a head. Luke was loose jointed, easy in the arms. He was swarthy, with eyes coal black. He wore a white shirt open at the collar. His Levi's fit snug. Luke was delicious.

"Trouble," was what Mom said, when on rare occasions she spoke of Luke Lane. She'd preach to me: "Nothing but trouble. He's a mucker. Not that he doesn't know how to speak well, but you watch out, young lady. Don't you go givin' that Luke Lane the time of day. As your grandma would say, he's just a bit too choppy."

Not for not wanting had I not given Luke Lane the time of day. And "choppy"? It wasn't his fault every girl in town wanted him for a beau.

Luke was supposed to have graduated with the class of 1910. He graduated in 1912. Because my mother was the secretary at Gaitsberg High School, I knew all about Luke.

I knew he had rarely done his homework and if he did, he didn't turn it in on time. I knew he skipped classes. I knew he frequented Bierly's Bar even before he turned eighteen. I knew he paid an enormous amount of attention to the high school Harvest

Queens. And, I knew the rumors that there were teachers who regularly failed him so he could continue to play sports for the Gaitsberg Comets.

I was absolutely and completely aware that in his two extra years of high school, when Luke was a senior for the second time, he grew from a lanky, athletic boy, to a man. He starred in football, basketball, and baseball. Everyone thought it was a sad day for our school when Principal Madder graduated Luke Lane.

"Luke Lane is not what a woman with any brains would want, especially a Birnham woman!" Those were Mom's words. "Flirty. Doesn't know when to turn off the charm—if that's what you want to call it." My mother would go on and on. She made it clear that she thought I deserved more than the life of a farmer's wife, more than someone who was sure to end up with a run-around husband, and certainly, more than a Lutheran. "No Baptist would ever wish to end up with the likes of a Lutheran. So serious. So lacking in spontaneity. Keep your eye out for a nice Baptist boy."

It wouldn't have mattered to me if there had been an eligible Baptist boy. I couldn't remember the time when I didn't have my eye on Luke Lane. My constant, most urgent prayer was, "God, please give me Luke Lane." And miracle of miracles, only six weeks later, I was standing in Cramwell's Confectionary and he winked at me! Two days later there was a note stuck in the mail box. Thank goodness, Mom didn't see it. She would have pointed out with much severity that, "…he can't even spell."

The note? "How abot the Prom?"

And that's how I got asked to the senior prom. I planned and planned. Mom even relented enough to sew me a dress of the whitest, most beautiful pique.

This would be my very first date. Every girl in the whole school was jealous. At least that's what I thought. Except I really didn't know because that date never happened. I got chicken pox.

I was reassured when I learned Luke hadn't gone with anyone else. He went by himself. Danced with every girl. And this time, another note in the mail box, my Mom did see, "Get will." He didn't sign it. As Mom pointed out, he didn't have to. She thought the chicken pox was sent directly from the Lord.

Now, let me continue telling you about that day at the county fair:

The ticket line moved forward and wonder of wonders, Luke turned to look right at me. His eyebrows lifted. Black. Thick. His smile slipped across his face like a dog on a hunt. I so hoped he would leave Milt and come speak to me, but Milt nudged him to pay the ticket-taker and without looking back, the two of them walked away.

At least he had looked at me.

I got my ticket and headed for Lady Lazonga's Fortune Teller's Booth. Claire Sandborn was going to meet me there. We went to the fair every year since we were seven. We always met in front of Lady Lazonga's. Once we even heard Lady Lazonga's raspy voice yell at a departing farmer, "How dare you contradict me, dearie! I'm psychic!" As the man stumbled down the midway, his head bent, she continued to yell, "And your future is…" and she stopped yelling when she saw everyone was listening to hear this man's horrible fate. No way was she going to give her prediction away for free.

Okay, now back to Claire. Claire had vowed that this year she was going to learn from Lady Lazonga, her future. In spite of her mother forbidding it because, of course, God forbade it!

Claire ranted to me, words she would never have said to her mother, "You think God doesn't have better things to do than eavesdrop on Lady Lazonga? Besides, it's not my whole life I want to know about. It's when do I get out of this town? When do I quit babysitting Angelica? Do you know how embarrassing it is to be seventeen and have a four year old for a sister? What kind of God is in charge anyway? And if I roast in hell? So be it. I'll be dead."

Claire constantly defied her mother. Even when, or maybe because, her mother prayed long prayers over her every night. But then, I also prayed for Claire. Ever since Angelica, her little sister was born, Claire had become rambunctious. Once she even showed me a cigarette she had rolled—snitched the paper and tobacco from her Pa's tobacco jar. I envied Claire's wildness, but I never stopped worrying for her. It was one thing to be wild, but I feared the way Claire was headed, she was very close to being a wanton woman—the most horrible thing that could happen to a woman.

As I passed Milt and Luke at the ring toss, I walked with my head high, hoping Luke would signal me to stop, say something, call out my name. He didn't.

I continued past the Muscle Man Meter Booth, The Wonders of the World Freak Show, Sam's Wild West Shooting Gallery, and waited for Claire in front of the six-foot sign with three foot letters: LADY LAZONGA, PALM READER, FORTUNE TELLER, STAR GAZER.

After a few minutes I spotted Claire's head, a mass of red curls. As I watched, Claire stopped to greet Luke and Milt. The three stood studying a canvas panel covered with a painting of the bearded lady, her beard flowing over her bare breasts. Claire looked up at the painting, her hands on her hips, her head nodding yes, and then she laughed. Obviously, Claire had said something she shouldn't have.

It nearly broke my heart when I saw Luke turn his head to catch Claire's words. Laughed with her. He even put his hand on her shoulder.

Then, next to me, a bent wizened man pulled back the curtain of Lady Lazonga's booth and said in a scratchy voice, a near whisper, "Learn all. Know all. One nickel and the future is yours."

Before I could stop myself, my hand opened and there was one of my nickels. The old man reached and his filthy fingers curled around it and he pulled back the dusty-smelling, black velvet curtain. As if a magnet pulled me, I stepped into the darkness.

The inside smelled of cigarettes, peppermint, and sweat. My eyes adjusted and the dark gave way to a round table on which glowed a green glass ashtray. Smoke rose from the long ash of a cigarette. Seated at the table was an overweight woman draped in the same velvet as the curtain. Around her waist protruded a belt of bells. As I stood there wondering what to do, the fat woman picked up a granite-ware coffee pot and poured herself what appeared to be darkly steeped tea. Her brilliant orange head-wrap sat precariously on her black, black hair. "Right with you," she said with a hacking cough. "Got to take my medicine." And the bells jangled.

And without ever having smelled whiskey, I knew what she was drinking was evil.

Wiping her mouth with the back of her hand, Lady Lazonga reached for one last puff on her cigarette and scooted back into her wicker chair, the back of which was as high as she was wide.

"Sit!" she demanded.

I felt for the edge of a wooden stool and lowered my body. I held my hands tight in my lap. For this, would I be damned? Had I already sold my soul by being here? Was there any sin worse?

Lady Lazonga's yellowed fingers pushed aside the green ashtray. "Your hands," she demanded.

The bells she wore slipped under a roll of fat and they jingled as if from some distant spot in another time, in another country. Lady Lazonga opened my hands and parted my fingers.

"Ahhhh," Lady Lazonga said in a throaty, phlegmy voice, "A great love."

"What?" I couldn't believe her words!

"A great, great love."

I bent my head close and barely whispered, "A great love?"

Lady Lazonga grasped my elbows. Her black shimmering eyes stared into mine. "Soon!" she hissed.

In my confusion and anxiety, I swallowed wrong and a cough caught in my throat. Barely able to speak, I asked, "Who?"

"Of course!" Lady Lazonga exclaimed and leaned back, the bells protruding as if they too were looking for air. She scratched under her head-wrap with a little finger. She closed her eyes and said, "Yes, I can see him. Tall. Dark. Handsome. But…" and she stopped scratching and adjusted her slipping turban, "…this will take all of my powers. Powers cost. I need another nickel."

"I can't!" I exclaimed. "I wasn't supposed to spend even my first nickel on…"

"What? You question me? I've opened the doors to your future, and you can't spare a nickel! Of course you can!"

I stood. I had to get out of there. I knocked over the stool and stumbled through the parting curtain, fearful that bony fingers would reach out and grab me.

Out on the Midway, the air, the noise, the colors, whirled.

"You win!" Milt shouted. I blanched with embarrassment, ashamed that I had been seen and exposed by stupid Milt.

Then I realized I hadn't. Milt was yelling at Luke. Next to Lady Lazonga's, Claire, Milt, and Luke stood at The Shooting Gallery. Luke had just won a black bowler hat with red, white, and blue feathers. He planted it on his head, and snapped the brim with his finger—like a vaudeville dancer. He made a sweeping bow, as I approached.

"Hooray! She's here!" Claire took my hand, hooked it in the crook of her elbow and we walked toward the carousel. Milt and Luke followed.

"I was starting to worry about you. Where have you been?" Claire asked.

It was obvious where I had been. As we walked away, I asked, "Why are we leaving Lady Lazonga's? I thought this was the year you were going to find out your future!"

"Are you crazy?" Claire whispered. "We have the only two eligible men in Gaitsberg. I've already wheedled from them a promise to treat us to the carousel! Who needs Lady Lazonga?"

Being the good friend that she was, being the lost hopeless sinner I had become, I didn't say a word about my future. Claire pulled me close and whispered, "Which one do you want? Milt or Luke?"

I could feel myself blushing. Claire didn't have to ask. Claire and I had pulled dozens of daisy petals trying to discover if Luke would ever love me.

"Poor Milt. He is so ga-ga over you. But since I don't care, I'll distract him and Luke is yours. Maybe you'll be the one to tame him!" We walked around savoring our secret plans until we realized Luke and Milt had stopped at the Mighty Bravo Bell.

Luke rolled up his sleeves. With both hands he took the large wooden mallet, spread his feet and then he swung, a high curving arch, until the mallet hit, and the red ball flew up—past Outstanding, past Solid, past Splendid, past Mighty, past Magnificent, and the bell rang! The crowd cheered and then the carnie made a huge show of presenting Luke with a foot-high pink Kewpie doll, all feathers and sequins.

Luke held the doll out to the two of us and announced, "There's no way I'm going to walk around holding this thing! Which one of you will be the recipient?"

All I heard was the word 'recipient'. Unexpected. Lofty. Refined. Luke Lane had just asked if I wanted to be a recipient. He had asked both of us, but I reached to take the doll before Claire answered and with that Luke offered me his arm. Claire took Milt's arm, gave him a big smile, and as couples we walked down the center aisle of the fair where everyone could see. I was in heaven!

The warmth of Luke's arm, the muscle underneath the shirt, the smell of pomade—I thought I might swoon. I held on.

Soon we were at the line for the carousel where the horses rose and fell, rose and fell, and children squealed and laughed and leaned to grab the brass ring.

When the carousel stopped, Luke hoisted me onto a white-mane horse with red reflectors. Then the carousel slowly moved and picked up speed, the calliope pumped Camp Town Races, and my mind spun with the words: a great love, a great love, a great love.

Next, at the Center House Arena we watched the Nez Pearce parade their horses, everything beaded, everything majestic. Luke stood with one leg on the arena rail. I couldn't help but notice the roundness of his bottom. I didn't ever recall looking at any man that way. Maybe it was the angle of his leg, or the angle of his back, but he reminded me of the drawings in Miss Phinney's art class.

Miss Phinney had a large book on her desk: Gray's Anatomy. She assured the class that the naked bodies were God's art. The class only had the book for one hour and each student could only look at it at her desk. The students would draw at their desks and then when they got stuck they could ask to look again. No one got as many looks as they wanted. I never forgot the particulars of those men and I never told Mom about the drawing lessons.

At the Center House, it was a horrible coincidence that as we watched the Indians parade, directly in front of us, the male part of one of the horses protruded. It was astounding! I didn't know where to look. I certainly was not going to look to see if Claire had noticed. Or worse, if Milt and Luke had noticed.

Thank goodness, the parade passed and the announcer lifted his megaphone and said: "Next will be the Baby Animal Scramble! Three minutes! Five and six-year-olds first! Parents please stay in the stands!" A dozen or so bewildered children stumbled into the corral where baby chickens, baby pigs, three roosters, three ducks, three geese, and one skittish lamb, were let loose. Three children grabbed baby chicks. Six children ran around waving their arms. The other children stood stock still wondering why their parents were yelling at them.

Then, directly in front of where we stood, a little girl grabbed a rooster that was as big as she was. Seeing the bird was about to escape, Luke jumped over the rail and wrapped his arms around the bird's flapping wings. With the bird in one hand and the little girl's hand in his, Luke approached the official.

Pandemonium broke out! Parents yelled objections! Parents swarmed into the arena. One father grabbed a lamb his child had been chasing. Another father swooped down on a squealing pig. The voice through the megaphone demanded parents leave the arena. Now!

Three mothers surrounded the official, yelling, and pointing in Luke's direction. When one official handed the rooster to another official, the little girl screamed, kicked her legs, and thrashed the air with her arms. Only when the announcer announced that all parents of all the children would receive a free pass for the next day, if they picked up their tickets at the front gate immediately, did things quiet down. Luke walked back across the arena brushing feathers from his shirt.

I wondered at my response. For one second Luke seemed like a hero and the next he seemed as bad as all the other interfering parents.

"Time for corn-on-the-cob," Claire announced. "Millie and I will treat. You treated for the carousel." I couldn't believe Claire was so brazen, and, truth was, I was slightly annoyed. I had only one nickel left. I so wanted spun sugar. There was something about a day at the fair, being with Luke Lane, and spun sugar that seemed all a magical package.

We sat at a picnic table, near The Central Stage, eating corn-on-the-cob. We listened to a fiddler, watched an arm wrestling competition, and watched Theodore Abruzie win the belly bumping contest. One hour before closing. Milt said, "I've got a great idea! Let's all go see Lady Lazonga! I've one last nickel!"

Claire slipped her arm into the crook of Milt's arm and said, "Well, Mighty Milt, then you treat because I just spent my last nickel!"

Luke looked directly at me and asked, "And, what about you, Miss Millie, do you want to know your future?"

With a laugh I shook my head 'no' and said, "Fraid not. My mother places

Lady Lazonga somewhere between the Devil and President Harding."

"So, don't tell her!" Milt said. "Come on, let's go."

As we walked toward the fortune teller, Luke reached for my hand. He studied my palm and said, "Ah, ha! A great life line. A long, long life line and here, I think that's money, or maybe that's love. Guess we'll have to ask Lady Lazonga!"

As we stepped in front of the fortune teller booth, Milt said, "How about we all go in together. Get a group rate! Compare notes."

The skinny, black suited, dirty little man at the entrance of Lady Lazonga's booth sidled up to Luke, "Don't underestimate Lady Lazonga. The Future is not to be taken lightly. Serious. Serious she is."

Fearful the scary old guy would ask why I was back, I stayed close to Luke, half hidden.

The crazy man looked directly at Claire and said, "One at a time. A nickel each. You first young lady," and he pulled back the curtain, did a twisted little bow, and Claire disappeared. Milt paid the nickel.

"You'll be next. I'll pay," Luke said to me. "I promise not to tell your mama. But! One condition! You have to tell all of us exactly what she says about your future!!"

I didn't answer. No way would I tell anything to Milt, let alone Luke. Especially if she told me the name of my love, since I already knew the name of my love.

As we waited, we watched the shooting gallery across the midway. No ducks fell.

Luke watched the shooters and then said, "Lazonga better be good. I'm giving up another round of shooting. I should walk over there and show them just how it's done!"

I believed him. And, I agreed. Lazonga better be good.

Claire parted the curtain. She waved her hand, rolled her eyes, and indicated with a flick of her fingers that all of us should follow her.

"Where you goin'?" Milt demanded. "Claire, tell us! Too scary? You're not going to leave Gaitsberg are you? You're going to stay and marry me?" He said, but he was looking directly at me.

"Lazonga is pure blarney!" Claire declared.

"But what did she tell you?" Milt persisted. "You're hiding something. She probably told you and you're holding back. Fess up!"

"Okay. That dirty old woman held my hands. That was bad enough. But then she said, in this crackly, pretend voice, 'You will have a love. A great love.'" Claire bent over, made her fingers all crooked and looked up at the three of us with wide crazy eyes. "I asked, 'Who?' She does this…" Claire reached and grabbed me by the elbows, "…and pulls me close, her breath all burnt and heavy, and she says, 'For that you need another nickel.' So, I said, okay, and gave her my last nickel."

Milt exclaimed, "You fibbed! You said you didn't have another nickel!"

"Milt, you will always know what you need to know. Not a nickel more!" Claire laughed and bumped her hip against Milt's. "Now, let me finish. So, I gave her another nickel. And Lady Lazonga puts her hands to her head like this," Claire put her finger tips on top of her head and closed her eyes and said in a deep, Lady Lazonga voice, "Ah, yes, I can see him. A man. A medium sized man. He needs to shave. He speaks

English. He's...he's...almost, almost, I have his name. He wants you to know..." Claire's fingers dig into her forehead, "He wants, so very much for you to know his name. You learn his name and he will be the love of your life. Almost, almost I can see his name. The name begins with an L, or maybe it is a B. Only one more nickel and I will have his full name...yes! The name is becoming clearer and clearer..." Claire threw her arms up in the air, gave a hooty laugh, and said, "Guess what? I grabbed the nickel I had just given her, and walked out!"

"That's it?" Milt asked.

"Story's over," Claire said. She took Milt's arm and the four of us headed back down the Midway and stopped at the Cotton Candy booth where we, Claire and I, were treated. Heaven. A miracle of spun candy to end the day.

Much later, out past the lights of the fair, past the edge of town, the air grew cool. I walked beside Luke, holding the Kewpie doll, with my hand tucked in Luke's elbow.

The four of us stopped at the fence that surrounded my house.

"Milt, why don't you see Claire on home," Luke said. "I've something I want to talk to Millie about."

I could feel Luke's hand on top of mine, holding me there.

"Okay with you?" he asked. And I shook my head "yes" in disbelief.

There was no question Milt had been told to leave, to walk the half mile with Claire to Claire's farmhouse. A half mile out. A half mile back.

"See you tomorrow, Milt. Come by the house, we'll go hunting." And before Milt could say a word, Luke swung the gate open for me and guided me up the path to the front door.

I remember this as if it were yesterday.

We stood in silence. The smell of ripening apples, summer wheat, and blossoming alfalfa surrounded us. Frogs burped. Stars pierced the sky. Luke pointed out the Big Dipper.

I felt the warmth of his body as he leaned to show me Orion's Belt. Luke's fingers found my fingers and his hand enfolded mine. He brought my knuckles to his lips. For me it was as if that red ball ascended past Outstanding, past Solid, past Splendid, past Mighty, past Magnificent.

The screen door swung open.

"Time to say good night, missy. Nice seeing you Luke."

"Oh, Mrs. Birnham, I hope we didn't disturb you?"

My mother didn't have to say more. Her silence said it all.

It didn't matter. Luke was persistent.

CHAPTER SEVEN

GOING HOME

Mom sends another letter and it crosses my mind that Mom is protecting Grandma Millie. I'm not quite sure how this is going to work. A novel doesn't allow for much protection. I'll need to give this more thought.

Mom's letter:

10/11/1967

Dear Sarah,

Only a few more weeks, but I wanted to send you this reminder: Mom has her good days and her not so good days. Don't be surprised at how much she does and doesn't recall. She's still full of interesting stories. When she's in the mood. Hopefully she will be in the mood while you are here.

I love you,

Mom

Seattle, Saturday, November 15, 1967

Dear Mom and Dad,

Between classes, so just a quick note. See you next week. Northwest Airlines, Flight 806, 10:00 a.m. Thank you big time for the gift to fly home. Eight hours on a Greyhound is too many hours.

REMEMBER...THIS TIME WE'RE GOING TO WRITE DOWN THAT MINCEMEAT RECIPE! FOR REAL!

Love, Sarah

P.S. I have some great news!

I know that last P.S. will stop Mom in her tracks. I also know that going home will stop time. No, more than that. Going home will reverse time. I'll walk from the gravel parking space, past Mom's lilac tree, take two steps up to the back door, and I'll be ten again. The years from ten to twenty-one will vanish. Coming home to make mincemeat is worth the discomfort of becoming a daughter again, becoming a child. It is always worth it, being pampered and talked down to. Something soothing in not being responsible. And. I adore the whole mincemeat ritual: dicing, chopping, tasting, waiting.

And who knows? I plan to confess. Not about living together. But about Andrew. It will give me a chance to rave about him—how funny, how brilliant, how we are made for each other. How we share ideas. Talk for hours. How never in my life have I found someone who pushes me to question everything. Which is one reason I can't tell Mom or Dad what we talk about. God, for instance. Or sex. My parents will never understand. I live in a different world from theirs. What we discuss probably never entered their minds.

I sleep on the flight home, exhausted after a long night of saying goodbye to Andrew.

"It's only five days," I reminded him this morning.

"Yea, but it will be a long, long five days," and Andrew pulled me back on top of him.

Now the 707 is fifteen minutes from touchdown.

Below the clouds, wheat fields give way to the neat grid of Spokane and the plane bounces onto the runway.

I hurry from baggage claim to find Dad at the passenger pick-up, standing proudly beside his white-finned Ford. He hugs me a big hello. Then he steps back so I can admire the glow of the car—the clean, sparkling car—his way of welcoming me. A ritual. A tradition. What a father does. And it's that very minute I know I'll have to keep Andrew a secret for a little while longer. Andrew's ramshackle Dodge has probably never been washed.

Dad puts my bag in the back seat and we head down Sunset Highway. As we drive, Dad whistles. It's something he does when he can't quite figure out what to say.

"So, how's Grandma?"

"Your grandma?"

I don't answer. He'll get to the conversation in a minute. I wait. As I wait, I study Dad. He wears a flannel plaid shirt whose turned cuffs expose the quilted sleeves of his long underwear. I've spent hours studying my parents' family photo album and I wonder how Mom, who had once worn smart platform shoes and a wispy silk dress with silk flowers in her hair and Dad, who wore a Fedora tipped at a jaunty angle as he stood in front of his first Model T looking like Humphrey Bogart, had turned into such old fashioned parents. I made Andrew promise we would never get old like that. We would never stop talking. We would never get out of shape. We would never, ever go a day without sex.

And then Dad finally starts to talk. He talks about the beanpoles he's rigged. He talks about the pies Mom made this morning. He talks about the neighbor's kids not being much disciplined. He ends his part of the conversation as we turn off Division Street to Napa. These last few blocks, he finally says, "Grandma is doing okay."

I know from the short sentence and the clipped way he says it, that the sentence is code. Grandma is not doing okay.

I fill the final blocks with chatter: about the greenness and lushness of Seattle, about my classes, about my up-coming student teaching. And then we drive down the alley, turn at the tool shed and park beside the lilac tree.

Mom opens the back screen door and waits on the porch, arms wide. "Let me look at you!" She holds me at arm's length. "You are so tall! So beautiful! Turn around. So lovely. I know, I know, I'm just your mother, but believe me God has blessed you! And I like your hair short like that. You are God's gift to us."

Dad waits, holding the door, smiles. So proud.

"If it weren't for the Bingham nose, you'd look just like Audrey Hepburn. Right, David?"

Mom's compliments are always tempered. Since before remembering, my mother has protected me against vanity, lest the evil-eye of pride swallow me whole. Not good to dwell on any idea of beauty, or even quite believe such a possibility exists.

With that, Mom tucks her arm in mine and gives me a squeeze, and says in a low voice, "Grandma's here to welcome you home, but she's taking a nap. She's so excited to see you, but let's let her rest. We can have a few minutes for just the two of us."

"I'll put your bag and coat in your old bedroom," Dad offers.

Mom slips an apron over my head and ties it at the back. In her low voice she continues to say, "She's slowed. She's sometimes confused. Just don't get irritated if she repeats herself. Okay?"

"Sure, Mom. But tell me, you've sent those tapes. They are perfect. She doesn't miss a beat. How does she do that?"

"Yes, there's something about the tape recorder. It sends her back. She doesn't repeat herself. She remembers tiny details. It's like she has slipped back to another life."

"That's so strange."

"More than that. It's like a miracle."

Dad watches from the doorway. "Nice to have you home, sweetie," he says and waves a rolled newspaper, by way of saying he'll be in the front room. There's no need for him to tell us, but he says, "I'd stay and help but I've got an appointment with a football game."

"We'll do just fine without you. But, please keep the sound down. Mom needs all the sleep she can get."

"Not to worry," Dad says and disappears.

Mom hands me a chopping board and a paring knife. I ease onto a kitchen stool. It *is* grand to be home. In the kitchen. The sun bursting through the pine trees into the breakfast nook. In front of me the counter overflows with parcels of wrapped meat, sacks of nuts, currents and raisins, a quart jar of molasses, two jugs of cider, a dozen canning jars, boxes of canning jar lids, and wrapped bars of paraffin.

Making mincemeat is a family tradition, as old as I can remember. Dad watches sports. We cook. The house smells delicious.

I wait for Mom's instructions, wondering how long before I might mention Andrew.

Mom hasn't changed that much since the last trip home. Last Easter. She's still peppy. Her hair is a mix of white and blond, the color of wheat harvest. She's the kind of woman who makes up for shortness by being decisive and orderly. She stands at the sink to finish peeling a dozen Winesaps. "While I finish the apples, you chop the citron. Quarter inch squares."

I reach for a pencil and a used envelope from the bill basket at the end of the counter. "I'll write down the recipe."

Mom turns from the sink, wipes her arthritic hands on her apron, and with a shake of her head, says, "Sweetie, you know there isn't a recipe." She wiggles her bent fingers in the air, "A pinch of this, a pile of that." At the stove she places a large black skillet on the burner and into it slips a large chunk of fat. "How many years have we been doing this? You probably know as much as I do," she says.

"That's nice. Nice you think…well, think of me as knowledgeable, mature." My words sound contrived. They are contrived. I think about what to say next.

"Huh?" Mom looks at me, one eyebrow cocked, pinning me with a quizzical, comic look. "I'm not so dumb. How did we go from knowing about mincemeat to being mature?"

"I meant, we—you and I—have been learning by doing. For a long time."

"Learning by doing?" she asks, just a bit incredulous.

And I'm on it, "Yes! This quarter I've been studying Dewey, and he's all about learning by doing, so learning by doing has been on my mind. A lot."

I stop talking and can still hear my words, hanging there like the spices Mom hangs in the window to dry.

I wait with my pencil poised.

Mom shakes her head and returns to the counter where she picks up a large cutting board and a bundle of oozing meat marked "BEAR HAUNCH." She saws at the string, removes the meat, cuts away a round, knobby bone.

I wait.

And then she gives me my opening. She says, "Sounds like we are *not* talking mincemeat."

I feel my face flush. I clear my throat and point at the package, "Dad's something, isn't he? Killing a bear."

"David didn't have much choice. It was either him or the bear."

"I know. But still. Dad shot it. The hunter. So manly." I stop chopping and rest my chin in my hand. With a calculated sigh, I say, "Must have made you fall in love with him all over again."

"A curious bear wanders up to a campfire and gets shot." Mom chuckles. She turns and looks directly at me and she says, "That isn't what makes me love your dad."

"I'm in love," I blurt. "I've found *the* one."

"Well, well, well. I could tell we were headed toward something. What happened to *the one* named Eric?"

"Mom, don't make fun. This is for real." And then the words tumble out, "His name's Andrew. He's *gor-geous*! He's smart. You'll love him! He's magical. I'm really, truly, for sure in love!"

I take one of Mom's apples, cut it in half, in half again, core it, chop it. My knife makes a *tock, tock, tock* sound against the chopping board. I finish the apples. I wait. A long silence follows. Mom gathers sprigs of herbs from the window, cans of spices from a drawer.

"Here's something you can write down: ten fall apples, but if you, for some unknown reason don't have good, tart fall apples, use cider and orange juice and skip the vinegar.

"Honest, Mom, you're going to love him."

"Him? We were talking about apples and orange juice."

"No, about Andrew."

"I was just getting used to the idea of Eric."

"He was just someone I chummed with."

"Make good amounts of cinnamon, cloves and allspice."

"What are 'good amounts'."

"Well, not pinches. Being generous is always a good rule of thumb. Generous but thoughtful," she says. "You're going to use an entire ten ounce bottle of molasses. So those spices have to do their job."

It crosses my mind she's saying something about Andrew and me, but she assembles the meat grinder and I'm not sure where we are in the conversation: Andrew or mincemeat. I pick up another apple.

"Chop precisely. With care." She gives me a stern look. I don't ask what she means. I just make smaller chopping motions and assume I'm doing okay when she nods her head 'yes'.

Mom takes the meat chunks from the stove and slips them into the oven.

"How much meat is that?" I ask.

"The right amount."

"How am I ever going to make mincemeat if at some point we don't write down some exact amounts? The *right amount* is a little vague."

"Well, I thought we were *having* a vague conversation." Mom turns down the oven. "Slow and easy," she says. "How about we say, five pounds? Now, Andrew?"

"Well, he's a lit major. Straight A student. He's got brown hair."

"What are his ambitions?"

"To write."

"Write? Write what?"

"Mom, don't use that tone of voice. He's going to be a great writer."

"Let's not tell your father about Andrew, just yet." She gathers the apple peels, stems and centers. She places them in a compost bucket under the sink. "We let that meat cook until it's tender. Couple of hours."

"One? Two? How long?"

"You'll know. You'll just know. Takes time. Bear meat you'll want to cook longer than deer meat. Beef, less. You'll learn. Certain things you do often enough, you intuit. You give yourself time. You practice."

This makes me stop talking. I wait. I know, from all the conversations I've had with Mom, that soon she'll say, "Practice makes perfect," and then, she does: "Practice makes perfect."

I answer, "Exactly. Andrew and I are practicing."

Mom doesn't answer. She checks out the spices. "Rosemary?" she asks. I can hear the question in her voice. "What do you do when you don't have rosemary?"

"I don't know. What do you do?"

"Choose with care. Something with memory. Something with history. And skip brown sugar because we are going to have plenty of molasses."

I scribble notes, totally lost.

"Here we go!" She scoops the different spices into the palm of her hand and drops them in the pot with the five apples I have chopped. I have fifteen more apples to go.

"Isn't this a lot of mincemeat?" I ask.

"It's for the whole family. That's why it's a family recipe! It changes a bit now and then, but family members get used to it."

I want so much to say, "Andrew?" but Mom keeps on talking.

"It's going to make for a very interesting batch. We'll call it, "Sarah's Learn by Doing Mincemeat."

"And if it tastes horrible. If it fails? If no one wants any of it?"

"My sweet, that's how we learn. Mostly we don't rush and we constantly taste. And as I just said, 'they'll get used to it'."

Frustrated that Mom doesn't follow my lead and ask questions about Andrew, I walk over to the refrigerator. I stand on tip-toe to study the shelf above and check the spines of the cookbooks. When I find the most worn, the most stuffed full of clippings and three-by-five cards, I pull it down. I open *The Joy of Cooking.* The innards spill into a pile. I check each card. Not one of a dozen cards claims a recipe for mincemeat. I check the cookbook index. Nothing.

"You won't find this recipe in a cookbook dear. I've told you a dozen times, cooking is in the hands and in the heart. Which reminds me...," and she gets down on her hands and knees and opens the cabinet door under the sink. She reaches deep inside and turns to extend her arm. She shows me a bottle.

"What is *that*?" I ask, knowing full-well what it is. I'm astounded.

"Gallo Dark Burgundy," she doesn't blush, or stumble, or appear as if she doesn't do this all the time. I can't believe it! As if our family wasn't all Baptists! As if she opens a bottle of wine every day.

"What will Dad say?" I ask in a soft voice and try not to show how incredulous this scene is. Unbelievable!

Mom empties the bottle, the whole bottle, into the pot. "Your dad doesn't need to know everything." With the empty bottle in hand, she looks directly at me and says, "Sarah, there comes a time you need to tell the truth. Reveal secrets. Let it out!" She wraps the bottle in yesterday's *Spokesman Review*, and pushes it behind the waste basket. "For your dad, now is not the time. About the wine, he'll never guess. He just loves the taste of mincemeat and I'll probably never, ever tell him why." She stands, hands on hips and gives me one of her Mother-Stares. "So with that, I hear some truth in your voice. Truth I haven't heard before. About Andrew. Does *the one* mean marriage?"

"Marriage? We just..." I hesitate. I know immediately I shouldn't have hesitated.

"Just what?"

I begin slicing the prunes.

"You didn't finish your sentence, Sarah."

"Well," I take a deep breath and let the words come out in a whoosh, "Andrew-and-I-are-going-to-rent-an-apartment." I blush at the lie and wonder if she will guess we are already living together.

"Well, well," Mom says, as if I gave her such news every day. "I could tell you were avoiding something."

"I'm not avoiding anything. I just told you."

"And now I'm going to tell you. You know exactly what your father and I think about the sacredness of marriage. I needn't remind you, you are a holy vessel."

Well, that holy-vessel thing stops me. Not that I hadn't heard it before, about a hundred times, but not in relation to Andrew. I don't know what to say. No other mother in the world talks like my mother. I end up saying the very first words that come to mind and I try to control the confession so it isn't quite so confession-y: "We've signed a lease."

"Well then, I guess it's time to talk about certain things."

"Mom, I don't think we have to talk about *certain* things. Andrew and I aren't children."

In the silence that follows, Mom slits open a box and currents fall with gentle plops. From a second box she scoops raisins and lets them slide into the mix.

"Mommm," I pull the word out like taffy, tentative and pleading. Then I proceed to tell her all about Andrew: what a good writer he is, how ambitious, how funny, how thoughtful, how he will graduate this coming spring with a degree in English Literature, how he is destined to be a great writer. In the middle of the description, I throw in the sentence, "Andrew's mom understands. She's very modern…she's already given us a set of silverware. She's…," I stop. I can see Mom wince and she holds her breath. I end the discussion with a sweep of words, watching to see how Mom will react. "We're going to apply to the University of Chicago."

"Who's *we*…?"

"Well, us. It will be great! Honest! I'll be teaching. I've already sent a letter of inquiry to the public school headquarters in Chicago. I've heard they are desperate for teachers and Andrew wants his degree from the U of C. Just to get in you have to be brilliant! He's brilliant, Mom. He believes he'll be the next Hemingway. We'll get married soon. He's not that much taller than me, but he *looks* taller. He wears a white silk scarf. He looks like a Hemingway character. Honest, Mom. Wait 'till you meet him!"

"Back up. The more you talk, the more I think your father is going to need to know. He just might have something to say about this."

"Well then, you better know. We live together. Already." There. I said it.

Mom turns from the stove and looks directly at me, holding my gaze until I have to look away. "Mom, believe me. We'll get married, soon. We've just been so busy. School and…"

"Pick a date. I'd suggest, if you're looking for a blessing from your father, you not only choose that date, but you make it soon."

"We will! We will!" Relieved, excited, pleased that everything is out in the open, I begin to explain our plans (hoping Mom will forget to call Dad into the kitchen). I tell her how we live above Bartell Drugstore. Only one floor up so it isn't hard to carry groceries. I tell her how I painted all the furniture white—furniture Andrew's mom gave us. Mrs. Althaus isn't happy with that, but she never told us not to. I tell Mom how the bathroom window looks out on the traffic on the busiest corner of the University District. How I can cook hamburger a dozen ways. How my two part-time jobs and his part-time pizza job pay for everything but tuition.

"That's very nice. Pick a date next month and maybe Dad doesn't need to know about this little living arrangement."

The initial excitement drains. I beg for understanding, "Mom, times are different. Everybody lives together. It saves money. We both cook. Andrew is a brilliant cook. He can make hollandaise. Real hollandaise. Living together is better than finding out later it isn't going to work!"

Mom gives me one of her squinty-eyed-you-better-listen-to-me looks and says with a sure, stern voice, "I don't think you thought about this quite enough…"

"He's *all* I think about!"

"Don't be smarty-mouthed! You're not quite so grown-up as you think you are."

She reaches for my hand and continues, "There are certain things in life that should not be improvised. Like who you live with and when. I know that making mincemeat seems to you like I'm improvising. But with improvisation, comes planning. You don't get to improvise until you know what you're doing." She gives my hand a squeeze as if the conversation is settled and done.

I've more to say. "You just said, just minutes ago, you said, I *do* know what I'm doing."

From her apron pocket Mom pulls a three-by-five card. She hands me the card.

GRANDMA MILLIE'S MINCEMEAT RECIPE

Meat, apples, currants, white raisins, dark raisins, prunes, suet, red wine, sugar, molasses, spices. Add assorted other ingredients in season and as needed.

"That's it? That's the recipe?" I ask in disbelief.

"Exactly. But remember Missy, my mom took a lifetime to perfect this. Then she showed me. Showed me for many years. Now, it's simple. It's clear. No fancy stuff. You know what you're doing and you do it."

"No measurements?"

"Measurements? You know when you know." Mom reaches for the recipe card and holds it in front of her as if it contained a thousand words of wisdom. She looks up from the card. "Okay. Write this down. I think some directions won't hurt. This is a family recipe and I don't want it to get lost. Or changed without thought. You're not to laugh…there's something sacred and sure about things that come down through the ages. I might not be so modern, but at least you and I will carry on something that has been important in our family. Do you understand?" By now Mom holds my chin in her hands and gently kisses me on the nose. "I love you."

"And I love you, you are the very best mother ever."

"Enough slathering. You still need to be thinking of a date. For the moment, write this down. Suet."

I write *suet* and ask, "Exactly what *is* suet?"

"Fat. From the butcher." Mom's voice softens. The air isn't quite so tense. "Tell the butcher you need about this much," she cups her hands to form a space the size of a grapefruit. "Suet is like faithfulness. It's the first ingredient."

Mom holds up a finger as if to focus my attention. She says, "The most important part of a recipe is care. But part of a good recipe is luck. Luck and care held together with faithfulness. That's the key. Faithfulness. That's what Dad and I have."

I don't ask for clarification. I have never considered my dad and mom anything but faithful.

Except once.

I was nine years old. I woke from sleep to hear my parents' voices. The words grew loud. Hard, sharp words and mumbled crying words. I sat up. Held my pillow against my thumping heart.

"You never should have..."

"It was for a piece of pie...for God's sake...very good pie, I might add."

"Pie? Alone with someone else's piece of pie? How could you? And I don't want to hear one word about her pies..."

"It didn't mean anything... I didn't mean..."

"Then, how could you ever have..."

"Please, please...it wasn't anything..."

I held my breath and tried not to listen to my parents yell. When I heard Mom sob, I pulled the covers over my head and hummed, "Oh My Darlin' Clementine."

I cried myself to sleep. I was sure my parents would be getting a divorce. I wanted to tell Freddy, but he was down in the basement in his own room. Tomorrow he would leave for Boy Scout Camp.

At the breakfast table, in the morning, when Mom and Dad were loading the car with Freddy's camp stuff, I told my brother, "I've got a secret." He finished his Cheerios, ran water over his bowl, and said as he headed out the back door, "Good. Keep it. That's why they call it a secret." And he left me to worry alone.

Things worked out. That Saturday, Mom baked four pies instead of two. She served pie for lunch and pie for dinner. Dad said they were the best pies he'd ever tasted. All week he asked for seconds.

I never told Freddy what happened. I didn't tell him because I didn't understand what happened. My parents yelled. Mom cried. Dad ate a lot of pie. I never recalled hearing the neighbor lady mentioned again. A month later a new neighbor moved into the neighbor lady's house. Life returned to normal.

I hold my pencil ready. Mom says, "Care." I write care.

Mom blinks as if to shoo away some errant thought. Then she continues, "And a little secret ingredient doesn't hurt."

"Like what?" I ask, fearful Mom might talk about black lace lingerie, or special ointments, or some strange ritual about which I don't want to hear. At least not from my mother.

Mom stands, lowers herself carefully to her knees, and once again rummages under the sink. She holds up another bottle.

"Slivovitz!" she says triumphantly.

"What's that?" I ask, realizing there are things about my mother I would have never guessed.

"Plum brandy. Like the coldest, best spring water. But stronger. Let's have some!"

"Mom, it's not even noon!"

"Yes, but we're making mincemeat and we're talking about you and Andrew getting married."

Mom places two jelly glasses on the kitchen table and carefully pours a quarter inch of liquid in each. She raises her glass. "Drinkin and clinkin," she says and our glasses chime.

I swallow and gasp, "Good God, Mom!"

"Don't you use such language!"

Then Mom laughs. She holds her glass for me to watch and instructs me, "Like this. Sip it. It gets better with the tiniest sips."

A loud rumble of a motorcycle fills the air and seconds later, Freddy clomps up the back steps. Dressed in black leathers, he pulls off his gloves, and pushes back his goggles. "Hey! Hey! Hey! Little sister's home! And…my goodness me," Freddy says and reaches for the bottle of Slivovitz. He pours himself a half-inch in Mom's empty glass. "I love coming by to visit to find the women folk tippling!" He turns one of the chairs around to straddle backward. "And just how are you except sweetly woozy?"

I think my brother is about the best renegade ever. By day he's a banker, and on weekends he puts on leathers and his helmet and takes to the road on his Harley.

"Your sister is getting married," Mom says.

"Let's drink to that!" and Freddy refills his quarter-inch of brandy. "Who's the unfortunate SOB?"

Mom slaps Freddy's arm, "That language is not allowed."

"His name is Andrew Althaus."

"Handy Andy! Great! When's the wedding?"

"Soon."

"Well, with that good news, I think I'll join Dad in front of the television. Dinner coming soon? I've got a Harley Club meeting later." He drains his glass. "Be sure to invite me to the wedding!" Freddy tries to knuckle rub my head, but I pull out of his reach and I grab his hand.

"Dad doesn't know," I say.

"And I'm not to tell?"

"Well, I'd like to do that. We haven't picked the exact date."

"My lips are sealed," he says and leaves us.

Mom waits for me to finish my drink. The sweet/sour smell of the beginning of mincemeat fills the room.

"One last thought. A very important thought...," Mom says.

My pencil is ready.

"Don't use walnuts. I heard of a woman once who used walnuts. Our family mincemeat never has walnuts. Some things just don't fit. Foreign objects—like walnuts, for instance."

"That's it?"

"I'm thinking. I'm thinking."

While Mom thinks, I luxuriate in the coziness of my parent's kitchen: the goofy salt and pepper collection of alligators and pigs, the week's newspapers stuffed in an old Easter basket in the corner, opened letters in a silver bread plate in the middle of the table waiting to be read a third and fourth time, ailing African violets leaning toward light on the window sill.

Then, unbidden, words pop out of my mouth, "Will you leave me the mincemeat crock?"

"Leave?"

"In your will."

"My will? Not quite so fast, young lady. I've years of mincemeat making ahead of me. But, when the time comes, yes. I can't imagine Freddy will fight you for it. It will be yours." Mom rubs her bumpy knuckles and works to straighten the ends of her fingers. "I do think of getting old. Older. Life brings changes. What you wanted and needed at twenty, your body might not want at fifty. Stiff joints make certain parts of marriage a challenge."

"Are we done?" I ask, fearful what Mom might say next.

"Oh! My goodness. I almost forgot. Write this down. Sugar! White sugar. Brown sugar. Molasses. The sweet part of the recipe! Sugar and molasses are like...."

"Why, Mom, sugar is like ... why it's like ...," and I almost say, but don't say, "Sex."

"I know exactly what sugar is like. And certain things about marriage are better left unspoken. Which reminds me of cranberries."

"Cranberries? You never put cranberries in your mincemeat."

"This year, I'm going to put cranberries in my mincemeat. No matter how old you get, you've got to be spontaneous!" Mom sighs and leans back. "I think that covers everything. I'll be anxious to hear how you and this Andrew work things out. If he's the right one, then you can marry the right one as easily as you can live with the right one."

"And who is this?"

I turn to see Grandma Millie in her bathrobe, eyes squinty from waking. Confusion is written on her face. "And drinking Slivovitz!"

I figure things can't be all that bad if she remembers the name of the most obscure brandy I've ever heard of. But I remind her with a hug, "It's me, Grandma. Sarah. I'm so glad to see you."

She holds me at arm's length and then gives me a big hug.

"Of course. My darling daughter, Sarah."

"Close. Granddaughter."

Thanksgiving dinner comes and goes. The mincemeat pie is the best ever. And then it is time to fly back to Seattle, to school, to Andrew. I arrive with a quart jar of mince-meat and I've promised Mom that there will be a wedding date. Soon.

Back in Seattle Sunday night, I report to Andrew everything I've said, what Mom said, and what my dad didn't say.

"What if we did get married?" I ask.

"I thought the guy was supposed to ask," Andrew says pecking away at his typewriter.

"But you didn't. You haven't."

"Now I won't. Surprise is gone. Besides, we've got to finish this year, graduate, get accepted at U of C, pack, take care of whatever needs to be taken care of in Chicago. All that stuff. Getting married on top of everything else would be crazy. I don't have time."

"I'll take care of it."

I do take care of it. And I think, in truth, Andrew is pleased. He has enough on his mind finishing his last year. If it hadn't been for me, we probably wouldn't even have gotten to Chicago. From the day we began living together I had said, "We should apply to the University of Chicago's Advanced Writing Program." He never finds time. I get the application. I fill it out. From his professors I get his letters of recommendation. Somehow, somewhere, someone must have been impressed, because the University of Chicago accepts Andrew. Accepts him with a scholarship. A little scholarship, but it's money we'll need with only my teacher's salary.

Oh, and yes, I applied and received a teaching position in Chicago. Once I have the job, I register us for Student Housing for Couples. Then I plan the route from Seattle to Chicago.

And the wedding? I know it sounds horrible, but I find my own engagement ring. I find a minister. Then I write Mom and Dad to plan on a June wedding.

Mom writes back to tell me Dad is pleased. I will also follow Mom's suggestion to come home for Easter and try on Grandma's wedding dress. Mom describes it as ivory, silk, not extravagant, no train, no veil, a classic, ankle-length dress with covered buttons and rows and rows of lace.

It is hard to let go of the idea of a tie-dyed cotton dress and a sunflower bouquet. Maybe there was a time when white meant something. Maybe there was a time when not wearing white was considered bad luck or worse, scandal. But ivory? Isn't that like yelling out, "I'm not a virgin? I can't wear white!" As for scandal and luck? Neither is even vaguely on my mind. Perhaps they should have been.

CHAPTER EIGHT

THE GAITSBERG ANNOUNCEMENT

Mom is watching Grandma's good days and not-so-good days, and when days are good they are wonderful. That's when I receive the best tapes ever. Grandma Millie even uses different voices for different words and different people. It is like listening to a dramatic production of her very own history, told just for me.

Saturday, August 1, 1914

Luke was very persistent. We saw each other almost every day for the next month.

And when he asked? Well, it wasn't too romantic, but I think of it being just right. We took Babe and the buggy and rode all the way to Soap Lake. We sat under this giant weeping willow. And then he said these words: "I can't wait any longer." And then he added, "You know what I mean." And guess what? My mom had told me about angels singing, and I guessed I knew what he meant. And it wasn't but a bug-bite minute, I said, "Yes!" And then we kissed a good many times.

Two days later, I walked up the front steps of The Gaitsberg Daily's office, pushed open the solid oak doors, and followed the polished brass arrow up the stairs. Through a wall of glass, I could see huge rolls of paper being transformed into newspapers. Below, at one end of the room a workman in coveralls checked the taut paper, his hand inches from the rolling sheet as if in blessing.

The acrid smell of a cigar made me look up. Above, on the landing was Abe Wiseman, Milt's pa. He was stocky like Milt. He wore a white shirt with a stiff collar and a pin-striped vest. His stomach pushed against a gold watch chain from which dangled a gold coin. His sleeves were rolled. He removed his cigar and called in a gruff and demanding voice, "Millie! Millie Birnham! Come up here!"

I was amazed that he even knew my name and I had no idea why he wanted to talk to me. Flattered, I followed him up those stairs.

"Well, you took your time, but I'm glad you made it. Never too late." His cigar stabbed the air like an exclamation point. "I told Milt to keep telling you. That boy is always looking for reasons to get your attention anyway. So! It worked! You are finally here." Abe Wiseman's voice boomed, "We need talent. Like yours!"

Mr. Wiseman turned his back to me and kept right on talking. I hurried up the stairs to try and figure out what, as Dad would say, the "H" he was talking about.

He talked as he walked, waving his cigar.

"Solid. That's what you are. Solid. Think I don't know? I heard your valedictorian speech. You've got what it takes! Some learning to do, but that's why I'm here."

"I'm here…"

He ignored me. Kept right on talking.

"Get this job hammered out. I've got some ideas. Bet you have some too!"

"I don't have ideas. I have…"

"Now, no false modesty. Milt raves about how smart you are…," and speaking around the cigar he added, "…no question, you're smart. But before we get started, let me explain how this operation works!"

He pointed to the machinery below, and over the noise he shouted, naming cylinders and cradles, rotary press, moveable type, more bins of type, the folding machine, capacity and volume, tack and bulk, and compact low-bulk paper.

I didn't dare interrupt. I wondered exactly when and how I might hand him my announcement.

"Okay?" he asked.

I nodded a yes, only because it seemed he needed an answer. He turned and said, "Well, then, follow me!"

At the end of the hall, Mr. Wiseman opened the door to the second floor offices. With a sweep of his arm, he explained without introduction that the four people seated there were his reporters, his secretary, and his bookkeeper.

They barely looked up from their tasks, but I noticed the reporters (men, of course), glanced at each other and it crossed my mind they too might think he was crazy. Or? Or maybe they were wondering why I was there.

Abe Wiseman snapped at the men, "Back to work! Get used to it!" He stepped back to usher me into his office and as he held the door he said, "Don't pay them attention, Millie; they think this is their domain. You'll give them some competition!"

"I…," and once again Mr. Wiseman either ignored me or didn't hear me. He pointed with his cigar at the chair in which I should sit and continued in his staccato voice, "Let's get down to business."

"You don't understand…"

"Don't understand? Don't you tell me what I don't understand, little lady. This is my business!" He pulled a stack of papers from a file cabinet and splayed them across his desk: The San Francisco Chronicle, The Spokesman Review, The Yakima Herald, The Portland Gazette. *He slammed his hand down on the papers with a*

thud. "Every one of these papers—every one—has a woman reporter and that reporter writes women-stuff: weddings, funerals, bake sales, just the kind of reporting women understand. Good writing! Every one of them. And that's what we need here at The Gaitsberg Daily*—a woman with a handle on the soft side of things! You!" He leaned over and stared right at me. I scooted back.*

"Soon. You'll be on your way. You and Milt."

"Milt?"

He stubbed out his cigar. "I've got news. Ernest O. Holland. You know Ernest O. Holland? Of course you do."

I must have indicated I didn't, because his next words were said in absolute disbelief.

"You don't? Can't imagine: Besides being important, he's a friend of mine! A close friend of mine. Come on now, his name should ring a bell."

Mr. Wiseman looked at me like I'm not that bright valedictorian he thought I was.

"Well, little Missy, he's the President of the State College. Where, as I have heard it rumored, you want to attend college. Right?"

Of course he didn't wait for me to answer.

"Well, guess what? Ernie? He loves my idea. Wait until you hear this!" Mr. Wiseman didn't wait. Whether I wanted it or not, another idea was about to descend.

"September comes around, you and Milt will be on your way. Home for weekends. You'll report. Write about school." He lowered himself into his cracked leather desk-chair, "Trust me, we might be a small town newspaper, but we're growing! You'll be part of it! An important part of it!"

He sliced the end off of a new cigar and pointed it at me. "'Word to the Homefront,' great title for a column, eh?" He leaned forward with both hands on his desk. "Can't tell you how pleased I am that Milt's got his eye on you. Think of this…" he waved his cigar in an arch, "…you two finish school, and see how it goes! Who knows? Things happen! I'm not going to push. You're young. Wide open future." He leaned back until his body was near horizontal, and clasped his hands behind his head. "But, things do happen!" And then he was silent. Waited. One minute. Asked, "What do you think?"

I swallowed, pushed forward in my chair, clasped my hands in my lap, and got out five words, "First I've heard of it."

"Well, yeah. Everything just came together these last few weeks. Milt didn't have permission to offer you a job, but he was to tell you to come by. I just heard from Ernie and he'd love to have you in that new School of Journalism. All you have to do is apply. Scholarship coming!"

He raised his eyebrows. Put his fat hand out, palm up as if I might place my life in it.

It was time for me to dive in:

"Mr. Wiseman. Please listen to me for a minute?"

"Yes, I'm all ears," he said with a huge smile.

"I'm not here to apply for a job."

"No, of course not. I'm offering you a job. It's yours! What would stop you? Right? You're the one! This paper needs fresh blood. I want a young person's point of view. A young woman's point of view. Maybe you want the column to have your name on it? I've thought of that too. How about Millie's Musings? Birnham's Beat. Whatever you want. I'm flexible. Tell me what you want."

"Please, Mr. Wiseman, you don't understand. I came here to put something <u>in</u> the paper."

"A story? You got a story and I haven't even hired you yet! Well, I have now. Right now!" Again, his hand hit the pile of papers. "Tell me! What's the story?" He leaned forward and smacked his lips: "mmm…mmm, I do love go-getters."

"It's not a story."

"Well, maybe it's a little story. It's still a story."

"It's not a little story."

"So, what's happening? You walk up a flight of stairs, you listen to the entire explanation of my newspaper, and you come into my office. So, why are you here?"

"It's about the wedding."

"What wedding?"

"My wedding."

"I don't understand."

"I'm getting married."

"To who?"

"Whom."

"Don't you get smart with me young lady! I know who and whom. What are you talking about?"

"My wedding."

"Wait, just you wait one god-damned minute. Milt said I should offer you a job. I was going to offer you this job and at the same time Milt was going to start courting you!"

"Milt courting me?"

"Yes, that idiot son of mine, Milt!"

"No. I'm going to marry Luke."

"Luke?"

"Luke Lane. Here…" I handed him the announcement, "I've written everything down. The church. The witnesses. The date. The time."

Abe Wiseman didn't speak. He pressed the edges of the handwritten note into the center of his green desk blotter. He looked up. His silence and squinty-eyed glare were enough.

I stood and without another word, I left.

The announcement was printed in the church bulletins: The Lutheran Ledger *and* The Baptist Beliefs.

CHAPTER NINE

TO TELL THE TRUTH

Spring quarter I begin student teaching. My novel hasn't received much attention. It's okay, because I finished *In Cold Blood* and Andrew raves about this new kind of writing. Literary Non-Fiction. Turning real lives into literature. That's me. That's Grandma Millie. Thank you Truman Capote. Soon as I can, I'll begin re-writing. Juice it up.

Easter Sunday, April 14, 1968

Once again, the folks send me a round-trip ticket and Andrew drives me to Sea-Tac. As we wait for my flight, I step back so he can get a good look and I ask again, "Are you sure?"

"Beautiful. You look beautiful," he pulls me close. "Perhaps a bit junior-league-y, but beautiful."

"I'm working on *mature*."

"You've got it nailed."

I go to swat him and he grabs my wrists and kisses my nose. For a second I lay my head on his shoulder. People around us seem to stare and I wonder if they think I'm more Jackie Kennedy-looking than hippy-looking and do they wonder why we are a twosome?

Student teaching has made me change my look. My supervising teacher suggested I might want to follow her example. Look more professional. I could have died, I was so embarrassed to have not been as professional as I thought I was. I bought a jacket and the minute I finished reading Capote, I purchased and devoured Molloy's *Dress for Success.*

I do feel more professional. I even bought panty hose and a bra.

Andrew hasn't changed. In fact, he's attempting to grow what may one day be a beard and he's got that worn look, thanks to me, in his jeans. I put them through four washing cycles. It's his pony tail that doesn't quite look right. I wonder if I would've ever pushed for our wedding if he had that ponytail when I met him.

I know one thing for sure. Mom and Dad will be very pleased at my new look. It has been hard for me to admit, but people really do care what other people wear. What's funny is that I remember dressing up for Easter when I was a little girl. I'm back to "Go."

I pull my sleeves to my wrists so the cuffs show just under my beautiful new coat. To get this coat, I had to stand in line for an hour at the Bon Marche coat sale. The women in front pushed right by this, the most beautiful coat in the sale. And only ten dollars. High-waisted, buttoned to the side, a buttery yellow. Having purchased such a bargain, I splurged on a pair of white gloves, stitched with the tiniest of yellow flowers. They cost as much as the coat.

In the coat department, I studied myself in the three-way mirror and felt conflicted. My hair now touches my shoulders. Sometimes I still part it in the middle to recapture a little of my Joan Baez look. But since student teaching, I've set my hair with sponge curlers and gel. Mom and Dad will love it, but Grandma Millie? I just hope she remembers who I am.

"Wish you were coming with me," I say to Andrew as my flight is called and the line moves forward.

"That's a frightening idea," Andrew answers. "Once we're married, they'll just have to accept me, and you can go back to looking like who you really are."

At which moment, I'm up to the ticket-taker and I wave and walk down the accordion ramp to the plane. With that last remark, I'm glad to be by myself.

The forty-five minute flight gives me time to make the transition from girlfriend in Seattle to daughter in Spokane. I wonder if I'll ever become my own person—be comfortable wherever I am, whoever I'm with. Why had Andrew's last words seemed so mean? Like he doesn't change his entire demeanor for his mother? Gets all boyish. And I accept that.

But now? I hate it when an edge appears between us. I want a perfect engagement. A perfect marriage.

We still have a few things to work out.

In Spokane, at the load zone, the front seat of the Ford appears to overflow with flowers. It's Mom in her Easter bonnet—a bountiful bouquet of silk roses and silk lilies and silk snapdragons—ruby to pink. A good foot and a half wide.

Uncle Oscar has come to visit from Montana. He's Mom's twin brother. The most unlikely of twins. Mom is short, slightly round, with tiny feet and small hands, quiet and soft-spoken, with always a bit of worry about her. Oscar is tall and slender, with a long nose and ponderous earlobes. He is outspoken and irreverent; always saying whatever comes into his head. He readily compares himself to Walt Disney's Goofy.

He greets me with, "Happy to see y'all!" He often plays the role of a drunk or a southern hillbilly. This morning it is all Tennessee/Arkansas.

He's clean shaven and reaches with his large, long-fingered hands to give me a hug hello. He looks me up and down and says, "Well! Aren't you the fine lady! Gloves and all!" He makes me turn around. "And! A bit of the Kennedy about you!"

"You are looking pretty good yourself! Rather Eastery!" I say as I tug at his shirt-tail that isn't quite tucked in.

Mom calls, "Come give me a kiss hello and get in the car. And Oscar, of course she's beautiful. And, notice! She's wearing gloves! It's Easter. Some people honor Easter by dressing appropriately. It wouldn't have hurt you to wear a tie."

"Ties look awful with Hawaiian Easter shirts!" he says and winks at me.

"Here, dear." From her lap, Mom passes me a hat, half the size of her hat. Yellow daisies galore. Soon enough I'll put it on—at the church door. I know Mom well enough, that the fact that it might not fit doesn't matter. Whether to wear an Easter hat is not discussable.

We have exactly thirty minutes to get to Born Again Baby Jesus Baptist Church. Freddy will meet us there. Grandma Millie will come to the house after her service at St. John's Lutheran Church.

When I ask how Grandma Millie is doing, Mom explains that when she's at her best, she insists on driving. There is no stopping her. Mom hopes she remembers how to get to church and back home. As far as *if* she should be driving, I am told, the subject is hands-off. Then Mom reminds all of us that at dinner, "There will be no comparing of Easter services with Grandma Millie. The subject of sermons, beliefs, traditions, altars, flowers - anything, everything about Baptists and Lutherans - will not be discussed." Mom turns to look over the front seat at Oscar. And at me. We nod in agreement. Subject closed. Grandma Millie has made it quite clear that she might have been a Baptist at one time. But now? Now she is a Lutheran. No more said.

At The Born Again Baby Jesus Baptist Church, where they sing, and clap, and wave their arms as they praise the Lord, everyone stretches to see Pastor Jones around the sea of Easter bonnets. I try to pay attention to the blustery sermon (about the rapture), and I envision all of these Easter bonnets trying to get by each other in a rush to heaven. And by now, near through the last chorus of *Bringing in The Sheaves,* all I can think about is how much my forehead itches where the Easter bonnet has made an indent and I can hardly wait to remove it—like pulling off a too tight girdle.

Back home, as the front door opens, I drink in the sugary, sweet scent of Easter lilies. Mixed with the perfume of the flowers is the smell of the Easter ham roasting. I know without having to turn on the oven light that the ham is weighted with canned pineapple slices, pierced in the center with maraschino cherries, all held in place with small, spear-like cloves. I relax into the feel of home and hope that if the rapture does happen, the Lord will wait until after dinner.

Mom and I leave hats and gloves in the back bedroom and head for the kitchen. Dad loosens his tie and pushes back into the depths of the Barcalounger. Oscar follows us into the kitchen to start Easter with a beer. And surprise of surprises, Dad calls that he wouldn't mind a beer too, if someone had been courteous enough to ask. Nothing like a good cold beer to get ready to float up to heaven!

"Sweetheart, just don't stand there. Grab an apron to protect your dress. Never thought I'd see the day silk would replace denim! You are looking so grown up!"

I can't wait any longer. I unclasp my hands from behind my back, and extend my left hand—it may be small, but it *is* a real diamond.

"Oh, goodness, gracious! David, David, come here! Right this minute!"

Dad and Uncle Oscar come into the kitchen as if there's been a huge calamity.

"Look! Look at your daughter's hand! And when is the date?"

"Soon! Very soon." I should have lied and given them a date, but I'm not good at lying, and should I say a date, Mom will get the calendar marked and Andrew will wonder, once again, why he wasn't consulted.

"Oh, sweetie, I'm so happy."

"Well, good," Dad says. He takes my hand in his and gives it a squeeze. "It's about time."

And I wonder if he hadn't figured out everything already.

"Couldn't be happier…but next trip you bring that husband-to-be with you. No excuses. He's supposed to ask me for permission!" Dad is all smiles. "Oscar and I have a football game to watch." And after Oscar kisses me on the forehead, they leave for the front room. Mom wipes away tears.

"Sweetheart, this is so wonderful. The ring is beautiful. Just perfect. Not that I doubted your letter full of hints, but it is nice to see the proof. And tell me, what's his name again? Andy?"

"Andrew."

At just that minute, Freddy bangs on the door and enters carrying a two-foot-tall plush Easter rabbit.

"Did I hear something about Andrew? Isn't he someday going to be the betrothed to be?"

"*Is* the betrothed," I flash my diamond for him to see.

"Lordy be! A child in this family is finally getting married."

"You forget...you were married. Once? Twice? How many?"

"So long ago, I can't recall."

"You can't have forgotten them?"

"They forgot me first."

"Stop it, you two. Let's focus on happy times. Like today. And the wedding to come! Besides, it's time to cook. Sarah, please peel ten potatoes. Freddy, please create one of your wonderful salads. Grandma Millie will be here any minute, and she will be hungry."

"When's she going to be here?" Freddy asked. "I'm starved...but a beer will do," he says as he pulls a Rainier from the refrigerator. "Oops, I forgot it's Easter and she'll get here when and if that Lutheran minister stops talking. How they do like to talk."

"Now, now," I remind him, "House rules. No bad-mouthing the competition."

"Well, when are you going to do the dastardly deed with Andy?"

"Andrew, if you don't mind," I say.

"You call me Freddy. I'll call him Andy."

"But you're a Freddy, not a Frederick. And he *is* an Andrew."

Mom pops back into the kitchen, rummages for the good silverware and calls, "Children! Stop that. Right this minute. No arguing. No fussing. This is Easter and we are going to act like a real family."

"We were acting like a *real* family," Freddy says.

Mom bonks Freddy on the head with a silver serving spoon and we get busy.

But first, I get myself a beer.

A half hour later, Grandma Millie drives up. Before she can park her Hudson Hornet, I'm out the door to greet her. I wait patiently as she maneuvers the car back and forth, over and over, until it fits exactly one inch from the sidewalk. Inside the car she finds her purse, her gloves, and then pinches her cheeks as she looks in the rear-view mirror.

She inches out of the driver's seat. It surprises me to see how Grandma Millie has aged. The change has been steady. Like watching a time-lapse camera. Grandma moves a bit slower. Her hair is whiter. Her shoulders more rounded. But her lipstick is bright red and matches her fingernail polish.

What is left of Grandma Millie's youth is in her eyes—black eyes which she lines with black liner. Her eyes are full of defiance and her mouth has always been full of quick, smart, sassy answers and a laugh that makes her teeth clatter. Her body is slightly arthritic, and she has slender ankles melting into log-like feet. Her waist has slowly grown.

But, even now, Grandma Millie has never been like any of my friends' grandmothers who are decorous, proper, modest, demure, restrained, age appropriate. Grandma Millie isn't much like anyone I know. She smokes. She swears (at appropriate moments and places). She has a laugh like thunder. And now, with the recordings, Grandma has stories to tell.

And as soon as dinner is over, I'm going to get her alone and see if she won't tell me more about Luke Lane, the mystery man.

I did hear about him, once, but not from her. I heard the tiniest bit about Luke Lane. I was supposed to be asleep, and I heard Uncle Oscar say, "Damn him. Damn that bastard. Leaving Mom. Three of us and he left her for the neighbor lady." And Dad interrupted him to say, "Better watch how you talk. You know how your sister feels. Talk like that and she'll wash your mouth out with soap!"

And that was what I knew. It seemed impossible to me that anyone could have left Grandma Millie for any reason, let alone, for the neighbor lady.

Out of the car, I offer Grandma Millie my hand. She readily takes it. Grandma takes a minute to rest against my arm. With her other hand she steadies herself with her ebony, duck-headed cane. She smells of White Shoulders and Marlboros. She leans back as best she can and gives me a good once-over.

"Mighty sassy, my little one! Something must be going on. I don't remember you ever looking so grown-up!"

I tuck my hand inside my grandmother's elbow, and lay my other hand on her arm to show off my ring.

"Glory be! Your mom said it was going to happen, but she thought maybe it was sometime in the far future. And here you are. With the ring."

Grandma Millie studies my finger, turning the ring to catch the light and when she does I feel a slight sigh pass through her body. "My, my, my," she says and looks directly at me, "It's always nice to practice."

"Grandma! Andrew and I are not like that!"

"Like what?" Grandma Millie's smile fades.

"Like …other people, like, I don't know, like anyone else! This is forever."

"Forever is formidable."

"Not for us!"

"Well, as this family has always said, 'Put one foot in front of the other and you never know just where or when you'll arrive.' You! Us! Them! Whatever! I wish you luck."

By now we are up the steps and at the door. I walk her through the front room. The men wave and nod hello, but the three of them, Dad, Freddy, and Uncle Oscar, hardly take their eyes off of the television. They are deep into a golf game. How could golf be that exciting? And a re-run probably. Who plays golf on Easter? And Grandma Millie doesn't miss a chance to chastise them, "Gentlemen, it's always a pleasure to see you so intellectually challenged!"

They laugh. Stand. Accept her hugs and air kisses. And return to their television.

In the kitchen, we finish with dinner preparations.

"Sweetie, tell the men to wash their hands. We're almost ready. And, it's time for the candlesticks."

In the sideboard, I find the soft silver bags that hold the candlesticks. I love these candlesticks. Grandma Millie has never said, but I wonder if she and Luke got them at their wedding. Will I get them at my wedding? I hope so. Freddy doesn't care and they should be mine, if for no other reason that this family has seen Grandma Millie and I as a matched pair, separated by time: the old and new version of the same woman. Both voracious readers. Both Scrabble players. Both quick to know the answer to *Name That Tune.* Both crazy about those candlesticks. And for a split moment, I think, if we are so much alike, what does that say about marriage?

I check the table. Immediately I turn two knife blades toward the dinner plate, with the ever-present words of Grandma Millie guiding me: "The blade goes toward the plate, otherwise it means you wish the person to cut themselves and die."

And Mom? She has her own set of admonitions and superstitions—never trust a man with a mustache; once you're married, if he doesn't kiss you goodnight, check his collar; men who wear hats are always gentlemen but they take off that hat and cheat; if he whistles under his breath he's dreaming of another woman. Mom's admonitions and Grandma's marriage failure aren't all that reassuring.

At the dining room window, I let the sunlight play off the facets of my diamond. A prism of color slides over the ceiling. I promise myself, tonight when I take left-overs to Grandma Millie's house for dinner, I'll ask the biggest question: "Why did your marriage fail?" Not that I think for one minute Andrew and I will fail, but there's that nagging twin-ship thing.

The marshmellowed sweet potatoes pass from hand to hand. Grandma Millie asks, "So, Sarah, I understand you'll be heading for the big city?"

"Yes! Chicago! The University of Chicago." I look to see if the family is impressed. Hardly.

"We'll be working on Andrew's graduate degree," I say.

"*We*?" Freddy asks. "What is this *we* stuff, masked man?"

Then Grandma Millie asks, her eyebrows high and questioning, "Sarah, I thought you were going to teach."

"I am! Someone has to pay the bills!" I meant it as a light-hearted comment, but except for Mom, no one smiles.

"And I understand from your mother that Andrew will be getting some kind of a degree in books and reading," Uncle Oscar says and I check to see if he is being sarcastic. Who knows?

"Creative writing," I answer.

"How nice. So sad he wasn't able to join us."

"He wanted to come. But, he's swamped. Of course, you'll all get to meet him at the wedding."

"Too bad. If he had shown his face, we could have voted on him," Freddy says.

"Hush. Don't tease your sister. Please pass the Jell-O," Mom's voice commands.

"What a beautiful Jell-O ring, Mama. I always love your interesting Jell-O rings." Freddy's sarcasm is so drippy, Mom answers with a laugh, "Made it just for you!"

I could tell the subject of Andrew was over. Conflict was to be avoided. Conflict of any kind. And, of course, conflict was never avoided. I wondered how long before Uncle Oscar would be chastised. Freddy would think it was funny, and then he'd be chastised.

What is it about holidays? I dream of a Norman Rockwell Easter. Norman Rockwell must have had an entirely different family. I can hardly remember a family gathering where, at a certain point, Uncle Oscar wouldn't over-step some hidden line, and leave. The first time I remember Uncle Oscar leaving was another time I heard the wee-ist bit about Grandpa Lane.

I was ten. I gently placed each plate on the milky white table cloth. As I tip-toed around the dining room table filling crystal water glasses, I listened to Uncle Oscar and his then wife, Aunt Juniper. From the living room, their voices slowly built to sharp exclamations.

Uncle Oscar's words slurred, "You don't know what you're talking about! He deserted us!"

I reached for a water glass and moved it a half inch. I turned a knife edge toward a dinner plate and worked my way around the end of the table. I almost dropped the butter dish when Uncle Oscar loudly spit out the words, "That son of a bitch left Mom for a round-heeled-whore!"

At those words, Grandma Millie stormed into the front room and said in words like steel: "Oscar! Hush! You hush or you leave! You hush or I'll wash that mouth of yours out with Naptha!" Aunt Juniper glared at her husband. My mom must have held her breath, because the whumping sound of potatoes being whipped in the kitchen stopped. It would have been a tableau like a game of 'freeze,' except Uncle Oscar glared at Grandma Millie and yelled, "I was defending you!" and then he stomped out of the house. He pounded the car horn until Aunt Juniper gathered her purse and her coat and joined him. At which moment Freddy arrived, walking briskly through the kitchen to the living room, demanding, "What happened? What happened?"

Mom pointed to the bathroom and told him to wash his hands. Dinner was mostly silent. By the time pumpkin and mince pies were served, Uncle Oscar's exit was ignored, and Grandma Millie suggested we all needed a little port. She toasted the turkey, her dear grandchildren, and the Rose Medallion dinner ware. Mom immediately served steaming cups of coffee. And so ended a non-Norman Rockwell Thanksgiving.

Today, with dessert comes 'family stories' and, for once, the mood and words are more calm than I ever remember. Our stories seem to have quit precipitating exits.

Mom starts first. She tells how the minister once came to dinner and she made it all through the dinner, nervous as a terrier, when at the serving of the dessert, she asked Pastor Grunwald which pie he wanted, "Pince or mumpkin?"

Grandma Millie tells about the time when she was named princess of the grange dance. She was sixteen. She wore a sky-blue dress with an eyelet collar and dyed her white shoes with blueberry juice and didn't realize until she got home that her feet were blue.

Oscar tells about grooming his horse, Babe, to a fair-thee-well, and braiding leaves into his mane. Leaves that just happened to be poison oak. Horse didn't notice. Seemed to like being beautiful. Oscar had a few miserable days.

Dad reaches to give Mom a hug and he tells how he found his sweet Sally at the Five and Dime where he ordered toasted cheese sandwiches and crinkled pickles every Saturday for two months before the cute-little-thing behind the counter accepted his offer for a date. Mom just loves Dad telling how he tried to get courageous enough to speak. And, all the time, she waited.

I listen, wondering what would happen if I said, "I know! Let's someone tell the story about why Grandpa Lane left!" I don't, of course. I don't want everyone to 'freeze.' But I remain ever curious. Which leads me to ask, "Grandma, are you up for left-overs later? We can visit before I head back home." And Grandma Millie beams. I can tell she is so pleased I want to spend time with her all by myself.

CHAPTER TEN

UNCOVERING TREASURES

Later, Easter Day.

Grandma bids us all goodbye. Freddy roars out the back drive. Uncle Oscar naps in front of the football game. Dad watches. Mom and I finish dishes.

"It's time!" Mom announces. She is near giggly. "Hike yourself upstairs and look in the round topped trunk. It's wrapped in tissue. I'll finish wrapping the candlesticks and be right up!"

I can't believe Mom is suggesting I open that trunk—the trunk with the photo she had snatched from me. I'm more than curious. I climb the stairs to the attic and from under the eaves I pull open the round-topped trunk with its leather straps and pressed tin lid. Under a pile of hand-stitched quilts full of memories of childhood forts and picnics, I find a package wrapped in tissue. It is tied with a ribbon the color of caramel. It barely holds dried flowers. At my touch, the brittle bouquet of lilacs breaks into pieces. I carefully, carefully pull back the tissue to find a card with Mom's writing: *Millie's wedding dress.*

I stand and gently pull the dress against my body. The dress drapes over my extended leg, the layers of tiered lace end in scallops at my ankle.

"Mom," I call down the stairs, "Are you coming?"

"Be right there!"

I shake out a quilt and place the wedding dress on it. I kneel at the trunk. A circle of Victorian children, swags of flowers circling them, decorates the two curved compartments in the trunk lid. Each half of the lid opens. One half is empty. The other holds an album; crusty glue and black corner stickers hold each photo.

Seated on the floor, leaning against the trunk, I open the album. I find bookmarks, advertising cards, a high-school diploma, a see-through envelope with a curl of blond baby hair, a dance ticket, a Christmas program, a tender black ink footprint of a baby, train ticket stubs, and a Pullman car baggage claim. I find two photographs on the last page.

The first photo is of Grandma Millie, marvelously young. She is poised. Tall, slender, her wedding dress a perfect fit. On her head, as if to take flight, is a hat of bird's wings.

In the second photo, Grandma has aged. She stands with her head high. The photographer must have stood below the porch on which she stands. The angle makes Grandma Millie look monumental: tall, strong, the wind pushing against her ankle length dress. One child stands as if molded to her body. A second child peeks from behind her, holding a gather of dress in her hand. A third child, heels hooked over the bottom rung of the porch railing, wears bib overalls. In his lap he holds a rifle with one hand, cupped as if it were a child. I know immediately by the distant look in his eyes that the child is Uncle Gabe. His mouth is slightly open, head tipped back. The other two children are Mom and Uncle Oscar, looking nothing like the twins they are.

On the back of the photo is written: The Lane family on the Gaitsberg front porch, June, 1920. Then I notice a shadow at the bottom of the picture. The shadow of the photographer covers the porch steps—a man's shadow, with wide shoulders, wearing a wide brimmed hat.

When I hear Mom coming up the stairs, I slip the page with the two photos behind the trunk. Even if Mom knows about the photos, I need to study them by myself. Alone.

"Well?" Mom asks. "Put the dress on. Let's see how it fits." She pulls a peer mirror from the end of the attic. She dusts the glass and waits for me to slip into the wedding dress. I turn to look over one shoulder. I look over the other. Mom gives a gentle tug to the bias-cut satin.

"Stand tall," Mom demands.

I suck in my stomach and vow to only eat carrot sticks and grapefruit forever.

I groan, "I can't believe Grandma was ever this small. I'm huge. I'm a giant. I've got two months to lose ten pounds. At least. " I can feel the strain of buttons down my back.

"Dear, you're not big. You're just right."

Mom pulls at the bottom of the dress so it just hits the top of my Frye boots. "Well, the dress was an idea. A silly sentimental idea." She tugs again. "You're not big. You're healthy."

Somehow, as much as Grandma Millie and I look alike, no matter how much I might diet, I fear I will never be able to capture the lean, lanky figure of the grandmother in that photograph.

"Okay, enough torture and humiliation. Get me out of this."

As Mom unbuttons the ten top buttons on my shoulder and the twenty buttons down the back, I hold my hair up and away.

Mom opens the trunk lid and places the dress inside as if it were a sleeping baby.

"Hard to imagine your grandma so tiny."

She pats the tissue and closes the lid. When she turns she faces me with a bright, (forced) cheery smile and says, "Or maybe it's admitting you are grown up! My little girl all grown up. Forget the dress. I'm not even sure why I've kept it all these years."

For this moment, I believe we are on the edge of solid neutral ground. In this moment of closeness, I take a chance. I say, "Grandma's wedding must have meant a lot to you. Grandma must have told you…" I let my voice trail off.

"Weddings always mean a lot! *Hit Parade* is on." Mom turns and heads down the attic stairs. Like the trunk lid closing, the subject of Grandma Millie's marriage once again slams shut—a sure, firm, dropping of the subject.

I find the two photos behind the trunk and tuck them inside my blouse.

Back in the kitchen, I try once again: "I thought about wedding ideas, Mom. We want everything natural. Natural and real. Wild flowers in my hair and in my bouquet. And not wearing Grandma Millie's wedding dress is okay. I thought I'd wear a dress I'm making. A magenta tie-dyed dress. What do you think?"

"A little tradition would be nice. That's what made me think of you and Mama's wedding dress. The idea of a real wedding dress."

"Mommmm, tie-dye *is* real. Times have changed. Please understand. We need to own our wedding."

"Own? Own your wedding? What kind of a word is that?" Mom rarely gets bristly. It isn't often that her voice gains an edge, but I know enough to stop talking about a wedding in a park, my hair wrapped in wild flowers, vows spoken spontaneously.

"Don't get me started with your made-up vocabulary."

Dad comes into the kitchen. Looks at us quizzically. Retrieves a Rainier from the refrigerator. I try another tactic: "What do you think, Dad? Andrew and I thought of having our wedding in a park. Outside. It'll be free."

"What happened to weddings in churches?"

"Well, we thought it would save some money…"

He gives me a peck on the check. "I can think of better ways to save money."

"Like?" I ask. And immediately realize that wasn't the right thing to say. He does one of his lips tight, eyes tight, looks and walks back to the front room. "The quarter break is over. You and Mom decide. I'm pleased that you are engaged. Choose a date. Whenever, wherever you want. Just get married!" Somehow he has figured out our living arrangement. I'd let it slip that we was "us" and I had said something about "our" kitchen. He was not pleased.

With Dad in front of the television, Mom and I finish doing the dishes. In a subdued voice I try to tell her our plans: a small, very small service in Seattle at Golden Garden, out in the open, with a view of the Olympics.

The conversation slows almost to a stop, which makes me talk faster. All the time Mom remains silent. I explain that having the wedding in Spokane makes no sense. My high school friends no longer live in Spokane. And those that do wouldn't understand a small, intimate wedding. And at what park? Manito? I didn't think they did weddings at parks in Spokane. And then I begin to plead: if she and Dad would just drive to Seattle, they could take a nice vacation—eat at the Dog House, stay at the 6th Ave Motor Inn, go to the Pike Street Market. They would love Seattle! My enthusiasm and list of the wonders barely keep Mom's tears away. I don't add that we probably wouldn't even be getting married if it weren't for them.

I dry the silverware in silence. I'm learning that there is no way to talk about the meaning of marriage. If you love someone, isn't that enough? Ceremonies have so little meaning. Living in the moment is what Andrew and I try to do. I want to tell her that Andrew and I work at being honest and open. Being sincere. Being truthful. Having no secrets.

Finished, I announce to Mom, "I need to take a little nap before I head over to Grandma's. Please don't worry. It will all be fine. One step after another and all of that. Right?"

I slip under the covers and think that getting my parents to understand modern times is never going to happen. When Mom left the attic, she was just about ready to cry. Just now she was wiping her eyes. If she cries, I'll cave in—do the whole wedding thing like a good Baptist daughter, in a Baptist church. Mom's words romp around in my head and I can still see her tying the ribbon around the tissue, around Grandma Millie's wedding dress, and I regret my words, "It isn't that I don't think the dress is beautiful. I do. It's just not the real me."

I turn. I toss. Finally, I study the two photographs of Grandma. In the young photo she looks strong and hopeful. In the farm porch photo she looks burdened and sad. It crosses my mind that the second photo must have been taken by Luke Lane. And I wonder, how many days after this did he leave her? Leave his children? And I fall into a dream of dreams of women with large wedding hats—hats so large eyes are hidden. Out of the crowd appears my childhood minister, Reverend Torbat. From under the rim of his black fedora, he demands, "Well?" and again, "Well?" My voice catches and I cannot bring myself to say, "I do."

I wake full of anxiety and go to the kitchen and prepare Tupperware left-overs to take to Grandma Millie's.

Left-overs. What a strange word.

CHAPTER ELEVEN

CLOSER TO THE ANSWER

Easter evening.

I borrow Mom and Dad's car. I drive down Mission Avenue wondering what the evening will reveal.

In Grandma Millie's small black-and-white tiled kitchen, I add garlic to the mashed potatoes, add rosemary to the gravy, and top the Jell-O with real whipped cream. If the food is just right, the thermostat a cozy seventy-four degrees, everything perfect, maybe Grandma Millie will finally talk. I unfold the wooden TV trays, turn on the television, and join Grandma for dinner. Talk will come when *Wheel of Fortune* comes on. Grandma hates *Wheel of Fortune.*

We watch *Name That Tune,* and compete for who gets the answers first. She wins with *Sentimental Journey.* I'm first with *Tip Toe Through the Tulips,* and we tie for *Red Sails in the Sunset.* During the commercial, I serve the Jell-O in pale green Melmac bowls. With the first bite of dessert, Grandma Millie gives a huge sigh and says, "Have you been watching *The Ed Sullivan Show*?"

"Grandma, we don't have a television."

"Oh, that's too bad. I just love that Dick Cantino! He gives me goose bumps! And can he ever play the concertina!" Without hesitation, as if one man had reminded her of another, she demands, "Tell me again, where's Andrew?"

I'm pleased with the question. If I can talk about Andrew and our upcoming marriage, and marriage is the topic, maybe we can talk about her marriage and maybe I'll start to learn about Grandpa Lane.

"Andrew's in Seattle, finishing his finals."

"I would have liked to have seen him. The real him. We've all enjoyed the pictures you've sent, but the real thing would be nice. Maybe if we saw him in real life, we might not mind his pony tail."

I laugh. I'd tried not to expose that dumb pony tail in any of the pictures, but it appears that Mom and Grandma Millie have colluded about Andrew's appearance. I reassure her, "Not to worry. He's talking about shaving his beard."

"Tell him to keep trimming. I never could tolerate a man who hadn't shaved. Clean. I like a man with a clean, smooth jaw."

I take a chance, "Grandpa didn't have a beard?"

"Grandpa?"

"Your husband. My grandpa."

"How strange. I'm definitely your grandma, but never, ever, have I thought of him as your grandfather."

"Why not?"

"For obvious reasons…"

"Tell me…" I can barely speak.

"Are you ready?"

"Yes."

I turn off the television and scoot our trays across from each other. Grandma Millie spreads her napkin over her red and white candy striped dress and picks up her fork. She presses the tines of the fork through the whipped cream, cuts into the Jell-O. She brings the fork to her mouth, but instead of eating, she gazes past the television out the picture window. The Jell-O wobbles. Grandma begins to speak, "He…Luke…he was something. A catch. That's what everyone said, 'Luke Lane? He's a catch.'

I watch Grandma Millie's face. The softness of her cheeks seems to pull back, her eyebrows lift, and her dark eyes grow wide, her lips with crinkly lines pull into a smile. I had expected tears or terseness. I never expected a smile.

"You won't be shocked now, will you?" Grandma asks and doesn't wait for my answer. "Luke was something else. I wasn't the only one who thought so." Grandma leans forward, pointing her fork at me. "Don't you tell your mother I said so, but having children with Luke was fun. A lot of fun. Fun, of course, after I taught him a few things. It's after that…" She places the un-eaten Jell-O back on her plate, pats her napkin into place and demands, "If you think you're ready to hear, I think I'm ready to talk. Before I leave this earth someone ought to hear this story. And there's probably no better person than you."

Grandma nods toward the bookshelf where books bulge, tightly tucked. So many books fight for room, a few have slid to the floor.

"Get the Goode's Atlas. On the bottom shelf. Under the National Geographics."

I find the atlas and slip it onto Grandma's lap where it teeters for a moment and then falls open to reveal a smudged envelope full of photographs. I move to sit on the arm of the horsehair chair, my body warm against Grandma Millie's shoulder.

She holds each photo to the light, studies it silently, and holds it for me to see. She doesn't speak and I wait her out. Together we look at each photo:

- a farmhouse in a field of oats
- three girls in full-body bathing suits leaning against an Oak tree
- men with flat hats and skinny bicycles
- baby in a bonnet and a cascading christening dress
- men in suits sheltered from the sun under the Hennessey's Feed Store sign
- women in flowered hats and men in bowlers at the Number Sixty-nine Grange Picnic (identified by a sign held by two kneeling girls, braids curled on their heads)
- a wagon with three children, their faces blurred as if the speckled horse had shied
- a Victorian house with scalloped shingles
- a horse and fringed buggy with a woman holding a curly headed child
- a man posed beside a Roman column holding a pocket-watch draped from a vest
- a wedding photograph of Grandma Millie in a lace cap holding a bouquet of spider mums, her left hand, delicately placed on the family bible, showing her wide gold band.

Grandma shuffles the photos and chooses the Victorian house.

"That's *her* house, and my best friend's house," she says and gently pulls her finger over the photo. Grandma's smile disappears. Her shoulders slump. Just as I thought I should hug her to reassure her somehow, Grandma Millie sits up straight, her rounded shoulders taut. She picks another photo and demands, "See there in the buggy? All those curls? I saw her grow into a woman. Angelica. That's who Luke ran away with. Makes me hurt in my bones. I never knew how he could have left. Maybe me. Leaving me I could understand. I'd run out of steam, if you know what I mean. But how could he have left our beautiful children?"

She searches the pile for the blurred photograph of the children in the wagon and she holds it out in front of her. "Feisty bunch! Hard to get them to sit for a picture. Oh, they were such wonderful children. We did well. All but Gabe. Poor Gabe. Sorry you didn't get a chance to visit him this trip."

I stay quiet. It has been at least five years since I last visited Uncle Gabe. I hate visiting him. He never speaks. Doesn't even know who I am.

When I was little, we would drive out to visit Uncle Gabe at Medical Lake once a month. All I can remember is the whiteness of the building, the sour smell of old men, and the silence.

Grandma sighs. She pats the picture. "Yes. He slipped away from us…" She tucks the picture under the pile of the photos. She replaces it with the photo of the women in bathing suits. She points to the third woman over. Shorter. Hour-glass waisted. One hand on her hip.

"Angelica was a looker," Grandma says and places the horse and carriage photo next to the picture of the women in bathing suits. I study them. It dawns on me that one of the bathing suited women is the grown child. "...a looker. And by then, I wasn't..." Grandma's voice fades just as there is a knock on the back door. She slips a photo to the bottom of the pile.

"I'm here for dessert!" Uncle Oscar calls and the screen door slams. "Sarah! I've come to celebrate your engagement! Again!"

He bangs around the kitchen. I hear him open a cabinet door, followed by the clink of jelly glasses. He enters the room holding a tray like a French waiter, the three glasses teetering next to a half-full bottle of Jack Daniels. "We'll toast your success and hear about this trip to the big city, to the big university!"

Uncle Oscar places the tray on top of the television and fills the glasses. I notice he stumbles slightly when he offers me my portion. He stops mid-reach with Grandma Millie's drink when he notices the atlas.

Grandma's eyes and Oscar's eyes catch and then Grandma looks away, delicately sipping the dark liquor. Oscar slumps onto the couch, places his booted feet on the coffee table. He raises his glass, "Here's to that SOB. Mom, you telling lies again about that no-good father of mine?" Then Oscar turns to me, raises his glass and says, "Don't believe a word she says."

Oscar takes a huge swallow of the Jack Daniels and wipes his mouth with the back of his hand. "He was mean!" Oscar emphasizes each word with a jab of the empty glass. "He was nasty. And he got what he deserved." Oscar raises his glass higher, "So here's to you and here's to him and don't give me the evil-eye, sweet Mama. If we don't tell Sarah the truth, no one will."

"And just what do you know about truth, young man?"

"I know enough that, with a little Jack Daniels in you, *you* might let some truth out. Just a little. Not a lot. But you might admit you once said he should have been mangled by a hay mower. You see, Sarah, Mom's sentimental and forgetful now that she's wiser. But I can remember the days I could get her to share a bottle with me and she'd get riled and crazy and all the time I'd egg her on and wonder why she didn't hate him more!"

"Oscar! That's enough! He was your father."

"My father? What part about him was my father?"

The tension in the room is brittle. I have never seen Grandma so angry.

"He certainly wasn't mean and ugly, and unforgiving! Your father never, ever was vulgar or rude. You can just leave if you can't show some respect."

"Respect? That son of a bitch leaves you with the three of us and a farm to run and you think I should show him respect? Why? Give me one good reason!"

Grandma Millie sits as straight as a plumb bob. "Well, look at you! You're handsome. You're fit. You've had more women fawn over you than any man deserves. Martha! Just think of Martha. Which one was she? Second wife? Or the not-yet wife? You talk about your father and you seem to forget you haven't much room..." Grandma slows. She wheezes and huffs until Oscar jumps up and tips her forward and pats her back. I run to the kitchen for a glass of water.

"Let's think about something else. *To Tell the Truth* is on in two minutes."

As the television flickers, I watch my grandmother and my uncle. All this commotion, and I haven't learned anything. A grandfather leaves because his wife "*ran out of steam*?" That's it?

Grandma waits until after the Ajax commercial then says in a measured voice, "Oscar, of all the people in the world who shouldn't be judging a marriage, it's you. Each time you choose a new one, each time, I tell you what I learned about marriage and each time you just plow forward. True?"

Uncle Oscar raises his glass, "Mama Millie, you do know what's true."

"I am not Millie to you. I am your mother. And what is true is that you get a new woman and you just trade troubles."

"Yes, Mother, one does trade troubles, one woman for another, but you forget you also trade pleasures!"

"But, why trade? Why not just make it work?"

"You're treading on mighty soft ground, little Mama."

"I think we've covered the subject."

I can't resist, "One more question? Please?"

Grandma looks at me over the edge of her glasses.

"Is that why you didn't marry again?" I ask.

Grandma pushes back in her recliner. She sighs. "Not trading troubles. Not quite. But I can tell you this—once you've had the best, it's hard to settle for anything less."

"The best? The only person got it right is Gabe!" the words spit out of Uncle Oscar's mouth.

"Conversation over," Grandma Millie snaps and pushes herself upright. "Finish your drink." She means it. I watch as they look at each other, sealing their secret. Oscar drains his glass, slaps it on the tray.

Grandma turns sideways to talk to me, "My dear, this has nothing to do with marriage. What it has to do with, is that your marriage will be yours, and you'll do with it whatever you'll do with it."

"Bad odds, however," Uncle Oscar says, sitting cross-legged in front of the television, not looking at either one of us.

"Oscar! Stop that. Mind your own business."

I don't want this crazy conversation to end. This is the most I have ever heard. "What about being angry? What about hating him?" I ask.

"Only so many days, so many years, you can be angry and hateful. Eventually, what you remember are the good times."

"How'd you do that?" I ask.

"Do what?"

"Stay strong. Be positive. Learn to be who you are."

"I'm strong and positive and know who I am? How do you know that?"

"Any grandmother who wears red nail polish has got to be strong."

"Bingo! No question. Every time I paint my fingernails I feel like a woman ready for battle. Here's what else I do. You feel low? You feel like another day will be one too many? Do this—buy something red. Nail polish. Shoes. An apple. A big, juicy apple! It's magic. Life is all myth and magic. That's a glimpse at how to be strong." She turns to Oscar, "Turn on the news, Oscar."

I do dishes and listen from the kitchen. I make out a few words over the newscast: we will agree to disagree, you don't know everything, we are family.

Before the news ends, Uncle Oscar comes through the kitchen, kisses me on the forehead, and says, "Probably just as well you don't know. What you don't know won't hurt you." He is out the door.

I dry my hands and tuck the dish towel in the handle of the refrigerator. I don't know what he means. I want an answer. I want to think there has been something pure and strong about Grandma Millie—beyond red nail polish. I want my grandfather to have been weak, and stupid, and wrong. Or, I want the two of them to not have loved each other. If they'd truly loved each other, then how could it have ended? So badly? What was marriage if it didn't last? One day a marriage, the next day none? First one mate and then another? I ache to know the answer. By the time the dishes are done and the kitchen is neat and orderly, in the living room, Grandma is sound asleep.

I wait through the commercials and run my finger over the crepe-like skin of Grandma's arm. I whisper, "Time I should get home, Grandma."

She wakes with a sleepy smile. "I always love our times together," she says. She reaches for the photos that have slipped down the side of the sofa pillow. She taps them into a neat pile.

I take a deep breath and call up the nerve to ask her, "That last photo?"

I can see she knows exactly what I mean. She re-taps the photos and says, "Someday. Someday you'll learn it all. But for now, you hurry home and tuck yourself into bed. Sleep tight. I love you..."

I stuff my arms into my coat sleeves, find my purse, and dig out the car keys.

Grandma Millie holds out her hand for mine. She holds my diamond ring up to the light of the television. She says with a sigh, "It's a promise, that ring. But sometimes life is just life."

I repeat her words hoping she will say more. "Life is life?" I ask.

"Not all. Your life is your life. My life was my life. We each do the best we can, one step at a time. Remember though, there are those times when life happens to you. When it does, go buy something red!" Grandma smiles a big smile and squeezes my hand. She pulls me close for a kiss goodnight. I know when I look in the mirror in my childhood bedroom there will be a smudge of red lipstick on my cheek.

In my bedroom, as I drift off to sleep, I know that photo was Luke Lane. I know that picture.

CHAPTER TWELVE

MY WEDDING

Saturday, July 20, 1968

Andrew sleeps. I'm so excited I can't sleep. Over the back of the couch I spread my tie-dyed dress and Andrew's black high-school graduation suit. I polish Andrew's shoes. I clean my ring, again. I read over the vows we've written just to be sure I have them memorized.

Andrew: I promise to be the person you need and want: to laugh at your jokes, to share the shower, to learn to cook, to explain the purpose of Literary Criticism.

Sarah: I promise to be the person you need and want: to laugh at your jokes, to share the shower, to teach you to cook, to explain why I can read Jane Austin more often than I read Sartre or Kant.

Too nervous to eat breakfast, I leave Andrew a note on the kitchen table: "I'm off to pick up my bouquet. Be ready by ten thirty! Or else! This warning comes from your soon-to-be wife! (I can hardly wait!). And, yes, you have to wear the suit!"

I sign the note with loopy *x's* and *o's*.

When I return, Andrew sits at the kitchen table reading the Wheaties box. He hasn't dressed, or showered, or shaved. If I hadn't found him so gorgeous in his bare chest, plaid boxer shorts, and hair all askew, reminding me of a six year old dreaming of being one of those Breakfast of Champions, I would have screamed at him. Instead, I wrap my arms over his shoulders, kiss his head, and nestle against his back. With a lick to his ear I whisper, "Just a few more hours and we'll no longer be sinning."

"Speaking of sin, your parents called. From Spokane."

"Called! They should be here by now!"

"Your dad broke his ankle. They would have called earlier, but they were in the emergency room all morning."

"But they have to be here! It's my wedding."

"You spent a dozen phone calls assuring them they didn't have to come and now, they aren't. You got your wish."

I can't help it—I sob. "No! No! Mom convinced me that families are families. Forever! And I tried, but I just couldn't fit into Grandma's wedding dress. Without them, it won't feel like a real wedding!" It's all I can do to stop the tears. If I don't, my eyes will be all red. On top of a half-real wedding, I'll look horrible.

Andrew scoots his chair back from the table and pulls me onto his lap. "It will be okay. Just like we wanted. Small and intimate. With only our friends. Don't be silly. And you'll be beautiful in your dress."

"I can't believe this," and then the tears flow.

"The least you could do is ask how your dad broke his ankle."

"How?" I sniff and blow my nose.

"Your mom beat him up!"

I push back from Andrew's hug. "You're crazy!"

"Well, right. Crazy about you. Your dad broke it playing basketball with the Baptists. Your mother's words were, "He's a little old to be playing basketball." Andrew pulls me close, begins to unbutton my blouse, "But since I've got you here, let's sin a little."

I giggle, "Andrew, we sinned all night!" I whack the side of his head with a gentle slap. "I'll shower. Then it's your turn!"

He finds me in the shower. And we sin with delight and purpose.

And, we end up with time to dress and fix the flowers in my hair and finally, finally we are ready and we head out the door.

"Andrew, hurry up. We're going to be late. What if the chapel is locked or the organist forgets and our friends are late, or…"

"They never lock that chapel and no one's going to be late. And if you hadn't changed your mind about the park, we wouldn't be worrying about a locked chapel!"

I ignore him. I had vetoed the park. It could have rained. It could have turned cold. My parents and Grandma would need to sit down. And then I think about all of my family not being at my wedding and concentrate on not crying.

"Slow down," Andrew calls behind me as we hurry down University Ave.

I turn to grab his hand and he says, "Once we're married, it's two steps behind me! You'll need to obey! I'll be your lord and master!"

"Bullshit!"

"I can't believe it. My sweet, pure wife-to-be just said bullshit."

Andrew gives me a hug and we walk to the steps of the Universal Life Chapel.

Outside the double-wide doors of the cement block building, on the wide porch where students park their bicycles and smoke, wait our witnesses who are also our best man and maid of honor: Jake Blakely and Cynthia Schwartz. Jake was Andrew's last roommate and Cynthia is Jake's latest girlfriend.

Jake Blakely is dressed in black jeans and a black turtleneck and a black jacket. He calls, "Hey, hey! Ex-roomie! Get this show on the road!" Jake throws his half smoked Marlboro into a ceramic pot and gives Andrew a bear hug. Jake winks at me and proclaims, "Lamb to the slaughter!"

Cynthia Schwartz plants air kisses and bats the conversation back at Jake, "No negative anything, Mr. Jake. Sarah, you look beautiful. Jake's jealous. Nobody'd marry him in a million years."

"I get what I get without getting got!" Jake responds. Cynthia gives him the finger and heads for the door of the chapel.

I grab Andrew's hand and we follow.

Inside, the late afternoon sun shines through the cobalt blue windows making the pews, alter, and lectern an eerie under-water color. The last time we were here was for the wedding rehearsal. Bridget Barnett, the minister, explained how everything is moveable. She explained that sometimes they sit in a circle for sing-alongs and sensitivity sessions. Sometimes they put mats on the floor for yoga or therapy sessions. Today the eight short pews are in rows, filled with our friends. Someone has laid a bouquet of lilacs and rhododendrons on the bare alter, probably picked on the way through campus. I rummage behind the alter and with great luck I find a tin-foil wrapped coffee can. The flowers will shortly be dead with no water, but at least they will be upright.

As I arrange the blossoms to face forward, Reverend Barnett bursts through the doors, calling, "So sorry, I'm late." She holds up a wrapped finger. "My cat bit me. Ended in the emergency room. Me. Not St. Augustine. Now, there's a life lesson! 'Cat Scratch Fever'!" She looks around as if we all know what she's talking about. She realizes everyone is staring at her and she pulls her long black coat/robe over her ample frame, hides her hand, smiles a smile that takes in the entire room, and says with ministerial authority, "But I'm not going to die. Everything is going to get better!"

A squat, suited man peers around the door and Reverend Barnett throws out an arm in greeting, "Here's Olaf the organist! Sarah, Andrew, just like we rehearsed, please stand at the front door."

She looks over our assembled guests. Jake and Cynthia stand waiting.

"These must be your witnesses. All four of you go to the door. Witnesses first. Olaf, to the organ!" With that she strides up the aisle while pulling a long green scarf from around her ample waist. She places the scarf around her neck in ceremonial fashion and reaches deep inside her coat to find her notes.

Olaf the organist plays a bubbly version of *Sunshine of Your Love.*

All of my doubts about not having a real church, with a real organ, with a real minister, fade. The disappointment over my absent family melts. Our friends are all smiles. Olaf literally bounces as he plays the organ.

"You look sooo great!" Andrew whispers. I hold his hand tightly. It isn't until I look up at the large form of the French-Norwegian minister that I realize she has for the occasion added rainbow colored sparkles on her eyelashes and down the part of her hair. I erase the thought that it looks stupid.

The sermon is short:

"I send you into the adventure of marriage with the words of Ezekiel the Prophet, the words of William Shakespeare, and the words of William Faulkner. In Ezekiel 10:24 we read: The newly betrothed have the strength of horses bound for war. They run. In glory they run the race. Like warriors they charge, their flags the flags of Isaac and Jacob. The battle is theirs to win.

And William Shakespeare in Coriolanus says: And you the wedded two remember this, treasure all things rightly, love judiciously, give of yourself generously."

She looks up as if to accept our approval. But winks as she says, "We'll skip the parts where everyone dies or gets their arms cut off."

Satisfied with the half-smiles coming back at her, she continues: "William Faulkner has this to say: The past is never dead. It is not even past."

Again, the look, the chuckle and she ends with, "These three quotes I give you as a gift: one speaks of the strength you will garner, the second of the love you will share, and the third of the community which supports you. Marriage has been handed down to us since the beginning of time. I commend you to be ever vigilant. Ever watchful. Ever giving. The power of this churchly tradition is its longevity. In these times, when so many forgo the transformation of the marriage ceremony, I commend you for doing what will give you power and peace. And with those words, the words of generations, I ask you Sarah, do you take Andrew…"

And, so we are married.

Back at the apartment at the reception, I stand in the arched doorway studying our old roommates, old lovers, new friends.

Jake sidles up to me. He puts his arm over my shoulder and gives me a squeeze. "Fool around much, my little chickadee?"

I back away. Sometimes Jake is a real pain.

"Joke, Sarah! Relax. Just joking!" He plants a sloppy kiss on my cheek. "But I do like to fool around with married ladies in case you ever get bored!"

At which point Cynthia comes to the rescue, "Jake. You leave Sarah alone. Your jokes sometimes just aren't jokes."

Jake does have a reputation, no matter that Andrew teases him about being a virgin. Hard to imagine. No, impossible to imagine.

I check to be sure there are plenty of animal crackers and Twinkies. I retrieve another bottle of champagne from the refrigerator and as I fill outstretched glasses, I realize that while most guests sit on sofa arms, or perch on window sills, or sit on the floor, Andrew leans against the arched doorway on the other side of the room. He leans close to Luella Hard. Head bent as if to catch what she is saying, it looks to me as if Andrew's eyes are focused directly on Luella's abundant chest.

My head fills with remembering the huge fight we had a week ago. While Andrew was studying at the Suzzallo Library, I cleaned a closet and found a pile of *Playboys*. The June, 1968 *Playboy*—the *Playboy* he'd promised he wasn't buying anymore.

I went to work. I left Andrew a note on the apartment door, "They're all yours."

And here's what he finds—down the hall, on the roll of the roll top desk, in his typewriter, on each stove burner, floating in the day old coffee pot, on every chair back, on the toilet tank, in the refrigerator—every available space is filled with the double round cutouts of women's breasts. The entire collection of *Playboys* lies in a ragged heap on the living room floor.

Andrew finds me at the Coffee Corral. He's pissed. But given the time it has taken him to find me, it is long enough for him to realize my little art installation was pretty damn funny, and he does beg, please, please, please to come home because it's cold outside and the heat is off in the apartment again, and he just wants to crawl in bed. He whispers, while snuggling into my neck, that I am beautiful, that he loves me, and won't I please, please quit pouting and come home. We get over it.

Back to our wedding night.

Finally, finally we close the door on the last guest and tumble into bed. And for once, with too much champagne in his belly, Andrew falls asleep.

I lay thinking about the magic of the ceremony. One minute I'm one person and the next minute I'm a different person. Then my head fills with the image of the old elephant at the Woodland Park Zoo who walks around and around the circular path he's worn over the years even after the chain connecting him to a center spike has been removed. Is that what comes of vows and giving up my name? Do I start walking and walking around a stake called marriage? I turn. I toss. Finally I sleep, dreaming of elephants.

In the morning, while Andrew sleeps, I call home.

"Oh, sweetheart, I'm so glad you called." Mom's voice is full of good cheer, "And you're all married?"

"Yes, all done."

Is she asking if I'm still a virgin? It is the kind of question that I'm always afraid Mom will ask.

But, Mom chatters on. She worried all night that perhaps the wedding wouldn't happen without them.

"Let me get Dad."

I wait, growing ever more anxious. When Dad's solemn and strained voice says hello, I rush to tell him everything went perfectly. I tell him how sorry I am that he couldn't travel. I ask about his ankle and I suggest he think of giving up the Baptist basketball team.

Mom comes on the other line with the words, "Tell us everything." I tell her there was singing and hand clapping, and that the minister gave a little sermon based on the book of Ruth and I finish the lie by telling them that all the wedding guests are seriously considering joining the church.

I get on the "lie train" and I can't get off. I figure out later it was all in preparation for telling them that when we drive from Seattle to Chicago, we will only spend a single night with them. But I didn't have to lie. I just never tell them. Later, when that day arrived, we just drove into their driveway, had dinner and left in the morning. Mom cried. Dad wiped his eyes, glaring at the thief who had stolen his daughter. They never did adjust to Andrew. Ever.

When Andrew finally stumbles out of bed, I insist he call his mother and thank her for the Tupperware.

"You call her. You're her daughter-in-law."

"I hardly know her."

"Me either."

"Andrew, don't do that. She's your mom. It's probably not uncommon that mothers-in-law consider their only son, stolen. At least she sent us a gift. She'll get the spelling of my name someday. Probably soon. Maybe." I sit on Andrew's lap. I hold him close. I don't want to talk. I just want to be quiet, and hold each other, and feel married.

Andrew finally gives in. "I'll call her. Say thank you. Then I'll give you the phone and you can say thank you and I won't have to talk to her all morning."

So we did.

The next day after Andrew leaves for work, I take out the envelope with our marriage license. With it is a copy of Reverend Barnett's sermon. I reread our vows. I reread the sermon. After I finish studying both, I open *The Book of Wedding Memories*, a wedding gift from Cynthia and Jake, and I write:

Even after a day, it's difficult to remember how large the wedding loomed. I felt how Dorothy must have felt facing the curtain in the *Wizard of Oz*. I was nervous, excited, frantic, joyous, everything! And then yesterday arrived so quickly and we walked over to that dreary little chapel, and fifteen minutes later I was Sarah Althaus. I remember standing there at the altar trying to hold on to what Minister Barnett said. Today, I reread the sermon and tried to look up the quotes. I couldn't find any of them. It has crossed my mind that the minister made up the quotes. Like marriage is something made up. Not magical at all. And the magic that I thought would happen by getting married eludes me. I don't feel it's true that one minute you're one person and the next minute you're a different person. I don't feel changed. And walking up University Ave to the reception at the apartment didn't feel magical. It rained. And something about the heaviness of the rain made the smell of onions and garlic in the hallway of our apartment stronger. At least, at the reception, because I insisted, we didn't have Hawaiian punch with vodka. We had champagne. Cheap champagne, but at least it was champagne. We drank all six bottles! And just as I worried would happen, Andrew got a little bit tipsy. Guess that can be expected on a wedding night. And we had been living together, so it wasn't like a real, real wedding night.

I'm trying to figure out why this minister seemed to focus on the past. Why? I wonder if she really is a minister with her made-up quotes, maybe she just made up she's a minister! And if she isn't a real minister are we really married? The past was exactly what I didn't want to think about. Not on my wedding day. All during the vows I tried to keep my head empty, but five minutes after saying, "I do" and the goofy minister announces, "It is my pleasure to present to you Andrew and Sarah, now married, blessed by the Universal God, transformed into Mr. and Mrs. Andrew Althaus," all I could think about was at what point does a man, who has vowed until death do you part, run away with the neighbor lady?

In the next few weeks, I pack boxes of books for the move to Chicago. I slide the wedding book between two cookbooks. I wrap the wedding book in heavy rubber bands and then I pop the rubber bands and reread what I've written. It makes me wonder if Andrew will ever guess my worries about marriages dissolving. Part of me wants him to read everything I've written, but part of me wishes he would intuit my fears about faithlessness. I want, and I don't want, to tell him about Grandma Millie's strange marriage, a marriage that failed. And whose fault? I rarely let it happen, but sometimes I consider that maybe my grandmother was the one who failed. In that photo with her children she looks tired.

Once, Andrew and I talked about jealousy. He'd had coffee with someone in his English class. An hour's conversation. Nothing meant by it. When he told me, I grabbed my coat and headed for the Coffee Corral. He found me there. He held my hands in both of his. He said, "Sarah, listen to me. Don't be jealous. It's a waste of emotions. Jealousy is a construct of the last century. Jealousy can be erased. You love someone enough; you want them to have as much love coming at them as possible. Love fosters love. It's a matter of erasing jealousy. Replacing it with generosity. It's something we should work on in our marriage. This is a different time. We can control our world."

His words brought back a memory of a party we'd had with our friends at Golden Gardens beach. Andrew's words: "That evening was one of the best ever. Remember what happened? Jake slobbered over you. It's obvious he's always been crazy about you. And what was my response? Not jealousy. It made me proud to be with you. Made me love you even more."

But lately, I often wake in the middle of the night. I turn to study Andrew. Where would I be without him? What would I be without him? Even now, married, he'll look up in the middle of a conversation and watch a woman walk by. Why? Why does he do that? Since our first night as a married couple, I regularly wake and wonder what it means to be a husband and wife. And, what does one do with jealousy? With insecurity? With fear?

For the moment? Absolutely nothing. I never say it, but part of me thinks Andrew's ideas about jealousy are nuts.

CHAPTER THIRTEEN

CHANGING FAITHS

I pack the final box of our belongings and as I pack (Andrew is finishing his final day being a pizza delivery man), I listen to a tape. Grandma Millie's voice runs the gamut of a wavery voice near tears to short snorts of laughter. Listening to her remembrances is like being in the middle of a comic tragedy!

Saturday, August 1, 1914

This was a day I'll never forget. We took the wagon and Babe to Soap Lake. Walked half way around the lake. And? Luke asked, "What do you think about marriage?" I answered, "I think about it a lot." He replied, "What do you think about marriage with me?" I answered, "Yes!" And then we kissed many, many times. I was the happiest person on earth.

Sunday, August 2, 1914

There was a slight complication. I was a Baptist. We were a family of Baptists. We attended Come to the Lord and Rejoice Tabernacle. Regularly!

Our go-to-church schedule was something like this:

Sunday—Early morning—Adult and Children Sunday School
Mid-morning—Regular Service (we called this 'Church.' The service probably had a real name, like Sermon Service, or something, but we called it Going to Church. Ignoring the fact that every day was going to church).
Late afternoon—Immersion and Regeneration Gathering
Evening—Songfest
Monday—Choir Practice
Tuesday—Family Potluck

Wednesday – no going to church, but we most often had Bible Study at home during dinner
Thursday—Mission Society, Youth Fellowship, Deacons
Friday—Growth in Grace Prayer Meeting
Saturday—Choir Practice

And of all these, Sunday evening was my favorite: everyone sang. Loud. With hand motions. Brother Obadiah Jones, the assistant minister, moved back and forth between the piano and the lectern. The missing five keys on the piano bothered no one. We all shouted and stomped and waved our hands. Hymnals never opened. Everyone knew "Bringing in the Sheaves," and "Take Me in Your Life Boat," and "Amazing Grace." Hands clapped. Miss Rena Redman tapped her tambourine. Claire and I sang harmonies with full throats. Being a Baptist was glorious, fun, and full of grace.

Luke was a Lutheran. We didn't discuss my Baptist-ness. The next day he told me to meet him in the vestibule of Pilgrim Lutheran Church.

That very day I told Mom, your Great Grandma Sarah, I wouldn't be attending the Baptist church. I remember her clutching her chest and wiping away tears. My announcement was not taken well.

That very morning my mother and my grandmother wore extra-large hats. I pulled on white gloves. I wore a white hat with a single callalily. We parted at our corner and not a word was spoken. Not one word.

I walked the ten blocks to Pilgrim Lutheran Church. With each step I repeated vestibule, vestibule, vestibule, concerned because I hadn't asked what a vestibule was and where in the church I was going to find it. When I arrived at the church I found Luke standing next to his mother inside the front door—in the vestibule. Mrs. Lane greeted me with the words, "Thank goodness you're not late." And with that bit of nothingness, I entered a different world: dark wood, amber windows, white lit candles, red-wine carpet, a silent congregation, and a wheezing, groaning organ grinding out solemnity.

Mrs. Lane took the arm of the usher and they walked down the aisle past a dozen pews. Luke and I followed. As we walked down the aisle, I was aware that my perfect Baptist hat was larger by half, and whiter by far than any other hat on any other head. The Lutheran hats tended toward flat in shades of navy, gray, black, and none. Mrs. Lane's black hat was smaller than most, with a wisp of a veil and not a single feather.

I felt all eyes on me. Thank goodness, I felt rescued and taken care of when Luke tucked my hand in the crook of his arm.

When seated, Mrs. Lane handed me a hymnal and nodded to the list of hymns posted on an arched plaque next to the lectern (didn't know it then, but learned the preacher didn't move around, didn't lead the singing, stayed right there in his pulpit...a Lutheran lectern). With the striking of a single chord, everyone stood, the minister entered—from what appeared to be a secret door in the wall behind the altar—and down the aisle proceeded the choir, in black gowns, stepping in unison, heads held high, singing A Mighty Fortress is Our God.

Not one bit of joy.

A dirge.

After singing all six stanzas, everyone sat, and all attention was focused on the minister. I tried not to stare. I tried to look as if I knew ministers wore white satin scarves embroidered with gold crosses, over a sheer white night gown, all over a long black dress.

The minister raised his hand with three fingers extended and made a cross in the air, then read a long, long prayer. No one amen-ed. No one said, "So be it, Lord," no one called "Hallelujah!" When he finished he pulled the voluminous dress around him and settled like whipped meringue into a carved wooden chair with wine-red velvet tuffeting.

The organ wheezed and moaned and it crossed my mind that it was a good thing Lutherans could afford an organ, because the pumping, pounding sound covered the barely singing voices. Mouths hardly opened. Even the choir sang discreetly and solemnly, "Just as I Am." It was a long, long hymn about blood and sin and more sin. There was no clapping.

I bit my lip during the sermon to stay awake. Reverend Handshue had a similar message to Brother Jones' message—all about heaven and hell, but no one reacted! I wondered if anyone cared. An hour and fourteen minutes later everyone stood as the choir exited and Pastor Handshue walked down the aisle all smiles. It seemed to me that he was also glad the service was over.

At the vestibule door, Reverend Handshue clasped my hand in both of his and said as he said to each person in front of me, "How nice of you to come."

Outside where people gathered in small discreet groups, Mrs. Lane said, "Next week, you'll be interested, Millicent, in the fact that Reverend Handshue begins a new catechism class."

That moment, called by my full name, perhaps the only time in my life, I realized I had been enrolled to become a Lutheran. There would be no Luke without being a Lutheran.

CHAPTER FOURTEEN

HEADING EAST

Thursday, August 22, 1968

I fill the trunk of the Dodge with four boxes of books. I tuck sheets and towels around the spare tire. I drape clothes over the boxes and wrap my winter coat around the six silver-plated wine cups our friends gave us for our wedding. Our Goodwill pots and pans protrude higgly-piggly and our Melmac dishes are so tight, they won't clatter. I place Tupperware containers in every empty space. The last container holds tuna fish sandwiches and Oreo cookies just in case we need a snack on the road.

Friday, August 23, 1968

We are up at sunrise to cold, bright air. By eight o'clock we are on the road. Headed east. A new penny of a day!

Crossing the Mercer Island Floating Bridge, misty clouds lay soft on Lake Washington. By the time we reach Issaquah the windshield wipers are beating away the rain. As we curve up over the hills to Snoqualmie Pass, the rain eases; and at the summit, there is nothing but blue sky. As we pass Lake Keechelus, I finally get up enough nerve to say, "Pretend you like sports when you meet my dad."

Andrew drives in silence. We take the Cle Elum exit for breakfast at the Bakery. Inside, full of regulars, we are greeted with smiles. We order and Andrew leans back and stares at me.

"Tell me again. I'm to pretend something I'm not? I thought you said your parents were going to be crazy about me."

He adjusts the collar of his shirt as if to make a point and then bites off the words, "I plan to wear my scarf."

"No!" pops out of my mouth before I can think. "It's buried under boxes of books!" It's a lie. I know exactly where his magical scarf is. I wrapped all my beaded macramé necklaces in that scarf.

Andrew doesn't answer. He stares at me like he's never seen me before. Like I'm some kind of apparition.

Thank goodness the waitress arrives with a thermos of coffee and cinnamon rolls draped in pecans and oozing butter.

I try to explain. "We're not even going to be there for a whole day. I thought you might get along better with Dad if you let him think you shared something in common. And if you wear your silk scarf it will…well, he just won't understand that it's your good-luck scarf. In fact, he won't understand the luck thing. Luck is right up there next to Voodoo. Please try to understand. Please?" I reach for his hand and am relieved when Andrew kisses my knuckles.

"Settle down. I can pretend sports as good as anybody. I just didn't think that would be the first thing to worry about. So, tell me what I should and shouldn't say. What I should and shouldn't do."

I honestly can't tell from his voice what he means. Every once in awhile in the middle of one of our long talks, Andrew pulls back like he's watching the conversation from a distance. I hate when he does that. It makes me feel weird. Like an alien.

"My parents already know you are going to be the next Hemingway."

"Good. I don't want them to have low expectations."

I ignore what is obviously sarcasm. I pretend we are having a reasonable conversation.

"There's one thing." I take a deep breath, and finally I say what I fear my parents will bring up when they meet Andrew. "Not for you to worry, but they are a little concerned if my salary will be enough to live on in Chicago."

"They know about your salary? Our budget?"

"No, I didn't tell them about our budget. I told them we're going to be okay."

"But they don't think so? They think I'm living off you?"

"No, no. I've told them about your scholarship. I told them you'll probably find a part-time job."

"I am? I'm going to find a part-time job? Well that's interesting."

Andrew swipes a chunk of cinnamon roll through the puddle of brown sugar and butter. He chews while he looks at me, squinty eyed, as if he were studying a map or filling in blank spaces of a crossword puzzle.

"Sarah. I thought we had this straightened out. The graduate school thing was your idea. You talked me into applying. You created a budget. You said everything was fine. Now it isn't fine? Never once did you say anything about a part-time job. Not that I'm not good at part-time jobs, but the whole idea was to get me in and out of graduate school and get published. How can I write, go to school, and hold down a job? No question, I can, but it's going to make things a whole lot harder."

I squish the center of the cinnamon roll under the tines of my fork. I look straight at Andrew and say, "We can do it! Don't worry. Just go along with the part-time part of it. What I'm trying to do is avoid a lecture from my father."

"A lecture?"

"Believe me. We don't want a lecture. Dad knows how to lecture. Just be agreeable. We're going to be there *one* day. Please." I reach for Andrew's hand. "Please, please, just get along with them."

"Of course I'll get along with them! What kind of a person do you think I am?"

In silence we drive past Ellensburg and Vantage, across miles of flat land to Moses Lake. I pretend to sleep. Andrew keeps blowing air out of his mouth as if to rid himself of everything he isn't saying.

Just past Dry Falls State Park, because we aren't speaking, I don't mention the fact that we have passed the exit to Gaitsberg. If we hadn't been in such a hurry to get in and out of Spokane, I'd thought of suggesting we stop. I don't say a word. I don't tell Andrew that Gaitsberg is where Mom was born, where Grandma Millie got married. Where Grandma Millie got left.

Soon we pass Medical Lake. I can't bring myself to say word one about Mom's older brother, Gabe. I remember those horrible Sundays sitting in the Sun Room at Medical Lake. All of us pretending it was a normal everyday thing to do – sit in the reception room of a psychiatric hospital attempting to make conversation with mute Uncle Gabe.

To break the spell of bad memories, to give us something to share, I take out the tape recorder and insert a tape. I watch to see what Andrew thinks. This is a first. He kind-of knows I'm writing something. He kind-of knows tapes exist. But he's busy. He had to graduate (well, so did I). I watch to see his expression as Grandma Millie's voice fills the car.

August 20, 1968

Dear Sarah,

I'm really getting the knack of telling my stories. I hope you like how I've done the dialogue. I find myself very entertained and I think you'll enjoy this bit about my wedding dress.

August 18, 1914

The Sears Roebuck package was stuffed in my tapestry bag which was stuffed in the bicycle basket. I propped the bicycle against the rock wall fronting Claire's house, grabbed the package, and ran up the front stairs. I called through the open door, "Claire, it's Millie, I'm here!"

Angelica, Claire's little sister, skipped down the hall toward me, her hair a bouncing mass of blond curls, her green eyes wide, her gingham jumper flouncing to reveal her white lace petticoats. She wrapped her arms around my legs. "Auntie Millie!" she called and buried the rest of her words in the folds of my dress.

Claire appeared, grabbed Angelica by the hand and turned to take her back to the kitchen. She called, "Be right back." Claire's mom peeked around the corner. "You have at least two hours to work on the wedding dress. I'll keep little Sweetness out of your way."

Claire rolled her eyes at her mother's name for her little sister. "The most spoiled four-year-old you'll ever see!"

"But cute."

"Embarrassingly cute. I'm the only seventeen year old in the whole county who has a baby sister!"

"I am not a baby!" Angelica called. "Not...not...not..." her voice faded as Claire's mom closed the kitchen door.

Claire reached for my package, "So show me!"

From the string-tied paper package we removed a lace trimmed chemise. Claire ran her hands over the under-garment, "How wonderful! Too bad Luke will be the only one to see it!"

"You are so naughty! Just when I think I can't get more butterflies, you say something like that and it makes my heart stop!"

"All in preparation for angels singing!" Claire threw her arms in the air and danced around the table.

"I should never have told you that. It's no joke!"

Claire reached for her sewing basket, found a needle and slipped the thread thorough the eye. "Think a needle sings when the thread goes through?"

I felt myself blush. If it weren't for Claire, I would never have known what to expect on my wedding night. Claire gave me so many details I wanted to put my fingers in my ears. Mom had told me: "Angels Sing!" She also told me that my wedding night would be miraculously guided by God. I was too embarrassed to want to learn more details. Nothing my mother told me seemed real. What Claire told me was frightening. But between Claire's giggles and hand waving and the wonderful times Luke has pressed his body against mine, I had begun to figure things out.

"Enough!" Claire stated, reaching for the package. "Time to change the subject."

She removed the top layer of silk cloth and let it unfurl—the cloth floated like a cloud. "Then this, I gather..." she said and unwound a roll of lace, "...will be for the hem." And last, a ribbon of tea roses bloomed in a line on the dining room table.

"Close your eyes," Claire demanded.

I waited and as I waited I heard Claire roll the dress form from behind the Chinese screen. "Now! Look!" Before me was the dress form with a wooden knob for a head. It held a long slender dress, cut on the bias, as angled and elegant as a calla-lily. Claire knelt to place the lace along the scalloped hem. "It will be beautiful!"

"It's already beautiful," I whispered, tears filling my eyes.

Claire reached for the strawberry pin cushion and attached it to her wrist. "Time to try it on!"

I stepped behind the screen, she handed me the dress, and when I stepped out, I twirled to let Claire see how the scallops lay straight and true.

"Okay, stand on that stool." Claire pinned the lace along the hem. "So, tell me! Tell me all about church yesterday. And Mrs. Lane. I bet you're just going to love her!"

"Luke's mom? You want the truth? She smelled like Smith Brothers Cough Drops and she kept patting me like I was a cat."

Claire laughed. "You know she's in mama's quilting group. She's full of stories about Luke's dad, and how much they loved each other, and that she'd never, ever marry again. Not that there's another man to marry in Gaitsberg." Claire reached for additional pins. "You'll get to love her when you know her. Besides, she said to Mom that you are 'perky' and you have 'twinkly' eyes."

"She said that? From how she acted at church you'd think I was stealing her son. She found a dozen times to hold Luke's arm. Squatter's rights."

"She's got to be feeling a little insecure."

"She's feeling insecure? What about me? I'm going to have to share her house!"

"Goodness! Goodness! I can't believe I've forgotten to tell you! I have great news! But because it isn't for sure, sure, I'm not supposed to tell you, but..." and Claire dropped her voice, "Mom said that Mrs. Lane told her Reverend Handshue has asked her to take care of the parsonage, the vestments, the whole church! And for that, they are going to let her live in the carriage house behind the church! It's almost a done deal. You know how Luke's mother loves everything Lutheran. She already talks about her new life in town. Isn't that just the greatest news?"

I stepped down from the stool. "Sure. It will be great to have the house to myself...but..." I stepped behind the screen. "Don't you think it will be a bit lonely? Me, by myself at the farm? Almost as scary as living with Mother Lane."

"You won't be alone! I'm here—a hill away. Maybe we'll both join the quilting group. You'll have the Lutheran Missionary League. And you'll have Luke. What more could you ask for?"

I didn't hold back a sigh. I was pleased with how easily Claire had reassured me. Best of all, she said nothing about all the warnings I'd gathered: Luke with a roaming eye, Luke with a bit of a drinking problem, Luke not being that good of a farmer.

"There's one good thing to say about your converting to Lutheranism, you get to wear this real wedding dress, in a real church, and walk down a real aisle."

I handed Claire the dress and Claire slipped a dozen stitches in and out of the hem. "I'm almost finished!" She held up the last yard of lace. "I do do good work! And I have one week to finish the hem and then I'm going to finish my dress. So watch out! No one is going to miss the maid-of-honor!"

"Just don't you dare out-shine me!"

Claire looked up with a worried look, "No way will I look more beautiful than you. But tell me, are you sure about the crème color? Did you ask? What if there's some kind of Lutheran white-dress rule?"

"If there is, it's a little late. Besides, I'm giving up Baptist singing and arm waving and taking on Lutheran somber like a litter of kittens. So a little crème won't hurt."

"What will Luke say?"

I folded the chemise and let my fingers feel its fine, filmy beauty. "Luke just wants this dress off of me!"

"Millie! I can't believe you just said that! You, the sweet little Baptist-turned-Lutheran girl, are becoming a brazen hussy!"

"You're right! The closer this wedding gets, the crazier I get. I can't sleep. I talk to myself. I have crazy dreams."

"Time for tea and you can tell me all about your dreams," Claire said and slipped the dress back over the form.

We sat at the dining room table, the tea cozy hugging the teapot. We each sipped from a two-handled Blue Willow cup, swirled the tea, waited for the leaves to settle.

"I have wild dreams: running, yelling, swearing—words like snakes falling out of buildings. I wake up, my heart pounding, fearing I'll go right back into the same dream, and I do. And guess what I've learned? Did you know dreams have meanings?"

"Like what?"

"Honest. I read it in The Saturday Evening Post. *There's this new kind of doctor, a German. Can't remember his name. But he says things like snakes have to do with men's genitals! Can you believe that?"*

"That's crazy! Dreams come from eating sauerkraut before you go to bed."

"No. This is serious. Maybe my dreams are trying to warn me about getting married."

"You've got to get married! The dress is almost done!"

"Maybe I should be going to college. Take that scholarship."

"What scholarship?"

"I wasn't going to tell you. In case Abe Wiseman ends up being your father-in-law."

"Now I know you're crazy! It would take more than The Gaitsberg Daily scholarship to keep me here!" Claire poured more tea. "Believe me, soon as Angelica and Mom don't need me, I'm leaving town. Spokane or Chicago, or New York! Anywhere, but here. I'll get a job in a big store, not some small town thing with a soda fountain. I'm looking for some place like Stewart's in New York or Marshall Field's in Chicago. And I'm going to be the best sales woman they've ever seen!"

"You just promised me I wouldn't be lonesome," I pleaded. "That you'll be a hill away!"

"Not for a year or two, dummy. Besides, by the time I leave, you'll have a little one."

"Don't talk like that! Don't rush me! I'm not even married. And what if I do and what if I end up like my mother, or like your mother?"

"Never. We know more than our mothers. Don't let Luke touch you after the

first one. One is enough. You think I ever wanted a baby sister? Mom is ancient and now she's got a four year old! Never, ever, is that going to happen to me!"

"Poor Milt. He hasn't a chance?"

"Absolutely right, Milt hasn't a chance."

"I'm so relieved you haven't changed your mind about Milt, because when I went to The Gaitsberg Daily to give them the wedding announcement, Abe Wiseman implied that Milt and I were destined to be a couple. He's crazy! I've never encouraged Milt. But that's what the scholarship thing was all about. Abe Wiseman somehow had visions of Milt and I taking journalism classes together. He might be the most powerful man in this town, but he sure isn't observant."

"Let's celebrate with some more cookies," Claire said and headed to the kitchen.

"I'll never get into that dress if I have one more cookie."

Claire returned with a fresh pot of tea. She filled our cups. "So, tell me about being a Lutheran."

I slid down in the chair, balanced my tea cup on my chest and gazed over the lip studying Claire. "I've been kidnapped by a bunch of Lutherans. I thought we spent a lot of time in church. The Lutherans are a match. But they are solemn. Serious. They never laugh. For instance. Do you remember Hilda Geist, Pastor Handshue's wife?"

"How could anyone forget Hilda Geist! So perfect. So beautiful!"

"Shows what we knew." I put my cup on the table, stood, and placed my hand against my stomach to make myself taller and I said in a breathless voice, "Hilda Geist, the Harvest Queen, Tatiana in the Senior Play, lead in the Spring Celebration. And," I spread my arms wide, "Remember how she sang in "The Pirates of Penzanse," her hair all wild and wonderful?"

"Yes, absolutely unforgettable."

"Well, she isn't the same Hilda. No more wild hair. Her hair is screwed to the back of her neck in a bun. The top of her head is so slick it looks as if it had been polished with Shoe Shine Lacquer! Her black clothes are dowdy and her brown shoes are ugly, and she has red, red cheeks, like they've been painted on."

Both Claire and I knew that no matter what Vogue Magazine might say about the liberated woman, in Gaitsberg the only women with painted cheeks were the ones who danced at the Rivoli Theatre when the carnival came to town.

"Pay attention. Here's what she said to me at the Sunday school teacher's meeting." I leaned over the table and glare at Claire, "Millie! I've told you what to do! I can't imagine that you can't do this lesson. They are six year olds!" She didn't add, "For God's Sake!" Lutherans don't get to say "For God's Sake." But, she meant it.

"Maybe she's jealous," Claire says.

"Jealous? Of what?"

"How about, jealous of you! Hilda got old, frumpy, and mean. Then there's you! You got Luke Lane. You'll marry him in her church!" She raised one hand palm up, and declared, "Luke!" Then she raised her other hand. "Pastor Handshue!" Like the angel of justice she let one hand go up, the other down. "Wouldn't you be jealous if you weren't you?"

I considered the comparison. Pastor Olaf Handshue is short and squat. Rounded out. All parts of him seem to be rounded out—his belly, his bald head, his bulgy neck, and his fat fingers. And then there is Luke. Beautiful, wonderful Luke.

"Time I get home. Walk with me, at least half way."

I pushed my bike. We cut across the large front yard where dahlias the size of dinner plates bloom. Claire stooped to pick a bachelor button and pulled the petals to He loves me, he loves me not, a ritual we have performed through all of our childhood. At the edge of the orchard we stopped under our favorite tree.

"Amazing isn't it. Another two weeks and we'll be neighbors. At least for awhile." We wrapped our arms over each other's shoulders and we gazed out over the rounded hill of newly planted winter wheat.

"I've got an idea," Claire said. "Skip Luke. Come with me! We can be girl-reporters, or girl-Fridays or something truly wonderful. Together."

We sat with our backs against the huge maple tree that we have forever called our 'wishing tree'. The edge of the trunk is worn smooth from all the years we have shared secrets here. Grasshoppers snapped and jumped in the wheat. The air smelled ripe with summer warmth.

"You know I've waited for Luke all of my life. He's everything I've ever wanted. He's everything anyone would want! Don't you agree?"

Claire patted my knee and said with what I think was conviction, "Of course, my dear friend. How could I not."

Onthis day, in the sweet warm late-summer sun, I didn't ask Claire if she really meant what she said.

"What if we did one last crazy thing before you become a serious married Lutheran lady?"

"Like what?"

"Something crazy. Like put some Baptist zip into your wedding."

"Besides my cream colored dress and that green shimmery thing you're going to wear? Something more than that?"

"Sure."

"Like what?"

"I've been thinking about the music thing. What if you asked them to add one romantic song, something like 'Just a Song at Twilight'?"

"I'm sure Lutherans aren't allowed to sing those kinds of songs. Certainly not at a wedding."

"Okay, okay," Claire said brushing the air with her hands as if to be done with any objections. "I've another great idea! What if you asked Hilda Handshue to sing at your wedding? She's the minister's wife; she could sing anything she wants!"

I sighed with a bit of longing, "It would be nice to have at least one sing-able tune." I stood, straightened my skirt. "But, for now, dear friend, it's time to go." I gave Claire a hug and a kiss goodbye and said, "Let me think about that music idea."

I rode the half-mile home wondering the whole way if there was any chance in the world of making that Lutheran ceremony more zippy.

I look over at Andrew. Wait for him to say something.

"Are they all like that?" he asks.

And I know from his question, that he's not curious. Doesn't care to hear more.

Silence and sadness fill the car. Thank goodness, we are heading into town. I point to the Division Street exit and we head north. We pass by St. John's Lutheran Church and I look for Grandma's Hudson Hornet. Not there.

I point to turn down Sharp and there we park.

I stop humming and realize Andrew is looking at me quizzically. Even he must have noticed the song I quit humming was, *I Wish I Were Single Again.* Not a good sign.

CHAPTER FIFTEEN

HOME AGAIN, HOME AGAIN

Friday, August 23, 1968

Mom sits on the front porch, her hands wrapped in her apron as if to contain her excitement. As we pull our overnight bag from the backseat, she calls, "David, they're here!" Dad joins Mom and they wait for us to walk up the path. Dad has a Rainier beer in his hand. I can tell by the way his head is tilted he is still listening to the television, whatever the game.

I hug both of them and then from the top steps the three of us turn to welcome Andrew. From where we stand, five steps above him, I see Andrew from my parents' point of view—Andrew is short.

And before I can introduce them, Mom exclaims, "Why, Andrew, you're so young!"

Oblivious to the strain of the moment, Dad sticks out his hand, pulls Andrew into the crook of his arm and leads him into the house, saying, "Andrew! Welcome to the family. You're just in time to watch an interview with Red Kerr."

Mom and I pick up the overnight bags. I leave them in my old bedroom, so very aware that Mom and Dad will probably stay up late to play cards and they will hear every word and turn and sound from our bedroom. So we won't: turn or talk or make a sound.

In the living room as we head to the kitchen, Andrew already sits on the couch directly in front of the television. From his Barcalounger, Dad asks Mom, "How about another beer for the men?" And Mom gets them beers. Was it always like this?

With the beer in hand and feigned interest (at least I think it's feigned), Andrew leans toward the television at the very same angle as Dad. Andrew looks at the television as if he is as interested as Dad. I hear Dad ask, as if it was the saddest thing in the world, "What'd you think of last season? Losing the Western Division to the Hawks?" And before Andrew can concoct an answer, Dad continues, "Thank God for Rodgers and Sloan, wouldn't you say?"

I can't stand watching this tableau. I join Mom.

I help her cook dinner: pork chops, mashed potatoes, canned peas and carrots. Before we call the men, Mom hands me an envelope from her apron pocket. "Here, Sweetie. I want you to have this. A little secret stash. Good, for those bad times."

"Mom, how can you say that? The bad times! We're hardly married. Saying that is like putting a jinx on us."

"No! I didn't mean it that way. We're happy for you. Really. I just want you to have something to fall back on."

"But that's your fun money." I know that Mom's stash is money she regularly wins when she and Dad play poker. It has always surprised me that quarters add up to such a substantial amount. It's crossed my mind that Dad's ever hopeful wish to win is what keeps my parents a twosome.

"There's nothing more fun than helping you get off to a good start. I've also a gift of sheets, all white, of course, because you can never have enough sheets, but this, this little stash is just for you. Believe me; you never know when you might need a little extra."

Thankful and reluctant, I stuff the envelope deep into my fringed leather bag, all the time feeling conflicted. Andrew and I have promised to be open with each other. Not to have secrets from each other. And now I have a secret in the bottom of my purse. I didn't ask and I didn't look, but I wonder just how big a secret Mom has given me.

Dinner's ready and we sit to say grace. Mom announces, "Grandma Millie is expecting you to drop in for a minute."

"Why didn't she come to dinner?"

"I didn't want to worry you while you were finishing up your classes, but Grandma hasn't been doing well. Harder and harder for her to get around. I've packed a little bit of Jell-O dessert for you to take over after we finish eating. And, of course, she'll want to meet Andrew. You might have to explain exactly who he is."

I can hardly finish dinner, concerned about getting to Grandma Millie's. It helps when Dad looks at his watch and announces, "Sorry, you won't be able to watch the Yankees, Andrew, but Grandma waits. It's great to see you're the good sort you are!" Dad stands and announces, "If you'll excuse me, I think I'll go catch that game. Sweetheart, I'll take my coffee in the living room."

Thirty minutes later, we stand in the clutter of Grandma Millie's front room.

"So this is Andrew?" she says and reaches out her blue-veined arthritic hands and brings Andrew toward her as if to get a good look.

He takes her hand in both of his, as I announce, "Andrew, this is Grandma Millie, the best grandmother in the whole world!"

"So pleased to meet you."

I've never seen him so prim and proper. Another side of Andrew. Nice.

I reach for her hug hello. I sit on the arm of the horsehair chair where Grandma Millie is propped with pillows, her ebony cane by her side. I hold her hand and play with the single gold band that for a reason I do not understand still claims her slender bony finger.

"Mom says you've been a bit under the weather."

"Well, not to contradict your mother, I'm doing just fine. A few more aches and pains, and I seem to sleep a little more often than normal, but I'm doing just fine. Especially now that you are here! Tell me about your wedding. And tell me about your friend, here." I'm tempted to say 'husband' but let it pass.

Grandma Millie pats the arm of her chair to invite Andrew to sit on her other side.

And then I describe Andrew and the chapel, Bridget Barnett, the quotes, the Twinkies, the Champagne. In the middle of the description, I nod toward the kitchen and Andrew, I assume, gladly disappears to bring back the Jell-O dessert.

"Who is he, again?"

"Andrew."

"Your husband, right?"

"Indeed he is my husband."

Andrew serves us small cut glass bowls full of the bouncy red squares. I continue telling Grandma Millie about my tie-dyed wedding dress. I tell her about the accidental flowers, the rhodies and the fragrant lilacs.

"I had lilacs at my wedding!" Grandma Millie says pulling back, with wide eyes, as if surprised by her memory.

"I know."

"How do you know?"

"Here's how it happened: Mom had this idea that I could wear your wedding dress. So, when I was last home, we headed for the attic. There in that round-topped trunk, wrapped in tissue, tied with a silk ribbon, were the remains of your bouquet."

"Well, how nice! And just what was wrong with my dress?"

"Absolutely nothing. What was wrong was me. I'm too big. It didn't fit."

"Oh, I'm so sorry, that would have been so nice to have that dress worn again. You know it was made with my best friend. Claire. Claire Sandborn."

"It's a beautiful dress. Tell me more."

"More?"

"About your wedding."

"Well, it was a very small wedding. Lutheran, of course. Not much to tell but it was quite lovely."

"And what is your advice?"

"Advice?"

"About marriage. You've given me advice my whole life and now…" I turn to bring Andrew into the conversation, "This is the grandmother who told me everything: how to wear lipstick, how to curl my eyelashes, how to not wear horizontal stripes! Right Grandma? You've taught me all the important things about life. Now it's time to tell me about marriage."

Grandma Millie pulls the afghan tight around her legs. She turns the wedding band around her finger and she looks at Andrew and then she looks at me. "Okay. Here's my advice. Make it work. You think grass is greener? It's just grass. A different patch of grass, but trust me, it's not greener." Grandma slaps her hands together as if her advice were dust on her fingers. "That's it!"

"That's it?"

"That's it. If I knew more, I'd tell you. I'm not much of an expert." Grandma sighs, "…a tiny wedding in a white clap-board Lutheran church in Gaitsberg, Washington…" and then she stops. Her mouth smiling, but her lips closed. Subject over.

As we drive back to my parents' house, Andrew asks, "Your grandmother's advice went from being absolutely sure of what she was saying to a sigh. What was that about?"

"She never talks about her marriage. I've asked, but no one ever gives a straight answer."

"Why not?"

And I decide it's time to share with Andrew my biggest fear. "All I know is one sentence, 'Grandpa Lane ran away with the neighbor lady.' "

"He what?"

"That's it. That's all I know. My whole life I've tried to find out what happened. No one says. Makes me a wee bit nervous."

"About what?"

"About marriage."

Andrew reaches for my hand and gives it a squeeze. "Silly girl. There's nothing to worry about."

"Ever?"

"Never, ever."

I hold Andrew's hand. Just before we turn, I see the tower of the Episcopalian cathedral up on top of the South Hill. It glows in the fading sun and I wonder if marriages in a cathedral last any longer than marriages in a Lutheran clap-board church or a pretend service with a pretend minister in a student chapel.

In the morning, as we get in the car, Mom hands me another set of tapes. Then she and Dad step back, arms snug around each other and they wave goodbye.

CHAPTER SIXTEEN

LET IT SHINE

Saturday, August 24, 1968

It's Saturday and we just drove through Post Falls, Idaho. We're on our way.

"Mind if I listen to another tape?"

"Be my guest."

"You could listen if you want? I don't have to wear the earphones."

"Then play the tape. Now that I've met her, she's way more interesting. I'm going to put her in my 'Portrait' book. So, let her rip!"

"Hi, my little pumpkin. This tape is mostly just for you. Your Mom asked me to describe my wedding day….so here it is:

Saturday, September 26, 1914

I wore the dress Claire and I sewed. We sewed every stitch. I thought I looked beautiful. Luke was in his dark suit. Hate to say it, but I think he stole the show. No one could believe he was finally settling down. Making a choice. Giving up his rambling ways.

But before that, I want to tell you one more story about the felt board and my Sunday school class.

Sunday, August 30, 1914

I remember the day so clearly: I can see the children in their small chairs, a crescent circle around me where they wait to have their turn to place on the felt board of Jesus their choice of felt tears, spear, drops of blood, crown of thorns. Finished with the gruesome lesson, I directed their attention to the Sunday school pamphlet. I asked if they didn't think the hills around Golgotha looked just like the hills around Gaitsberg. I thought if they realized the felt Jesus walked similar hills to their hills, they'd have more faith. No one answered. No one blinked.

"Okay!" I closed the pamphlet. "I've got an idea!" The crucifixion didn't seem all that good for six year olds, anyway.

"What if we sing a song?"

Not one child responded. Eyes darted to the door, to the window, to each other. Then Mary Jane, always the first to volunteer, shot her hand in the air.

"Yes Mary, what would you like to sing?" I asked, relieved at this interest.

"Mary Jane."

"Yes, Mary Jane. Next time, I promise I will have all your names memorized. Now, what would you like to sing?"

"We don't sing," she said, folding her arms, frowning her face. "We don't sing in this room," she corrected herself with a huff.

"Well, we only have a few minutes left, so I thought we could sing."

"Not in Sunday School," Mary Jane says with a nod of her head, making it a very forthright 'no.'

"It will be fun! Do this," I said and stretched out my right hand in a fist and covered it with my left hand.

Four children tentatively followed my lead.

"Come on, everyone! Hands out!"

The other children reluctantly extended their arms. Mary Jane didn't budge.

"Follow me," and I began to sing softly, "This little gospel light of mine…" and when I got to the phrase, "I'm going to let it shine," I let my thumb pop out and I raised my voice and raised my hand! By the time all of us got to "…all around the neighborhood," the children were singing and Mary Jane had uncrossed her arms. Then children shouted, "I'm going to let it shine!" Thumbs danced over their heads.

I stood. I called out, "One more time!" And Mary Jane followed the rest of the children. She stood up!

And then? A solid knock on the door brought singing to a halt. With my right hand still in the air, I opened the door with my left.

There stood Hilda Handshue. She snapped, "Millie Birnham! What exactly are you doing? What exactly happened to the lesson? In case you didn't know, what happens in the basement of this church is my responsibility."

"Well, I…"

"What happened to the lesson?"

"We finished the lesson."

Hilda glared. She appeared to be stumped. The children slowly slid down into their chairs. Their hands disappeared between their legs, behind their backs, under their bottoms. They ducked their heads. Mary Jane's eyes welled with tears.

Without hesitation, I suggested, "You could join us!" I turned to the class and with all the gumption I could muster I said, "Let's sing a verse for the pastor's wife!"

Silence. Tears dripped down Mary Jane's cheeks.

Hilda snapped at the children, "Each of you. Re-read your Sunday school pamphlet. Miss Birnham and I have something to discuss. In the hall!"

I wished I had said the obvious: Except for Mary Jane, the children didn't know how to read.

Instead, I turned to follow Hilda and as I turned, I stumbled over the small chair on which I had been sitting. With the hand that seconds ago was a shining light, I grabbed Hilda's strong straight arm pointing to the hall and we both fell down.

On my knees, I offered Hilda a lift up. She ignored my offer and clung to the leg of the easel that held the felt Jesus. I thought she and the easel would collapse and Jesus would fly about. No such luck. Hilda stood on her very stout legs and without missing a beat, demanded, "I'll see you in the parsonage. Before the coffee hour." And she left.

The children looked at me with pity. I took my coat and my purse and softly said, "Goodbye." The children whispered, "Goodbye."

To gather my thoughts and put off the confrontation as long as possible, I took the long way around the church. I walked down the alley off Concord, I pushed open the gate, and I walked past the carriage house my mother-in-law would soon occupy. I studied the flagstone steps at the back of the parsonage and considered knocking on the back door.

I didn't knock, fearful that coming to a back door might appear to be too neighborly. Instead, I walked around the side of the house and just as I passed by the kitchen window, I heard a clink of glass on glass. Through the window I saw Hilda Handshue. She must have felt my presence, for she turned holding a glass high, and I smiled a tentative greeting. Hello, I called, and that's when I saw what I wasn't supposed to see: in one hand Hilda Handshue held a jelly glass. In the other hand she held a bottle. An emerald green bottle with a round bottom. It was the very bottle Henry Highman generously gave to everyone on Thanksgiving. It was a bottle of his home-made, sweet-sour, lime-yellow, green-apple wine.

Hilda Handshue's hand released the bottle and I heard the crash of breaking glass and I heard Hilda Handshue exclaim, "Oh, Hell!"

My spirits soared. I knew immediately that the conversation I was about to have had just taken an unexpected turn.

On the front porch I turned the brass doorbell in the center of the carved door. I waited. I turned the bell again. Waited. I was patient as I imagined her cleaning up the wine mess.

Eventually, the door slowly opened.

Tears streamed down Hilda Handshue's face. Hilda stepped back to let me enter and without saying a word I followed her into the kitchen. I knew it was a cruel thing to do, but I made an audible sniffing sound.

Hilda blinked. Blew her nose. Knelt. From under the sink, the very place my mother kept our bottle of wine, Hilda produced a second bottle. She took two stemmed glasses from the cupboard and poured generous servings. We sat across from each other at the pine table. With the slightest smile on her lips, Hilda raised her glass to meet mine.

In the mid-morning sun we sipped wine. It was as good a communion as the two of us could have asked for.

Hilda finally spoke, "I guess there's not much comparison between what you were singing with the little ones and me at my worst."

"For worsts, it's not so bad."

Hilda laughed a snorty laugh, a defeated laugh, a laugh on the edge of despair. "It's not even noon," Hilda said her head bowed, both hands held her glass like an anchor.

"Not even noon..." I responded, with the dawning awareness that this was more than a single Sunday slip for Hilda.

"Don't make fun! You don't know what it's like to be a minister's wife. A minister's wife with no children!" Then Hilda cried. Through her sobs she said, "We've been married five years. We've tried. I'm so tired of trying."

Her words startled me. I reached for her hand. She squeezed my fingers and said, "Millie, I shouldn't be talking like this, you're only days away from marrying Luke, but you need to be sure. Are you really, really sure? Marriage is hard. So hard." Hilda's words ran together in a rush, "At least when I married I thought I'd get out of this town. We, Olaf and I, were at the seminary when they announced the calls. Olaf's best friend got a call to San Francisco. His worst enemy got a call to New York City. And Olaf? Olaf got a call to Gaitsberg. To return to this place was so horrible. At least I didn't cry during the call service. But oh, have I cried since."

Hilda held out the bottle, "Some more?"

We continued to sip and Hilda continued to talk. She told how she had always wanted to be a singer. An opera singer. In a big city. In a concert hall. With lights and costumes. Instead, she was a minister's wife leading a horrible choir. No one sings. Really sings. And if they did it was always the two Senter sisters, totally tuneless, insisting God had called them to the choir.

Hilda was not stoppable.

"When I heard you singing with the little ones, I couldn't bare it. Those poor babies. Soon their dear voices will be cemented with hymns of sin and blood and guilt. I've had enough wine to ask right out: Why? Why not say whatever we want? Why can't we at least sing? If I could just sing, maybe being here in this dreadful town wouldn't be so bad. Sometimes I think not singing makes me not have babies. Does that sound crazy?"

I didn't tell her that it did sound crazy, but then my best friend's words came to me and suddenly Claire's suggestion seemed a perfect fit for the problem at hand. I asked, "Would you sing at my wedding?"

"Sing? At your wedding? You want me to sing at your wedding?"

"Yes. I'd be honored."

"How wonderful!" Then as if having second thoughts, Hilda pressed her handkerchief against her bottom lip. "But I can't. I just can't. It will be dreadful. Lutheran's sing the most mournful, solemn songs. Even at weddings."

"All of them?" I asked in disbelief.

"Even if the words aren't solemn, the organist plays them like they are."

"You could sing without the organ."

"I don't think that's ever been done."

"Another good reason to do it!"

"But what?"

"Anything! You could sing Amazing Grace. Just pep it up a bit."

"Lutherans don't sing Amazing Grace."

"They don't?"

"It's not in the Hymnal."

"How Sweet Thou Art?"

"No."

"Just As I Am?"

"Yes. But do you know the words? You want to sing about blood being shed? At your wedding?"

"Sing it like a waltz. Change the words. Lots of hymns come from folk songs. Somehow, over the years, you Lutherans rewrote nice old songs and put dreadful words to them and then you got to singing slower and slower."

"A waltz?" Hilda asked as if she was considering the idea. She hummed two lines. "My word! My God. It is a waltz!"

"So we just have to change the words."

"How?"

"Just do it! You're the minister's wife, for goodness sake!"

"You're right! I'll do it! Let's drink to that!"

So there you have it! I clearly remember Hilda singing. Shortly afterwards I remember she became pregnant. And our children and her children had a couple of great years. All of us being best friends.

Oops…at the end of….

The tape ends and it is time to stop for coffee. I can hardly wait to hear about the wedding. Andrew even seems to be enjoying this last one…his comment? "Interesting. Very interesting."

CHAPTER SEVENTEEN
THE HONEYMOON

Saturday, August 24, 1968

We pass Coeur d'Alene, Idaho. And? While hunting for coffee, Andrew does only what my Andrew would do. He pulls off at Bide-a-While Motel and gloriously, slowly, loudly we make up for last night in my childhood bed.

As if there's some need for balance in our newly wedded state, we have what is almost our first fight. It happens like this: for lunch we stop in the City Park in Kingston. I present the Tupperware container with the sandwiches and cookies. Andrew opens the container, turns his head in disgust, and throws the sandwich and the Tupperware in the trash.

"Andrew! That was our wedding present!"

"Right, and it smelled like someone died. Let's go find a Dairy Queen." Andrew leaves me at the park picnic table. He waits at the car.

It isn't that I am overly upset about throwing away the Tupperware. We'd even made fun of his mom's gift. What makes me angry is that Andrew didn't ask. He didn't acknowledge that I was half owner.

At the Dairy Queen we order double-cheese burgers and Frosties. Andrew doesn't seem to notice I'm not talking. By the time we cross over into Montana, Andrew has taken to reading the Burma Shave signs out loud. I'm brooding over the Tupperware, trying to think of the words to let him know I should be included in decisions about our shared stuff. But it's hot and I nap ignoring this some-other-day-to-be-decided argument.

I wake hot and sticky.

Heat off the highway curls over the road.

We drive through Missoula, Butte, Bozeman, Billings. The radio announcer's voice is all we've heard since breakfast. Out the window are endless cows, tumbleweeds, fences, falling down barns, road-side-attractions, and, of course, Burma Shave signs. We drive and drive and Montana never ends.

The radio announcer declares in a nasty, cutting voice, "In our great state someone declares, 'The greatest good for the greatest number?' Communist drivel! Real Montana men don't…" I push the "Off" button and not tolerating Andrew's silence any longer, I ask, "Do you think there are any women in Montana? Except waitresses? Just like the road in front of us evaporates, the people behind us evaporate. The anti-commie radio guy must be the God of Montana. His irritating voice has followed us across the state. No one else exists!"

"Who cares? I've got you." Andrew says as he makes smacking noises and says in what, I'm sure, he thinks is a seductive voice, "You know, my tasty thing, you're something. Want to stop?"

I give him a "you're crazy" look. I'm sore. I'm exhausted. "No, I don't want to stop. I want to get out of Montana."

"Here comes another one!" Andrew points at the stubby sign sunk fifty feet off the road in an expanse of dun-colored land.

WOMEN LIKE MEN WHEN THEY LATHER AGAIN AND AGAIN WITH BURMA SHAVE!

"Write it down!"

Playing the Good Wife, I write it down.

Ten miles later, a silhouette of another sign appears ahead.

"Get ready! Here it comes!" He shouts, A SMOOTH MAN IS REAL BUT DON'T LET HIM STEAL BURMA SHAVE!

And on the other side of the road, another: FEELING DOWN? NOT LONG IF HE'S FOUND BURMA SHAVE!

The wheels make a shush sound like the car is sucking up the highway. I wipe the sweat from my forehead, tuck a towel under my legs and another behind my back to absorb the sweat and ease my soreness. I fan myself with the tablet on which I've written the Burma Shave slogans.

"Why are we writing these down?"

"I'm a writer. It's material. Nobody writes about Montana. Maybe I'll write about Montana."

Before I can tell him there's a reason no one writes about Montana, he yells, "Get ready!"

JUST WAIT LITTLE MAN THE DAY WILL COME WHEN YOU CAN USE BURMA SHAVE!

Andrew laughs and grabs my knee. "Little man? My little man is just aching to…" he pinches my thigh. The Dodge jerks over the center line, and then straightens. "Let's stop. Here. Do it here. We've never done it in a desert."

I study the map. Wyoming is only a hundred miles away. Maybe there will be air-conditioning in a real restaurant in Sheridan. Without looking up, I say, "I'm sore."

"You're sore? What from?"

"What do you think?"

"Oh," Andrew says.

I push the auto-find button on the Wonder-Bar radio. I hear snatches of a John Birch editorial, a Hank Williams waltz, a Dodge Power Wagon sales pitch, a come-to-God- tirade. I settle for Patsy Cline singing, *Crazy*.

The T-shirt that I've stuffed in the window to block out the sun flaps, balloons, and pulls free. It lopes down the black pavement behind us as if it runs for its life. Andrew doesn't stop.

I close my eyes. I wake with a start when Andrew puts his finger in my open mouth.

Signs begin to dot the fields along the highway. The car thrums and Patsy Cline sings and sings. A tumble weed crumbles under the tires making scratchy noises as if crying for help.

The round clock on the dash reads four-thirty. The temperature is in the high nineties. In the distance appears a large billboard, a real billboard. The sign grows from a postage stamp size to postcard size to trailer house size. From the billboard glowers a cowboy. On his hip he has roped a cowgirl, bursting out of her bustier. WELCOME TO WYOMING.

Andrew's hand is sticky on my leg. "That cowboy had a hard-on."

I don't answer.

"He did. You want to go back and see?"

"No! Don't you dare go back."

'Well, that's just what you women do to us men."

Andrew drives another ten miles. "Look at that!"

"What?"

"The mountains, what are they? What are they called?"

I unfold the map and run my finger along the red line of highway. "Big Horn Mountains. Maybe the Tetons."

"No, it's got to be called 'pussy!' "

"What are you talking about?"

"See! There between the mountains." Andrew wiggles his finger, follows the silhouette of two mountains. He ratchets up his eyebrows, leers at me.

"Is there nothing else you think about?"

"Nothing! Not if I can help it!" Andrew says with a laugh and turns the steering wheel until the car moves from one side of the road to the other. He makes kissy sounds and bounces up and down. "Uuuu-wee!" he gives a cattle call.

I grab the arm rest. "Stop! Stop driving like that! Right now!"

Andrew swings back into the right lane, smiling.

I'm furious. I push the auto-find and Arthur Godfrey sings *I Warm So Easy So Dance Me Loose.*

Andrew points at the dash, "See? Even that old fart's singing about sex!"

I push the button, again. Paul Harvey's twangy voice comes on and Andrew snaps off the radio. "Now, that's obscene."

"You told me your mother loves Paul Harvey."

"She does. That doesn't make him any more interesting, correct, entertaining, or anything. What else? He's boring. He's what my mother stands for before she didn't stand for anything. So if you don't mind I'd just as soon not listen to Paul Harvey."

"We could have used that Tupperware."

"Tupperware? You're still talking about that Tupperware? Why didn't you say something?"

"I did."

"You did not!" Andrew slams on the brakes and I slip on the sticky leatherette seat, hitting my knees against the dash.

"We'll go back! You want that stupid-burping-keep-every-damn-left-over-in-the-world Tupperware? Great. We'll go back."

"That hurt!" my eyes fill with tears and I rub my knees. "I'm hot and sticky and sore, and I wish this trip was over."

"This trip is our honeymoon!"

I don't answer. Andrew has never yelled at me. He's yelled at other drivers and he's yelled at the stupid television, but he's never yelled at me.

"Exactly what would you like to do?" Andrew asks.

Tears stream down my face. I scrounge around for a Kleenex and then I really cry.

"Oh, God, Sarah, don't cry."

Which makes me sob.

In desperation, Andrew asks, "It's your period coming on? Right? Geeze, honey why didn't you say so." He holds the Kleenex box for me. He eases off the road then he scoots over and holds me.

I don't push him away. I mumble into his sweaty neck, "It's not my period. It's just everything. I'm tired. I feel bad about your mom. She doesn't even want you to be married. To me. We've driven a thousand miles and we're still nowhere."

Andrew holds me tighter. I snuggle into him. We hug until everything is better.

I check my knees. I touch the red spots on each, "I really did hurt myself."

"Let me kiss the hurty," Andrew says and leans over my lap.

"It's okay, honest."

"Just a little kiss?" Andrew asks, his eyebrows up like he's Groucho

Marx. His voice gets low and sexy, "Let's do it!"

"No, no, no, no," I laugh and squirm away.

"In the middle of the road," he sings and looks out the back of the window while he reaches to unbutton my blouse.

"Andrew, don't."

"You know you like it."

I push hard and Andrew's back bumps into the steering wheel. He sucks in his breath and stares at me.

"Drive," I plead. "It's too damn hot."

"It's supposed to be hot. You're supposed to be hot."

"You're nuts! You're crazy!" I laugh, but it is an uneasy laugh. "We could fry eggs in the middle of this road."

"Okay," Andrew says as if to give up the idea. He turns the key in the ignition. "I'll start the car and," his eyebrows do the Groucho thing again, "I've got an idea." Andrew leers. "It's hot. Take something off!"

"While we're driving?"

"Why not? I want to look at you."

I moan, but the idea of taking something off, anything off, isn't such a bad idea. We'd played, 'take-something-off' before, but in bed or in the Dodge at a drive-in. I giggle and check the map wondering how long it will take to be naked and Andrew wouldn't be able to stand it. And for the moment I don't feel all that sore.

"Here's the rule. Every ten miles, you have to take something off." Andrew checks the odometer. "I'll tell you when." He wiggles the car back and forth across the center line and leers, "Umm, umm, you know how I love your bare feet."

I take off one sandal. I wiggle my toes.

By the time we cross into South Dakota, I'm near naked. And I'm not all that comfortable. My feet are hot on the bristly floor rug. My rear-end is sweaty and clings to the plastic seats. I still have on a T-shirt, my bra, a watch, sunglasses, a charm bracelet, and my wedding ring.

Andrew watches the odometer.

I keep the map in my lap and place it strategically whenever we pass a trucker. My peddle-pushers and panties, sandals, and socks are in a pile. Andrew yelps as he calls out miles. I know he won't think sunglasses and a watch count. I wiggle my wedding ring at him and he moans.

Andrew rubs his crotch. "Ten more miles. Get ready!"

Then the car swerves and I see that Andrew is studying his rear-view mirror. "Oh, fucking H Christ! Get dressed." In the rear view mirror red lights flash.

"Quick! Quick" Andrew yells. His voice is tense and angry.

I ignore my under-pants, grab my peddle-pushers, and put a foot in one leg and then the other. I push back against the seat and pull at the side zipper. The zipper catches and won't budge.

Andrew slows the car onto the embankment. The door of a cruiser slams.

"Get your God-damned clothes on!" Andrew hisses.

Frozen by his words and his anger and the stuck zipper, I grab the map.

"Where you two headed in such a hurry?" the trooper asks as his arm braces him so that he can peer inside the car. I sit up straight. Study the map.

Andrew hands the state trooper his wallet, a ten dollar bill folded neatly under his license.

"Just your license will do," the trooper says as if talking to a ten-year-old. He smiles a big smile and looks directly at me.

"Honeymoon," Andrew says and although I can't see his face, I can see the trooper's and whatever signal Andrew sent, the guy smiles and shakes his head and says, "Well, I'd suggest you slow-down a tad so you don't cut anything short!"

The two men laugh and he hands Andrew his wallet. "This warning is a wedding gift!"

We wait until the police car drives away. The patrolman waves. I finally get the zipper to pull free and I button the top button of my blouse.

At the city limits of Pierre, we pull into the Lazy River Motel. There is no swimming pool. There isn't even a river. There is no air conditioner. The room smells of Pine-Sol and cigarettes. Andrew sinks into the deep V of the bed. I ignore his "come here" wave and head for the shower.

The water shoots out in a dozen harsh spikes, first too cold and then too hot. Once I've soaped myself with the miniscule bar of soap, the water turns into a dribble. I sit on the edge of the cold porcelain tub, and twiddle with the faucets.

"Andrew! There's no water!"

Andrew doesn't answer.

I turn the hot and cold faucets again. The water sprays cold. That's when I notice that someone had written on the bathroom door, *Life is preparation for Hell.* The words bleed into the cream colored paint. The soap starts to burn.

I yell, "Andrew! Do something!"

I can hear him mumble as if he's just awakened.

"Go to the office and tell them there's no hot water!"

I turn on the cold water. I'm freezing, but at least I can wash off the soap. I dry myself with a towel generously frayed on every edge. I dress quickly and come out to find Andrew reading *Playboy.*

"Andrew!"

"What?"

"You promised. And it's our honeymoon!"

"Yes, caught me." He closes the magazine. "You ready for dinner?"

"Andrew, you're reading *Playboy* on our honeymoon!"

"It's nothing. I've told you a dozen times, it's nothing."

"How can you say it's nothing?"

"Nothing," he repeats and moves over, patting the bed. "Come on, it's a magazine, for God's sake. You're you." Then just when I think I'll walk out the door and keep right on walking across South Dakota, across Wyoming, across Montana, across Idaho…he says the magic words, "I love you."

So there in South Dakota, in a cabin with no air-conditioning, in a bed with a huge dip in the center, on a chenille blanket that smells of Ivory soap and Brylcreem we make love and I make sure to wrestle and bounce enough to forget the rash from the soap and how sore I am from making love before, and Andrew doesn't even notice when I catch my heel in the centerfold of the *Playboy* and give it a good twist.

The next two days on the road to Chicago, we find motels made of quaint separate houses with geraniums in window boxes. No one can hear how much fun we are having. We share reading our copy of *The Kama Sutra* and we brilliantly rename positions: *The Twist, The Stopper, The All or Nothing, The Winner, The Yes-Right Now- Right There!*

CHAPTER EIGHTEEN

MILLIE AND LUKE'S WEDDING

Our last night on the road I play a tape that is marked, WORDS I'VE NEVER DREAMED I WOULD EVER SAY. YOU HAVE MY PERMISSION TO SHARE THIS WITH THAT NEW HUSBAND OF YOURS.

And so we both listen.

September 26, 1914

We married on a Saturday. After the ponderous processional of The Church Has One Foundation and after the congregation sang A Mighty Fortress Is Our God, and before the congregation sang with a little more gusto, Onward Christian Soldiers, and after Luke and I said our vows, and before we sealed the vows with a kiss, Hilda sang her solo:

Just as we are
We come to be
Gathered here to vow that we
Will live together
Constantly
Oh love of my life,
I come,
I come.

Just as we are
We come to wed
To love and honor
Till we're dead
Our love will grow and

Flood the world
Oh, joy, oh, joy
We come, we come.

Just as we are
With love to spare
We give our hearts
To each with care
And through life's trials
We'll be a pair
Oh joy, oh joy,
We come.
We come.

I'm glad Claire was standing next to me and blocking my view of Hilda, because if our eyes had met I would have burst into unstoppable giggles. It appeared the rest of the wedding guests didn't notice the strange words. And thank goodness Claire and Hilda had only written three verses and not six!

And, once again I compared Milt (Luke's best man) to my handsome, handsome husband. How did I ever get so lucky?

After the service, after the reception, after the shivaree (where the rowdy town boys did not kidnap me, but sang and pounded tin cans with wooden spoons), after Luke served the crowd small servings of Henry Highman's wine, and finally, finally, after everyone went home, I went upstairs and dressed in my flower embroidered, lace trimmed night gown.

I could hear Luke downstairs, shuffling about, knocking down the fire in the Monarch, pumping a glass of water, stacking wood in the wood box. I knew he was being discreet. I so wanted him to run up the stairs, throw open the door and grab me. I listened, and finally I heard his steady steps as he climbed the stairs. When I realized he was stomping on each step to announce his arrival, he found me with a huge smile on my face.

Luke ducked his head and entered the slope-roofed bedroom. The sculpted outline of his shoulders glowed in the dim light. He turned his back to me. There was a rustling as he unbuttoned and removed his stiff starched shirt. He hung each piece of clothing on the wooden pegs of the closet. He stood on one foot and then the other as he removed his shoes. And with his back still towards me, he stepped out of his trousers and then his shorts.

His hand reached out, pulled back the covers and he slid in beside me. With the expert skill he brought to shearing and skinning and milking, his large farmer's hands gently, carefully, pulled my night gown up over my head and he let the gown fall to the floor like cottonwood down.

Skin to skin—his skin cool, my skin warm—until neither knew where each began, until his body cupped mine, until my hands held him, until he enfolded me, until my body joined to his, until he entered me, and I felt pain so sweet, I cried for the staccato pulsing that made us one, until he sighed, and I lay staring at the moonlight slipping through the window, until all of that, I had not felt married. Now we were married and Luke slept and I lay wondering at the magic. In the early dawn I woke to sparrow chatter and crows' calls. The birds swooped and folded themselves over the corn fields. A rooster called his raucous good morning. I could smell the pungent acrid smell of nasturtiums and dahlias, above which sunflower heads bent under the weight of their summer seeds. Luke slept.

Tenderness radiated from between my legs and I felt everything could not be more perfect. Everything I had wished for had come true.

Perfect. Even the pledge, that had seemed balanced towards my new husband, the love, honor, and obey, it didn't seem wrong. I turned the wedding band on my finger round and round. I retraced each step on the path to becoming a wife: the fun of rewriting the hymn with Claire and Hilda, the smell of my lilac bouquet, the tin cans clanging on the buggy bumper, the rutted drive, the whiteness of the moon, the cold, creaking farmhouse, the wooden stairway up to the bedroom, the hollow knock of Luke's knuckles on the bedroom door, the undressing. Perfect.

I thought of my mother's promise: angels would applaud. But everything went so fast, and later I listened to Luke's soft snores and wondered, did angels applaud? Before I fell back into the last of the morning sleep, I wondered just how long it would take to repeat applauding angels.

CHAPTER NINETEEN

CHICAGO, CHICAGO

Wednesday, August 28, 1968

I'm the navigator. I've marked our route and so far we've not made one mistake.

I jump when Andrew yells, "Smell that? Smell that gas? I can't believe it! We're in Chicago! OOOO-WEEEEE!"

His right hand pounds the steering wheel and I point, and just in time, he swings out and around a Pabst Blue Ribbon truck and maneuvers into the right lane and we follow the arrow off the JFK Expressway to the Dan Ryan.

He sings, "Chicago, Chicago," in his totally atonal voice and then as if to grab the city, he sticks his hand out the window to scoop in the heavy, humid air.

I can't believe it when he yells, "Tear gas! It *is* tear gas!"

I think he's nuts. I reach for the steering wheel. My voice matches his in loudness. Except, I'm irritated. "Watch what you're doing!"

Once the car is back in its lane and Andrew isn't cheering and yelling, I smooth the map and run my finger along the crinkled surface searching for Grant Park. And because we have been following the demonstrations on the radio, I say more to calm myself, than to convince Andrew, "We're nowhere near the demonstrations."

"We have to be! My eyes itch! Hot Damn!"

"Not from tear gas! Smog. Probably big-city smog." I measure the map with my thumb, end to knuckle, end to knuckle. "Three miles. We're at least three miles away."

"Wind carries that stuff," Andrew sniffs the air. "God, this is exciting. To be right in the middle of a revolution!" Andrew turns up the volume on the radio. The chant of demonstrators fills the car: "THE WHOLE WORLD IS WATCHING! THE WHOLE WORLD IS WATCHING!"

Over the chants the announcer declares, "A RAG-TAG ARMY OF HIPPIES AND YIPPIES ARE PUSHING AGAINST LINES OF ARMED, EXHAUSTED POLICEMEN. CHICAGO'S FINEST ARE DETERMINED TO KEEP THE DEMONSTRATORS ON THE PARK SIDE OF MICHIGAN AVENUE. INSIDE THE HILTON HOTEL, DEMOCRATIC CONVENTION DELEGATES IGNORE THE GROWING, CHANTING CROWD. WITH TEAR GAS FILLED AIR, CANDIDATES ARE ANGRY AND CONCERNED. AN UNNAMED SOURCE DECLARED DELEGATES ARE REQUESTING ESCORTS AND DEMANDING THAT MAYOR DALEY TAKE CONTROL. IN THE WORDS OF OUR SOURCE, THIS CROWD HAS UPSET THE DEMOCRATIC PROCESS. THE OPPOSITE POINT OF VIEW CAME FROM PEACE RALLY ORGANIZER, RENEE DAVIS, WHO, BEFORE BEING CLUBBED UNCONSCIOUS AND TAKEN AWAY IN AN AMBULANCE, DECLARED FROM THE GRANT PARK STAGE THAT THE GATHERED TEN THOUSAND DEMONSTRATORS REPRESENT THE TRUE SPIRIT OF DEMOCRACY. THE CONVENTION IS ONLY HOURS AWAY FROM CHOOSING THE NEXT CANDIDATE FOR THE PRESIDENT OF THE UNITED STATES. HUBERT HUMPHRY LEADS. MAYOR RICHARD DALEY HAS CALLED ON THE GOVERNOR DEMANDING MORE NATIONAL GUARD. WHILE TENSION MOUNTS OUTSIDE, INSIDE THE BUSINESS OF THE DEMOCRATIC CONVENTION CONTINUES."

"Damn! We should be there!"

"We've got to find our apartment."

"The apartment can wait. Check the map. Get us to Grant Park."

"No! You want to go to Grant Park? Go tomorrow."

"It'll be over."

"Revolutions last more than a day. Besides, it sounds totally out of control."

"Right! Material! The most important event of my life and I'm driving around with a car full of shit looking for an apartment that can wait."

I scoot across the front seat to rub the back of Andrew's neck. I tuck a strand of hair from his pony tail behind his ear. I whisper, "But I can't wait. That apartment will have a bed. I'll put on brand new sheets…" I run my finger along the edge of Andrew's ear, ". . . and you can take off my brand new teddy."

Andrew reaches for my hand and guides it between his legs.

"Ummm-ummm, almost as good as a revolution." Andrew pushes my hand against him. The Dodge swerves.

I pull my hand away. "Watch it, Romeo."

I love it when he lets me know how much he wants me. Just thinking about the last few nights makes me smile. Our honeymoon has been delicious. Even though my hips ache and I'm dozy from lack of sleep, I couldn't be happier.

But, for now, I am so ready for our apartment. Getting away from the car. Taking a walk along Lake Michigan. Then I remember that the lake shore is inhabited by screaming protestors.

We both have negative thoughts at the same time. Andrew asks, "What if our apartment is full of cockroaches? I've heard Chicago is full of cockroaches."

"Andrew, you go from saving the world, to being amorous, to cockroaches." I giggle and reach to rub my palm up and down the inside of his leg. "We can get cockroach killer. There will be a fire escape. We won't be murdered in our sleep. We will get your degree."

I tuck my fingertips under the curve of Andrew's leg. "Don't close your eyes. You're driving."

"Then be careful with your hand or we'll end up doing it in the middle of the road."

"All hot and sticky. The whole world watching!"

"You think I joke!"

I laugh and scoot back against the door. I flap the map to stir the air, dry the beads of sweat on my forehead. Then I check the map. "Next turn should be Highway 55 toward Lake Michigan." Soon, tall apartment houses slap shadows over the freeway and I watch hoping to get a glimpse of the Lake. Buildings block any view as we head further south and I begin to count turn-offs and watch for the off-ramp to the University of Chicago.

"There! There! Turn!" I yell as we whip past the Fifty-Ninth Street Exit.

"Shit, Sarah. You weren't paying attention!"

"Who wasn't paying attention?"

"You're the navigator!"

"Okay, okay. We'll take the next exit."

Andrew slows the car. On his right, tall, sparse apartment houses give way to the backs of three-story brick buildings. Laundry hangs off balconies. Cars and car parts lay scattered in vacant lots. Plywood covers windows. The streets are littered.

"What a mess," Andrew says. "How do people live like this?"

"What people? Those buildings are empty."

"You know what I mean. Why do you do that?"

I ignore the irritation in Andrew's voice. I gaze at the passing buildings and then my eye catches the rounded breasts of a naked woman leaning out a window, her partner holds her from behind.

"You sure we are near the University of Chicago?" Andrew asks, his voice full of disbelief. "We're going to get lost? Get trapped? Murdered?"

I don't mention the couple. I answer with irritation, "If we're dead, we won't care."

Something about the couple repulsed me. Was it because those people were poor? Or because they were black? Or because it wasn't the two of us making love? I block the image and watch the street numbers slip by: Sixty-fifth. Sixtieth. Fifty-sixth. In front of us appears a broad expanse of green. On the other side red brick buildings line the street.

I point with one hand, follow the map with the other. "Almost there! BLACKSTONE AND STONY ISLAND WAY. Get ready to turn."

"You sure?" Andrew asks, doubt riddling his question. "Check the map."

"I am checking the map! And unless you want to go to Gary, Indiana, turn."

I hate when our conversations get cranky. I hate when Andrew becomes tentative. I hate being irritated and impatient. To erase my bad thoughts—I call on a childhood trick. I close my eyes and hum *Oh my darlin', oh my darlin', oh my darlin' Clementine.*

Andrew turns to go around the Midway (we learn later that this is the dividing point between the University and where I'll teach). And then I realize the buildings to our right are the campus and we've gone too far.

"So where is the apartment?" Andrew asks.

I stop humming and check the map. The cross streets slip by. The tires make a ripping sound as if the hot blacktop might ooze up and pin us in place. We're headed further south and the Dodge rolls over a plastic drink cup. Andrew swerves to avoid the remains of a broken bottle.

"What a garbage pit."

I return to my humming.

"Look. Look around you."

I hum louder.

"Stop that stupid song and take a good-god-damned look."

"And?"

"We're the only white people."

"So? They're people."

"They're staring at us."

"They're not staring at us."

I smile at a group of men leaning against a store window. I raise my hand to wave and then, hesitate, deciding they don't look that friendly.

"Would you quit gawking and tell me how to get the fuck out of here!" Andrew spits the words out.

I bend over the map. "We need to circle back on Lake Shore Drive."

"Roll up your window!" Andrew demands and pulls the car closer to the center of the street.

Three teenagers in hair nets and white sleeveless undershirts lounge in front of a hotdog stand: MOISHA PEPIC'S CHICAGO FRANKS. The hotdog stand appears to lean against an abandoned hotel. Above the hotel entrance, a lifeless neon sign hangs cock-eyed from its bracket. It reads: BLACKSTONE HOTEL.

A rusted orange Vega, with missing wheels and smashed windows, straddles the sidewalk. Graffiti strewn plywood covers windows of the next four buildings.

"God, Sarah, what if your assignment is down here?"

I don't answer. I fold the map. "Two more blocks and you can turn."

Down the sidewalk, an older Negro woman and a young girl push a cart full of clothing. A fringed scarf falls from the cart. The girl runs to pick it up.

"Moving day," Andrew says.

"Don't make fun."

Two black men rest their haunches against the window frame of a liquor store. They look up as Andrew stops for a light. One waves a long-fingered hand and yells, "Hey, Whitey! You lost?"

Andrew grips the steering wheel with both hands. He hisses, "Sarah! Roll up your window."

"We'll suffocate," I answer through clinched teeth and then I roll up the window. Our car jerks forward in anticipation of the light change.

"What if we get a flat tire? What if we hit a dead-end street?"

I snap, "What if, what if, Chicken Little…just drive." Sweat slips down my sides.

"I'm the one that has to protect you," he says as he looks both ways. We pass a weather-worn granite sign, OAKWOOD CONFEDERATE CEMETARY, CIVIL WAR VETERANS.

"That's ironic, huh? We're in a ghetto and the only trimmed lawn surrounds dead confederate soldiers."

Andrew reaches for the button to lock his door. "If you get a job in the ghetto where you can't possibly teach we won't have any money and if we don't have any money I can't go to the University of Chicago and if I don't go to graduate school I'll get drafted, and Vietnam, here I come."

"Stop Andrew! You say one more word and I'll scream!"

"Lock your door."

"Andrew," I hiss, "we're driving next to a cemetery and a vacant lot. There's nobody here! It's a thousand degrees. I can't breathe."

"Better than dead."

"Turn!" I yell.

Miraculously, we are back on Lake Shore Drive. I roll down my window, lean my head back, and close my eyes. I put my arm out the window to let air slip inside my sleeveless blouse. The car slows and comes down the ramp; once again we're back at the Midway.

Andrew points and exclaims, "There! There's the campus. Thank God." He rolls down his window.

I open my eyes to see Gothic buildings of red brick and pale cream granite. Peaked roofs. Students walking in twos and threes. In the Midway, a group of students play football. White students.

I sigh, slightly ashamed at my relief. And then I think about the two sides of Andrew. His 'what-if' side that always ends in cataclysmic disaster. His warm, sexy side that pulls me in, turns me on, and makes me feel safe. Even irritated, I think we are a pretty good couple. Andrew does the worrying. I do the action stuff: sending his application, getting letters of recommendation, forwarding transcripts, typing term papers, reading the map.

His job? Study. Make good grades. Graduate. Write the great American novel. Be famous. Teach somewhere. Win a Pulitzer.

A horn honks. A Negro man leans out the window of his dented, head light missing, Ford truck, inches from our bumper. His hand is raised and to me he looks like he is about to slam into our car. He yells and jabs his finger at us. I can see his hand is meaty and huge, black fingers with an eerie, pink palm. And as I grab the handle to roll up the window, it snaps off in my hand.

"Back off, buddy!" Andrew yells.

At the very moment our front wheel begins thumping. The man points down. By the time we understand what he's yelled at us, "Ya got a flat tire!" he drives away.

The Dodge bumps against the curb. Andrew's head slumps to the steering wheel, his forehead rests against his crossed hands. His muffled voice says, "He didn't have to yell."

I pull my hair up away from my damp neck. "It's too damn hot," I say and flap my hands as if I could scatter the humidity.

"If you'd been paying attention…"

I throw the map on the floor, push the door open, slam the door behind me. I walk a half block down the street under the splattered shade of oak trees with large heavy leaves. The leaves droop as if they too, can't bare the heat. Above me two crows dart and slip inside the branches to find shelter from the sun.

From where I stand, in the shade of the trees, I can hear the trunk lid pop open. I walk slowly back toward the car, pretending not to hear Andrew's grumping. I don't offer to help as he unloads boxes to find the jack and the spare tire. I sit under one of the oaks and close my eyes.

Eventually the trunk lid slams shut. When I feel the rounded glass edge of a pop bottle against my bare arm, I open my eyes to the gift of a warm Nehi Orange. Andrew squats down and kisses my nose.

"Friends?" he asks.

"Well," I say, letting the liquid slip down my throat and feeling his thigh against my hip, "I'd probably settle for lovers."

"Good, good, good," he says and his tongue catches a drop of orange Nehi from the edge of my mouth. "God, it feels good getting out of that car."

We stand in silence enjoying the shade and the slight breeze off of Lake Michigan.

"Look down the street," Andrew points. "That has to be the Robie House." We stare at the flat-roofed, low-slung building two blocks away. "And if you hadn't been pouting, you would have noticed…" and Andrew turns my shoulders, "…that's Rockefeller Chapel."

Across the street, past a large expanse of lawn, stands the largest church I've ever seen. Spires pierce the sky. I crane to take in the bell tower.

"And look behind it!" I point to where dark clouds bump against each other. Thunder rumbles, and immediately a cool breeze pushes away the heavy humid air. Within seconds, rain splatters the sidewalk making small dust puffs. Andrew runs to open the door and calls, "Get in!"

Inside, rain makes hollow tap-dancing sounds on the roof.

I search through my fringed purse for the envelope with the keys to The Adler Arms. Room 308. The apartment is only three blocks away. We drive down Woodlawn passing Fifty-Third.

Are you sure you have the right address?" Andrew shouts over the exuberant rain storm.

"Absolutely!" I lean forward to catch signs and numbers as the wipers smear the windows. "We're close."

"Then where is it?" Andrew's voice has gone from a yell to a bark.

"Don't use that voice. I hate it when you use that voice."

"Damn it, Sarah. It's raining. I use that voice so you can hear me for God's sake."

"Well don't."

"Then where in the hell are we? We're at Fifty-first. Have we gone too fucking far?"

"Drive around the block. It must be behind us."

We drive in silence. I strain to see the numbers tucked in doorways. The buildings all look alike. The numbers are impossible to see.

"Ooops. It's not 5212. It's 5220. Keep going."

"God…" Andrew says with disgust. "You've had a week to read all that shit. Now you…" A car honks and the driver of a postal truck waves his arms.

"All right! All right already!" Andrew shouts.

I point for Andrew to turn the corner. Sweat puddles under my breasts.

"All this and we could have gone to the park. We could have demonstrated. We could have stopped this stupid war."

"And had our car broken into? And everything stolen? And no place to stay? And tear-gas everywhere? And…"

"You sound just like me!" Andrew laughs and he reaches for my hand. I pull away. It's hard to hold my words back—not to snap that he never once went to a demonstration in Seattle. *I did!* I helped carry the PEACE NOW banner. I was there! Proof on the front page of *The Seattle Times.* My face a blur, but I circled that blur with a magic marker and put the article on the refrigerator. I sent a copy to my parents. And Andrew? Andrew was busy. Andrew had to finish his degree. Andrew had to get some sleep after pulling all-nighters. Andrew didn't even look like a demonstrator. He couldn't grow a real beard. He had a skinny pony-tail. And if he did ever get arrested? He'd have a nervous breakdown without clean socks.

The car inches down Woodlawn. Students run to get out of the downpour. A couple snuggles under a green awning, deep in conversation.

"Now where?" Andrew shouts as he inches the Dodge down the car-jammed street. I call out street numbers. Fifty two ten. Fifty two twenty."

Miraculously, at that very moment, a parking place appears. We park in front of The Adler Arms.

"There is a god," Andrew says with a sigh.

I sit without moving. I listen to the slap of the rain. I watch the drops bounce off the hood of the car. This moment has been so long in coming. Where is the celebration? Where is the fun? Seattle seems a long time ago. I feel numb and wonder how the joy has vanished. I can barely remember why we are here, why we bothered. The rain isn't Seattle rain.

I hug myself. Shiver. The temperature has dropped twenty degrees.

Two hours later, inside the third floor of our barely furnished apartment, I've finished fitting our clothes into a three-foot closet. The kitchen stuff is in a four-foot-square kitchen. Towels and bed sheets fill three board shelves in the bathroom. Six boxes of books line the two-tiered cement block bookcase left by the last renters. Eventually, I fix Campbell's Chicken Noodle Soup while Andrew plugs in our twelve-inch television.

Sitting on a spring-sprung couch, hunched over our bowls of soup, we watch as the television camera jerks and speeds through the demonstrators. Chants grow louder. Crowds of kids with bandanas over their mouth run from advancing police and clouds of tear gas. Some stumble and fall. Angry mouths shout, "Pigs! Pigs! Pigs!" Batons rise and fall like a thrashing machine and the crowd scatters. The television doesn't mask the sound of wood on bone. Another camera catches the back of the crowd where demonstrators appear oblivious to what is happening to the compressed bodies near the stage. Another camera focuses on arm-linked demonstrators chanting louder and louder, THE WHOLE WORLD IS WATCHING! THE WHOLE WORLD IS WATCHING! Then the tear gas divides the masses and people break and run stumbling, covering their eyes with their T-shirts, scarves, and handkerchiefs. Then the news reporter coughs and the camera whirls and shows a scatter of lawn, of sky, and of running feet.

I fear for the demonstrators. In Seattle, though I had heard there had been scuffles and arrests, my part of the parade had been a singing, chanting community. The sky had been blue with white tufts of clouds. As we marched, arm in arm, we called out to the police to join us. As we came off the freeway exit into the downtown, we sang over and over again, "All we are saying is give peace a chance…"

I can't watch the television anymore. I scrub kitchen shelves, the refrigerator, the sink, the black and white checkered linoleum.

Andrew leans inches from the television, switching channels, searching out re-runs of the falling bodies, the bloodied heads. Without looking up he says, "Damn, I wish I had been there."

I go to the bedroom, find our new sheets and instead of the new teddy I had saved, I find an old T-shirt of Andrews. I lay on top of the covers in front of the open window trying not to listen to the angry television. When the eleven o'clock news ends, Andrew joins me.

No rain. Humidity makes the air fat and heavy. Even with wide-open windows, the curtains hang slack.

Andrew touches my back and for once, it is just too hot.

CHAPTER TWENTY

HOW DO YOU KNOW WHO YOU ARE?

Chicago, Tuesday, September 3, 1968

"Oh, Mary Mack, Mack, Mack, all dressed in black, black, black…" A girl in a crayon-red shirt and denim cut-offs lifts her ebony black arms, pats the air to the rhythm of the rhyming words and slips inside the double-dutch ropes. She crosses her feet, slaps her heels, bounces on her toes—left foot, right foot.

"With silver button, button, buttons, down her back, back, back."

A second girl joins her. Together, they lift their heels higher, push out their bottoms further, chicken-wing their elbows faster. Their bright voices slice the air: "They jumped so high, high, high, they reach the sky, sky, sky and they never came back, back, back till the Fourth of July, ly, ly."

I think the children might look in my direction. Wave or smile. They don't. I walk out and around the churning ropes, push open the heavy oak doors of Tesla Elementary School, and escape Chicago's heat and humidity.

Inside, waxed floors gleam. A locker door slams. The hall smells of carnauba wax, orange peels, sour milk, and chalk dust. Directly in front of me black letters shimmer on a frosted window: PRINCIPAL. An image waffles behind the obscure glass.

I knock.

A military voice shouts, "The door's open!"

I turn the knob, peek inside and call, "Hello?"

"Back here!" the voice barks. From behind a metal file cabinet, like a giant pop-up figure, a formidable woman appears. Broad shoulders. Blond hair on its way to gray. Blouse pushed forward by mammoth breasts. With her right foot she slams the file drawer closed. In her left hand she holds a box of Triscuits.

"Breakfast," she says, and pops a cracker into her mouth. She looks directly at me and demands, "And you are?"

I flinch. I stutter. "Ah, Sar, Sarah. Sarah Althaus. The new librarian."

"Principal Goodwin." She brushes crumbs from her fingers, extends her hand, and states firmly, "No library."

The strength of her grasp stops me from insisting Principal Goodwin has to be wrong. I *am* the librarian.

"Give me your SAC."

"My sack?" I ask.

"School Assignment Card. From Central. You must have it. You got that librarian idea from somewhere."

Inside my fringed leather bag, I push aside my lunch, a pack of Kleenex, *The Adventures of Augie March,* and find the assignment card stuffed between my diploma and a box of magic markers.

Principal Goodwin gives the card a cursory glance. "Damn. Library? It's been ten years. 1958. Maybe 1959. And *that* library? A coat closet! Twenty books max." Then she asks with a skewed smile, "What grades can you teach?"

"I have a Bachelor's of Arts in Education. Any grade through fifth." For a minute I consider handing her the diploma from my purse. Proof.

"And what grades have you *taught*?"

My knees go loose, as if marionette strings have been snipped. "I student taught. I taught…"

Principal Goodwin interrupts, "Doesn't matter. You're here." She extends the Triscuit box. While I savor a single salty cracker, I notice a list of names tacked to a bulletin board directly above the principal's head. Around the list are dozens of children's photos. Gleaming teeth. Pigtails. Stretched smiles. Every child a Negro child.

Following my gaze, Principal Goodwin says, "Let's see what we have here." Her finger goes to the last name on the list. She reads out loud, "Jennie White. Kindergarten. Room 101."

"Kindergarten?"

"Kindergarten. We can use you in the kindergarten." Principal Goodwin's statement is crisp and certain.

"Kindergarten." I say, defeated. I know nothing about kindergarten. I student taught third grade, and every child in that third grade was white. "Use me?" I barely whisper.

Principal Goodwin slumps into a wine-red swivel chair. She rubs the bridge of her nose. "They do this, the assignment office. Assign librarian so you'll show up. Some stay a week. The brave last to the first paycheck." As if filled with a bright new idea, she tilts back in the chair, slips her hands behind her head, and says with perfect precision, "Not you, of course. Not you. I can see you are made of steel."

I hug my bag to my chest. Hold it like a shield.

"So to work. You're the first teacher here this morning. First teacher makes coffee. End of the hall. Jennie will be here at eight-thirty. You'll find the kindergarten. The chairs are real little." Principal Goodwin chuckles, stands, walks around the desk, takes my arm firmly, opens the office door, and points down the hall—a dark, cool, tunnel. "Umm, umm, love that smell of a clean, shiny hall. Don't you?" She doesn't wait for me to answer, but points and says, "You can do it, girl!"

The door shuts. I fight back tears. What am I doing here? I feel white and pale and sickly and inadequate and ill-trained and out of place. Girl? I feel like a baby.

The door opens. Principal Goodwin leans out, one finger raised. "One thing," she says. "I need someone to teach an after-school class. One hour. Math. Fifth and sixth graders. Twice a week. Twenty bucks an hour. Let me know by tomorrow."

"Math?" I ask.

"Trust me. You're going to love it here. And the math? Anyone can teach it. Besides there's a guide. And it will be good for the older kids to be around a white person. Besides me, of course!" She chuckles and then as if to encourage me, she walks with me down the hall. "This will all work out. Jennie's a great teacher. She'll show you the ropes. She's been in that room for twenty years. Of course, you'll be her assistant." She chuckles again. "You'll be glad you're the assistant."

We walk past an empty room stacked with tables and chairs pushed against a dusty chalkboard.

"Tesla's a great school. White teachers don't stick around long enough to learn that. You leave and you'll never know what you missed." A phone ringing catches her attention. "Keep going. End of the hall. I'll talk to you later!" Principal Goodwin hurries back to her office.

I wanted to call out, "Don't leave me!" I don't, of course. I walk the length of the hall to the last room. Inside are stacks of red, yellow, and blue chairs. Little chairs.

Jennie arrives exactly at 8:30.

"You must be Sarah. I'm Jennie White."

Jennie is short, compact, trim and tailored—dressed in a navy blue polyester suit with severely centered silver buttons. She is the color of burnt toast. Her black hair is oiled in a marcel wave. At her right temple the crimped black hair is shot through with white. She stands back on one heel, her arms akimbo. She studies me. Her eyes take in my Indian print blouse, my leather mini-skirt, my Doc Martens. Without hesitation, Jennie demands in an in-charge voice, "Unless you want to give one hundred and ten five year olds an eye full, wear slacks tomorrow. Something in which you can sit on the floor." Jennie's voice is smooth and precise. "Enough about dress.

In the closet you'll find last year's supplies. Place five tins of crayons on each table; find a ream of eight-and-a-half- by eleven-inch paper, cut 110 nametags. Pins are on my desk." Jennie pulls a list from a manila file. "First names only. Not that they can read, but it gets them used to the idea of letters and names. Then when you finish the name tags, set up easels and fill paint jars."

Jennie picks up a notebook brimming with vaccination slips and registration forms. "I've a home visit and some paper work to do in the office. I'll be back in time for lunch and introduce you to the staff." At the door she turns to say with a broad smile, "Looking forward to working with you." And she is out the door.

I lower myself into one of the little chairs and study the list of children. Fifty-five in the morning. Fifty-five in the afternoon. Corin, Tamika, Ebony, Cama, Tawana, Leppart, Aisha, Leny, Ali, Rasheed, Gabeua, Kareem, Galiano. My head drops to my knees. I close my eyes and try to block the panic that slides down my spine. I sit curled over thinking I will just have to adjust. There is no way I can't work. We have a degree to pay for.

The tiniest tug. Fingers pull my hair.

Startled, I turn just in time to see one of the jump-roping girls run down the hall. Voices cheer when the child opens the heavy oak door. I hear her triumphant voice call, "I touched her hair!"

Just as she promised, Jennie returns at noon and invites me to join her in the teachers' room. Jennie introduces me to six teachers. Two men tip their heads. Four women barely smile. Jennie and I find two chairs at an empty table. Jennie offers to share her three Tupperware containers—red beans and sausage, cornbread, and sweet potato pie. I thank her and then pull from my bag a tuna fish sandwich.

Jennie delicately eats her lunch with a sterling silver fork. I unwrap limp waxed paper. As we eat, Jennie places the class list between us and circles every fourth or fifth name.

"Twana Freeman—I taught three of her siblings. Same with Kareem and Galiano. The more I know the families, the better the children behave." Jennie laughs quietly, "With fifty-five children, they don't have much room for mischief. But you'll be surprised. Last year Corinthia Jackson led four children up to the elevated tracks to watch the trains go by. A born leader. Her little lemmings all trooped back ecstatic over their adventure! Miss Goodwin was not pleased."

The rest of the afternoon, Jennie and I scrub chairs, stack nap-mats, finish name tags, and cover the corkboards with cut-outs of orange and brown fall leaves. I pin WELCOME letters over the chalkboard.

"Sorry about the library thing," Jennie says as we end the day. "You might be surprised how much you'll enjoy the little ones. And should you not … I got a full day's work out of you!"

"You think I won't be back?"

"You wouldn't be the first."

We walk down the hall. Out the front door, under the awning, Jennie and I maneuver through four girls playing jacks, two girls re-chalking their hopscotch pattern, three girls waiting their turn to jump rope. There are furtive glances and turned heads. Two voices call out, "Hi Mrs. White! How you doin'!"

"Fine! Thank you for asking!" Jennie answers.

The tiniest of the girls slips her arm into Jennie's. "I wish I wasn't first grade. Wish I was with you again."

"You'll do just fine, Jasmine. And you can come see me!" She gives the child a hug and a kiss on top of her head. The child smiles and sighs with pleasure.

At the curb Jennie turns to me, "That's what keeps me coming back. A good hug."

"My reason?" I answer and point to Andrew waiting in the Dodge across the street. "My husband has two years of graduate school ahead of him. You'll see me tomorrow. And the next day."

Jennie's back straightens and I realize that my words have an insensitive note. I try to reassure her, "I'm sure I'll enjoy kindergarten. Honest!"

"You give it a try, you will," Jennie answers. "Here comes my bus!"

I wait until the accordion doors of the bus close and the heavy smell of diesel fills the air, then I walk over to the car where Andrew waits and I slump into the front seat.

"That bad?" Andrew asks.

"You won't believe…"

"Look!" Andrew says and leans back into the seat so I can see around him.

The children have gathered at the curb edge. They point and whisper and nudge each other. We hear one child yell, "Look at white teacher's husband! He white too!" Shouts and hoots and whistles follow us as Andrew slowly drives away from Tesla Elementary School.

"So, tell me," Andrew says and reaches for my hand.

"I don't know what I'm doing," I say.

In the kindergarten the next morning, seven children have already gathered around Jennie. She bends to hear each child's name, and before pinning it on, repeats the name as she guides one small hand after another over the tag.

More children arrive. Mothers, reluctant to leave, help find places for their children around a circle painted on the floor. The first child I help, Carol Lynn, is brittle-boned small, with a pink pinafore, white starched lace collar, new Mary Janes, pink stockings. Her small breakfast-jellied hand reaches to clutch mine as I lead her to an open space in the circle.

Children descend in droves. Four mothers stand outside the door, tearful and anxious. They stay until Jennie assures them all will be well, and they leave reluctantly.

Finally we have checked in all of the children. I realize the name tags are for my benefit. Jennie already has all of the names memorized. Once the door closes, Jennie sits at the piano. She hits a C chord. She waves the children to stand. She plays a Chopin mazurka. Over the music she calls, "Skip!" She turns to me and demands, "Skip!" I grab the hands of the two nearest children and I skip. We make our way around the room. With a final chord everyone sits. On the floor. Including me.

The piano guides the next two and a half hours. When Jennie isn't at the piano, she and I help the children discover the toy bin, the crayon tins, the painting easels, colored paper, snub-nosed scissors, and the bathroom. Intermittently, Jennie strikes the piano keys. To waltzes, arms swing. To marches, feet march. To lullabies, bodies sleep.

The first hour I think the children are cute. So many pigtails. So many happy faces. So many cute first day dresses. I've never seen so many adorable children. By three o'clock, they are no longer adorable. They are people. Little people. People with specific needs: sticky hands, spilled paint, hoarded crayons, snack too small, snack spilled, no snack at all, name tags lost, torn pictures, wrinkled pictures, runny noses, wet pants, easels knocked over, easels not gotten to, turns at chairs. And yet? All in all it is a very good day. The best part is that the children don't seem to notice that I'm white. Children need me as often as they need Jennie. I'm pleased.

Driving home with Andrew, all I want is a hot bath and a large glass of wine. Instead, Andrew tells me he has made arrangements to meet another student and his wife for pizza and beer at Kafka's—Gustaf and Bunny.

At a booth in the smoke filled bar, the men debate literary theories of Northrup Frye. Bunny talks home decorating. In a voice miniscule and jarring Bunny tells me how she plans to decorate residences on the near-north-side when she graduates. It isn't until the second pitcher of beer, Gustaf asks, "And Sarah, what do you do?"

"I teach. Elementary school in Woodlawn. Kindergarten."

"How brave, teaching in the ghetto," Gustaf says.

Bunny exclaims, "My goodness! That's amazing. I hope they appreciate you. Poor little things."

Words tumble out of my mouth before I can stop them, "Those poor little things are not poor little things. They've more energy than this entire bar! And believe me, the only amazing thing is how strong and bright they are!" I take a long drink of beer. And then since no one has responded, I continue: "Don't say one word to discourage or encourage me. I have a God-damned job and it's going to pay my husband's God-damned tuition to the God-damned University of Chicago."

The silence that follows my exclamation lets me know I'll be making up to Gustaf and Bunny for the remainder of the year. I start that apology with the very next sentence, "Forgive me. I'm tired. It's been a long day."

Gustaf appears to speak for both of them, "We understand. Teaching in the ghetto has got to be exhausting." He lifts the half-full pitcher, "Here, have some more beer."

I don't answer. I sit quietly, trying to listen like a good wife. Trying to look attentive. Trying not to feel totally removed from the conversation. Trying not to feel irritated. Finally, finally it is time to leave and we say quick goodbyes in front of Kafka's Bar.

In the car Andrew takes my hand. We don't talk. Three flights up, back in our apartment I brush my teeth, wash my face, and go to bed. I drop into a deep, dreamless sleep. I couldn't tell you when Andrew comes to bed. I could care less.

The next day, in the office where each teacher has a mail cubby, I find a note from Principal Goodwin: *Math class. Thursday. Room 204. 3:30. Please confirm.* It appears I have an after-school job. We need the money.

September 5, 1968

On this day at 3:15 I hurry upstairs to find on the teacher's desk in the front of Room 204, seven workbooks, a teacher's guide, pencils, and one broken piece of chalk. With relief I read the guide: addition, subtraction, multiplication, and division. Nothing I hadn't taught third graders.

At 3:30 there are no children.

At 3:40 I think perhaps I'm in the wrong room. I check the hall. Nobody. I decide to wait five more minutes.

At 3:42 the door bursts open and four tall, gangly, raucous boys enter. They yell, open-hand-slap, call, "Hey bro!" and "Check it out!" and "This be my desk!" until one pushes the other out of a chair which allows the two biggest boys to pull each other onto the floor where they wrestle to the enthusiastic encouragement of their friends.

I clutch the math workbooks in my arms. At the door, two petite, slender twins wait, holding hands. At their appearance, the four boys stand, brush off their dust covered jeans, and grin sheepishly. They tuck in their shirts, pick up the fallen chairs, and step back to let the girls enter.

"We're here..." says the first twin.

"... For the math class." The second twin finishes her sister's sentence.

"Come in," I say, pleased at their composure and their influence. "Find a desk." At which request everyone finds a place to sit with a minimum amount of desk banging.

I pick up the broken piece of chalk and write on the board, *Mrs. Althaus, Math.* As I write, someone makes a hollow hooting sound, and another boy calls, "Hey, hey, you white!"

The chalk snaps. I turn to face the class. I'm not sure what I expected, but I didn't expect what I just got. Every student sits quietly, eyes on me, waiting for me to say something.

It takes all of my strength, but I force a smile and I say, "You're absolutely right. I'm white. Now, I'd like to learn your names. Let's start with you." I point at the largest of the four boys.

"Ali Oops!"

The boys laugh and slam their hands on the desk. The twins giggle and bend their heads in embarrassment.

Then the large kid stands and as if to direct his words, he says as he points at himself, "My name be Jerome. He be Telly. That's Franklin and over there, that's Jethro. The twins? They Sallie and Sue. You need me to whop anyone upside the head, you just ask!"

Over the loud guffaws of the boys, I say, "Thank you, Jerome."

I need to take control. I place a math workbook in front of each child. When I get to Jerome, he says to me, "Yeah, he right. I'm not Ali Oops. But I *be* Ali, if I could. You know Ali?"

"We're here for math. Time's passing. Write your names on the book and..."

"You white. You probably don't know Ali."

"I got no pencil," Telly yells.

I hand him a pencil.

"Ali! He the best!" asserts Jerome.

I stand at my desk. I open the guide book. I press the pages flat. "Maybe another day we can talk about Cassius Clay. Today we are going to study math."

"He *Muhammad* Ali," Jethro says.

"He *is* Muhammad Ali," I correct, feeling I am on very shaky ground.

"We say, '*he* Muhammad Ali.' He the one an' only Muhammad Ali!"

"Maybe some other time we can talk about Muhammad Ali."

"Why? You scared Muhammad Ali?"

I slowly walk over to Jerome. I place both hands on the front of his desk and lean until I make contact with his coal black eyes and I say in a quiet voice, "Jerome, you signed up for this class. No one made you come to this class. So… if you don't mind, open your book to page two."

I walk back to the front of the room, surprised to see that everyone had turned to page two. "Please do the first four problems. You have five minutes."

For a brief moment, the children scribble, sneak peeks at someone else's book, or sit scowling. I check the teacher's manual: "*Write the answers on the board. Let the children check their own work.*" I do exactly that. "*When the children have checked their work, don't look at their books. Let them see where they need help. We suggest you respond with these words: 'How did you do? If you got four right? You're a winner! Three right? You did well. Two right? Don't worry; this class will put you on the road to being a winner. Missed them all? You're here! You're interested! Attitude is everything! Our goal is to make you a winner!'*"

I use the words, more or less, in the way they are written. The class appears after a bit more erasing to get the four correct answers in their work books.

Jethro's head rests in his book. He pretends to snore. Telly laughs and follows suit. Franklin pumps his arm in the air and yells, "Yes, Yes, Yes! I be the best!" Sallie and Sue sit with folded hands and wait for further instruction.

The door opens and Principal Goodwin asks, "Everything okay? Thought I'd see if you needed anything."

"We're doing just fine," I answer. "Just fine." I wave the answer book to let the principal see I have the guide and I'm using it.

Principal Goodwin smiles, and after slight hesitation, she leaves closing the door behind her.

I check the clock. Four-twenty-six. When I look up Jerome is staring at me.

"Time up?" he asks.

"A few more minutes."

"End of this class, we get Talking Time."

"Talking Time?" I know I am being pulled into some ploy of Jerome's but I'm too exhausted to challenge him and I feel totally defeated trying to teach math to children when from all of their scrambling and peeking and pushing to see each other's answers, can't pay attention and half can't add.

"Tell me about Talking Time."

"We choose the talk. Then we talk."

"If it's about math, I guess we can talk. That seems reasonable."

"Good! This about numbers." Jereomes's smile grows huge. "How many fights Muhammad Ali win?"

I ease myself into the teacher's chair and say, knowing I've been out-done, "I don't know. How many fights has Muhammad Ali won?"

"He won *all* his fights! He the greatest!" Jerome exclaims and jumps around the room throwing punches. Franklin kicks him, and Jerome howls, grabbing his leg.

"I gonna be Ali!" Jethro declares.

"You no Ali. You gonna get your ass whupped!"

"Today, I win!"

"Ten minutes you be dead!"

"You bet? You wanna bet?"

"You gonna lose. You gonna lose sooo big! He bigger'n you!"

Everyone yells at each other, except for the twins. They listen with wide eyes, and nod their heads when they agree.

"Stop!" I finally interrupt their nonsense. Then my stomach clinches in shame. All during my student teaching I had never yelled. Ever. Teachers, good teachers, did not yell at children. Teachers stood silent until all the children became silent. Up until the moment I yelled, I had stood waiting. No one noticed.

"Stop yelling, right this minute," I demand. "You must take turns! Someone, please tell me what you are talking about. Jerome, explain!"

"Five o'clock! A big fight!"

"Muhammad Ali?" I ask.

"No," Jerome laughs and pounds his desk. "It be Franklin! He be fightin' Big Eddy. Big Eddy, he real, real big!"

Telly yells, "He not that big!"

"He bigger than Franklin!" counters Jethro.

I look at Franklin. Franklin sits straight in his chair, his chin held high. I can see his small arms, and for the minute he is no longer a large, loud kid, but a very slight twelve-year-old.

"Franklin? Is this true? Are you going to be in a fight?"

Franklin gives his head a quick 'yes' nod.

"I think Principal Goodwin needs to know about this."

At that, the boys shout and hoot and slam their hands on their desks. Jerome yells, "No! No way! You tell Principal Goodwin, that be bad! It just a fight!" Jerome wiggles his hand in the air dismissing my words. "It nothin'! We always be fighting."

"Wait. What do you mean, you always *be* fighting?"

"Every night, most nights, there be a fight."

"Why? Why do you fight?" I ask.

The boys look at each other like I had just asked the most stupid question—the most stupid white question—they had ever heard.

"You know. When you was a kid, you fight!"

"No, I don't know. I didn't fight."

"You didn't fight? Why you didn't fight?"

"We just didn't. Why would I fight?"

Jerome answers, but every ounce of his voice indicates he doesn't believe I haven't been in a fight. He asks in a slow, thoughtful voice, "How you know who you be?"

Confused, I shake my head and ask, "What do you mean? How do I know who I am?"

"You fight. You know who you be. Big Eddy? He win last week, he be first. Franklin? Maybe Franklin be first tonight. Jethro he be first last month."

Somehow, I thought the girls might bring some sense to this conversation. I ask, "Sue? Sallie? Please say something."

Sallie giggles, "Sue be first last week."

"The girls fight too?!" I ask in no way hiding my disbelief.

"You need to fight! You have to fight!"

On that sentence, the 4:45 bell rings. The children jump up. Jerome knocks over his desk. The boys push each other getting out the door. The twins wait for the boys to leave and just as they are at the door, Sue turns and says, "You welcome to come to the fight, Miss Althaus. It be by the basketball hoop. You be the only white person, but it be okay. We take care of you."

In awe, amazement, disbelief, I mumble, "Thanks. I think I'll pass."

After the children have left, I gather up the books, set the chairs upright, grab my coat, and head out of the building.

At the front of the school, four sixth grade girls are at their usual place, jumping rope. I can't imagine them fighting. And maybe by sixth grade they don't have to fight.

As I skirt the slapping ropes, one girl calls, "Jump, Miss teacher! Come jump!" The ropes whip the air and two girls slip out leaving an empty space.

I eye those ropes.

"Go! Go!" they call.

"We'll make it slow," one of the turners yells.

"Don't you dare," I call and run across the street to pass my bag to Andrew through the window of the car.

"Sarah, what are you doing?" And as I run back, I hear him yell, "You're a teacher for God's sake…!"

At the curb, I stand for only a second, waiting for the churn of the ropes. I scoop the air with my hands in time to the ropes' rhythm. I wait and then I jump into the arch and the girls sing, " … and she jumped so high, high, high, she reached the sky, sky, sky and she'll never come back, back, back till the Fourth of July, ly, ly."

As the song ends, I skip from between the ropes. I wave and I run to join Andrew. A girl with a dozen pigtails and bright white teeth waves and calls, "Miss White Teacher! You jump good!"

There is a moment's pause, and then she adds, drawing out the words, "Re-al good!"

CHAPTER TWENTY-ONE

A BLACK BORDERED ANNOUNCEMENT

Friday, September 28, 1968

Andrew went to his Friday-night writers' group. For once I don't care. I have a new tape. First in forever. I'm pleased to be back in the world of Grandma Millie.

Pumpkin, you would think I wouldn't remember this sad, sad news so well, but I kept the folder with Luke's cut-outs about Milt. I want to be correct when I share these dates with you. It was a difficult time for many reasons. The war years were hard years.

President Woodrow Wilson declared June 5, 1917, "National Army Registration Day." It didn't take long for the local boys to sign up. By the end of the month, Milt signed up for the army and reported for duty. At the Northern Pacific Station, half the town came to cheer him and wave goodbye. I remember this clearly because Luke and I were there.

From that day on, Abe Wiseman detailed Milt's experiences on the front page of the newspaper. The column was called "Over There." Milt's adventure began with the Northern Pacific Railroad trip to Camp Sherman, Chillicothe, Ohio. Milt made friends on the troop train to New Jersey; on The Queen Victoria in high seas, and at the final days of preparation for the front-line battles in France.

Each week Luke borrowed my kitchen scissors and cut out "Over There." He read the articles to me after dinner while I did the dishes. Then Luke would disappear into the parlor. When you started this project, I found this long-forgotten folder tied with a shoestring in the bottom drawer of my roll-top desk. There in Luke's writing were the words: Milt, My Best Friend. It wasn't so much what Abe wrote, but how the articles were saved. And cherished. Because I don't remember much of those letters. You see, my life got busier and busier.

Beloved Gabe was born June 16, 1915. My pregnancy was a bit difficult, for both Gabe and me. When he was small, we worried about him. He seemed so quiet. Played alone. Thank goodness two years later it became very apparent that I was pregnant with twins and I hoped having siblings would help Gabe. He needed company!

Dr. Swanzy gave me over to the care of the nearest neighbor, a midwife, Mrs. Roosted. Strange that having two babies was easier than Gabe's birth. And, within days of delivery, Oscar and Sally were all puddly fat and full of baby coos. It took a while for me to catch on to the demands of twins, but they were such good fun, such bright little sprites. Those three little ones did keep me busy. Thank goodness for what I thought at the time was a blessing: Angelica, a six year old going on twelve. A 'little mother.' She would visit often and she would sit with them, play games, walk them down to see the new hatched chicks, teach them the songs she knew. They loved her. Especially, Gabe.

Life as a mother and wife suited me. I was surprised how much I enjoyed the children and how much I enjoyed the farm. My green beans won first prize at the Inland Empire County Fair. My baby quilts got blue ribbons three years in a row!

Luke and I settled into a life of planting and canning, birthing lambs and tending baby chicks, harvesting and gardening, shearing sheep, and raising our little family (well, not that little!). The silly song from my childhood bounced through my head as I accomplished each day's tasks: Monday, washday; Tuesday, string beans; Wednesday, soooup, Thursday, roast beef; Friday, fiiiish, Saturday, payday; Sunday, church. Is everybody happy? Well I should say!

The only thing missing from the song was something that stopped. Dr. Swanzy had warned me and I took it to heart. The glorious 'applauding of angels' should happen rarely. We tried, but there were many months I worried wondering if I was with child.

Back to Abe Wiseman and his newspaper: after each of the births, I checked the paper each day for the announcement of the arrival of our children. I finally quit looking. Life got busy and I hardly listened as Luke read the columns about Milt. And then came bad news. Luke could hardly bare it.

Here's the story: It was May, 1918. May is usually a glorious time of the year. But on May 30, Luke brought home The Gaitsberg Daily. He called me to join him at the dining table. I, as usual, had dessert in the oven, potatoes boiling on the stove, Gabe demanding I tie his shoes. I glimpsed at Luke sitting at the dining room table. From the slump of Luke's shoulders, from his not giving the twins their usual hugs and chuckles, from not coming into the kitchen, I knew there was bad news. I just didn't expect the news to be what it was. He demanded, but softly, that I give him my full attention. His words were plaintive, "Please. Now."

"Be right there," and I quickly poked a broom straw into the chocolate cake and let it continue baking. In the dining room, I pulled Gabe up on my lap to tie his shoes and then I reached for the paper. The news could not have been more tragic: a black border surrounded the front page of the paper. The headline was extra-large: THE BATTLE OF CANTIGNY CLAIMS THE SON OF GAITSBERG.

"You've read it?" my voice choked.

"No, I couldn't. You read."

I read out loud the letter printed inside the black borders:

"Dear Readers,

As you know, every day we list those brave men who have registered for the military. Up until this day we have not had to write about any of those young patriots giving his life.

There is no way for me to be the objective, disinterested editor for this story. This story is about my beloved, only son, Milton Wiseman. As many of you know, I lost my dear wife to the virulent influenza pandemic only a year ago. That was tragic. And many of you shared my grief when you also lost a loved one. But now to lose my only son, a son who should never, ever have died so young, is near unbearable.

Milt was one of the twenty-four million brave men who completed their draft registration card. He loved his country. He was a true patriot. He proved to the likes of those who President Wilson called shirkers that he was not a shirker. His green registration form hangs over my desk. Milt was not only one of the first to register to serve; he was one of the few who actually was called to duty. He went bravely.

Many of you will remember President Wilson's call and when we all traveled as a Gaitsberg family to Yakima. Five wagonloads of friends and neighbors joined us in front of the newly built Yakima Opera House and watched Milt register. We heard later that the registration board had to enlist extra volunteers there were so many young men ready to be counted, even though there was only one that day from amongst our youth from Gaitsberg.

In Salt Lake City they deputized a registrar to go to Sacred Heart Hospital to register those who were unable to leave their beds. In New York City, young men unable to speak English, had interpreters on hand to help with registration. Many registered. Few were called. Even fewer chose to go.

Milt made a brave choice. He left with your blessing and your voices harmonized as we sent him off with a song: "When Johnny Comes Marching Home Again."

In the few short months of serving his country, Milt showed his prowess and leadership abilities. His letters home wrote of the camaraderie, of the challenge, of the glory, of the satisfaction in being a soldier in a mighty cause. Never once did Milt mention that he had given up college, had given up his budding career here at The Gaitsberg Daily, had given up friends, had given up all, for his country. He represented all of us on that battlefield. He gave his life that each of us, each citizen of Gaitsberg, might receive the blessings of Democracy and Freedom.

Yesterday, Lieutenant Lawrence Lord came to my office. He brought the terrible news of Milt's final days. I asked for all of the details. I proudly share the last hours of Milt's life with you.

Milt was assigned to one of the units to be deployed for the purpose of aiding the French in the attack on a small German-held town in Western France: Cantigny. After a two hour artillery barrage, Milt's unit followed twelve French tanks into the small village of Cantigny. His unit took one hundred Germans prisoner. However, it took the lives of one thousand American boys to capture one hundred of the Huns. Milt was one of those one thousand. That brave, strong son died for all of those who chose not to be by his side. He died a brave, quick death. These words are my tribute to one of us who gave the most."

And it was then that Luke exploded, "That son of a bitch, Wiseman! He's accusing me!"

Over the cries of Gabe, Luke shouted, "He thinks I'm a shirker. I'll go to his office and beat him to a pulp! He's made me look like it was my fault Milt died!"

Luke snatched the paper, tore it in half, and threw it on the floor. He pushed over his chair. The door slammed behind him.

The twins burst into tears. I jiggled them into a restless silence until I could lay them back in their cribs. Gabe sat at the top of the steps, eyes wide and fearful, hiding from the outburst.

I placed the two halves of the paper back on the round oak table. I reread the entire page. Abe Wiseman's choice of words made my stomach clinch. Luke was wrong. This article was not directed at him. It was directed at me. If I had not married Luke, had accepted Abe's suggestion that I give Milt a chance, then Milt would have never, ever gone to war. Milt would have been the father of my children. Milt would still be alive.

Luke returned home long after I was in bed. Liquor on his breath. The next morning he was up early, the remains of a cold breakfast left on the table. I knew to leave Luke alone when he was troubled. Given time, Luke always returned to the easy-going, care-taking farmer I loved and relied on. Late morning, waiting for Luke to return from the fields for noon dinner, I re-read the article. The more I read, the more I didn't know. Maybe neither of us was right. Maybe it was only a father grieving for his son.

Over a lunch of hog-hocks, lentils and fresh baked bread, Luke spoke of farm chores and errands to run. He didn't mention Milt. After he returned to the fields, I cleared the table and tucked the children down for their naps. I sprinkled the day's laundry, wrapped each piece of clothing tight, and tucked the full laundry basket behind the Monarch's hot water tank. Then I stoked the fire box and placed four flat irons in the center of the stove. Before beginning the ironing, I picked up Gabe and hugged him and told him how much I loved him. I told him he was beautiful. Together, we settled into the slat-back rocker Luke had made to celebrate Gabe's birth. I hummed and rocked and forgot all about the sadness of the article and the anger of my husband. If only I could sit and rock and hold Gabe all day. How heavenly, to hold this child, who I hoped would become the perfect miniature of my beloved Luke. He held on tight. I was aware of how infrequently he received this singular attention now that it was attention shared.

There were pleasures during the war years. Saturday's were wonderful. I'd pack up the three children and spend the day with Elsbeth Sandborn. Angelica was there for the children and Elsbeth and I canned or knitted or just found time to visit. Time to ourselves. I luxuriated in hearing about my best friend's adventures in Chicago.

In the years that Claire had lived away from home, she had worked at Carson Pirie Scott. She had become the principal buyer of ladies fine clothing. She had enrolled in evening classes at Loyola University. She continued her buyer's position and became a freelance writer for neighborhood papers. Shortly after, she wrote home to say she had secured a position of junior editor for The Chicago Tribune*. Six months later she had her own column: Society Sensibility. Elsbeth and I each received a newspaper subscription for Christmas.*

Occasionally Claire found time to write to me. Here is one of her letters:

"Dearest Millie, I'm soooo busy. All is well. It is so very fortunate that Luke Lane is around to help Mom out, what with Dad's hip so bad. I can hardly wait until Angelica is old enough to visit Chicago (and you too, of course). Tell her to start thinking of a college somewhere close to me and then we can see each other! I know I'm way overdue for a visit home, but it's just impossible to get away, what with all the events I have to attend and the demands of a daily column.

I'll try to make it home, soon, I promise. Please write! Love, Claire."

I didn't find time to write. Claire didn't make it home. Angelica barely remembered her older sister. Elsbeth was proud of the columns Claire wrote, but she never understood what was so important about who wore what designer. I thought occasionally about my lost friendship, but I was too busy and it was too hard to find time to miss what wasn't there.

CHAPTER TWENTY-TWO

AN EVENING WITH EVIAN

Saturday, October 5, 1968

The first weeks of my teaching make the days fly. I am the only white teacher. Maybe not a librarian, but I love working with Jennie and the children are bright pennies in my life. They are interesting and fun and, oh so full of it!

On the home-front, the busier I get, the less we make love. Usually Saturday mornings are our stay in bed till noon day. However, this Saturday Andrew stays in bed forever. He is dead to the world. We had beers with a couple of other graduate students and their wives last night. Drank too much. Came home too late.

By eleven-thirty, I'm beyond restless and I head downstairs to check the mail. I take a single envelope out of the mailbox. I hold it up to the light—the paper is thick, the handwriting is swirly. I'm so tempted to open it, but, it is addressed to Andrew. I run up three flights of stairs, and call to Andrew, "Wake up! Wake up!"

Andrew pulls the sheet over his head.

"You've got to wake up! If you don't, I'm going to open this without you!"

Andrew grumbles, "What? What? What time is it anyway?"

"It's noon, for God's sake. The day is half-gone and you should look at this." I flash the envelope in front of his face. Andrew reaches for the letter. He scrutinizes the hand-writing. "What?" he asks, turning it back and forth.

"Let me!" I pop it out of his hand and open the thick vellum envelope. I read aloud:

Dear Mr. and Mrs. Althaus, please join me for a slight repast,

Saturday evening, October 5, at my pied-a-terre. 7:00. See address on the envelope. I'll buzz you up!

Dr. Evian Cush, your graduate advisor.

(Yes, Andrew, I know you are well aware of who I am, but perhaps, not your wife, who I am so looking forward to meeting.)

I hold the letter to my chest. "Oh, my God! His pied-a-terre. A repast!"

Andrew groans, "This guy is just a bit over-the-top. Lovely? A pied-a-terre? Give me a break"

"Andrew! He's your advisor. He could make your future."

"Future, what?"

"Writer, dummy. Think of it this way. He could introduce you to the whole world of writing. Become your mentor." I study the invitation again. Back and front. I study the envelope. "Has anyone else been invited?"

"I don't know. Probably. Who knows? I haven't a clue how advisors are assigned, or who else he advises, if anyone. I've met with him once. He's weird. Asked me how we met. Lectured me on "coincidence" in Tolstoy. I hardly got to say two words."

"Well, this invitation has to mean something special. I bet he saw your brilliance. Your potential."

I jump up and pull back the accordion door of the closet. "What will we wear? Do you think the red dress is too much?"

Andrew slides under the sheet. "The red dress will be fine. I need sleep." He moans into the pillow, "Don't ever let me drink again."

I push through the closet of clothes until I find Andrew's graduation suit. I spend the next half-hour sponging a spot out of one pant knee.

On the appointed day, I pull my red bias-cut dress over my head and slip my arms through the string straps. I check my new lipstick, Red Revolution. Perfect.

Andrew uses the bath towel to polish his shoes. He ties his tie. Studies himself in the mirror. Removes the tie. Puts it in his pocket.

In the kitchen I wrap a grocery bag around our house gift of Chianti. Andrew asks for the third time, "Are you sure?" To which I answer, "Of course, I'm sure. Who wouldn't want a beautiful wicker-wrapped bottle? When it's empty it will make a wonderful candleholder."

Outside we walk east toward Lake Michigan and then turn north until we arrive at 5700 Lake Shore Drive. At the locked double-glass door, in a yellowed plastic panel, we search the dozen names until we find *E. Cush.* Andrew pushes the button.

A hollow voice echoes from the slotted box, "Yessssss."

"It's Andrew and Sarah Althaus."

"Please. Come up."

The buzzer hums and when the elevator delivers us to the sixth floor, we step into an amber, sconce-lit foyer with tapestry-covered walls of charging horses and princely banquets. Elegant oriental rugs hug the parquet floors and a cut glass vase embraces six plumes of pampas grass.

Across the hall a door opens and there is Professor Cush. Arms wide.

He wears a crisp white cotton shirt under a beige V-necked sweater, pleated caramel colored pants, and woven sandals. He is trim, tall and elegant. He accepts the bottle of Chianti, holds it out to read the label, like it is the best wine he's ever been offered. He beams at me, reaches for my hand, and brings it to his lips. He winks at Andrew as he pulls me into the crook of his arm and mock whispers, "We've got to quit meeting like this."

We all laugh. I resist wiping my hand on my red dress and blush at Professor Cush's intense gaze.

Andrew pulls back his shoulders and I see him stand taller as if his heel-lifts aren't quite enough. Behind his recently acquired Buddy Holly black-rimmed glasses, his eyes are static and dry. He holds his hands behind his back, which gives him a scholarly look, a look I've watched him practice in the bathroom mirror. Tonight, on our way here, he told me that I'm engaging and beautiful enough, without flirting, so please, would I not flirt with his graduate advisor. "This is *our* evening," he says. I hear, "This is *my* evening, don't hog the lime light." He's made it clear that he wants Professor Cush to see him as a serious writer who plans to write a great, powerful, and certainly long, novel.

Professor Cush ushers us past his collections of masks, spears, baskets, and totems. He points to labels. Pronounces African tribe names: Malawi, Lusaka, Bulawayo, and Vereeniging. Once in the living room, we stand at the picture window. Before us Lake Michigan is a blanket of slate gray.

To the right of the heavily embroidered curtains stands a black lacquered liquor cabinet surrounded by a collection of framed photographs. I am about to ask an appropriate conversational question, when Professor Cush opens the cabinet door to reveal a good dozen bottles and he asks, "What will it be?"

Andrew leans slightly forward to read the labels and answers as if he were a connoisseur of sherry, "Harvey's Bristol Cream." And in the tiniest glass the professor pours the tiniest amount of liqueur.

I ask for white wine not realizing Professor Cush will have to go to the kitchen to get it.

"Be right back."

Andrew glares at me and through clenched teeth asks, "Why'd you do that? Why couldn't you just choose? Like I did?"

I can't believe we are having an argument right here, right this minute. I don't answer. We wait in silence as we hear the refrigerator door's soft close, the cork's plump release, the gurgle of wine poured.

When Professor Cush returns, he extends a slender stemmed glass of white wine. I accept. With my brightest smile, I ask him to tell us about his extensive display of photographs.

Professor Cush beams and describes each.

- Dwight Eisenhower at the Capitol
- a very large dead elephant
- Lady Ashland in the Himalayas
- Dorothy Lamour at Sardi's
- Errol Flynn in the Caribbean

Before we proceed, he takes a minute to refill our glasses and we follow him around the room as he identifies a Mondrian painting and a Calder circus figure.

At a glass-topped side table he points out which is the most rare snuff bottle and which is the oldest silver fish slice.

"You might think they are fish servers, but the appropriate word is "fish slice."

I wouldn't have thought either, as I hadn't a clue they even existed up until this moment. Already, I'm a bit weary of the long, overly precise explanation of not so much what something is, but how it came to be in his collection.

We follow Professor Cush down a hall and he suggests we retire to the study.

Great. I'm so ready to sit down.

Professor Cush steps aside, and we follow his outstretched hand into the dim light of the library.

"This," he announces, "…is my limited, but well-chosen library."

He gestures toward two over-stuffed leather chairs. "Please, sit."

I sit and immediately feel as if the chair has swallowed me. Andrew sits in a matching chair. His legs extend to a fat ottoman. He holds out his wee glass for about the tenth refill. My hand covers my glass to end, as the Professor says, a "refresher." I am not feeling refreshed.

He continues with a slowed, detailed, precisely enunciated description of his unending collection of stuff. I am so ready for dinner. And I try to remember the invitation. Maybe there isn't any dinner.

Professor Cush perches on the edge of a highly carved, four-foot by four-foot, mahogany desk. He tamps his pipe. The smell of cherry tobacco floods the room and for the next half hour he tells us more about where he has traveled, what he has written, who he has met, what treasures he has collected.

While Professor Cush speaks, I pretend I do not see him slip his hand in his pocket and rearrange himself. It is a habit Andrew shares and it makes me crazy. Andrew always says it is because of me. I excite him. Well,

I hate it and I am not flattered. And what is Professor Cush's excuse?

It's time for God's sake. Time to eat! My eyes burn. My head hurts.

"Your collections are amazing," Andrew says for the fourth or fifth time.

"Thank God for research and sabbaticals," Professor Cush answers with a chuckle. "There's more! Let me show you."

I follow them down the hall.

My right eye begins to throb.

Professor Cush's bedroom is maroon and mauve, with heavy black curtains held in place with gold tassels. Mirrors reflect into infinity. Shelves bulge and sag with more of Professor Cush's collections.

"These are Northwest—Tlinget baskets. The china is Meissen." He turns over a milk pitcher to show us the mark, explaining the under glazed blue crossed swords. "And those," he points to a leather umbrella stand spiked with glass canes, "Those are my favorites—French, English, Bavarian, American! Here. Feel how lovely they are." He hands a long slender cane to Andrew and laughs as if there is something to laugh about, which there decidedly isn't.

I have begun to think that Professor Cush's look, words, gestures, mannerisms, lectures, are beyond strange. I am way past being interested. The wine tastes sour. What kind of a man uses the word "lovely" anyway?

I am exhausted. The conversation is exhausted. Back in the study, we are surrounded by a heavy silence. And then, thank goodness, Andrew takes over! He points at an arrangement of golden plums in a woven basket and then he says something totally stupid: "How lovely. So large, they look like apples."

"They are apples! *Evangelista dominicus.* Miniatures. Rare. Come here." Professor Cush says and signals Andrew to join him at the window. He drapes his arm over Andrew's shoulder and he points to a balcony garden three stories below. "I picked them just yesterday. Still a bit tart and hard at the moment, but in ten days or so, they will be perfect. I will be sure you and your lovely wife have some." He pulls back and looks directly at Andrew, "If you would like?" he asks.

"Great!" Andrew exclaims. "Sarah is a great cook."

"And you, Andrew, do you?"

"What?"

"Cook. Do you cook?"

Andrew sips his sherry, holds it in his mouth. Then he swallows and says, "Well, with someone like Sarah around, I don't want to compete."

Professor Cush gestures to me, "Come look." He steps back to make room between the two of them. "See, see our little garden? When you get the apples—when they are perfectly ripe, I'll expect a return invitation. Or perhaps, since cooking is something I quite adore, perhaps we could cook up a little something together. Perhaps a quince/apple flambé or an apple galette. At your place."

I think, how does one cook quince? What is a quince? And what in hell is a galette?

"That would be wonderful!" Andrew says. "You could probably teach us a few things."

"That I could!" Professor Cush answers and waltzes in front of us, turning as if he has a partner. "I believe that calls for a refill!"

We are back in the living room. I stare longingly at the kitchen, wondering, hoping that food is waiting.

"I think we are going to find ways to get to know each other in the days to come," Professor Cush says, lifting his glass. "Let's drink to that."

"I couldn't be more pleased at the prospect of studying with you." Andrew exclaims. "I'm excited. Truly excited."

Professor Cush asks me, "And you, lovely Sarah, are you excited?"

"You know, it's getting a little late," I answer. I place my glass on the desk.

"But, the evening's young," Professor Cush says and turns on one foot, his arms out to me as if he is asking me to dance. "You make me feel so young…" he sings.

I can't stand it anymore. I walk to the front alcove next to the hall tree. "Truly, we've had a wonderful time. It's been a pleasure, but we have a big day tomorrow."

"Tomorrow's Sunday," Professor Cush says, with a mock pout, "The Lord wants you to rest on Sunday."

"I've hours of preparation. Andrew has his first proposal due. For your class."

"Well, ain't that the truth?" Professor Cush says with a big laugh and steps back and bows to Andrew, "Andrew, please proceed. I believe we are no longer in control."

I reach for my coat. I yearn for fresh air. I yearn for bed. I yearn to be a couple. To fold into Andrew's arms. In our bed.

"Well, that leaves the second bedroom for another time," Professor Cush says with a wink. His eyes first on Andrew, then on me.

"If for any reason you should have to stay the night, there's plenty of room here."

I'm totally confused, and totally off balance. This guy is totally nuts.

"Don't look so doubtful," Professor Cush laughs and says, "It did happen once. A student dinner. A huge snow storm. It was like summer camp! But then there's no such storm tonight."

"No, not tonight." I can hear the relief and exhaustion in my voice.

Professor Cush walks us down the hall and waits with us for the elevator. As the elevator door opens, he waves his fingers in a farewell gesture and says, "Well, then, you two, it's been lovely."

I step into the elevator. Andrew follows. As the door begins to close, Professor Cush says, "The apples! Just a few more days and I will call. Be ready! Be ready…" He raises his arms, extends a leg, toe pointing, and the last we see of him is his back as he dances down the hall with his invisible partner.

I push my back against the mirrored wall. I wait for the brass arrow above our heads to move. I pretend I don't hear the muffled voice of Professor Cush singing, "Wouldn't it be lovely…"

Above our heads the arrow slowly moves to the left. Andrew says, his voice not critical, not disparaging. "That was something. Don't you think?"

I nod my head yes and then I say, "Lovely, just lovely."

CHAPTER TWENTY-THREE

CLAIRE COMES HOME

October 12, 1968

Back at the apartment, we eat peanut butter sandwiches. Andrew watches the late-night news and then he goes to bed.

I sit at the kitchen table. I know if I started talking about that idiot professor, the conversation will never end. How can Andrew not see he was hitting on us. Both of us. It gives me the creeps.

I, oh, so want, out of here. Out of this new, stupid, strange life. To get away from it all, I put on a tape that arrived today.

Hello, my Dear One,

Friday, August 29, 1928.

This scene has a twist. Claire rarely wrote home. She had never returned home. It was as if she couldn't tolerate the town she left. But then things changed. Elsbeth died.

I took a break from baking pies and picked up Rita Roosted. We would meet the four o'clock Northern Pacific. She needed to pick up her Avon orders (talc, perfume, toothbrushes—those glorious products all of us so enjoyed touching, trying out, sometimes buying).

I was with Rita because of the letter I received three days before. I had shared it with no one. Why? I was so excited. Claire was coming home for the funeral. Everyone said she wouldn't. That she had forgotten all about her roots and Gaitsberg. But they were wrong. This day, the Avon delivery day, was also delivering Claire back to us.

At exactly four o'clock the Great Northern rumbled in. Right on time.

While we were enveloped in the noise and rush of the train, the stationmaster, Brew Sexton, bustled out of the ticket office. He went directly to the mail car and pushed open the sliding door. Before removing any of the mail sacks and packages, he turned to ask Rita to please wait under the eaves.

"Don't want to get you run over by no train. Just government regulations. We got to obey the government."

No matter what Brew said, Rita stood her ground. Brew kept right on talking, "Certainly the government wouldn't have made such strict rules about mail delivery if they thought it was okay for just anyone to handle this mail. Now, if you'll step back, I can proceed." (And, you guessed it. Later they fell in love!)

Rita glared, but she stepped back four steps. The same four steps she stepped back every month. Rita and Brew rivaled each other as to who was the bossiest. As Rita waited for Brew to load the flat bed hand truck, I watched the passenger car and just then Claire Sandborn stepped from the passenger car.

"Claire! Claire!" Rita called all excited and pleased as if she hadn't been one of those who spread rumors about Claire not returning.

"Miracles will never cease! You've come home! Of course you're home. Even big city people come home for funerals."

Mrs. Roosted bustled over to clasp Claire's gloved hands. "Amazing. Here you are. If only your mother were here to greet you!"

Claire winced and turned from Rita to greet me with a smile tinged with tears.

Brew stood waiting after dropping Rita's package at her feet. He extended a hand to Claire and in a mannerly voice said, "So sorry about your mom."

"Thank you," she whispered and slipped a dime into his hand.

I took Claire's hand in mine, and with my free hand picked up her small leather suitcase. It was only later when the rumors flew that I was made aware of how she was dressed and how bright was her red lipstick and how a bit show-offy was her hat.

Inside the station, Claire's dad and Angelica waited and it was apparent that Angelica stood in awe. The big sister had returned. She took tentative steps and when Claire opened her arms wide, Angelica snuggled in. Within seconds I called, "Talk to you later!" and with a leather-gloved hand Claire blew me a kiss.

I had promised Rita I'd drive her to make deliveries.

By afternoon, every clerk, teller, store-keeper, in-town shopper, and home-maker had received their Avon order and everyone knew that Claire Sandborn was home. For some, her return was accepted without comment. What was most spoken of was that Claire had arrived in black alligator shoes and a black fur muff, with black leather gloves. And although Rita couldn't say for sure, she believed it was very likely that Claire wore black false eyelashes.

Back home, exhausted, I walked out to meet Pete Sounds, the postman. He greeted me with the latest Sears & Roebuck catalogue and two words, "She's home!"

I didn't have to ask who was home. I walked back to the house wondering how long before Claire would have time for me. But tomorrow's funeral preparations demanded that I continue baking pies.

Over dinner Luke told me that everyone at Hennessey's Feed Store had something to say. Called Claire a real la-de-da lady. Hoity-toity. High hat.

But, at least she had come home. Finally. It appeared there was no one in the city of Gaitsberg who did not have an opinion.

Up early, sleepy from a cascade of dreams draped in black, I tied black grosgrain ribbons to the ends of Sally's pigtails. I did not let Oscar wear brown corduroys. He had to wear his black wool pants, no matter how much they itched. Gabe was ready before everyone, dressed in Luke's hand-me-down suit of black worsted. Gabe's hair slicked back with Wildroot.

Strange idea, Gabe getting grown up. I accredited my son's interest in grooming to his sudden awareness of Angelica Sandborn. It bothered me that Gabe didn't realize Angelica was dressing, preening, and primping for older boys. She had left behind her awkward elbows, her plump round face, her coltishness. She was on her way to being a tall, elegant young lady, and Gabe had noticed.

With the children dressed, I hurried upstairs. I removed the white sheet from over my black crepe dress, the one I ordered for Mother Lane's funeral, and I pulled from the top shelf my black hat—the hat no longer sporting red poppies, but encircled with a somber black Jacquard ribbon. Black gloves. Black hose. My single strand of pearls. My newly purchased screw-back earrings. Single pearls, up to the ear. Nothing fancy.

Out the window I could see Gabe and Luke wrestling the canvas tarp from off the recently acquired 1928 DeSoto. Even Luke seemed to be in the mood to impress Claire. He'd polished the car—made it shine. It had a couple of scratches, but Hennessey had taken good care, and when Luke purchased it second hand (just too darn fancy for Hennessey), with the money from his mother's estate, it had only a thousand miles on it.

I secured the pies in the car trunk. Gabe sat in the front seat. Sally, Oscar, and I squeezed into the back seat. As we drove the half mile, it pleased me to see how Gabe studied his father. He watched as his dad shifted gears, watched how he drove with one hand, studied the angle at which his father tilted his head and raised an eyebrow to avoid the smoke from his freshly lit Camel cigarette. I almost chuckled when Gabe put his elbow out the window, in the exact way Luke had his elbow out the window. All that was missing on Gabe was the fedora Luke wore at a jaunty angle, but even with no hat, Gabe's head tipped just right. Oscar's fingers moved silently in time to the song that I imagined was running through his head as we drove to say our goodbyes to Elsbeth, "So Long, It's Been Good to Know You." It ran through mine.

Mostly horse and buggies surrounded Sweet Baby Jesus Baptist Church. The cars, certain to startle the horses, dropped off their passengers and parked back on Main Street. Everyone wore their best. Their best black. But no one out-did Claire.

Straining to see the Sandborn family in the front pew, heads undulated, like the wind tipping stalks of wheat, first this way and that. Everyone wanted a glimpse of the daughter-come-home. Claire sat tall and still in her large veiled hat, black gloves, seamed black hose, black laced high-heeled shoes, black bias-cut silk dress, curved bun of hair held at the nape of her neck with a tortoise shell and jet barrette.

In contrast, next to her older sister, Angelica twitched, her blond mass of curls barely contained under a black band. Their father sat between them, his shoulders seemed to hold sadness and defeat. Everyone worried how he would survive without Elsbeth. He dabbed his eyes with a newly pressed handkerchief.

The red mahogany and brass casket lined with tuffeted sea-foam green silk, held Elsbeth Sandborn in serene repose. No one would have known looking at the still and placid body, that Elsbeth's last days were full of pain. Nothing of those hard, last hours showed on her powdered, composed face.

In time, Reverend Billy Ohnly spoke solemnly of the great goodness of their departed sister. As for the singing, it stayed controlled. The recently replaced out-of-tune piano no longer inspired good Baptist singing. The small, sonorous pump organ made even the Baptists sing in hushed tones. To me, it was strange and sad that today, Baptists sounded more like Lutherans.

The following hour, at the graveside, our singing voices slipped through the stand of silver birches. Hilda Handshue and I carried the sopranos:

Abide with me
Fast falls the even tide
The darkness deepens
Lord with me abide
Heaven morning breaks
And earth's vain shadows flee
Help of the helpless
Oh abide with me

As the shovel passed from Mr. Sandborn to Angelica to Claire, the hollow thud of dirt echoed on the coffin lid. Reverend Ohnly asked all to join in the Lord's Prayer. Overhead, crows cawed raucously in the long-needled pines. Something about those outrageous birds pleased me. My friend and confidant, Elsbeth, was not a timid soul. The crows seemed to say, 'Pay attention! Death may be black, but death is loud and demanding! It's good to shout! About death! About life!" I took it as an omen, and by the time everyone arrived at the Sandborn farmhouse, people had loosened up, and in their remembering of Elsbeth, chatted and laughed—subdued, perhaps, but no longer somber—full of fine remembrances.

In the kitchen, where dishes of food accumulated, I took charge. I directed and accepted all of the potluck offerings. On the front porch, the receiving line finally ended and as I maneuvered between the kitchen and the dining room, I stole glances as Claire moved through the crowd.

I'm glad she stayed occupied. She seemed to me to be from some future time. She appeared to float through the crowd, like something out of the latest Vogue or from the illustrations of the beautiful French women captured in Godey's Lady's *Book.*

My dress started to feel too large, the buttons too generous, the hem too long, and even the pearl screw-back earrings too plain. They pinched and made my earlobes hurt. I wondered if my old friend and I would have anything to say to each other.

In the dining room, the lion-pawed round oak table, stretched to its full twelve foot length, filled with emptying pie tins, pedestal cake plates, cookie platters, and cobbler pans. In the kitchen the sink, the dough table, and the round side shelves filled with pottery, porcelain, and china empty of macaroni and cheese casseroles, Jell-O, three bean salads, sliced ham, fried chicken, and barbecue ribs. I washed dishes and silverware. I refilled empty serving plates and arranged the desserts.

The late fall sun slid toward the end of day and Angelica sat with her friends in the front yard cupola where the girls soon forgot to be decorous and solemn.

Theodore Sandborn sat with the men. He remained silent. Stared into space.

The men friends smoked their cigarettes and spoke of the new two lane highway cutting through prime farm land.

Inside, the women filled the parlor, complimenting each other on the food they had competitively prepared for the last few days.

Gabe and the other teenage boys stood on the front porch, pretending not to sneak looks at the girls.

At sunset, exhausted, I asked Luke to drive the children home. I needed to stay. I wanted to stay. I'd walk back over the hill later. Without saying, I knew Luke would understand that I'd waited all day to have time with Claire.

Finally the last family accepted their cleaned serving dish, gathered their children, and said their goodbyes. They hitched up the horses. Started their cars. Mr. Sandborn sat alone on the front-porch glider, as if he dreaded going upstairs to an empty bedroom.

Claire and I were finally alone in the kitchen. Claire gathered the remaining dirty dishes. I scraped them clean. A white cotton apron covered Claire's black silk dress. I washed. Claire dried.

At first reticent conversation cut holes in the silence. We each made small observations: Miss Hildegard's tuna casserole, Mrs. Hales' miniscule hat, the heat of the dishwater, the number of people who attended. Eventually Claire said, as she placed a felt pad between each gold-rimmed china plate, "It feels as if everything has changed."

"It has changed. Fourteen years. That will do it," I answered as she re-rolled her sleeves, keeping them free of the dishwater.

"I never dreamed I'd be gone so long."

"Me neither."

"Strange not having my mother here. If someone had only sent word earlier. But then who could have guessed. She had such little time. I guess there was no way for Doctor Swanzy to know."

"It took us all by surprise," I said.

Claire set each cut-glass cup upside down on a bleached towel. She dabbed at the bottoms of the cups. "I always thought it would be Dad who went first. I've tried to talk to him, but he appears to need time alone. It is as if he doesn't remember who I am. Thank goodness Angelica is here to help him through the days ahead. But, tell me, what do you know about Mom's illness?"

"No one seems to know. You know how that is. Parents hardly admit they have

a body, let alone have something wrong. Even at the end, she'd say, 'I just need a little nap.' She never spoke of her pain or discomfort. If it hadn't been for Rita Roosted, none of us would have known anything. I think Rita was the one who finally confronted Dr. Swanzy. Went to take him his wife's Avon order, and demanded that he at least stop the rumors of cholera and flu. No one ignores Rita. Did Dr. Swanzy tell you?"

"I had a very few words with Dr. Swanzy today. He said he hadn't been quite explicit with the family, because he didn't want to violate Mom's privacy. Can you believe that? For God's sake, she was our mother! If I'd known, if someone could have told me how serious it was, I would have been home earlier. The first diagnosis was consumption! Consumption? Consumption is a euphemism for 'I'm a stupid country doctor and I don't have any idea why people die'." Claire brushed tears away. "Dr. Swanzy did mention to me today that she had this mass. A tumor. Not just one. He didn't mention the hemorrhaging. Rita told me about that. He said there was some talk about sending her to Seattle for surgery, but it was too late. He said at the end he increased her morphine so she could sleep, and from sleeping she just never woke up."

Claire's voice was full of sorrow and sadness, almost an apology. As if her mother's death was her fault. As if Claire had heard all of the gossip of her being the uncaring, errant daughter. As if Claire was ashamed of putting me in the position of accepting her apology. Claire picked up a gold rimmed serving platter. She wiped it dry and then said, as if to change the subject, "I think my mom never used these plates. Can you imagine? They were her 'good' plates." Claire held the plate like a mirror. "You see? We hide everything. Our bodies. Plates. The truth. You name it."

And then I reached to hug Claire and I sat her down on a kitchen chair and I was able to say, "No need to cry about the plates. Your mother did use the plates. More often than you might think. These past years she even brought them out for the quilting group. She used them at Thanksgiving, Christmas, Easter. When we lost Mother Lane, your mom adopted us for holidays! She used the good plates."

"Oh, thank you, Millie. That makes me feel so much better. So, no crying over the plates!" She sighed with a certain relief. Looked up as if she was seeing me for the first time today, and she asked, "How about you? Catch me up. Tell me everything."

"Well, things are fine, just fine."

"Fine? Three kids and fourteen years? If 'consumption' is code, then I think 'fine' is code. Tell me what you aren't telling me."

I don't.

Claire held both of my hands, and said, "Well, just look at you! All this farm life's got to be agreeing with you. You're so healthy!"

"Healthy? Now there's a code word! You mean plump. Do you know how hard it is to even be in the same room with you?"

"Millie! Shame on you. You have a real life. You have children. I thought of all of you so often. I thought of coming home. But, believe me, it isn't easy leaving a job, even for a week. Once the Tribune hired me, it felt as if there was someone just wishing I'd fail. It takes time to establish your name, and then once people began counting on my column for all the gossip, I couldn't let them down. And then I couldn't leave because

there were, are, six women selling ads who would just love for me to disappear. They would love my job! It's not like being you—secure, on a farm, with a husband, with children. Believe me, sweet Millie, you have an enviable life."

"True! There's no one in line waiting for my job!" And I wondered, even then, without knowing what I would later learn, how Luke and I were really doing. Who knew? Later I would learn it certainly wasn't me.

"Here's the strange thing. I'm conflicted about where I am and what I left. Part of me loves the city. The rush! The uncertainty. And part of me fears coming back to Gaitsberg—afraid somehow this town will reach out and grab me. Look at my mother! She was bright, and when she was young she was beautiful, and I know if she'd had a chance she could have done so much more. I feel like I did what she might have done. She loved my column. Even if she didn't know anybody, she loved it. Did you know that?"

"Of course! She would read your words at every gathering. You seemed so exotic to us! And from your columns we'd try to decipher your life. Your wardrobe. Your men friends. Or just your vocabulary. I remember the time you wrote a whole column about a diamond parure worn by some Lake Michigan matron. We finally figured it out! It meant a set! Reading your columns brought a little of the big city to us. Yes, we love what you write."

"But didn't you think Mom was waiting for something? Something more? Something different?"

"I think she loved her life. She was proud of you. But, she loved this farm. She made things happen here. If it weren't for your mom, we'd never have had a quilting group!"

"But listen to what you've just said! She made a quilting group! That's it! Then she died. Makes me so angry for her. Sometimes I think my leaving was all about making up for her just being a farmer's wife."

"Careful. You are talking to one of them."

"One of what?"

"Me, Claire. You're talking about me. I'm just a farmer's wife."

"Oh, Millie. I didn't mean you. You've made a real life out of staying here."

"How do you know that?"

"Mom wrote me. Wrote me about your beautiful children. She always let me know about how you had three children and, of course, by saying you had three, she made it very clear I had none. And she told me how wonderful Luke has been. Not just to you. But to our family. How he helped with the harvest. Helped with spring planting. As Dad's health worsened, he depended on Luke. And about you? She always wrote about you. Said you made the best pies. 'Adventuresome pies' she called them. Mincemeat and quince! Like where in heaven did you ever think to use quince? Where did you even find quince?" Claire didn't wait for an answer. She slipped silverware into cloth pouches and continued talking, "Not many farmers' wives get to be known for adventuresome pies. I'm certainly never going to be known for pies. Any kind of pies."

I raised my hand and demanded, "Stop! Look at you. Look at me. No, don't look at me!" I pulled the front of my dress down where it had bulged over my belt. "You know how everyone refers to you? They call you The Big City Girl!"

Claire laughed and climbed on a kitchen stool. I passed her the remaining china plates and Claire eased them on to the top shelf. "Well, that's one thing to call me, but I think a number of those older Baptist women think of me as The Prodigal Daughter."

"I've heard it said!" I say. "But mostly, they envy you. Admire you. Jealous even."

Claire closed the cupboard door, stepped down, and pulled her sleeves to her wrists. One sleeve covered a slender diamond watch.

She turned to study me. She asked, "Do you know how wonderful it is to be here and not worry about every word I say? To be here where every inch of my clothing isn't being judged? Honest, Millie. Writing a society column, I know it may sound trivial when compared to raising a family, but it's demanding. And when it gets called a gossip column, it makes me furious! I try to be a real reporter, but the things that I get to cover? If I have to go to one more charity ball, note every fabric of every gown, the weight and size of every diamond in every ring, all the time making out like the rich of Chicago are not themselves one generation from the farm. It's exhausting. And the worst part? I have to pretend, just like them, that I didn't grow up milking cows and shoveling horse manure. We all pretend like we aren't who we are. So, I do envy you. You are you! You're a real mom! A real wife!"

I drained the dishwater and scrubbed the sink. As I wiped my forehead with the back of my hand, I wondered what Claire used on her hair to keep it perfectly in place.

"I love being here! Everyone is so at ease. So down to earth. So real."

"But not so real that you'll be coming home to stay."

"Come back? No, no, Millie. I have a life there."

"It's not like people here don't have a life."

"Oh, I know that. It's that things have changed. I've changed. For example, look at this," Claire splayed her fingers, the red of her nail polish bright as a cherry. "I've got a life where nails have to be perfect. It seems trivial and stupid, but just go a week without a manicure, and you won't have a column. People won't give you the gossip you need, if you don't measure up. My whole life is about measuring up."

I held out my hands and studied my short cut nails. "Me too," I say with a laugh. It sounded stupid, but I didn't take it back and Claire didn't respond.

One year later I thought of that sentence and wondered if she had suspected; or if perhaps there were already rumors that were being kept from me, about Luke, about his other life. Did Claire even suspect the tiniest bit that horrible things would happen later when I didn't measure up?

"Sit with me," Claire said, "Let's have a little Henry Highman's." From under the sink Claire brought the round-bottomed bottle. The sound of the gurgling wine as it poured into the jelly glasses filled the kitchen.

Claire raised her glass. I raised mine. Without words we toasted each other. As we sipped, Angelica appeared at the door wrapped in a chenille bathrobe.

"Caught ya!" she called and pulled up a chair. "What is it with Baptists? They wait until everyone's gone home and then they bring out the booze?"

"Would you like a little sip?" Claire asked.

"Mother would die!"

Silence set like a giant block of ice, and then Claire giggled, and seconds later Angelica giggled, and then all three of us laughed until tears ran down our cheeks and Claire poured her young sister a glass of wine.

"You see," Claire said, gasping for breath. "This would never happen in that other life. That Big City Chicago life. Nothing there would make me laugh like this."

"I'll tell you what everyone envies," Angelica said, her glass already half empty. "What everyone envies here in Gaitsberg is Millie."

I shook my head in disbelief. "What in heaven's name are you talking about?"

Angelica lifted her glass, drained it, stood and said, "I'll leave you two. I know you won't say anything interesting in front of a little sister. Thank you for the sinful liquor. It'll help me sleep." She pulled the belt of her bathrobe tight, and turned to leave.

Claire called, "Wait, little one. Tell us what is it that everyone envies about Millie?"

Angelica stopped and faced us, "That's obvious. Everyone envies Millie. Luke—handsome, charming Luke. That's what everyone envies."

The next day Luke and I drove Claire to the train station in the DeSoto. Angelica came along to say goodbye. I noticed that Luke opened the door for Angelica and even offered her his hand. Angelica wore a pale yellow dress and yellow shoes that matched her out-of-control blond hair. She had dressed as if for a special occasion.

CHAPTER TWENTY-FOUR

KROCK AND BRENTANOS

Sunday, October 13, 1968

For once I splurge. While Andrew sleeps I slip out to buy the *New York Times.* Back at the apartment, over Folgers, I study the front page picture of Jackie Kennedy. Her head is draped with a white mantilla, eyes downcast. She towers over Aristotle Onassis. He looks tired.

No matter what Andrew says, I know Jackie loves Ari. She'd have to! Why else would she be with a wizened, little old man? Not money. She already has tons of money. Whatever it is, I admire Jackie Kennedy's faith. Not her Catholic-kind of faith, but her faith in going on. Getting married. Building a new life. Falling in love.

Sunday is our "together" day. But not until 1:00. Andrew still sleeps.

I take a break from the paper (it's an all day job) and I clean. Bored with cleaning I page through *Catch 22.* Ten pages later I try reading Andrew's copy of *Herzog.* Andrew has told me it is important for me to read *Herzog* because it is just a matter of time before we run into Saul Bellow on campus and then, should I have read his book, we'd both be able to carry on an intelligent conversation with him. And I didn't say so, but I just can't slog my way through Bellow's book, no matter how important it is, just to slather my admiration on the author. I'm just not up to all those words.

Finally, finally Andrew's up. Sits at his typewriter. In his pajamas. I'm not supposed to talk while he's typing. It's a new rule.

I settle on *Steppenwolf.* I love Hesse. If *Steppenwolf* had been a smell, it would have been patchouli. If *Steppenwolf* was a city it would have been Alexandria in Lawrence's Quartet. If *Steppenwolf* had been something to eat it would have been papaya and mangoes. I love Hesse. In my estimation, no matter what Andrew proclaims, Bellow isn't Hesse.

I check the kitchen clock. Only ninety more minutes before *our* day officially begins. While Andrew writes, I continue reading. He looks up every once in a while as if I am doing something annoying, like turning pages too quickly. I take Hesse to the bathroom to read. I don't want to disturb Andrew's writing but mostly, I didn't want him looking at me like he wishes I would disappear. I understand. He's at a critical place in his novel. But then it seems he's always at a critical place in his novel. I wrench open the bathroom window to check the weather. Two inches up the window jams and all I can see is the brick wall of the air shaft and no weather.

On top of the hamper is Andrew's newest copy of *Playboy*. I've quit complaining about *Playboy*. Once I even yelled at him, "Then you get a job so we can afford that stupid magazine!" He looked at me like I'd lost my mind. Our agreement, he reminded me, is to get his degree. Not stifle him.

I look at the center-fold. The woman is a Swede with bulbous bullet breasts that she holds with Bubblegum Pink fingernails. No question, by Hugh Hefner's standards I am less than adequate. Andrew says he never compares me to the centerfolds but I wondered what he would think if I kept magazines with naked men with exposed penises. Long penises.

I place the magazine on the window sill and as I stand, I brush it with my elbow. The magazine falls out the window. I didn't push it. It fell.

I study myself in the bathroom mirror. I unbutton the two top buttons of my blouse. I fold my arms across my chest and make my breasts bump up. Not much help. I go back to Hesse and can't shake the thought that lately we go to bed at different times. Often, when we go to bed Andrew wants to tell me the latest plot point.

I check the time. Only thirty more minutes. I go to the kitchen to make a tuna fish sandwich. At his typewriter Andrew eats from a can of Spaghetios. At twelve-thirty Andrew takes his twenty minute nap. I sit at Andrew's desk. I don't touch one thing. I read the page of his novel in the typewriter. It is one long sentence. It is about the burden of mothering on the mothered. It makes no sense.

At exactly twenty minutes, I know Andrew will open his eyes and finally, finally, the day will be ours. We have made a pact that no matter how much work he has to do, Sunday afternoon is sacred. We made the pact ten weeks ago. September 2. I remember the day because there had been a huge earthquake in Iran and we were at home for the holiday. I ended up yelling at Andrew that 10,000 dead Iranians didn't get to choose what they were ever going to get to do again in their life, so couldn't he just once make a choice about us.

I demanded, "You choose!"

"Like what?"

"Anything! Something! For once, you be in charge!"

A flick of puzzlement settled in Andrew's eyes. He said, "Okay. How about we go downtown to Krock and Brentanos?"

Before he changed his mind or suggested something else, I grabbed my coat and waited at the door. And that is how "together" Sundays began.

Outside the air was crisp and clear. The sky held one lonely cloud that seemed to wait patiently for other clouds. It wasn't until we had walked through a golden blanket of kickable, crunchy leaves, and not spoken, that at the bottom of the steps at the end of the Midway where we caught the elevated train, I reached for Andrew's hand.

"Thanks. For us. Today."

"You're welcome," he said.

I didn't know if the argument was over or not.

Twenty minutes later we were in the Loop.

At Krock and Brentano's Andrew studied the crumbling spines of the books locked in the first edition case. I went upstairs to look at prints in search of something to hang in our bare apartment. I flipped through the floppy sheets, tempted by a Sister Corita-Kent's Wonder Bread print. Corita-Kent was not one of Andrew's favorites. I let it flip forward and studied a Klee of blue and green spheres with faces, then a Miro of black lines and a single eye with legs. I studied a Chagall with a married couple flying through space. Andrew came up behind me and looked over my shoulder.

Outside the elevated train pounded by. I pointed and over the noise I asked Andrew what he thought of the Chagall. We shouted back and forth until the train passed. The shouting continued. But not about the print. Andrew was shouting about the wad of one dollar bills I had in my hand.

"Where'd you get that?" he demanded.

"Money I saved. Don't shout."

Andrew lowered his voice and asked, "Saved from what?"

"It's not important. It's just some extra money, and I thought I might buy a print. What do you think of this one?"

"Sarah, why are you being so secret about this huge amount of money?"

"It's not a huge amount of money. It's thirty dollars. It just looks like a lot of money. They're ones."

"That's weird. Where'd you get a bunch of ones?"

I stuffed the money in the bottom of my bag. I walked back to the record department. I pretended to be interested in LPs. What did it matter that my mother gave me secret money? Why was Andrew being so strange? He came up beside me.

"I think you should tell me where you got that money," Andrew demanded.

"Why are you being so weird?"

"Because we share everything, and now you're being secretive. What kind of a marriage is that?"

"What?" I asked, avoiding his accusation.

"We're married. We're a couple. We live together. We should choose whatever we are going to live with, together. And it should be *our* money."

"Well, we will choose it. Here," I thrust the roll of bills at him, "Take it. It's our money."

"It wasn't our money two minutes ago. I think we need to talk."

"Well, not here, not now. Not with people staring at us."

Andrew looked up to see an elderly couple sorting through a sale bin of 45s. Definitely watching us.

"Alright, already. But we *will* discuss it later."

I didn't answer. I went back to the print bin and pulled up the Klee. "What about this one?"

"It's not solid. It's not strong. How about Goya," he held up a Goya print.

"You're joking. A bunch of dead people in a firing squad?"

"You're the one who's always saying our lives should be relevant. Goya? Relevant. Klee? Light weight."

"I'm not going to spend my money on something I don't like!"

Andrew stared at me as if I'd just shot him. He hissed at me, "What is it with you? Secret money. Trying to control everything. You're always controlling everything."

I ignored him. I looked at more prints. Angry. What a mean, stupid sentence. And what if it was so? If I didn't control everything, nothing would happen. Besides, why were we fighting in public? We rarely fought. Maybe a couple of times. But over nothing as stupid as this. Once, on our drive to Spokane, somewhere between Vantage and Moses Lake, we discussed why didn't men take women's names instead of the other way around. It wasn't that I didn't want to be an Althaus. But in August when Jackie Kennedy had been photographed with Onassis on his boat, the question was asked as to what her name might be. I was sure that even if Jackie wrote Jackie Kennedy Onassis, she'd always be Jackie Kennedy. It didn't even enter the discussion that she'd already been a Bouvier before she was a Kennedy. Andrew said it was stupid to discuss it one way or another and I decided it wasn't worth arguing about. Somehow choosing this print was worth arguing about.

"Come here," Andrew called two bins over. He held the Goya print at arm's length, "Can't you see the strength in this painting? It's a painting about injustice! About good and evil!"

"And guess what? I'd like something less good and evil in our rather drab apartment."

"I thought you liked our apartment."

"I do. What's our apartment got to do with bad art?"

"Goya? Goya? That's rich. Goya's bad art?" Andrew threw his hands in the air and stomped down the aisle. The older couple retreated to the first floor leaving Andrew and I alone in the balcony. I walked up to him and said, "So you want to wake up every morning and look across to our one wall and see a dozen people screaming and bloody and guns firing. Besides, everybody in that painting is a man! Aren't all the dead guys in Vietnam enough?"

"How in the hell did this get to Vietnam? How? If you start up again about my not marching, not protesting, when I'm trying to write…let's just forget it."

"What's 'it'?"

"Sarah. Forget it."

I was near tears and I couldn't even figure out why we were arguing. I found a rumpled Kleenex in the bottom of my bag. I pulled the lint bunnies from it and blew my nose. I stood at the edge of the print bin and tried not to cry. My fingers peddled through the prints: Mary Cassatt, Picasso, Modigliani.

Andrew said over his shoulder as he went down the stairs, "Your money. You choose. I'm going next door for a beer." He pushed through the revolving door and I realized that every person had heard him and they were watching to see the next act.

I found the ladies restroom and waited and waited. When I came out most everyone who had seen our little scene had left. I quickly chose a Jim Dine poster.

"Nice," the clerk said.

And I had one last look at the print before it was rolled and put in a bag.

Whatever made me choose a print with a dozen split, shattered, scuffed, broken, smudged, battered, cracked, crushed, scribbled-through hearts entitled "Love." Don't ask.

I found Andrew next door in conversation with the bartender. He seemed to have totally forgotten the print, the argument, the roll of bills. He reached to give me a smooch and he introduced me to Alphonse, the bartender. I suggested we might want to eat in a booth over against the wall. Reluctantly, Andrew picked up the half empty pitcher of beer and followed me to the booth. Alone together, he reached for my hand. "What'd you choose?" he asked.

"Something simple. A bunch of hearts."

"Great!" Andrew said, his eyes wide and glistening. "I know whatever you choose, will be just great. You make the best choices in the whole world."

He didn't say I made all the choices.

So ended our first Sunday set aside for "us."

CHAPTER TWENTY-FIVE

COTTON CANDY SATURDAY

October 15, 1968
Another tape arrives. It is wonderful to hear Grandma Millie's voice.

Sarah, this tape is a little what we called in my day "risqué" but it's so telling; I cannot but share it with you. Most difficult to share are excerpts from Gabe's diary (but how important). You'll see how sensitive he was. How poetic. He was such a beautiful boy. And you'll learn a little bit about me. I'm, as they said in my day, 'busting out all over!'

As I recall this was mid-September, 1929

Luke, after all our years together, on occasion had words that are hard to forget:

"Millie, come on sweetie. You know I love you. I'd do anything for you. Come on, turn over. God, you feel like velvet. You smell like honey. You are the best woman a man could ask for. Your curves just right. Your hair beautiful all messed like that. Give me a kiss. Come on. Just one little kiss. Insy-weensy kiss. Don't laugh. You can't laugh. You laugh, I'll catch it and swallow it and then I'll have to burp. You know you hate my love-burps. Here, now doesn't that feel just right. Feel good? I'd say that feels perfect. I can hear you purring."

Luke was smiles all week. And, again I was relieved when I knew all was well the next month.

On Saturday, Luke called Gabe to hitch Babe to the wagon. They sat up front together. The twins and I sat in the back. On our way to town, Luke made big about Gabe holding the reins, two men going to town together. Off to buy feed and seed.

"We men, we got to stick together." Gabe, only fourteen at the time, sat up straight. Proud to be with his father, or so I thought.

In town, I did my errands. The twins got sodas.

Luke gathered the bags of feed inside Hennessey's. Gabe stood by Babe, holding the reins, keeping the horse steady as sacks dropped into the back of the wagon.

I didn't see the whole interchange, but I saw enough to know this is what happened:

Luke showed off a bit and I'm sure Gabe was a bit embarrassed. Luke liked putting on a show for the locals—men who braced themselves against the railing at Hennessey's and watched. The locals were a great audience. The men rolled cigarettes and shared snuff and called "Luke! Lookin' good! Feed sack like air! All that energy! Where's that come from?" Luke would have pretended he hadn't heard a word.

Eventually he went inside to settle-up the bill. He came back out with the last sack over his shoulder. He braced himself with his free hand and dropped three feet to the ground—as smooth as a circus acrobat.

The men clapped and whistled, and Luke winked at Gabe as if to share the glory. That's all I saw, delivering my packages to the back of the wagon. It was only later I learned more. Learned what happened when I wasn't there.

I confess. I read Gabe's diary for that day (I know I shouldn't have, but it was there, by his bed, as I changed the sheets), and this is what I learned:

Dad embarrasses me. He thinks he's some kind of god. Gives everyone a pat and a wink. Even me. I hate being treated like everyone else.

In the middle of his 'stupid show,' a car horn bleated. Babe shied. I grabbed the halter. A Model-T bumped into the space next to us. Babe balked. Pulled back. Eyes white.

I didn't yell at that stupid driver. I didn't yell because I saw whose car it was. Old Mr. Sandborn got out. He walked to the passenger's side. He opened the back door. I tried not to stare.

I saw her ankle. A white shoe. A lacy dress. She had a blue sash. Her hair like cotton candy. All curls. Angelica Sandborn.

I admit it. I stared. Angelica Sandborn is like a drink of cold, cold water."

Before I go further, let me explain something you would not know: when Gabe was five and Angelica Sandborn was ten, her hand held his as they walked to Cramwell's for hoar-hound drops.

When Gabe was seven and Angelica Sandborn was twelve, they sat together on one or the other of their wagons waiting for their fathers. She made math problems for him and he learned to do multiplication.

When Gabe was eleven and Angelica Sandborn was sixteen, older boys pushed Gabe away to get closer to Angelica.

When Gabe turned fourteen, Angelica Sandborn was well into being a woman, a shapely woman. From Gabe's diary I learned that he imagined her nipples like pink jelly beans. I have a hard time admitting it, but Gabe's diary was pure poetry. Here's more.

I watched Angelica get out of her father's car and when her father took her hand, the armpits of her pink dress were dark scallops. She smiled at me and in that instant our eyes held and a dozen butterflies filled my mouth, and pink cotton candy dissolved on my tongue, and I smelled the smell of ripe raspberries, and my breath caught like gauze in my chest.

Then a horrible thing happened. I looked up and there Dad stood on the loading dock and Angelica's eyes looked, not at me, but at Dad. Time stopped. My chest caved. I couldn't breathe. Above me, I swear I saw a gold thread between my dad and Angelica. As I watched, Angelica closed her eyes and she took a deep, deep breath.

That's when Dad winked at me. Like water the reins slipped through my fingers and my body turned cold and silent while inside words like nails drilled my soul: the bastard the son of a bitch i hate you i hate you i hate you

Through Gabe's diary, I became aware of two things. Gabe began to save all of his words for his diary and Gabe's father no longer saved himself for me.

That night things between Luke and I changed. My words?

"No, Luke. No. Not tonight. You know what Dr. Swanzy warned. We can't take any chances. No more babies."

CHAPTER TWENTY-SIX

GOTTA HAVE A GUN

October 22, 1968, my birthday

Before I start the tape recorder, I want to thank you, my darling girl, for the birthday card! Hugs, kisses and please come home soon! I miss seeing you, talking to you, and I want to hear and see how our book is going. Time to continue….

October 22, 1930

So, I will begin by remembering what should have been a wonderful day, a day not about my birthday, but about Gabe and a gun.

I woke to the sound of the twins helping Luke stoke the Monarch. When they called me to come to my birthday breakfast I knew what to expect: eggs scrambled, coffee boiled, wild flowers in a canning jar, handmade cards. I turned to touch the cold sheet where Luke had slept. For now, all is fine. Luke's promise as he left our bed was that he would wait, but not for long, before the subject of Gabe and a gun would be addressed again.

I tried to explain my concerns about Gabe—his poor grades, his sullen silence, his outbursts of anger. When I discussed my worries, Luke brushed me off, "That's what teenagers do." I disagreed. Gabe's diary was full of beauty and sorrow and anger. Gone is the Gabe who was my child of brightness and light.

After breakfast silence surrounded us. Earlier, Luke had said we would discuss the gun. I decided, since we weren't speaking that much anyway, I'd bring up the subject. I'd confront him. I'd wait for just the right moment. I wanted to tell Luke how Gabe disappeared into books or into the attic or into the fields for hours at a time. I would remind him that there was a time Gabe was full of words. He confided in me. Told me everything: how to catch pollywogs, how he knew the best time to fish, where to dig for the biggest and best earthworms. Or he told me I had to read his Tarzan books. They were the best! He'd leave copies lying around, open to a particular page, hoping I couldn't resist.

Now all of Gabe's words are in his diary—a diary that I am not supposed to read. A diary about which I will certainly not tell Luke.

The birthday breakfast had been okay. The twins were chattery and Gabe wasn't so sullen. It was Luke who was quiet. He didn't tell Gabe to sit up straight. He didn't insist the twins clean their bowls of oatmeal. After breakfast he walked the children down to the turn-off where they cut across the field towards the schoolhouse, I watched from the porch stoop. The gesture that caught my eye was Luke straightening Gabe's collar and Gabe jerking away as if he had been struck. Luke watched the children until they were hidden by the drooping branches of oak trees and then he headed for the coop to feed the chickens.

I worried about Gabe and Luke. For the past few months, they had quit being a pair. I thought they had been close, sharing chores. Now they rarely spoke. The silence was like a dark pit that we walked around.

At noon, I heard the cut-off of the tractor motor and minutes later Luke walked into the kitchen. He smelled of wheat chaff, dust, and warm sun. At the table there was something in the tilt of his head, the lift of his eyebrows, something in the way he sat back in his chair that made me curious and cautious. I served him a crockery bowl full of ham bone and navy beans. I cut slices of newly baked bread and served them on the cutting board with a square of pressed butter. I was surprised when he reached for my hand.

"Come join me."

I did and I wondered what was coming. It was so unlike Luke to invite me to sit with him at lunch. Usually Luke reached for the Grange News or flipped through catalogues. Usually I finished kneading the bread for the day, or continued pressing the jam, or shucking and stripping the corn—did whatever was at hand.

"We have to talk."

Part of me was relieved. I wouldn't have to bring up the subject of the gun. I waited for Luke to begin.

"Look at me, Millie. You get that faraway look and I feel like you've cut me out. I've tried hard this last year to please you. Finished the attic, just like you asked. Planted those lilac bushes, even though they aren't doing so good. I think I have the right—and it's time—to bring up Gabe and the gun. Don't pull away. Listen to me!! Gabe's birthday's coming up. If I'm going to have a gun here in time, I've got to order it now."

I watched as he opened the Stokes Kirk Catalogue and pointed to the gun he had circled on page twenty-four. He placed the order form in front of me. From his pocket he unfolded forty single bills and placed them next to the catalogue. His hand pressed down on the huge pile of money, money he'd silently saved all these months. There was nothing to discuss.

That night after dinner, while Gabe read in his room, Luke sat beside the Monarch oiling his Winchester. "Gabe!" he called, "Come in here. Have something to show you."

Gabe appeared at the door of the kitchen. He leaned against the door jamb.

"See this?" Luke held the gun for Gabe to see. "Good as new. Model 52. Rimfire bolt action. I bought it the year they made them. Twenty bucks. 1918. Big money in those days. Just smell that wood. Cherry. Beautiful. A gem. Doesn't get any better than this."

Gabe's diary later brimmed with angry words:

he's so stupid touches that stupid gun like it was Babe or a new calf it's a stupid, stupid gun it stinks smells like him oily and dirty

However, this morning, Luke wouldn't let up. He made Gabe take the gun in his hands.

"Hold it. Not like that! Like this! Now, sight down the barrel. That's it. Perfect! Bet you can hardly wait till you're old enough to have one of your own. Growin' up! Getting taller than your mom! Millie, see how he handles the gun. Like it was his own.

Luke reached for the gun, continued to rub down the stock. Gabe sat in a chair, as far away from his father as possible. Gabe paged through the worn pages of 'Tarzan of the Apes.'

I reached for the darning basket. Occupied myself. The twins played Checkers in the front room, away from the harsh tone of their father's words. The room was heavy with the smell of linseed oil. Luke wrapped the gun in an old quilt of his mother's, and concentrated on the Kirk's catalogue. With a furrowed brow, he paged through, checking out canteens, cartridges, compasses, fish knifes, lanterns, packsacks. He finally focused on the ten pages of rifles, displayed like soldiers at attention. With a knife-sharpened pencil, Luke circled the ammunition he'd need. He added the bullets to the total. He addressed an envelope: 1627 N. Tenth Street, Philadelphia, Pennsylvania.

I watched as Luke sighed, coughed, cleared his throat—small actions to get Gabe's attention. He even made a production of licking the envelope, licking the stamp, pounding it with his fist as if to seal the deal. Gabe never once looked up from his book. He saved his words. Days later, he spilled the bitter words from his diary, spilled them like a rainstorm at its cusp. But just to me. Luke could not have heard them without a back-handed swat.

The next day, from the side of the wagon, I waited until Gabe was at the turn of the far corn row. I watched as he dug at the earth with the vengeance he kept for cutting the head off the occasional snake that crawled into the chicken coup.

I called, "Gabe, honey, you sure you don't want to join us? Chores can wait!"

Gabe waved his hand without raising his head and disappeared behind the heavy headed stalks.

Luke wasn't waiting any longer. He slipped the harness on Babe. Sally and Oscar scrambled to get in the back of the wagon where they arranged piles of empty feed sacks. They placed one sack in the center as a table and began a game of Old Maid.

Luke didn't come around to offer me a hand. He waited, the reins at the ready. The envelope protruded from his overall pocket.

I kept my voice low, hoping the twins were distracted in their card game—distracted enough not to hear what I feared would turn into an argument.

"Luke, I know I promised, but please, listen to me. Gabe's too young."

"I had my first gun at ten! He's going to be sixteen for God's sake."

"Don't blaspheme! He's a very young fifteen."

"Young, 'cause you protect him! You want a momma's boy? You want him a joke? It's time he grew up!"

"He's different from other boys."

"You want a namby-pamby faggot for a son? That what you want?"

"Don't you dare use that word!" I lowered my voice and in a whisper full of venom repeated, "Don't you ever use that word."

"I'm ordering that gun."

We didn't wait another minute for Gabe to join us. The clop, clop of Babe's hoofs on the dirt road filled the silence.

In town, the gun order got mailed and then Luke went to filling the wagon with feed and corn. The twins grabbed my hands. It was treat time. I gave them each five pennies, and they headed to Cramwell's to choose their treats. While they chose, I ducked into Conklin's to buy a bolt of blue denim. I inquired about the health of Mr. Conklin and thanked Mrs. Conklin for the extra yard of ribbon. On the ride home, the only sounds were the slap of the cards, the murmur of the twin's secret language and the constant rhythm of Babe's hoofs. The only sound.

I hated that silence. Silence followed us home. Followed us into our bed. Silence and not touching. And the only salve was repeating over and over before I slept, "No more babies. No more babies."

Silence continued. It wasn't just Luke. It wasn't just Gabe. I also learned to use silence. Silence kept Luke away. In bed I turned on my side. Pretended to sleep.

Then Luke started using silence like a truncheon. He'd yell and then cut me to the quick with hours and days of silence. Only the twins seemed not to have joined in the deadly game.

The rifle arrived in a wooden box. Luke crowbarred the lid free and, as the nails pulled from the wood, a high pitched screech filled the air. Gabe stayed in his room. I had visions of him covering his ears so as not to hear the cry of the wood and I imagined the staccato words I'd read later: ***I hate that sound   He shot and shot and shot everything dead   the duck screaming overhead   its mate dead   the bastard   yelling I'll never be a real man if i cry over a stupid dead duck***

The twins slipped out the back door. Anything to get away from the scene that even they knew was going to happen.

I worked at the sink, scrubbing and rescrubbing pots and pans.

"Get out here!" Luke demanded.

Gabe stood at the door. Stared at the gun nestled in wood curls.

Luke gently lifted the gun to the light of the flickering Monarch.

Luke stood and placed the gun in Gabe's hands.

Fearful he would drop it, Gabe cradled it in his arms.

"Give me that, you stupid idiot. You hold it like this. Level."

I stood there frozen.

"Hold it like I hold it. At your shoulder. Sight down the barrel. Treat it easy, slow, sure. You're in control. Not the gun. The gun should feel like its growing out of your arm, out of your brain. We'll practice 'til you get it."

I watched. I listened. Gabe's eyes held anger.

"Everyone to the back porch! This is a big day. The day Gabe becomes a real man. Has his own gun. Need to record this. I'll get the Brownie. The light's perfect. This will be a day you'll never forget!"

Each morning, before school, Luke made Gabe practice.

Then on a Saturday, Luke demanded, "Gabe! Finish up that stupid book! We're going hunting."

That night as he slept, I rubbed Gabe's forehead, and heard his mumbled words: "hate the bastard...hate him...never read a book in his whole damn life...thinks he's some kind of big shot with a gun...wish he were dead...his voice is what's stupid...coughs slugs shoots snot out of his nose...farts at the dinner table...how can she stand to live with him...wish he were dead...dead...dead...wish he were dead...wish he were dead"

And the next day I heard Luke's words as they walked into the field: "Don't know where your mother gets those stupid ideas about lessons. You? Music lessons? Can you believe that? Here's a lesson. Shoot that duck. I don't give a damn if it's got a mate. Shoot the damn thing. Now, go pick it up by its neck. See? Fun."

When they returned, Gabe barely hanging on to the slack neck of the dead bird, Luke kept up his monologue as if he wanted me to hear, wanted me to forgive him already.

"I love your mother, but I can tell you she has some very stupid ideas. Remember when she said we might share a gun? Where did she ever get the idea that men shared guns?"

They came up the back porch and emptied a gunnysack full of dead animals on my newly scrubbed floor: quail, pheasant, grouse, ducks, a Canadian goose, squirrels. The blood seeped into the wood.

The next day Gabe nursed his sore arm, bruised to the color of a mottled plum by the rifle's kick. He winced even as he picked up his Tarzan book. He scooted into the wing-backed chair, lost in the jungle adventure. He didn't see Luke's hand coming, but he felt the hurt in his arm when Luke snatched the book and slammed it into the wood stove. The iron lid slapped into place and fire consumed the book.

"I've had just about enough of this sissy stuff. Here! Read something worth

reading!" Luke threw the Kirk catalogue in Gabe's lap. The catalogue bounced to the floor. Luke stomped out of the house and I followed him. For the first time ever the children heard their mother scream at their father: "Don't come back in this house until you're good and sorry! You hear me?"

He left walking. That night Luke returned late and slept on the couch.

CHAPTER TWENTY-SEVEN

PEACE MARCH

Saturday, October 26, 1968

"Andrew, get up! You promised!"

Andrew mumbles and turns away, "Okay, okay. Ten more minutes."

"No, now! We'll be late." I pull the blankets from the bottom of the bed. "Come on. You promised. The march starts in an hour!"

Andrew scoots back against the headboard, pulling the blankets with him. "You go. I've got work and you promised from the get-go that Saturday mornings were sacred. My time."

"But you're not writing. You're sleeping."

Andrew jumps out of bed—buck naked to sit at his typewriter, as if to prove his point he rolls paper into the carriage. He types.

"I've really got to keep going. I'm at this crucial turning point."

I whine, "An-drew. This is important."

Andrew types. "My writing is important."

"More important than stopping the war? How can you say that? You flunk one class and you'll be in Vietnam so fast…"

"Exactly my point. If you'd just quit regulating my life, I'd get some writing done and then there'd be no chance that I would flunk and get drafted and go to Vietnam. So back off."

I grab my sign. Kick the NIX NIXON sign I made for him. I slam the door.

My fingers cramp as I brace against the wind that near wraps the cardboard sign around my body. And then the next gust of wind off Lake Michigan snaps the cardboard out of my hands and my STOP THE WAR sign twirls up and over the crowd and disappears into a sea of signs: STOP

THE WAR, PEACE NOW, HELL NO WE WON'T GO.

I step back looking desperately for my sign. Shoulder to shoulder marchers push me back against the plate glass window of Peacocks. Students in tie-dyed shirts, mothers with kids in strollers, old and young couples holding hands, veterans in wheelchairs, veterans in uniform, bikers in leather—pass me by.

I think of Andrew. Marching is no fun alone. Meaningful, I'm sure, but not fun. Then in an instant, my thoughts snap back to the march. Someone frantically yells, "Stop!" The corner light changes. The crowd pushes forward. From where I stand I see a teenage girl stumble. She yells frantically, "Don't push! Don't push!" When she steps off the curb, two policemen grab her by the arm and pull her toward a waiting van.

Five more people, unable to stop, step off the curb and instantly are arrested. I fear I will be pushed through the store window. Then the light changes and the marchers surge forward. I hold my breath. A young man with a beard and stringy hair yells "Chicago Pigs! Stop the Chicago Pigs!" One policeman's club comes down on the back of his neck. Another club smashes against his head. Blood streams down his face. He is pushed into the van with the others.

The light changes to green, and whether out of fear or whether the demonstrators are pushing to get away from the police, we all move forward. No one confronts the police or demands the people in the van be let go. I want out of here! The crowd pushes me forward. At the next light, looking for a place to escape, I step back and push through a revolving door. I'm inside Carson Pierre Scott.

It's a different world. Near silent. The chants of the demonstrators are muffled. On either side of the revolving door, cases brim with red purses and mannequins in red dresses wearing red pants, holding red paper flowers. Red the color of blood. I'm near tears. I lean on a counter next to a foot high column of red lipsticks, balanced like small sticks of dynamite.

I look up and I am faced with the cold stare of a store clerk. The clerk stands at the end of the counter. Arms crossed. Eyes narrowed. She glowers at me and I scoot on by.

At the Clinique counter I find a high stool. I lean against it.

"Hi! You're in luck today! It's Gift with Purchase Day," says the girl behind the counter. "Here, let me show you what you'll get. For a ten dollar purchase you get a blue plastic travel bag and coral lipstick and an eyebrow pencil and some vanishing cream and a single mask treatment in mint green."

The girl looks to be my age. She has flawless skin and a mouth so glistening she looks like a porcelain doll. She wears a pearlized blouse with her name stitched in turquoise on the pocket: *Tippy*. She wears creamy white pearl stud earrings and a flat gold chain that drapes over her collar bones like silk.

"Just looking," I say.

"If you found exactly what you wanted, what would it be?"

"I don't know," I answer, wondering that she doesn't recognize a demonstrator when she sees one. She probably doesn't even know there's a war on.

"Our new lip liners are wonderful. Here let me show you. Sit on the stool in front of this mirror so you can watch!" Tippy's voice is demanding but cheerful. "I'll give you a complete makeover! You have such a wonderful face. But wait until you see what I can do!"

I turn to look at the revolving door where marchers stream past and as I look I remember my jacket sports a huge round red button, the red of the very lipstick in the entrance display. The button reads: WE SHALL OVERCOME.

"I'm fast," Tippy says, nodding to the crowd outside the window. "Won't take me a minute."

I sit as I am told.

"I'd be out there if it weren't Saturday," Tippy says in a very low voice as she cleans my face with a moist cotton pad.

"You would?" I ask, stretching to see if the angry clerk is still guarding the entrance. She is.

"Your manager looks like she'd rather the demonstrators were dead," I say. Over Tippy's shoulder the woman glares at the two of us.

"Don't pay her no mind. She's retiring next week. She's angry over that, and then when there's a demonstration, there's no business. She's a crème puff under that exterior. She has no family and she worries, told me so herself, she won't have any life once she doesn't have a job."

"You'd never guess she had a sweet bone in her body."

"Well that's one of life's good lessons, isn't it? People sometimes aren't what they seem. Like you. Most people think all you demonstrators are dope smoking crazies. And here you are!" She gently presses my eyelid as she applies eyeliner. "Are you a student?"

"No. But close. I'm married to one."

"You left your husband in the march while you went shopping?" she exclaims, giggling.

It was all I could do not to lie, to tell her Andrew was a cripple or in bed with the flu or taking his doctoral exams. Something about Tippy's sweet innocence made me tell the truth, "No, my husband's home in bed."

Tippy squeezes a squiggle of foundation on the palm of her hand, then sponges it onto my forehead, nose, cheeks, chin. When she finishes, I glance into the mirror on the counter. My face is perfect. Tippy *has* worked a miracle.

Tippy leans close. "How did your husband avoid the draft?"

"Sheer luck. He has a good number. He'll never get called."

Tippy holds my chin. She draws an outline along my lower lip. "You really believe you can change things? Marching?"

"Well, sure."

"It's not just because your husband, had he not been lucky, could have been sent over there?"

"No! I think the war's horrible."

"Close your eyes," she says. "But didn't you read this morning's paper?"

"We can't afford the paper. What'd it say?"

"I hate to tell you this, but every time you march, Nixon's ratings go up. Did you know that?"

"No, that can't be true."

"Hold your lips still."

She draws a red outline on my upper lip.

Tippy stands back, the lip pencil poised.

"Are you sure?" I ask.

"That's what the paper said."

"Can't be true. We're stopping the war."

"Believe what you've got to believe."

Tippy pulls a soft brush over my eyebrow. I would like to sit here all day. I wouldn't care if Tippy had squeezed Crisco all over my face. It's just such an indulgence to have someone being gentle and careful.

"Relax your mouth," Tippy says and presses the tiniest brush through the tube of lipstick and then against my lips. "It isn't that you shouldn't march. I'd probably march if I didn't have two kids and Saturday wasn't my biggest commission day. Or it usually is."

Until that minute, Tippy has been more than friendly. I'm surprised to hear the edge in her voice.

"Here take a look," Tippy says and holds up a mirror.

I'm transformed! I run my fingers through my hair. My bangs separate into commas.

"You look great," Tippy says and lays all the different pencils and brushes and containers of makeup she has just used on a tray in front of me.

"What would you like to take with you?"

"Take?"

"Buy."

At this point Tippy hands me a check list of products.

From inside my jacket, I pull my charge card. It is wrapped in a ten dollar bill with my driver's license. I study the tubes, the pencils, the brushes. I point to every other item.

"I'll take those."

"Sure you don't want it all?" Tippy laughs like we've just shared a good joke. "You're definitely not boycotting cosmetics!"

I blink and think I've missed something important. "Should I be boycotting cosmetics? I just started boycotting grapes."

"You do what you got to do!" Tippy says and punches the sale into the cash register. She wraps each of the ten items in a square of red tissue paper. She pulls out a Carson Pirie Scott bag and more tissue. She gives me the Clinique Gift with Purchase. As she hands me the bag, she says, "Thank you. You will probably be my only shopper. Until the march is over."

I study the receipt.

"Anything wrong? I don't think I made a mistake."

"No, everything is fine." I slide off the stool. "Thanks again!"

It was the most I had spent on myself since the wedding. I feel guilty. I tucked the receipt deep in my pocket and headed toward the revolving doors. In front of the doors, I turn and with an outstretched arm and two fingers spread, I wave at Tippy. She waves back.

Outside the marchers continue to chant. I join a group of oldsters with linked arms. As we move forward my marching mates begin to sing in a slow, harmonious voice, "We shall overcome..." We march and sing, as if the mellowness of our voices will counter the aggressive chanting. I must say I also feel safer. Like what policeman would start beating on old people?

As I march, I see a man in front of me that looks just like Professor Cush. I drop out of line and wiggle my way forward. I tap his shoulder. When he turns around I'm startled and say, "Oh, sorry, I thought you were someone else."

I'm so disappointed and confused that it isn't Cush. I realize I want someone to see me. Someone to say, "Wow, you look so different! You look so pretty! You're transformed! Fifty-five dollars? It's worth every penny!"

I step back into the crowd, hold my bag close, and as I walk I sing, "*...deep in my heart, I do believe, we shall overcome someday.*"

And I get teary. And I feel great. And I feel pretty darn beautiful.

CHAPTER TWENTY-EIGHT

WHAT'S A MAN TO DO?

It's painful to remember. The words are like a scar. I'm not sure why I need to share these words, but I've found such solace in making these tapes. Perhaps it's the tone of your letters coming from Chicago and the sweetness of your voice in your responses. But I'm concerned. I plead with you, my dearest grandchild, to please be careful with your marriage. May what happened to me, never happen to you.

Late October, 1930

Luke had come home late two days in a row. An unspoken pattern had begun to shape our lives. Luke mumbled excuses and I was too tired or too scared or, maybe too sure, to demand clear answers to why problems at neighbors' homes, farm yards, machine shops were more important than his own home.

On this particular morning, Luke was gone before I got up. The kids finished breakfast and were off to school. I took Babe to town, anything to get away from the silence of the farmhouse. Back home, after lunch, I was surprised to see Billy Johnson drive up in his Model T.

Billy said he had come to ask Luke if he could borrow the tractor the next day or two. Or maybe that was a made-up reason. Maybe Billy, who'd always been a bit of a flirt, a widower, and not much liked by Luke, had come to see me. To see what I knew. What I didn't know.

He walked up the front porch steps, extending a jar of Henry Highman's strawberry wine. The children weren't due home for a couple of hours. Billy said he'd catch up with Luke sometime later, but why not share a drink with him? Seemed un-neighborly to turn him down. So we had a drink.

We talked. His words came to me as if I was watching a stage play. He didn't spare me. I think he wanted to get at Luke. I never figured that out. But this was the day I learned what I was near guessing.

Billy blurted out, "Luke's seeing Angelica."

I didn't respond. Held myself rigid and cold. I listened.

Billy continued: "Sorry to tell you Millie, but here's this morning's conversation at Hennessey's. Don't ever think women are the only gossips. Here's the conversation, best as I remember it:

We're all at Hennessey's like usual. George Hawks is sitting on the far end of the porch. He yells, 'What? Say again!'

That's when Jake jumps into the conversation, 'Luke's leaving her. Leaving Millie. He's pokin' that neighbor girl and he's leavin' Millie.'

Ralph Torgerson showed the most disbelief. He turned his good ear toward the line of us and asked, way too loud, 'Luke is what?'

That's when I looked up to see you coming down Main Street with Babe and the wagon and told them to shut their yaps. But, Jake was on a roll, like nothing would stop him from telling all of us his hair-brained thoughts. He declared Luke had changed and you had your hands full of children. Millie, believe me men compare. They start thinking about their own marriages, their own wives. I can guarantee you everyone was sitting there comparing themselves to the two of you. All these years and three kids. And I don't recall how, but we men knew you had a hard time birthing those twins. And somehow, not sure how, we all knew that Dr. Swanzy had given you full warning about not having another.

Billy refilled our glasses and I didn't object. He kept right on talking. Ralph said, 'Three kids? And he's banging out another?' Ralph asked that loud, as if the rest of us were as deaf as he was. And then for laughs, he adds, 'Doctor Swanzy'd cut Luke's machinery right off if he knew.' At about which time you came back from your errands and I told the whole lot of them to shut up. They did stop talking. They chewed and spat. Silence, cold as creek ice. You hitched the reins. You stepped past the sets of eyes staring and the mouths still. You held your head high, never looking right nor left. You walked past us like you hadn't heard our talking. I feared you had.

Once you left, though, the gossip continued. I must say that the men only half-believed the rumors. Such things just don't happen in Gaitsberg. Maybe in Yakima. For sure in Spokane. But here at Hennessey's? Hard to believe. Here's what we did know: Luke is neighborly. Always hallo-ing and complimenting the ladies. Then Angelica's sister stayed away in the big city, her mother died, and her dad got all arthritic and Luke took to dropping by to lend a hand.

About that time, and this is hard to say, but even I heard that you made Luke sleep in the shed. But, to put your mind at ease, I stopped that rumor front on. I told whoever was spreading such gossip, that no, Luke'd never sleep in the shed. It's too damn cold. Perhaps, just maybe, you'd make him sleep on the couch.

What you need to know Millie, this is where there was agreement. The men thought that if you'd done that, kicked him out of your shared bed, then maybe, just maybe, Luke had cause. And temptation was only one field over."

Billy drained his glass. Looked right at me as if he wasn't tearing out my insides. He asked, "What's a man to do?"

I couldn't find an answer. Any answer. He kept right on talking.

"No one mentioned Angelica right out. But no one has missed how she changed from a girl to a woman in a flash. And comments followed:

'A husband has rights.'
'Says so, in the Bible.'
'What's a man to do?'
'Needs are needs.'"

I held myself as still as I could and I said, "That's enough Billy. Enough."

He must have heard the bite in my words, because he left and from that day on I limited every trip to town. And I began to plan. I needed to save myself. I needed to protect the children.

CHAPTER TWENTY-NINE

THE MEDICI, COFFEE, AND THOU

Thursday, October 31, 1968

While I watch *Maverick*, I carve two pumpkins. One to put by our apartment door. One to take to school.

I pour myself a glass of wine. Pop popcorn. I watch the nine o'clock news. Andrew won't be home from his tutorial for another hour. I sort my underwear drawer. I flip through *Anatomy of Criticism*, glad Andrew has to study Northrop and I don't. I try to read *Magister Ludi*. On the bookshelf above his desk, I find Andrew's "Free-write Folder." I glance through all of his short-story starts—the ones I've typed.

I know all about free-writes. Andrew will say, "Give me a word!" Or "Give me a phrase," and I respond with something silly, like "Rutabagas" or "Around the corner appeared…" and he writes with the kitchen timer going. Five minutes. Ten minutes. Twenty minutes. I used to listen to him read these impromptu essays or scenes, but they were generally pretty silly and eventually, he'd write longer and longer things, whatever he called them, and I'd go back to reading *Franny and Zooey*.

Then I notice something unusual. On the bottom of one of the papers I had typed was a yellow lined piece of tablet paper. Across the top Andrew has written: Late Night Thoughts.

The page, covered in his precise, tight script, is as if he'd written everything in a burst of anger:

"We applied to the University of Chicago's Advanced Writing Program. We? She uses me like I don't exist, like I'm a subset of her. When she insisted that Jack the Ass write my recommendation, it was just about more than I could handle. Jack and his

singular triumph of one story in the Atlantic Monthly. So what? But Jack was her professor and he wrote the recommendation. Then she filled out my application. She signed the lease on the new apartment. She packed the car. She chose the god-damned route we drove to Chicago. Since getting here, she's scheduled my life. We go to graduate school parties where I'm her husband and somehow I forget to remember not to drink too much and then we come home and she won't talk to me but she goes right to the typewriter where she types my drafts that need to be left alone but she thinks I'll be able to read them better if they are not on yellow legal pads and in pencil (which she for some unknown reason finds 'untidy') and then at breakfast there will be the draft next to my Cheerios and she won't say a word, because she doesn't know how to read my work and the next night, before she falls into a dead sleep and she says for the hundredth time, you're going to be even greater than Hemingway, and then she sleeps and snores and snorts in her dreams. Dreaming up how she's going to organize the rest of my life.

I don't know if I can take any more. She pushes and pushes and she doesn't realize that the last time we made love, she immediately asked, "How's the story going?"

Once, years ago, I happened to say after a couple of beers, "I'm going to be another Ernest Hemingway."

Now she slings that sentence around my neck like an albatross. And she's started asking if I'm such a Hemingway, why don't I send stuff right to the New Yorker instead of The Snowy City Review produced in somebody's basement and impossible to find at Krock and Brentano's.

I've tried to explain how the small literary world works but she just keeps saying, Go for the Big! And Don't Under Estimate Yourself! And Walk Proud! She sounds just like her mother who's three rowboats past a dingy and nice enough but thank God we live in Chicago and she lives in Spokane because she makes me absolutely nuts after about ten minutes of raised eyebrows waiting for me to say I've sold my first novel for a million dollars and when she doesn't hear that sentence she pats my arm like a puppy and says not to worry, everything works out for the best.

There are times I feel so weighed down with Sarah's expectations, I think I'm going to disintegrate. Instead, I do what I'm told to do. That's how I got here—doing what I was told to do: apply to the U of C, get accepted, write every day, get good grades, send out stories, get rejection slips, paste rejection slips on the bathroom wall. Lately I've taken to hiding rejection slips because I can see the disappointment and doubt in her eyes as she watches me open the envelopes.

Thank God for the writing group at Kafka's. Thank God for someone like Magda. Amazing. I just wrote her name for the first time. Magda."

I feel as if a two-by-four has just run through me. How could he have written something so mean? After all I've done for him. Isn't that what a wife is supposed to do? Take care of her husband? Be his help-mate? I'd worked so hard to get us to Chicago. Got him in the master's program. I've taken on the after-school math class so he doesn't have to get a part-time job.

I'm angry and I'm hurt and I don't have a clue what I'm supposed to do. I fill a wine glass and I go to bed and turn on the television and never once laugh at Johnny Carson. When Andrew comes home around midnight, I pretend to be asleep.

Things don't get better.

By the next Saturday, I still have not said a word about that free-write. The night before, when we usually go to a movie and have pizza, I came home from work, heated up a can of Campbell's Chicken Noodle Soup, claimed a headache, and went to bed.

This Saturday, Andrew sits at his typewriter for one of his 'do not disturb' writing sessions. While he writes, I clear the breakfast table, do the dishes, take the garbage to the garbage chute, take the laundry to the basement, iron Andrew's shirts, then I try to read. It is impossible to concentrate what with Andrew's incessant pounding on the typewriter.

In the kitchen next to the coffee pot I leave a note: *Gone for coffee. Be back soon. Sarah.* I leave no X's or O's at the bottom of the note. I grab my Hesse novel, my bag, and a sweater. Andrew doesn't look up. Apparently, he doesn't care whether or not I say goodbye.

I walk over to The Medici Coffee Shop, on Fifty-First. When I come in from the bright sunshine, my eyes slowly adjust to the cool, dark, cafe and there, under the gilt-framed crackled mirror, beside the philodendron, smoking a cigarette in a cigarette holder, leaning back, as if studying the room and all its inhabitants, one hand for the cigarette, the other hand for a fountain pen poised over a leather bound journal, is Professor Evian Cush.

He waves. He stands and I have no option but to sit in the curved iron chair he pulls out for me. He says with a laugh, "We've got to quit meeting like this!"

This time I get the joke. "How nice." And I steal his word, "What a 'lovely' coincidence!"

"The pleasure is all mine!" He reaches for my hand, and purrs, "What more could one ask for?"

For a second I think about Andrew back at the apartment. Too bad he said he had to write. He will be so jealous when he hears I have had coffee with his advisor. At the Medici, a place we have not shared. And now here I am, with his advisor. Alone. Well, except for the other twenty occupants of the coffee shop, we are alone. I look directly at Professor Cush. I smile.

Professor Cush signals the waiter and orders two double espressos.

"The only place for a double espresso. Where I come to think, to dream, to read, to…" and he leans forward and whispers, "…to meet a beautiful woman."

He pushes aside his *New York Times* and nods at the book tucked under my arm. "What are you reading?"

I slide the book across the table.

"My goodness. A heavy tome for such a slight lady!"

I wince. I want to tell him not to be a jerk. Before I can think of anything appropriate to say, his joking demeanor vanishes, and he asks with a note of seriousness, while flipping the pages of the novel, "I must say that of all of Hesse's work, *Magister Lude* is my favorite. Is it yours?"

In that moment, the tenor of the conversation takes on a note of respect. I go from being irritated to being flattered, "Too early to tell. Besides, I've not read everything he's written. This one is like entering a magical musical world. Strange, but dark."

"Oh, I agree. That book made me delve into medieval music. Hesse does that. Takes you into entirely different worlds." Professor Cush lays the book down between us. "The reason for reading, I believe, is for those moments when there is a distinct paradigm shift."

At which moment, the waitress places two delicate porcelain cups in front of us. "Your espressos!" She turns each cup so the handle is exactly placed. Shades of Grandma Millie!

The bitter taste is ambrosia. And I know, nothing about this moment will I be able to share with Andrew.

"Isn't this the very place to be discussing paradigm shifts?" he asks. "Dark. Mysterious. Things unknown. Things to be discovered. A new world."

I'm surprised at how warm and itchy I feel being with Professor Cush. I don't consider his attention as 'flirting.' I don't call my reaction, 'temptation.' I don't call the long-held glances, 'inappropriate.' I don't call what is happening by any kind of name. But when he touches my arm and I grow warm between my legs and I am conscious of the blurred edge of his eyebrows, the darkened cleft of his chin, the plumpness of his lower lip—an imaginary sign glows over his head beating to the rhythm of my heart, SEX, SEX, SEX.

At eleven forty-five, Evian Cush checks his watch and says, "I hate to end this bit of enchantment, but I have a lunch date. I'm always here on a Saturday morning. So if that husband of yours doesn't feel as if he needs to protect his treasure, and you want to spend a few stolen moments of sheer enjoyment—at least that's how I have felt about this accidental meeting—you are more than welcome to join me. And next week I'll try not to have another engagement." He lifts my hand and brushes it with his lips. "Auvoir, my liebchen, to mix a metaphor!"

Walking home, I can't stop blushing. I'm worried that I will not be able to keep this experience from Andrew. Should he learn, he will be upset. I try to think of a nonchalant sentence to cover this strange meeting.

Back at our apartment, I slowly turn the key and then push open the door. I call softly, "Andrew?" Andrew harrumphs in his sleep, turns and curls into a tangle of sheets. Relief slips through me.

I put on a kettle for instant coffee.

As I wait for the water to boil, I stand in the doorway to the bedroom and watch Andrew sleep. He makes soft snoring sounds; a small slip of drool makes a dark patch on his pillow. Back on the kitchen table, I open my book and try to read. The sentences make no sense. I stare at the words and slowly review all that has happened. Why was I so pleased and excited to meet up with someone until now I had barely liked? Why did I feel excited and scared at the same time? Professor Cush had talked about Andrew's career as much as anything. But why did he touch my hand, and why didn't I pull it away? Why was I feeling as if my pulse had doubled? I wasn't supposed to feel this way. I'm a married woman. It hasn't been six months and I feel as if I don't have a clue what marriage means. Did I ever know what marriage meant? Why did I feel so unfaithful? What did it mean to forsake all others? One and Only? Cleave to what?" I can't quite remember my marriage vows. I memorized the marriage vows. Knew them like I knew the Twenty-third Psalm. Now they are scrambled, out of order. When I start the mantra, 'Do you Sarah, Take Thee Andrew?' what happens? The words are a mess. To have and to hold? To beg and to borrow? To wed and to shed? What was it I had promised? What's a promise? What's a vow?

When I was ten I crossed my heart and hoped to die and never, ever told anyone that Meggie Pryor had watched her brother through the bathroom keyhole. She said he was furry down there. She said he pretended to conduct an orchestra with his thingie until his thingie was hard and straight. The image was monstrous, exciting, forbidden, funny, and serious. I never told anyone what Meggie had told me, but then I barely believed her. And still, I never broke the vow not to tell.

When I took sex education in junior high it never crossed my mind that what Meggie's brother did and how babies were made, were related. What I didn't realize was that I could barely admit to myself the reality of what Meggie had said. Sex was secret. You did it but you never talked about it. Now even as a grown woman, sex still seemed to be strange and secret. And all the feelings I was having now? Weren't they supposed to be reserved for marriage?

Home, I don't tell Andrew about the morning meeting. I thought I would tell him, but the right moment never happens. The longer I don't mention it the more impossible it becomes to say anything and I avoid even walking by the Medici.

Then one day I open a white envelope addressed in an elaborate flourish to both of us. *Please share a meal with me. Friday night? 7:00? Unless I hear otherwise, the wine will be chilled and ready.*

I ask Andrew, "Did the rest of the grads get an invite to dinner?"

"Not that I heard of."

"Do you think it means anything?"

"Like what?"

"I don't know. Like he thinks more of you, of your writing, than the rest?"

"Well, hopefully he does. But quit thinking everything means something. It's a dinner invitation. No big deal."

"But it is a big deal!"

"Sarah, give me a break. The guy's a professor. If he was such a great writer, he wouldn't be teaching. It didn't take me long to figure him out. We'll schmoose, he'll open some doors to publishers he might know, he'll pass on manuscripts, so it's certainly a good thing to have dinner with him. But when it comes to his writing, he's back in the 50s. He might know a few crafty tricks, but he can't possibly capture the emotion and spirit of the 60s."

When Professor Cush opens the door of his apartment, his arms fly wide. He kisses me on both cheeks. He holds me at arm's length.

"What a pleasure! So lovely to see you again!"

What does it mean when the professor holds me too long? What does it mean that he winks at Andrew as he holds my hand? As he ushers us into his apartment, I feel as if I am watching myself in a play.

After dinner of angel hair pasta with crab, and very fine chardonnay (as we are told), we carry tiny cut glass liqueur glasses to Professor Cush's study, after Andrew excuses himself to go to the bathroom, I have no time to think it is strange when Professor Cush doesn't say a word. We sit in silence like we are wrapped in a warm blanket. Our eyes catch and hold. We sip the thick, sweet liquid. He smiles slightly as he holds my gaze. He lifts his glass as if to toast something.

I know what is happening. I pretend I don't. At least, this evening, I pretend everything means nothing. So why do I blush? Why do I grow warm? Why do I ache? Why, without ever saying a word, am I slightly irritated when Andrew re-joins us?

And then there is one incident branded in my brain. While Andrew wasn't in the room, I watch as Professor Cush 'rearranges himself.' His hand at his crotch. While he 'sorts himself out' I immediately study the row of leather bound books over his right shoulder all the time aware of how he moves, how he watches me. I ignore the most prominently displayed book on the bookshelf, the *Kama Sutra*, and I ignore Professor Cush's hand on himself and I let *Oh My Darlin' Clementine* roll around and around in my head until Andrew re-enters the room and says, "Great shower you have!

Big enough for ten!"

"Big enough," Professor Cush laughs and Andrew laughs and I laugh, but I don't know why.

"You're one lucky man, Andrew."

I stare at Professor Cush. I panic, fearful he will say something about the Medici, about this moment when Andrew has been gone, or how he finds me attractive, how I turn him on, how Andrew will fly through graduate school if only…

Instead, he says, "You've exciting years ahead of you."

The Professor and Andrew fall into a wordy discussion about literary criticism. Professor Cush shows Andrew his signed first edition of *For Whom the Bell Tolls*. He shows Andrew his maps where he's marked out Kerouac's cross-country trip. He shows Andrew his own manuscript in progress. I watch them and see how often his hand rests on Andrew's shoulder, how he gives Andrew small pats on the back and I wonder if maybe I'd imagined Professor Cush's interest in me. Maybe I was wrong. Maybe Professor Cush is a homosexual. Maybe he pays attention to me just to get to Andrew.

And suddenly, I want to grab Andrew's hand and run. Go home. Save him. Save us. Save our marriage.

But the conversation drones on and with a second glass of liqueur thoughts of what anything means disappear. Finally, Andrew checks his watch. It is past midnight. It is time to leave.

Professor Cush walks us to the front of his apartment. He helps me on with my coat. His hands don't linger on my shoulders. Again, I think I've imagined everything. Professor Cush shakes both of our hands. The grasp is neither too heavy nor too long. We say goodnight.

Outside, walking home to our apartment, the crisp breeze clatters the maple leaves. The wind blows all of my worried thoughts away and when Andrew says, "When the time comes, he could possibly change our lives." I agree but I'm silent. As we walk Andrew whistles under his breath, "There'll be a Hot Time in the Old Town Tonight" over and over again.

I never tell Andrew I found his writing. Weeks later when I type five of his free-writes, and place them in his folder, I find that "Late Night Thoughts" are no longer there. Maybe Andrew threw those pages away. Maybe he realized he didn't mean it. Now we both have a secret.

CHAPTER THIRTY

LUKE'S GONE

My dear Sarah. This is the most difficult tape to date. I've started it over three times. Then I gave up, I closed my eyes and everything is immediate, and frightening, and full of sorrow; and I won't stop until this tape is finished.

Monday, November 10, 1930

Rita Roosted, the second nearest neighbor, plowed down the back path like a ship under sail. With a purpose. In a hurry. Full of intent. On her arm hung a woven wicker basket bursting with fresh baked bread. I smiled a welcome, pleased to have company.

"Coffee first!" Rita declared.

While the coffee grounds let loose their burnt, toasty smell, Rita sliced the bread. She bustled about my kitchen as if it was hers. She wiped the round oak table clean. She found embroidered linen napkins in the side board and folded them into neat squares. She even refilled the pressed glass jelly jar.

She was a master at building tension. Suspension. I can see she was bursting with news. Her eyes glittered. Her hands quivered.

After she poured the coffee, she scooted the ladder-back chair until her knees bumped mine. Then she reached for my hand. I didn't expect that–her gnarled bony fingers clasping mine.

"You'll never guess," Mrs. Roosted said leaning forward. Something about her pleasure in the news, her anticipation, the pressure of her fingers, let me know. I know before she said it, the secret I've been dreading was about to be revealed.

It was as if I watched the words fall from Rita's lips. She spoke five words. Slowly. Deliberately. Indelibly. The words dropped like round hard stones. The first three words were: "It's about Luke." And I knew the last two words:

"She's pregnant."

I didn't ask who is pregnant.

I didn't eat the slice of white bread spread with blood red jam.

I walked outside and looked at the fence on the hill.

Rita touched my shoulder. "Millie? Millie? Are you all right?"

I didn't turn toward my neighbor's voice. I didn't respond to the press of my neighbor's fingers. I held myself still.

"I didn't want just anyone bringing you the news."

I didn't say, "Thank you."

That day I started sorting. What will stay. What will go.

Tuesday, November 11

Some days and some moments you never forget. With the following words it is as if I am back at the farm, back at the moment everything dissolved.

Gabe slowly walked up the path with the mail, slowly turned over a fat, long envelope, and handed it to me. "What's it?" he asked.

From the heft, the cream colored stationary, the long list of names on the return address, Kennedy, Egan, Kind and Clark, I knew. "Nothing, nothing," I lied. "Farm papers."

Gabe's eyes grew small and angry as if he knew I lied.

He yelled at me, "The mailman said he won't deliver our mail anymore if we don't fix that falling-down mail box!" He turned and ran down the slope of yard to the creek. His words snapped back at me, sharp and mean, "Everything's falling apart here. I hate it! We live like a bunch of bums."

I let the screen door slide off my hand. I took the envelope to the parlor and placed it in the bottom drawer of the sideboard along with the farm mortgage, the children's birth certificates, our marriage license, my high school diploma, and a few photographs—life's markers. I studied my graduation picture. A stiff lace collar surrounded my neck. My slender arms draped over the back of a carved rosewood settee. A severe black dress hugged my breasts. It was hard to believe that photo. There was so little of me left in that young girl.

I slid the drawer shut. Later that night, when the children were safe in bed, I read the letter from the attorney.

I went to the front porch. I rocked in the rocker Luke made for me. In this rocker I had nursed my children. Today the wind hugged me as if it could tie me to this porch, to this farm, to the thought of Luke. But the wind was turning. The wind whipped dust devils along the border as if patrolling the two farms. Hers. Ours. A season ago I sat on this porch and watched the wind ruffle his hair. Only the night before I yearned for the length of him, the warmth of him. I rocked and wondered how everything changes.

The week before, I saw Angelica at Cramwell's Confectionary. I saw her through the window. Angelica's blond curls were pulled high off her face. Her face was full of calm. Her hand rode her waist, the slight swelling there. I knew it would take years for him to be bored with her. And I knew Angelica could not have resisted him. This day, I could not stem the hope that his eventual, certain marriage to her would shatter.

I studied the fields that surround our farm. Last August, the crops were stingy. Crows and weevils feasted on leftovers. Even voices were brittle. Then the wind hid, and the farm waited as if holding its breath. By October it seemed Luke was missing more often than he was home. Last week, the wind hurled rain. Today, the wind played tricks, and once again ladled out small bursts of almost warm air.

The farm was a constant reminder of Luke. The screen door's spring sagged. A porch step needed replacing. The curved drive had thrown itself away and needed another load of gravel. The chicken coup fence was torn.

I hated that I needed him. Two weeks ago, he returned for a day to show Gabe how to plant potatoes. After he left I found dollar bills stuffed in the crockery pot on top of the Monarch. A pay-off? Guilt money? I could barely come to touch it. Later, I will need it.

The twins appeared oblivious to their dad's absences. Perhaps it was because they had each other. I watched them and wondered what secrets they shared. When their heads touched, like two pale onions, they were salve for each other. They spoke in their own words and at night I heard their whispers. What will they say when they realize their dad has gone for good?

In Gabe there was slow sadness in his movements. I remembered when he was my child of hope. He ran with wide open arms at everything—joyously. Then the silence came. Then the anger. Now he lived in his own world.

The next morning, with no sleep and no hope, I sliced the last of the fall apples. I spread the slices in a fan and sugared them. I poured milk in three blue enamel cups. I placed crockery bowls of oatmeal on the pine table and filled a plate with buttermilk biscuits. In a blue willow saucer I scooped red currant jelly. At the bottom of the stairs, I called each child's name, and wished the wind could carry my voice out the window, over the hill, to Luke.

At the table, the twins scooted ladder-back chairs into place and bent their heads to their breakfast. Gabe joined us. He slumped in a chair and stared at his food in front of him as if he could magically read the liquid like Lady Lazonga might have read tea leaves.

Gabe lifted his head, his eyes distant. He said, his voice sharp and slow, "The chickens are out again." He put both elbows on the table, talked through a mouth full of biscuit. "I can't do everything around here."

"Gabe, please, please." My voice was as sad as his. Then, as if to remember my role, I said, "Please eat. Do not speak while you are chewing. After breakfast we'll round up the chickens."

Once again, I had said the wrong thing.

"It's not just chickens!" His words snapped like someone breaking brittle bones. He licked his fingers to taunt me. "Besides, you don't know anything about chickens!"

"Gabe! Enough! Sally, Oscar, finish your meal, dress and start your chores. Gabe, the minute you finish we will work on the chicken coup."

The twins scooted back, anxious to free themselves from the weight of the room.

The pounding of their feet on the stairs was all about escape.

"I hate this jam," Gabe said and pushed his plate away. "Everything around here stinks!"

"Gabe! Stop!" I held my arms tight against my chest as if to keep from exploding. I wanted to hold Gabe, but I was fearful I would crush his bones, crush his voice, or he would push me away. I stood and pressed my back against the cold iron of the Monarch stove. "Gabe, it doesn't mean he doesn't love you."

There, I had said it. For the first time. Outloud.

Gabe looked up, his eyes the same eyes as his father's eyes. I feared he would scream at me. But worse, as I waited, the horrible truth settled into him and his eyes dimmed, like turning down a kerosene lamp. I would gladly have traded the loss in his eyes for anger.

Gabe stood, and as he stood he braced himself against the table, slopping oatmeal. I watched as the river of liquid spread. "I'll clean it up," I said.

Without looking at me Gabe answered, "I'll go take care of the chickens." His slender shoulders folded forward as he walked out the kitchen door. He pushed the screen-door open and held the door as it closed in a whisper.

I fought back tears and I knew someday Gabe would learn, on his own, that love changes. Like the wind. Through my mind ran words like spikes, "Luke is gone. Luke is gone." I whispered the words out loud, "Luke is gone." Then I turned to the kitchen sink as if my words would splatter like vomit and I sobbed.

That night I retrieved the lawyer's letter and forms. I signed my name. Millicent Louise Lane. Once I wrote that name over and over on old envelopes and along the edge of the Farmer's Almanac. Then, I became that name. Now I would have to share Luke's name with Angelica and I hoped she would wear his name like a stone in her shoe.

Put one foot in front of the other. My mother's words. An old family cliché—words which over generations have been stitched onto pillows, burned into kitchen plaques, stenciled on the front of aprons. Once I thought clichés were stupid and vacuous and useless. But after I accepted the fact that Luke was gone, gone to me, clichés seemed powerful and full of truth and I knew that this cliché would sustain me through the months and years ahead.

As I stood alone in the kitchen, I heard the long slow whistle. The Northern Pacific. Headed for Spokane. Another cliché.

CHAPTER THIRTY-ONE

THANKSGIVING

November 28, 1968

"Exactly how will Band-Aids and Tums save us from freezing to death?" Andrew asks as he digs through the blue emergency duffel. He pushes aside the first-aid kit, folded scarves, pocket warmers, Tupper-wared matches. He extracts the bag of oatmeal cookies. He takes one out then shoves the rest in the pocket of his down jacket

It annoys me just about as much as the way Andrew folds the cookie and stuffs it in his mouth. I cannot believe this is the same man whose warm, wonderful body lay next to mine only an hour ago, who pleases me no end.

"Those are emergency supplies!" I snap.

"I've just dug through three feet of snow, which warrants at least one cookie!" he says as he stuffs the assorted items back into the duffel, slings it over his shoulder, and disappears down the hall.

"Honk when you're ready!" I yell as the door slams. Why? Why did he act that way? Chew food like a ten year old? Question my preparing an emergency bag? Why couldn't he see the purpose in it? It wasn't like he hadn't watched last night's news: snow so heavy people abandoned cars on Lake Shore Drive; a pregnant woman sitting alone in a deli with the owner hoping she wouldn't need an ambulance; ropes spread across Michigan Avenue to keep pedestrians from being blown into traffic.

And Andrew? Andrew just spent the last half-hour digging the car out of the snow. Something horrible *could* happen. Even in good weather it was an hour's drive to Lombard. We *could* get in an accident. We *could* get stranded. Disaster *could* happen.

I gather Ritz Crackers, Cheese Whiz, Twinkies, Sun Maid Raisins, and a checker set. We face a forty mile drive through three days of accumulated snow—the worst snow storm in twenty years. I pace the apartment, check out the window to see if Andrew is ready. I would give anything for a nap, but I know the minute I lie down he will honk.

I barely slept last night for the wind whipping off Lake Michigan, sending snow tap-dancing on the windows. Between worries about the snow, the pie, Andrew's ponytail, and visions of my barely remembered aunt and uncle, I woke exhausted.

At least, for the occasion, Andrew has shaved and he isn't wearing the jeans with the holes.

Outside the scrim of snow continues. Through the gauze-like light, Andrew stomps a path around the Dodge. He has dropped the bright blue duffel in a snow bank. He isn't wearing the cap I knit him. His face is bright red. He pounds his hands against his chest. Puffs of air plume from his mouth. He stamps his feet. He looks like the true outdoorsman! My irritation melts.

Instead of waiting for Andrew to honk, I decide to go down and give him a hand—scrape windows, pack the car. I wrap another layer of aluminum foil around my mincemeat pie. I zip up my puffy down jacket, tie an engine-red knit scarf around my neck, grab the full grocery bag, and head downstairs.

As I enter the vestibule of the apartment, through the beveled glass door I see that Andrew is digging out the neighbor's Mustang. The one with the black roof. The one he wishes he owned. The owner, a tall, enviably beautiful woman, chats and laughs at something Andrew says. She stands at the curb in her black leather boots with two-inch heels, arms folded under the flap of her Australian-Out-Back coat. Snow floats down to land on the enormous red fox hat that frames her face. I wait. Andrew tucks the shovel into the trunk of the Dodge and extends his hand to the neighbor lady. He doesn't let go of her hand until she reaches to open her car door. She honks a thank you as she drives away and I walk down the cleared sidewalk.

Then Andrew honks the horn of the Dodge.

"Andrew, I'm right here!" I say.

"Thought you were still upstairs."

"No, I've been standing here for a while."

"Oh, okay, well, let me help you."

Andrew reaches for the pie. I pull away and nod for him to open the car door. I hold the pie all the way to Lombard.

As we drive down the Dan Ryan, The Doors sing, "come on baby light my fire…." Andrew sings along, his voice loud and out of tune, "…try to set the night on fire…"

An hour later we arrive at the home of my Aunt Winnie and Uncle Vic. Their walk has been swept clean. Andrew pushes the doorbell and through the glass storm door I can see my uncle. The last time I saw him I was twelve. He looks like Dad—tall and slender, all lanky and easy in his body. Aunt Winnie joins him, plump, with tight curly hair, her walk quick and studied like a wind-up toy. Her welcoming mid-west voice calls, "Well look who's here! How tall you are! You've cut your hair! And this? Well this must be Anthony! Anthony, this is your Uncle Vic!"

Andrew offers his hand. "Andrew."

"Of course, Andrew, how silly of me," she says and on tip-toes plants a kiss on his newly shaved face.

As Uncle Vic shakes Andrew's hand, I can see that he is studying Andrew's pony tail.

"Well, come right in!"

Everyone troops down the hall. Aunt Winnie chatters, "We are so pleased you drove all that way. All that way from the ghetto, just to spend Thanksgiving with us.

"Hyde Park," I say, defending our home. She doesn't hear me.

"Pleased! Just pleased! Aren't we, Vic?" Her be-ringed fingers toodle the air and we enter an avocado green and Nehi orange kitchen. The counters brim with Thanksgiving fare: bowls of cranberries and cranberry jelly, a cupped plate of deviled eggs, a Beleek dish lined with cheese-filled celery, a tiered plate of assorted chocolates and pink almond candies.

"Right here! Right here!" Aunt Winnie directs as she pushes aside empty Jell-O boxes to make room for my pie. Gently, I pull back the aluminum foil, and Uncle Vic's eyebrows arch. He steps to the counter and pushes his finger into the center of the crust where mincemeat had bubbled through. He asks, "Raisin pie? Umm, umm, my favorite," and he licks his finger.

"It's mincemeat," I say.

And then, as if he can't hold in the words, Uncle Vic exclaims, "Mincemeat? Real honest-to-God mincemeat? Your mom's wild-deer mincemeat? Sarah, this is a treat! You are a treat. And you too, Andrew. " He stares, and then he blinks. If blinking could have cut hair, Andrew would have had a trim right then.

In the living room around the coffee table we eat all of the deviled eggs and drink tonic water in large cut-glass goblets. Soon, Aunt Winnie disappears into the kitchen, refusing any help. Uncle Vic sits with his hands around his glass of water and then as if he were inspired, he demands we follow him downstairs to the basement.

The light flicks on. Before us, filling the entire basement is an enormous train set. With a push of a button, four trains chug around a track through hills studded with plastic trees and lakes made of blue glass and snow made of sparkle-filled cotton. Then he points to the wall above the Styrofoam glaciers and the meandering trains, to a certificate: Twenty-five years of Service, Railroad Engineers' Union. We watch the trains make three more trips around their world and then head back upstairs.

We sit through a bit of a silence followed by another longer silence, which Andrew breaks by assuring Uncle Vic that he understands if they don't talk about the draft or the Vietnam War.

I could kill him. Miraculously, at that very moment Aunt Winnie calls everyone to the dining table.

"Sarah, why don't you say grace?" Aunt Winnie asks and reaches for my hand. We all join hands.

Then I pray a prayer I will forever regret:

"Dear Lord, bless this food." At that point I should have said 'Amen'. I didn't. It was as if I was possessed. As if Andrew had turned the day into a horrible joke, and I followed suit. I begin at one end of the table and say, "Bless the water goblets and bless the marshmallows in the Jell-O salad and bless the butter on the peas and bless the dinner rolls from the package and bless the fine stainless steel silverware. And bless the turkey and the dressing and the cranberry sauce and the cranberry jam, and all the Union brothers and …"

Andrew kicks me under the table.

"Amen."

The rest of the meal is nothing but tense. Andrew compliments every item we eat as if he might erase his self-righteous comment about the war and my horrid prayer. Nothing helps.

Aunt Winnie doesn't seem to notice that neither of us takes a second helping of lime green Jell-O salad. Uncle Vic refills water glasses as if the lubrication might help the conversation. I yearn for a large glass of wine.

Finally it is time for dessert.

I watch Uncle Vic as he chews his first bite of my mincemeat pie. I hear his teeth clatter.

"This isn't venison," he states and places his fork on the crocheted table cloth.

"It's *bear* meat," I say.

"Bear meat? You mean like Smokey the Bear, bear meat? What kind of mincemeat pie has bear meat?"

"Mom's! The mincemeat you love!"

"But … it's … it's …"

And then Andrew saves the day. He takes the bag of oatmeal cookies out of his pocket. Andrew offers a cookie to Uncle Vic. He nods to Uncle Vic to eat up, and Uncle Vic beams at Andrew like Andrew is a Union brother. He offers another cookie to Aunt Winnie. She smiles 'no thank you' and eats her piece of mincemeat pie. Andrew and Uncle Vic polish off the remaining cookies.

We don't stay for coffee. Andrew tells Aunt Winnie and Uncle Vic he has to get back to meditate. Why he said that, I haven't a clue. Andrew doesn't meditate. He isn't a hippie. He isn't a peace-nik. His draft card is in his wallet and it has never crossed his mind to burn it. He's never protested any war. He fears he might end up in jail and he wouldn't have clean socks. What Andrew has is a pony tail. And the ability to irritate relatives. But, then I haven't been on such good behavior, either. All in all the day is a disaster.

It is a long, slippery, silent ride back to Hyde Park. Miraculously, our parking place is still open. Andrew parks the car, opens the car door for me, and even guides me to the sidewalk, through a mix of ice and salt and drifted snow. And it is then, we both see, forgotten in the snow bank, the blue duffel.

Andrew exclaims, "See? We never needed the emergency supplies!"

Which makes me laugh. And then Andrew laughs. We throw huge handfuls of snow at each other until we are cold and wet and we hurry inside to take a long, hot shower. Together.

Later that night, while I wash the pie plate, Andrew's arms encircle me, and he whispers, "The pie was great." And the magic of this moment might have lasted, except he then says, "Next time you make a mincemeat pie, would you put walnuts in it? My mom always puts walnuts in her mincemeat pies."

CHAPTER THIRTY-TWO

MORE THAN A MEETING OF MINDS

Wednesday, January 15, 1969

I avoid all possibilities of running into Professor Cush.

Then he is invited to speak at the Student Wives' Group in January. A meeting I never miss. Even Andrew cares. He tells me to wear something very special. And so I wear my perfect red dress, but at the lecture I leave on my old, puffy, totally unflattering, down coat. And I sit in the back row.

Professor Cush charms the group. He gives a short 'fireside' lecture, comparing the use of 'road-trip imagery' in Kerouac, Hemingway, and Bellow. He pays equal attention to every woman in the group. He spots me in the back row. He winks.

He works the group like the smoothest politician. Somehow I am not surprised, when in front of all the other wives; he offers me a ride home. What's worse, is that I look directly at Cheryl, who has given me a ride over and she smiles a huge smile and nods her head to say "Go!" Her look (and not just Cheryl's) is full of envy.

I feel as if I have no option but to accept.

Outside, crisp snow whirls around us. The cold air catches my breath. Professor Cush's hand hovers near my elbow as I deliberately crack the ice puddles along the edge of the sidewalk. He joins in the fun. Once I slip and he catches me and we laugh as our bodies bump. By the time I'm tucked into the front seat of his Beetle, I am chatty and he is not.

He turns up the heater and by the time we arrive at Fifty-Third Street the car still isn't warm. Maybe he didn't really turn on the heater? Maybe he's going to try to hug me. I'm all questions and nerves. Cush slips the car into the Adler Arms load-zone. He keeps the car running as I reach for my purse and I check for my keys.

"That was a pleasant evening," Professor Cush says. "Andrew's a very lucky young man."

"Thanks for the ride."

"It's true."

I look at my watch as if I have some other place to be. Dark inside the car, I can't see a thing.

Professor Cush leans back in the corner, his body stretched out, "Very lucky." His fingers touch my shoulder.

I don't move. I dare not move. Or maybe I choose not to move. I'm nervous and I'm turned on. Heat between my legs, under my arms, over my face (and it's not the car!) My mouth is dry. It's exactly how I felt the first time Andrew and I made out in the back seat of his car. The only difference is that Andrew's hands had been all over me. Professor Cush's eyes are doing what Andrew's hands had done.

"I'd better go in."

"I'd like to go in."

Professor Cush's sentence sits salaciously in the space between us.

I sit up straight, re-position my purse in my lap, pull my coat tight around me and pretend he hasn't said what he has just said.

I block the idea of what he means by "in," although I know exactly what he means. I open the car door and call goodnight and call thank you and run as fast as I can up the slippery sidewalk to the door of the apartment, my key ready because I don't want to look back or appear hesitant, and all I want is to be not interesting or attractive to anyone but Andrew. Forever and ever.

The apartment is empty.

Scratchy writing covers a note stuck under the salt shaker.

"Have an unexpected study session. I'll be late."

It dawns on me he won't be home forever and I'm not to wait up for him. The note feels like a talisman for how far apart we've grown; each of us singular and separate, more often than I like, notes connect our worlds. The note's torn edge, the dashed sentence, mirrors our marriage. Separate. Separated.

Two days later, Andrew at another study session, Professor Cush calls to ask me to join him at Tender's Restaurant and Bar, for a quick glass of wine. I've been alone all evening. I accept. A week later Evian asks me to share an hour with him at the Chicago Art Institute followed by a quick sandwich at Hanson's on Fifty-First (this time Andrew is at his writing group). The next invite is not unexpected: Evian asks me to come up to his apartment to see his new Hesse first edition. As we ride the elevator and he reaches for my hand and he leads me into his apartment, past his study, past his bathroom with the huge shower, to his bedroom and the ruby and rust colored coverlet, already pulled back, and he says, "I want to see your white body on my black sheets."

Later when I run the water until steam makes the bathroom fuzzy and indistinct, I don't think of Andrew. I don't consider for a minute vows and faithfulness. I am satiated and pleased with how I feel. Desired and special.

"Sarah, all glistening and clean," Evian Cush stretches out his hand and I crawl back into his bed. He touches me in ways and places I never knew people touched each other. Then he leads me back to the shower. I wash his back. He turns me against him and makes me come standing there in the heat of the spray. It seems so natural. I believe him when he says he's making me a better lover, a better wife, and Andrew will be grateful even if he never knows and he certainly doesn't need to know. Now does he? And I agree.

The next week, when Andrew's at his writing group, I hurry to Evian's apartment where we tangle our bodies on the black silk sheets. After which I hurry home to make a late night dinner for Andrew. Andrew never asks about where I've been and I never say and he is pleased at how much better a lover I've become.

Except, I now have unsettling dreams. I dream of falling and I dream of being lost and I dream of forgetting names and who I am and who the person in the dream is and I fear there will be the moment I will call out in my dream and I will wake wondering if I have said *Evian* out loud.

Andrew doesn't seem to notice anything different and I pretend that nothing is different and I try to not remember my dreams.

Our lives get busier and busier. Andrew starts coming home later and later and all the excitement of not being faithful doesn't seem all that exciting. Probably six times, maybe eight I spent in Professor Cush's bed and then I notice the little role of fat at his middle and how shrunken his penis is when we finish making love—little and nubby and not wonderfully long and lanky like Andrew's.

And then comes the day Evian suggests Andrew might want to join us.

I go home knowing I never want to see Professor Cush again.

I miss Andrew and I miss being faithful.

And then comes the day I come home and find a note from Andrew telling me to meet him at Kafka's for a reading.

And I'm aware that I'm about to meet Magda.

Andrew mentions Magda often. Magda's writing is magic. Magda makes the whole class laugh. Magda challenges Professor Cush. Magda is a kind of muse. *A kind of muse?* He told me how Magda suggested he change his epic poem from the title, *Lace* to *Lace and Linguini.* My mind bubbles with the word "muse." As I walk out into the cold, brittle wind of Lake Michigan and my steps say the word, over and over: *Muse. Muse. Muse.*

Muse? I thought I was Andrew's muse.

CHAPTER THIRTY-THREE

THE LITTLE TALK

These recordings get harder and harder and I wonder if they are as hard for you to listen to as they are for me to tell. I've decided life is short and it is in the telling I will be able to leave this world in peace. I thank you for being my audience. My confidant.

Friday, February 27, 1931

I was in the middle of packing. The children were still at school, I heard a knock on the back door. I rinsed my glass, placed it in the rack, and went to see who might be dropping by in the middle of the afternoon. It was Luke. On the back porch. His hands stuffed deep in his overall pockets.

"We need to talk," he said.

My heart began to pound. I wiped my hands on my apron and hesitantly pushed open the screen door. I could not trust myself to speak. I could not trust myself to look at him, fearful for what I wanted, fearful for what I might not get. I stepped back as he walked into the kitchen. I stoked the fire and placed the kettle on the range.

Luke sat at the round oak table. He folded his hands and placed them on the table. My eyes were drawn to his hands. He still wore his wedding ring. Later, after he left, I thought maybe it hadn't been his ring. Maybe I had wished too hard for a sign. Maybe it was only a white line on his tanned hand.

I took a deep breath and asked, "Why did you bother to come here. Now?"

"Like I said, we need to talk. Figure things out."

I couldn't stand not to be busy. I ground coffee beans in the grinder. I waited for the water to boil on the Monarch. I threw in the grounds. And with my back to Luke, I waited for what he would say next.

I knew by the tone of his irritated voice, "Please. Sit down. Talk to me," that what I had hoped would happen was not going to happen.

Luke's voice grew impatient and I did not join him at the oak table.

"STOP RATTLING THOSE POTS AND PANS AND TALK TO ME! Look at me when I'm talking to you. I know how you feel. This is hard on both of us. So pour the coffee and come sit down and talk to me. GOD DAMN IT, WOMAN! THAT'S MY FAVORITE CUP! I CAN'T BELIEVE IT. YOU JUST BROKE MY GOD DAMN FAVORITE CUP! Go ahead. Clean it up and then we can have this little talk. Okay? Better. Oh, you missed a piece of the handle. There, under the range. Now, don't give me that look. What I'm trying to tell you is, I know you've received the papers. But it is important you know how I feel. I care. You know I care. I want to do right by the kids. By you.

That's one of our problems, you've made up your mind about something and we haven't even begun the conversation. SIT DOWN, FOR GOD'S SAKE, WOMAN, YOU'RE UP, YOU'RE DOWN. UP. DOWN. UP. DOWN. That's one of the problems. You're always busy. You're always thinking about Gabe or the twins. Never about us. What about me? It was like I didn't exist. I worked all day. I'm out in the fields. Alone. Ten, fourteen hours. I come in from working my butt off and not even a kiss hello. I felt alone, for God's sake. HEY, WATCH THAT, YOU ALMOST SLOPPED COFFEE DOWN MY FRONT. Let it be. Let's deal with what's important here. You sit down and we'll talk. Just the two of us. Get things straightened out.

Now, that's better.

Things change. Things happen. It's nobody's fault. PLEASE! PLEASE SIT DOWN. Okay, so stand there if you want to. I know you've been working all day, so I thought you just might like to sit down.

Good coffee. You've always made the best coffee.

Millie, Millie, please don't turn away from me. These changes don't change how I feel about the kids. And you. It's just changed things. Somehow, I got caught. It wasn't supposed to happen this way. DON'T TURN YOUR BACK ON ME WHEN I'M TALKING TO YOU. Oh, Millie, please, please don't cry. I can't stand it when you cry. Don't do this to me.

You think I planned this? You think I wanted things to turn out this way? I was just being helpful. She needed an extra set of hands. I know you won't believe this, but that woman seduced me. So, I made one mistake. One little mistake. And now, I've got to make it good. I haven't got a choice. Believe me.

When you settle down, I'll tell you the whole story. Unless you don't want to know the whole story. But some day the kids are going to ask what happened to their dad, and if I'm not around to tell them, you've got to tell them the truth. You've got to tell them I was there for them. I don't want them to think I ran out and didn't mean to take care of them. That's why this money is all yours. It should get you through the spring, into fall. I'll set the crops soon, next week, if you want. You can count on me.

OKAY! Okay. I'll send someone over. But, no matter, you'll have food until summer. Just listen a minute. Here's what I want you to do: get through the spring, into summer, the kids out of school, then think maybe about getting to a bigger town. Pullman, maybe. Or Spokane. It would be good for the kids. Good for you. Get you away from this place. You're a good cook. A damned good cook. There's lots of big houses in those towns need good cooks. LET ME FINISH, JUST LET ME FINISH, FOR ONE GOD DAMNED MINUTE! *You can get yourself settled and we can get a goodly sum for this land and in fact, her father is ready, next fall, maybe, pretty soon, to buy this place. There will be enough money for the both of us.*

I mean we'll have enough money for me and enough money for you. And the kids. All of you. Taken care of. You just have to say the word. When you're ready. No rush. Nobody's in a rush.

Think of it this way. It's about the kids. I didn't want to have to tell you this, but if her father comes after me, there won't be any father for anybody's kids. So, I'm begging you. I need your help.

DON'T SCOWL LIKE THAT! *You're acting like this was all my fault. It isn't all my fault. Think of us. You've been turning your back to me every night since I don't know when. Remember, you made a vow. A vow you broke. If a man has to look elsewhere, then maybe his wife should take stock. Take a look at her duties.*

Millie! What's come over you? You're not the woman I married! NOW WAIT, JUST ONE GOD DAMNED MINUTE! OKAY, *okay, okay, just simmer down.* ALL RIGHT! I'M LEAVING! *I'm going. Just hold-on a minute. Just hold-on. Think about the children. They need a father. Millie, please. Yes, I'm going. I'm out the door. Just put the god damned gun down!* I'M GONE. RIGHT NOW. DON'T DO ANYTHING YOU'LL REGRET. THINK OF THE CHILDREN!"

The door slammed. I sank to the floor, the gun across my lap, a sad numbness filled my body. He was right. I was not the woman he married.

CHAPTER THIRTY-FOUR

THE READING AT KAFKA'S

Friday, May 2, 1969

Half-moon stains bloom under my arms. My saffron colored silk blouse bleeds red and my palms ooze sweat—a crazy early summer day—Chicago ninety/ninety kind of day—ninety degrees, ninety percent humidity. The brass handle of the solid oak door is slick in my hand. As I enter Kafka's Bar and Grill, I stand tall and pretend to balance a tome on top of my head. I pretend I am the regal Jackie Kennedy.

But, I am filled with dread. I think this is the night I will know if Andrew and Magda are an item. My stomach clinches. An item. What a strange sentence. I wonder if anyone has ever thought of me and Professor Cush as an item. I doubt it. Who would know?

Inside Kafka's, frigid air swallows me. Goose bumps dance up my arms, behind my ears, between my breasts. The air is full of cigarette smoke, clamor, and loud voices.

Three older guys, meat-packers by the label on their hats, fill one end of the bar. In one corner a twosome hunches over a board, moving black and white stones. A chunky barmaid grips a gather of eight beer-mugs as she maneuvers between round oak tables. Clustered in the other corner, I see the writing group. They are a mix of tie-dyed shirts, head bands, jean jackets, peace symbols, long hair. And Andrew? Andrew is nowhere.

I walk toward the group. Composed. Serene. Tall. Slender. I walk in step with Carly Simon's husky alto: *You...just...call...out my name...and I know...wherever I am...I'll come running...to see you again.* Andrew's favorite song.

"Sar-AH!" The Cary Grant voice of Professor Cush calls and with arms outstretched he maneuvers around the tables to greet me. Today he wears wide-ribbed corduroy pants, a lavender silk shirt, and a white scarf around his neck. Gold glints off his snake ring. He grasps my elbows. His lips brush my cheek and he smells of Clorets.

"I've missed you," he whispers. "Two weeks is too long."

I cinch my shawl tight. His hands let go. Buddy Holly hiccups on the juke-box. Professor Cush's fingertips press my arm and I step aside to avoid his grasp.

I squeeze between two chairs, each filled with a burly man. One guy leans forward to make room. His shirt pulls out of his jeans. His rounded haunches glow white. Professor Cush squeezes my elbow as if we share a saucy joke.

Behind the writing group, mirrored walls reflect into infinity a Bruegel-like scene. There sits a woman with a Medusa head of hair—twisted corn stocks sprouting from a dark field. She reaches for Professor Cush. She pats the chair next to her. Magda. Without introduction, I know this is Magda.

Magda stands and perhaps it's the angle of her body, or the cut of her peasant blouse, or how insecure I'm feeling, but her abundant breasts appear to grow. Putty-like flesh protrudes. "You must be Andrew's wife," she says. "I've forgotten your name."

Before I can say "Sarah," Magda declares turning to face the table of students, "I'm Magda and this …" as if all she sees, she owns, "…is the writing group!" Her glass bracelets clank down her arm and the group cheers.

Thoughts ricochet through my brain:

She's loud.

She's huge.

I'm a school-teacher, in a shawl.

Her boots reach her knees.

Her eyes are green marbles.

I'm Andrew's wife.

She can't have him.

Magda taps fork-tines on a beer mug and announces, "Everyone, Andrew's wife!"

"Better half!" a ponytailed guy hollers.

"The back-up!" another voice adds.

"The editor!" a third voice chimes.

"Now, children," Professor Cush coos, his hand on my shoulder. "Be good to our guest."

Another ponytailed guy points and exclaims, "Here comes the man!"

Andrew works his way toward the group. His black rimmed glasses ride on his head in a mass of black curls. He's wearing the baby blue shirt I ironed this morning. It makes his eyes brilliant. His shirt is open at the neck, sleeves rolled. Over breakfast, when I suggested he might want to shave for tonight's performance, he said the scruffy look was in. Subject closed.

He stands by my side, and with a silly grin announces, "Sarah, my wife!" then he points to each person and calls out names. "Albion," "Hector," "Jocelyn." The rest of the names are lost in the noise of the bar. When Andrew comes full circle, Magda says, "Yes, we've met! And if you'll just let me steal your husband for a few minutes, we need to set the stage." Before I can say anything, Andrew has followed Magda to the corner of the room where they begin to sort through wires, microphones, the speakers list.

Albion pats the empty chair next to him as an invitation for me to sit. His hair is permed in a mass of curls. He has hairs growing out of his ears. I scoot the chair forward and as I do that, I feel my nylon snag and I look down to see my white leg protrude from the black stocking. "You okay?" Albion asks. "Oh, nothing! Just nothing," I answer. Albion pushes a basket of peanuts toward me and as I try to think of something clever or brilliant to say, he turns away to talk to the guy next to him. I stare at his ear.

Andrew returns from the staging area, slumps into the chair next to mine. "What took you so long?"

I want to tell him about missing the bus, about buying the saffron silk blouse, about unpacking the shawl. "You won't believe…" I begin. His eyes flick from me and he stares at the front door of Kafka's. I look to see what he sees. Two skinny women with bee-hive hair-dos, tight skirts and spiked heels stand in silhouette.

"An-drew!" I hiss. He knows how I hate his skittery glance, the way he checks out other women when I'm talking to him.

"What? What? I'm listening," he grabs my hand. Kisses it. He smiles a silly, guilty smile and I notice his pupils are dilated. "Nice blouse!" he yells over the noise. "How was school? How are all those little chillun?"

I try to think he doesn't mean to irritate me. He's had a few. But instinctively I reach for a napkin to wipe away the kiss in the palm of my hand.

Magda is watching. I take a handful of peanuts. I smile at her. Under the table I rub clean the palm of my hand.

Written on Magda's face is a look of "caught-cha." As if I had just rejected Andrew's amorous gift.

"School was great!" I say with false cheer. Then change the subject. "I even brought a poem to read."

"Really?" Andrew's face shows disbelief and concern. He's worried I'll embarrass him.

"It's a great poem. One of my sixth graders wrote it. She asked me to read it to the group. And it is an open reading, right? You said so. So I'm going to read the poem."

Andrew says, "Well, sure," but everything in his voice and face says the opposite.

The waitress places a brown crockery bowl of warty, lime green pickles on the table. Albion's hand reaches the bowl before four other hands. He pulls out the largest pickle and holds it over his head. He pumps it in the air and calls, "Writers rule!" The class members cheer. Albion takes a bite and hands the dripping pickle to Andrew.

Before Andrew bites the pickle, he yells, "Writers rule!" and then the pickle goes to Magda's outstretched hand.

Everyone cheers each bite as the slowly diminishing pickle moves from hand to hand. Somewhere in the middle of the raucous pickle passing, I realize that Albion is sitting much too close. His leg presses against mine. I scoot away. His leg follows. Andrew throws his arm over the back of my chair and yells in my ear, "Asymptotic!"

I am totally confused. "What?"

"It's obvious!" He's uses his impatient voice, as sour as the pickle everyone but me has shared. "Watch. Each writer takes a bite! The point is not to take the last bite. We do this every time we meet! Amazing, huh?"

I attempt to look amazed.

The waitress brings another round of beers. Andrew and Albion simultaneously reach, mugs collide, and beer sloshes across the table. Magda grabs a handful of napkins and her long-nailed, be-ringed hand sweeps away the oozing beer. She leans over the table. Albion and Andrew watch transfixed. Her breasts loll about in her peasant blouse.

"Nice work," Andrew says and signals the waitress to remove the paper mess. Magda sinks back into her chair and sighs as if exhausted.

Albion places his hand on my arm. "So, you teach?" he asks.

"Yes, yes," I answer. "I do. I teach."

"I understand you're one fast typist," he says and his fingers play my arm.

"You for rent?" The question comes from Hector, on Albion's left. Hector wears a psychedelic tie-dyed shirt of orange and purple. He laughs at his own cleverness. He looks to see if I agree how clever he is. His eyes are magnified behind glasses with wire rims and he leans against Albion and Albion's knee pushes against my knee.

The noise and the heat and the cold and the beer and the closeness weigh on me. I feel dizzy and disconnected. Why am I here? Why are we here? What happened to our dream of the writer's life? What happened to quiet evenings, intelligent readings, thoughtful writing, deep discussions? I press my legs together. I tug my shawl tight. I try to take up the smallest amount of space.

"Ten minute warning!" announces Professor Cush from the stage. Magda jumps up to join him. Writers reach for their notebooks.

Albion uses the opportunity to ask, "Where do you teach?" His shoulder presses against mine. "Who do you teach?" He's so close it makes my eyes hurt. I reach for Andrew's hand. Andrew's gone. Back at the stage, he holds the microphone stand. Magda repeatedly takes the microphone in and out of the stand and she and Andrew laugh. Co-conspirators.

I try to make my voice chipper and I make my eyes large and I say in my brightest voice, as if I could push Albion away with my cheerfulness, "I teach kindergarten! Black children. In Woodlawn. Fifty-five kids in the morning. Fifty-five kids in the afternoon. After school I teach remedial math."

"Wow," Albion says with awe. Magda and Andrew have returned and Albion yells over the din, "Magda, did you know what? Sarah teaches in the ghetto! One hundred and ten little black kids."

"Interesting!" she says and sits down next to me. She smells of patchouli–the smell of old socks and sex. She has thick, un-plucked eyebrows.

"Isn't the word, 'African-American'?" she asks enunciating each syllable. Not waiting for an answer, Magda reaches across me to press one bright orange fingernail against Albion's arm. "Albion, honey, you go to BPP breakfast meetings. Does Hampton say 'Black?' Ever?" Magda's voice is all lemon-sour. Snide.

Around the two tables, all eyes are on Magda.

I answer the question slowly, "Where I teach, we say 'black'."

"Then. . ." Magda lifts her glass. She looks at Andrew, at Albion, at Professor Cush, and then she turns to me and says, "Well, then, it must be 'black'!"

Andrew pushes his beer mug back and forth in the slip of spilled beer. He speaks as if he's talking to the table top, "Good. I'm glad that's settled." He opens his notebook and turns pages.

"It was just in *Newsweek*," Magda says.

Albion asks, "What was just in *Newsweek?*"

"If you read anything but Proust, you'd know. An article about Negroes, dummy. The correct terminology *is*, 'African-American'."

"You don't say." Albion's words drop like river rocks, one on top of the other. "I was just getting used to 'black'."

"Who cares?" asks Hector, pushing his glasses back up his nose as if to see the argument more clearly.

Andrew moans, "You're right. No one cares. Let's read."

My hands feel like ice around the cold beer. At lunch today teachers were discussing Ebonics. Everyone was excited about the idea of a black language, legitimate ghettoes. They seemed to argue their point for my benefit. For the white teacher. The outsider. The audience.

"Sarah, it's noble that someone like you helps those poor little kids," Magda says.

"Poor?" I ask.

"Poor. You teach in Black Stone Ranger territory, don't you?" Magda asks.

"We're ready to start," Professor Cush calls and claps his hands.

I ignore Professor Cush and say with a brittle edge to my voice, "I spent today with a hundred and ten five-year-olds and I can tell you they skipped and danced and sang and had a great time! Poor little things, they're not."

A pocket of silence surrounds the table.

Professor Cush leans over the table and enunciates each word precisely, "I think Sarah means—Sarah, interrupt me if I'm wrong—I think what she said is what we say about the essence of writing: death and resurrection; waking and sleeping; love and hate. A mix. We know the ghetto is horrid—drugs, shootings, poverty, but horrid exists side by side with happiness. Right Sarah?"

Everyone nods. Everyone wants this to end. Except me. I look from one set of eyes to the next as if I could gather this group for their own special story-time.

And then I begin my lecture, "Let me tell you about Jonathan. Today Jonathan wore new red boots. It wasn't raining. The boots were too big. He wore them into the classroom, making big, whapping sounds. He skipped in those boots. He about knocked himself over in those boots. Then he sweated the rest of the morning in those boots. Today was a day of pure joy for Jonathan. Nothing about today made Jonathan a poor-little-thing."

I take a drink of beer. I close my eyes and feel the cold deep in my chest.

"Nice, Sarah, very nice." Professor Cush says. "Great segue." He turns to point to the student sitting furthest away. "Hector, you're on."

I don't hear Hector and I don't hear the two readings after Hector. I think about Jonathan's new boots. I think about Andrew and I think about marriage. Is our marriage like those boots? New. Pure pleasure. Not the only boots you wear? Boots that get sweaty and grow old and worn out? Boots too big. You want to wear a different pair of boots?

Slowly, I return to the group.

Albion reads three pages about his mother and about how she'd like him to have real, natural hair. A copper-haired guy reads a poem about the University of Chicago, like Atlantis, lost. Two girls in black sweaters and black pants and black berets, read an 'echo-essay' about the wasteland of Los Angeles. Magda reads a tone-poem, "Love and War," full of moans.

Andrew reads a stream-of-consciousness, one page essay, on sleep.

"Anyone else?" Professor Cush asks at the microphone. "Have we missed anyone?"

I hold my poem in the air.

"Well, isn't this nice," Evian says.

As I approach the microphone, Professor Cush makes a slight bow, and steps back.

"This is a poem by one of my sixth-grade after-schoolers. She asked me to read her poem. She's curious to know what you think."

I read:

Black be beautiful.
Black be me.
Black ain't white, for sure.
White ain't hardly white.
I'd rather be black.
I know I be beautiful.
I know I be me.

Light splatter of clapping hands. No one says much of anything. I walk back to my chair. Andrew doesn't look at me. Professor Cush leans into the microphone, "Great!"

I fold the poem in half and then in half again, until it is a tiny square. I slip it into the side pocket of my purse.

Albion sits stretched out in his chair, his beer mug balances on his belly. He turns his head and smiles at me. "Guess 'black' is back."

By ten thirty the number of people in the bar has doubled. Magda holds court between Andrew and Professor Cush, discoursing on why she thinks Mercia Eliade is an anti-Semite. I catch Andrew's eye and nod in the direction of the front door. Andrew stands. I think we are leaving, but Andrew points toward the restroom.

I eat more peanuts. Bob Dylan's voice grinds on about his big brass bed. My throat hurts from the smoke. Albion argues with Hector about whether they should burn their draft cards or flee to Canada. Magda stands, stretches, and heads down the hall. Professor Cush slips into Andrew's chair.

"I miss you. I've missed you," he says, running the tip of his tongue over his lower lip.

"We've been busy."

I wish he would disappear. Did he expect me to yell over the noise of the crowd that the last few months have caused nothing but confusion? Tell him I couldn't keep my stories straight—where I was, what I was doing? Tell him Andrew didn't seem to care or notice? Tell him that all I wanted was hours and hours of sleep? Tell him, that if he asked me the definition of love or marriage or faithfulness, I wouldn't have an answer?

"The first strawberries are in the garden. Ripe. Luscious."

"How nice."

"Come over tomorrow," he says, his eyes never shying from mine.

"I work and tomorrow night I have a Student Wives' meeting."

"Ah, the wonderful wives' meeting! So, come by between your demanding appointments." He leans closer. "Come by on your way home. Come for tea. You can tell me about your class. Your teaching. Your passion. I love to listen to passionate teachers."

A sharp spike of pain whirls behind my right eye. "Evian, if you'll excuse me, I need to make a quick run to the bathroom." I stand. I've had more beer than I realize. I push back my chair, squeeze past the tables. At the bar I run into Hector.

"Seen Andrew?" I ask.

"Check the men's room."

As I walk down the hall, I run my fingertips against the rough boards that cover the wall. Slivers catch and I pull my hand away. As I near the restrooms, two guys come out of the men's room.

"Oh, gag," one says. The other guy grabs his nose.

Before the door closes I look in to see an open stall door. Inside Andrew kneels over a toilet. Magda stands beside him. She pats his back. She hands him a wad of toilet paper and with her free hand she flushes the toilet. Threads of vomit string from Andrew's mouth. Magda's voice mews, "Oh, sweetie, how many times have I told you, you can't drink this much."

I turn. I stride down the hall. I enter the smoke filled bar. Professor Cush half-stands and I ignore his gesture of 'wait.' I push open the door. I step out of the air-conditioned cold. The steamy night enfolds me, as if the air weeps.

CHAPTER THIRTY-FIVE

GOING TO MEDICAL LAKE

Thank you for continuing to listen to my tapes. Some days are fuzzier than others. This part of my story begins in the spring of 1931. March.

The silence grew. I became frantic. First Gabe at least would say "good morning" or "chickens are fed." Then two or three days passed and he'd not even say those words. Then there was a whole week when he said absolutely nothing, I became fearful. Then Gabe quit eating. As far as I could tell, he hadn't eaten for four days. Dr. Swanzy suggested that we ride out the problem. Gabe was an adolescent. He would eat when he was hungry.

I grew more concerned. Three days later I demanded Doctor Swanzy do something. While I sat in his office, Dr. Swanzy called the facility at Medical Lake. He made notes and I listened to his side of the phone conversation: "Yes, that appears to be the case. It is a crucial time. Yes, yes I'll tell his mother. I'm sure she will be glad to do that. Soon. I'll suggest she bring the patient as soon as possible. I understand you have a psychiatrist on duty. Okay, I'll confirm her visit as soon as I've spoken to her."

Dr. Swanzy leaned back in his chair, his hands locked over his protruding stomach. "They want you to bring Gabe over for a complete evaluation. You can take the Great Northern. Less than two hours. A little adventure for Gabe. Who knows, just going over might snap him out of it."

I gave Oscar and Sally a list of chores and instructions to call Doctor Swanzy if there was an emergency. I promised them Gabe and I would be back late the evening of his appointment.

March 27, 1931

As the Great Northern pulled into the station, I clutched the forms from Doctor

Swanzy. I was glad to get away from the town. I avoided Rita Roosted who had been waiting at the station when we left—there to pick up her Avon supplies. I handed the conductor my tickets and waited for Gabe to pull himself up the stairs and haltingly enter the passenger car. Gabe slumped in a seat and immediately fell into a deep sleep that lasted the entire trip to Medical Lake.

A hospital car waited at the station to drive the five miles to the low slung buildings at the north end of the lake.

The stairs to the hospital were wide, welcoming. The two-story brick structure had a scholarly look to it. Ivy. Large wooden doors. Brass hinges. I tucked Gabe's hand into the crook of my arm. Whether it was anxiety or fear or the analgesic Dr. Swanzy had prescribed, Gabe's body tensed.

In a soft voice, I told Gabe, "They are here to help you. Don't worry. We're going to find out exactly what will make you feel better." I held his arm and continued to say, "Hush, hush" as we approached the In-Patient Registration desk. We found seats in cracked leather chairs. I tried to ignore the acrid smell of ammonia.

And then words came. In a low voice I heard Gabe's string of words: ***walls the color of cat vomit if i push the chair against the wall if i touch my head against the wall if i lock my knees if i keep my legs straight if i keep my teeth together if i hold my breath if i don't move if if***

He braced his back against the slats of the wooden chair. He looked around the room as if to make sure no one was looking. He touched his head against the wall. He locked his knees. I patted Gabe's arm and cooed, "Relax sweetheart, relax. It won't be long. This is for you. Everyone is here to help you."

Chairs scraped. Magazine pages ruffled. Attendants rushed by in conversation. Nurses pushed carts of pills and white towels. And Gabe began again, his whispered string of words: ***watch woman in black she divides i'll be next I slit my eyes there are ten, no five, no ten sick sick one wipes his head two stares three has a notebook opens and closes opens and closes pages slap like thunder his bones bump like bombs four chatters and words run together she says dead children dead children dead children five plays his chin like a piano his fingers scrape his whiskers loud awful***

"Soon, sweetheart, soon. Just hold on. They'll examine you and tell us why those voices don't stop. This is all for the best. Everyone thinks this is all for the best. Just a few more minutes, my sweet, sweet angel."

A woman in a white coat approached us. She bent toward me and said in a loud whisper, "You must be Mrs. Lane. I see you have your paperwork ready. The doctor is waiting. I'll take your son. I imagine it won't be more than an hour."

"I thought I might stay with him. I'm afraid he won't do well if I'm not with him."

"He's going to be just fine, just fine. Come along, young man."

With a firm grip the nurse helped Gabe to stand and I watched as they walked down the green hall to a locked door. I heard the key turn and the door slapped into place.

An hour later a nurse asked me to join her. I followed her down the hall, heard the door slam behind me. The nurse ushered me into a room lined with books, papers in piles, a disheveled desk. And a doctor.

"Good afternoon, Mrs. Lane," the doctor said. "That will be all, Nurse Reim."

He wore a black three-piece suit. His skin was white. He held a folder in his hands, and tapped it against the edge of the desk as if straightened papers might mean a straightened life.

I did not understand the doctor's vocabulary. He used words I'd not heard before: pathological, cognitive behavior, electroconvulsive therapy, delusional disorder, depression. He said Gabe should stay for a couple of weeks, three, maybe four. I needed to sign some papers. They would take good care of him. I should make my goodbyes quick and assure my son that all is going to be fine. The doctor suggested that I be the one to ask for the patient's belt and shoe laces.

"Wait. Dr. Swanzy said I was to bring him here for an evaluation. No one said anything about leaving him."

"We made it quite clear to Dr. Swanzy that the evaluation would take a number of days. Your son's symptoms are severe enough to warrant his spending some time with us. I'm sorry if there was a misunderstanding, but I can guarantee you, our facility will be the best for his condition. This is not something you should treat lightly."

With that, the doctor led me down the hall past doors with small windows. He ushered me into a room where Gabe sat, hunched with his shoelaces in his hand. I embraced my son. Tears escaped me.

"Don't cry. I'll be okay."

"You see! He's speaking! He's not that ill, I think there has been a horrible misunderstanding," my voice pleaded and then an unspoken fear came out unbidden, "I don't know how we will be able to pay for this."

"Not to worry. We are a state institution. We have many guests who are not able to pay. I think Dr. Swanzy at least made that piece of information very clear. So now, if you are reassured, I do have other patients waiting. Gabe? Gabe, your mother has to leave now. Say goodbye."

I held him close. He seemed not to notice and he still whispered under his breath:
i didn't do anything wrong   I didn't. I didn't.

On the front porch of the hospital I folded the envelope that held a copy of the papers I had signed. I placed them deep inside my purse to hide the hospital name. I did not want anyone to see the letterhead: Eastern Washington Hospital for the Insane.

CHAPTER THIRTY-SIX

OUT OF HERE

Friday, May 23, 1969

Schools out. I'm free for the summer! I so wanted to celebrate with Andrew, alone. No such luck. We're to meet at Kafka's at six o'clock for the last reading of the quarter. In the school office, I call home, just in case I can catch him between his last class and Kafka's. I dial. No answer. Time to kill, I walk back through the halls, saying goodbyes to all the teacher friends I've made at Tesla. Jennie even offers to drive me home. I know that will take her totally out of her way so I hug her goodbye and I walk to the elevated. In Hyde Park I stop by Boo-tique and treat myself to a silk scarf. Cerise. Dresses me up! I'm ready to meet the Kafka crowd.

At Kafka's only regulars line the bar. I take a corner table. I have a beer. An hour later still no students. No Professor Cush. It's nice to nurse the beer, think of nothing.

Around five o'clock I look up to see Magda and Andrew coming in the front door. I don't have to see anymore. She clings to his arm. Laughs at something he says. She glows.

I know that glow.

I leave out the back door. I walk the six blocks. Determined. Angry. Alone. Finished. Was I rash? Was I stupid? I wait until eight o'clock and I call Kafka's to see if Andrew has left. He hasn't. The bartender says, "Hold on, I'll get him." I hang up.

At ten o'clock I call United Airlines.

At ten-thirty I call Aunt Winnie.

"Hi, this is Sarah, your niece Sarah. I know it's been a long time since we talked. I just wanted to tell you we are going to have to miss the Fourth of July party. I know we'll miss seeing you two. How am I? Well, I'm okay.

My voice? I've got a bit of a cold. Am I crying? Well…yes, I am crying. Well, things aren't going so good between Andrew and me. In fact I've made a stand-by flight for tomorrow. Nine o'clock. I'm going to Spokane. I'm not sure. Maybe for a short vacation. Well, maybe forever. No, no, don't say that. He doesn't mean to be a son-of-a-bitch. I'm to blame too, it's just, well, that's all I wanted you to know so you wouldn't worry about us."

I listen to her call Andrew a series of uncomplimentary names.

"Well, yes, I'd love a ride to the airport. But that's a long way for you to come. Oh, Aunt Winnie, I'm going to start to cry again. Yes, yes. If you could pick me up at eight o'clock that would be wonderful. Thank you so much. No, no, I won't do anything foolish. I'll see you in the morning."

At eleven o'clock I give up waiting for Andrew. The save-it-for-our-anniversary-bottle of champagne is now near empty. I haven't bothered with a jelly glass. I no longer have a jelly glass. All of the dishes, glasses, pots, pans, silverware, I have given to the neighbors across the hall. When Nancy, next door, asks with wide eyes, "For me?" I don't explain. I hand her the box, scoot another box with my foot, then turn and go back to our apartment before she can ask questions. Later I dump the Cuisinart and all its attachments in a box and leave it in front of the apartment on the other side of ours.

I make trip after trip to the garbage chute at the end of the hall. I push everything I can fit into the metal mouth: Cheerios, Saltines, Cocoa Puffs, a bag of sugar, a squeeze bottle of Brown Bear Honey, and the gourmet jar of blackberry jam. The next trip I dispose of a bottle of Heinz catsup, dead lettuce, three cinnamon rolls, a half quart of milk, four bottles of beer—Schlitz—his beer. Thud. Crash. Splat.

I grab a box of Andrew's *Playboys*, and every one of Saul Bellow's books (we never had met him, anyway). Into the garbage chute.

I don't think and I don't hesitate. I pull down the metal mouth of the garbage chute and let go of Andrew's typewriter, papers from every class, his ledger, his stories, and last of all, his satin covered baby book.

Photos and black corner tabs and pastel enclosure cards and blue ribbon ends and a curl of blond baby hair fly up and around the incinerator shaft as the book slaps the metal sides, bounces and thumps hollow thumping noises deep in the bowels of the apartment building until a final photo flies up, a baby hand reaches out towards someone who holds a camera some twenty years ago, probably Andrew's mother stepping back from her son's grasping hands, small pudgy hands that have grown into large men's hands wanting succor and hugs and security and safety, or some hidden, secret mother-thing that I cannot provide, and now Andrew hates our life and he will hate me even more when he realizes what a despicable thing I have done, throwing away the record of his first words, a curl of his baby hair, an imprint of his three inch foot—all those mementos given into my care when I had no need or desire to lug around Andrew's baby book, especially now that our life is over, done, finished, evaporated, stopped, ended, squelched, obliterated. It feels as if I have dumped two entire lives down that chute.

And by two o'clock in the morning, with no Andrew in sight, I have no more anger and I sit in the hall under the noise of the crackling incinerator chute and I wonder what happened to all those wedding plans and marriage vows and all the things we would do when Andrew became a famous writer and I would be by his side, his companion, his help-mate, his best-friend, and I know I have totally dumped my past and future life with Andrew.

I wonder as I think about our done-away-with life, what went wrong? Was I to be a cipher at Andrew's side with no identity other than the wife of the great writer? And where did that idea come from that I would be nothing and Andrew would be everything? Except, now he'd be everything without a baby book and I knew the burning of that baby book was just about as symbolic as anything could get because it wasn't just the stuff I'd pushed down the incinerator, it was all the stuff I'd pushed down inside myself that made me the paycheck and the housekeeper and the shirt ironer and the cook and somehow it wasn't enough. Andrew always saying what a great job I did, like always finding his socks three minutes before he is supposed to be out the door to his graduate seminar and he yells that if he doesn't find his socks, he'll be late and if he's late he'll get kicked out of grad school and if he gets kicked out of grad school he'll lose his draft status and if he loses his draft status he'll be drafted and if he's drafted he'll get sent to Vietnam and if he goes to Vietnam, he'll get killed and it will be my fault. So, I always find the socks, and I'm just the best little wifey and maybe that is what turns the page of our lives, not just his throwing-up at Kafka's where Magda, rounded, voluptuous Magda, held his head and cooed in his ear that she'd be right there, but, I need to admit what also changed was weeks, maybe months ago, when Andrew stopped calling me Sweetie, and started calling me 'wifey' which also began just about the time Andrew started coming home later and later, and didn't kiss me goodnight that last minute before sleep, and he didn't notice I had cut ten inches off my hair and he didn't mind that I went away on a teacher's retreat for a long weekend, the first time we'd ever been apart and he didn't seem to mind much of anything disappearing. Especially me.

I push my hands against the wall and slowly come upright to close the door of the incinerator chute and I walk back to the near-empty apartment. Except. I forgot the bottom drawer of the refrigerator. In a red plastic garbage pail I dump moldy onions, shriveled carrots, marble-hard radishes and two bruised potatoes.

As I bring the last potato to my nose, and smell its rough, earthy smell, I am suddenly overwhelmed with a childhood memory of a story Dad told me dozens of times—*The Potato Story*—a sweet-sad story.

I'd get Dad's snack of Corn Flakes, he'd throw a log in the fireplace, and we'd ignore Mom's reminder that it was bedtime. Dad held me with his chin on my head and he'd say, "Those were some potatoes." This is his wonderful story:

Early in the morning. Sun just up. I snuck from the bed I shared with your uncle Theodore and your uncle Edward. It was so early, your grandma hadn't stoked the kitchen range and Pop hadn't gathered the morning eggs. I pulled on long-johns, Levi's, and two sweaters. In a wool winter jacket I stuffed gloves and a wool scarf. Last came the potatoes. I placed ten potatoes in a pillow case. I pulled on lace-up boots and got my cap with ear flaps. I checked my back pocket to be sure I had the silver flask from Great-Grandad Theo. I slipped out the door, and I tried not to hear my mama crying. I'm sure Pop kept her tucked tight against his shoulder. We'd agreed that our previous night's goodbyes were all the goodbyes we could handle. I pulled the back-door shut and if I close my eyes I can still hear the screen door go whissh.

Always, here, I made the screen door sound.

Two blocks down Main, the railroad tracks crossed Union. I timed it just right. I could hear the distant rumble of the early morning Illinois Central. I held tight to the bindle and waited for the engine to slow for the switch. I turned my eyes away from the cinder and dust. I ran alongside the train. I threw my bindle ahead of me and like a miracle, a hand reached out and hoisted me into the dark, clattery car.

In the early morning light I could see ten, twelve companions. A strange family we became: sometimes a dozen men, sometimes three or four. Then, that late afternoon, just on the outskirts of a town whose name I never knew, someone yelled, "Camp!" And at that, each man slipped from the moving train and headed toward the remains of a camp fire on the outskirts of a town I never even knew the name of. That's where the potatoes came in handy and even though I was just a kid, those potatoes made me welcome. By evening there would be a bunch of us. We'd gather around the fire for warmth and for the large stew tin that nestled in the coals. I'd walk up to the stew and I'd drop a potato into the pot. I'd be welcomed.

Each night was a different family, a different campfire, another potato. Everyone'd gather round. Stories told. Songs sung. The whine of the harmonica would close out the night. And strange, but important, when the bottle went around, even at fourteen, I was included.

"Sing the song," I would whisper.

Dad didn't care he couldn't sing. His voice would vibrate around the words.

So long, it's been good to know yah;
So long, it's been good to know yah;
So long, it's been good to know yah.
This dusty old dust is a-gettin' me home,
And I got to be driftin' along.

Dad's voice would slow to a crawl and he'd sing the chorus again.

I would squeeze my eyes shut and imagine the clang of the train wheels, just like the Great Northern that squished our pennies. I'd imagine the smell of metal on metal. I'd see my dad approach the campfire. He'd swagger just a little. And after the stories and after the songs, before the men tucked into their blankets, my dad would offer his grandfather's flask. Each man would take a sip then curl into sleep, often with thanks for the kid who'd joined them.

"Enough for now."

Then Dad would ruffle my hair.

"That's it, my angel. Call when it's time to tuck you in."

I would move slowly, so as not to jar the story inside me. I'd hum the song and take the warmth of the fire and the warmth of my dad's arms to bed with me.

I take the last slug of champagne from the bottle. The champagne salves my soul. The sweet syrup of life. At the moment, it is the only sweetness in my life. Finding no more things to throw away, I wrap myself in the hideous orange and brown afghan Andrew's mother sent.

I dream of Dad and the churn of train wheels crossing the country. In the dream I magically smell spicy sagebrush, the snow-brittle smell of air off the Continental Divide, the sweet smell of Montana pines, the salty smell of the Pacific Ocean waves, and then a dream interrupted with the touch of that soft blue satin baby book. I wake and wipe away cold tears.

The apartment echoes emptiness. It is seven-thirty. I grab my single bag. Outside, the Chicago morning is silent and soft. I sit on one of the three boxes of books I packed last night. I move the FREE sign and flip through *Swan's Way*. I ignore *Ulysses*. Under the latest *Rabbit* book by Updike, I find *Titus Andronicus* and tuck it into my bag, a bit of mayhem to keep me company on the flight home.

My re-arranging of books ends with a horn honk and Aunt Winnie wiggles her fingers in greeting from the window of her dusty orange Vega. Aunt Winnie's hair is a mass of pink foam curlers wrapped in a yellow chiffon scarf. She jams the Vega into the loading zone, one wheel over the curb.

"Sarah! Hello! Hello! Get in girl! We'll make a proper get-away!"

I've never seen this side of Aunt Winnie. I have a sinking feeling that if I'd taken time to have been a better niece, I might have had a wonderful friend.

Inside, the car is toasty. My aunt wears a chenille bathrobe, and her ample figure still holds the smell of last night's sleep and this morning's Marlboros.

"You okay?" she asks, her eyes squinting with concern. As I turn to hide my red rimmed eyes, Aunt Winnie yells, "Car!" and jerks the wheel to skim by a sleek, silver BMW.

"Missed by a mile!" she exclaims and her red tennis shoe hits the pedal. We turn off Dearborn, head for the freeway, and hit the ramp to the Dan Ryan Expressway going sixty.

"O'Hare – here we come! Heading West! Sarah, it's a new beginning! I can't say I much liked that husband of yours anyway. But that Thanksgiving was one of the strangest I've ever had. Must have been the moon." She glances at me and waves her cigarette in greeting to a driver who passes with blinking lights. "He had no get-up-and-go, that husband of yours. Andrew? Right? Hard to remember the name of someone so faceless. I like men with umpf! Uncle Vic has umpf! You might not have seen it that day at our house, but let me tell you, before he gave up drinking he was something! He's a little more stable now, but sometimes I miss the old days. Now your father? That's another man with umpf! That Andrew of yours—as unlike your father as a man can get. First time around, women choose the opposite of their fathers. In my case, it worked the first time. So there you go! You're smart. I'm sure you'll get it right. But get yourself someone like your dad. He's a get-up-and-go kinda guy! Adventuresome! Exciting!"

"That's how you remember Dad? Adventuresome?" I ask, pleased at Aunt Winnie's take on my father.

"Of course! My god, girl, he left home at fourteen!"

"Yes, he told me he had to leave. Left because you were poor."

"We were poor. But that is not why he left! Sure, we didn't have money for a bus ticket. But hopping trains? He was always hopping trains. Started when he was ten! He'd ride a mile and then jump off and head back home. Practicing, he said. He was so full of it! By the time he was fourteen, there was no keeping him at home! I was there that morning. Saw him slip away. I grabbed an overcoat and sat with him along the tracks until the train came. He was off for the greatest adventure of his life!"

"Do you remember about the potatoes?" I ask.

"What about the potatoes?" she answers and flips her cigarette out the window.

"The ten potatoes he took for each night to help make the hobo stew?"

"Given the exuberance of your father, the potatoes were probably donated the first night. Who knows? Only took him four days to get to big brother Al's."

"He went to Uncle Al's? Didn't he herd sheep? Live in the mountains?"

"Yes, but that was summers later. Your dad was adventuresome but he came from a family of planners. You've seen Grandma and Grandpa. They're list makers. Your dad had to send a telegram back home the minute he got to Spokane. He had to finish high school. He lived with your Uncle Al and your Aunt Clarisse. He had a plan to follow, a plan the whole family developed. My goodness, girl, he didn't go off half-cocked."

I grow silent. In the distance, planes slide into O'Hare. I open the window, close my eyes and let the morning air tangle my hair. What was the truth about Dad? And the potato story? I had pictured Dad fighting all odds. It was near impossible for me to believe it was all planned.

"So tell me your plan?"

"A plan? I don't have a plan. I haven't even called my parents to tell them I'm coming home. I didn't call because I knew exactly what Mom and Dad would say, 'Stick it out, give Andrew another chance, talk it through.'"

I look over to see how Aunt Winnie is reacting. She waits for me to continue.

"I need a break. I haven't signed my teaching contract, but I have it with me should I decide to come back." I pat my purse to let her know I hadn't completely given up everything.

We pull into the United Passenger Drop-off. As we stand there, Aunt Winnie gives me a big hug, "You're smart. You'll figure it out. One step at a time. Now scoot."

Inside O'Hare, I find a pay phone and use the quarters I took from Andrew's change jar.

Mom answers the phone.

"I'm coming home," I say. "Flight 486. I'll be there at 1:50."

Mom is silent for just a second and then she says, "We'll meet you at the curb. Where we always meet you."

And then because my family only uses long distance calls for death and emergencies, she quickly ticks off questions to which all of my answers are "yes."

"You have enough money? You have a good book?"

She doesn't ask about Andrew. She must know.

I whisper, "I'm not sure what I'm doing."

"You're coming home…"

"I have all of Grandma Millie's tapes…"

The conversation ends. I'm out of quarters.

Flying over Chicago, headed west, I think about Dad's story. It was a sad, heavy, leaving story. The story gave me strength even though I had just learned he left with joy and a destination and strict orders from his parents. All this time I thought it was dark drama. Instead, it was a healthy amount of fourteen-year-old adrenaline. All those years, I imagined Dad traveling for days and days. I imagined him traveling for years.

Wrong. It was four days. A four-day adventure.

CHAPTER THIRTY-SEVEN

GABE'S JOURNAL

Saturday, May 24, 1969

On the airplane, with no one sitting next to me, I read a journal Grandma Millie sent with her last tapes. She said I had to promise to not share it with anyone. It's from the time Gabe spent at Medical Lake. What's strange is that his insanity soothes me. Like there are lives worse than mine.

June 1931

Nurse Melissa Ann. Walks with a waddle. Carries a ring of keys. They clang and bang. SHE IS TOO LOUD. I can't cover my ears because my pants fall down. She opens a door with a key. We walk down a hall. She opens another door with a key. It is a small white room. White floors. White walls. White table.

I have just come from one of their stupid reviews. Three people in white jackets and ties under their jackets, and stethoscopes around their necks, so they make sure I know they are doctors and they are the ones that think they know what is wrong with me and they think I'm getting better because I'm eating their food but I know if I eat their food they will let me go home so I eat everything on my plate.

It smells like piss. When I swallow I can almost taste the Pine-sol and vinegar and scrubbed wet wood. The Sun Room chairs are soft and tufts poke out like mice coming out of their holes. When I can, I sit in a wooden chair. It holds me in place. I push the back of my head against the white wall. Cold. Stops the headaches. Keeps

words from escaping.

Mom visited. She keeps saying, "Relax. It won't be long."

Why do some people divide and others don't? I'll squint and count the inmates they like to call us patients no way There are five. No, ten. No, five. The notice states *ATTENTION PATIENTS. Pa*tients, not inmates. You are required to stay in the restricted area. Do not leave unaccompanied. Do not tear pages from the magazines. Please leave all checkers with the checker board. Do not disturb the plants.**

My mother's hand is dry.

Who are all these people? Person number one: A red bandana from an overall pocket wipes a forehead. Person number two: Eyes stare straight ahead, focus on something far away. Out the window. Past the Oak tree. Person number three: A notebook opens. Closes. Opens. The pen scratches. Like tractor wheels cutting into frozen ground. The page turns. Like thunder. Like a thousand crows cawing.

Across the room a patient-inmate writes with a pencil. The pencil scratches across the paper. WHAT IS ALL THIS NOISE? WHY ARE THEY DOING THIS? I'LL PUSH MY HEAD HARD AGAINST THE WOODEN WALL. **There. There. Better. I can see the words all gathered on the back of my lids. I will rebundle them. Sort them. They sparkle with white lights.** WHERE DID THOSE SPARKLES COME FROM? **I breathe and white sparks on the back of my lids dart in rows. Hissing sounds. I hate the noise. What else do I hate?**

They have given me a form to fill out. It is a Weekend Visitation Form.

I fill out the form.

I check all the boxes.

The visitation form is folded neatly in the journal. I read the questions and I read the answers. The answers seem normal, but the writing is strange: tiny, precise, controlled, crazy.

Why do you feel you are ready for this supervised visitation home?

I no longer feel ill. I don't think I've ever run a temperature. I eat well. I sleep well. I talk with other patients. I attend all craft

activities. I miss my mother and my brother and my sister.

Have you, since admission to Medical Lake ever been violent?

No. Once the nurse said I had pushed her. I didn't. And one time I gave a torn magazine to an attendant who said I had torn the magazine in half and then threw it at him. I didn't.
Signature: Gabriel Lane

REJECTED was stamped across the application.

CHAPTER THIRTY-EIGHT

NEW BEGINNINGS

Saturday, June 14, 1969

I'm in my own bed.

I'm feeling stronger. Every day I try to write in my journal.

I try to make meaning from every minute. If Andrew has given me nothing else, he has given me this love of writing. The journal is what I'm not ready to say to anyone else. Here is my first entry since coming home:

My flight landed in Spokane on time. I grabbed my carry-on and headed to the curb-side pickup. Dad's 1959 Buttercup Yellow Pontiac waited at the curb. For a car that had always been an embarrassment, I was amazed at my tears, so pleased to see it and him. But lately everything brings tears to my eyes. On the plane I constantly wiped away tears (thank goodness I had an empty seat next to me). I cried when the stewardess asked if I wanted another drink. I cried when she offered me earphones for free. Then when Tom Jones sang *I'll Never Fall In Love Again* and Frankie Valli sang *Can't Take My Eyes Off You*, when I read the article in the flight magazine about baby gorillas, I cried.

On the drive home, I exhaust every topic of conversation: the Chicago Cubs, the weather, Dad's arthritis, Mom's excitement at my unexpected visit. At home, Dad stops in the driveway and I see our old family cat, Muggins, limps away, matted and lumpy. Tears again. Mom comes out to the car, hugs me, and says with assurance, "Hang up your clothes. Take a little nap. I'll call you when dinner is ready."

Over dinner, I continue a chatty monologue. Mom and Dad's eyes meet—a signal for me to explain exactly why I'm home. Alone. Finally, I stand, slightly hunched, belly full, and say, "Thank you for the wonderful meal. I'm awfully tired, time change, and all. I need to go back to bed."

Had it not been Mom's hand silently slipping to Dad's wrist, I think he might have demanded, "What kind of a daughter travels without her husband?" Instead, Mom calls as I leave the table, "You have a nice nap, Sweetie."

The smell of my room brings more tears: lilacs and Vicks Vapo Rub. It feels as if I have been gone a hundred years. The room is smaller than I remember. The cabbage roses on the wallpaper are bigger than I remember. I look at myself in the dressing table mirror, and see Mom at the bedroom door.

I almost plead with Mom, "Would you mind if I go to bed early?"

It isn't that the flight was so long—it wasn't. But all of a sudden I feel as if I might melt. My eyes are hot and heavy. I desperately want to sleep. And not think.

"Then we'll talk tomorrow?" Mom asks.

"Sure."

"Okay, Sweetie. You're sure you don't want some mincemeat pie for dessert?"

"No, Mom."

"Ice cream? Chocolate syrup?"

More tears. "No, Mom."

"Okay," Mom gives me a big hug.

I clinch my jaws to stop the tears. After her, I close the door slowly with both hands.

From my cosmetic travel bag I remove tiny bottles of hand lotion, moisturizer, shampoo, a lipstick, a tube of foundation. I place them in the left-hand drawer of the night stand. As I reach inside the bag for my toothpaste and toothbrush, my fingers feel slick plastic. I know immediately what I'd found. I hold the baggy with its singular occupant: a slender joint. It is a joint I had thought I would share with Andrew, but I could never figure out how to tell him where it came from—a gift from Professor Cush.

From the front room I hear the television. Dad softly snores. I look out the window to see Mom in her garden, pulling weeds. In the dresser drawer, under forgotten keys and rubber bands, I find a book of matches. I check the door to be sure it is closed tight. I sit down at the dresser and watch in the mirror as I light the joint. My reflection is something I never expected to see: myself, at home, smoking dope. It brings back the day I received the joint as a gift. The one and only day I smoked grass.

April tenth, while Andrew attended a writer's retreat, I spent a Saturday afternoon with Evian Cush. Naked, sitting in the sunlight streaming in the six-foot-tall windows in the living room, sitting cross-legged on a down comforter, across from each other, Evian said, "You need a small taste of life's other joys. In the next ten minutes I'll open a whole new world for you!"

From inside his glass-topped coffee table he removed a dragon-carved rosewood box. Carefully he pulled apart small squares of paper. From an ornate brass container he shook out assorted leaves, separating stems and seeds. He placed the marijuana in the crease of a paper and then deftly wrapped the tissue sides up and around the grass. With the tip of his tongue he licked the edge, sealed the paper, twisted the ends, and placed it in the palm of his hand and offered it to me.

He flipped on his Bic lighter. I inhaled. I coughed. I choked.

"No, my sweet. Like this." Evian demonstrated—held his head back, held his breath and instructed, "Hold it as long as you can."

My turn came a dozen times. My mouth grew dry. My eyelids felt heavy. My eyebrows grew heavy. My eyelashes weighed on my lids. I giggled at the pleasure of sunny skies that would never end. I studied the small tender joint. I tapped the ash into the translucent yellow bowl with the cobalt blue rim. I passed the joint as if I were handing my mother the Blue Willow creamer, Emily Post correct, with the handle ready for the recipient's hand. But then, my fingers touched his. His fingers were like Porky Pig fingers. His thumb was like a real big Porky Pig. I giggled.

Professor Cush leaned toward me. He chuckled and whispered "More. Deeper. More." My nostrils widened and the smoke drifted around my face in streams that slipped back into my nostrils. I held my body still and thought of how Evian held himself over me when we made love, followed by the release with eyes wide and smiling.

Later, Evian handed me a stemmed glass of red wine. I drank and lay back against the Moroccan velvet pillows thinking I felt as if I've just been poured over the cushions. My legs splayed open and he smiled and looked as if he were drifting on the words, "…I couldn't get much higher…." and I reached for the joint, ignored The Doors' final refrain, blocked out a sudden sadness, and we made love.

When it was time to leave, Evian walked me to the door.

"Here, a joint for you and Andrew. Make you think of me the next time you come."

I walked home not knowing what to do with unfaithfulness. I couldn't face the blank space in my heart that once was filled with Andrew. At home, I hid the joint in my cosmetic bag.

"Sarah, Sarah, Sweetie, are you awake?" Mom knocks softly on my bedroom door.

I nip the end of the joint, waved\ the smoke away, and hide the joint in the corner of the dressing-table drawer. A red crayon rolls down and I pick it up.

The door opens. "You okay?"

"I'm fine, Mom."

"I brought some lilacs for your room."

The lilacs spread their sweet silver smell. Mom hands me the bouquet. I bury my head in the fragrant, fat blossoms as if I could drink them.

"What do you have in your hand?

I look down and laugh. I hold the red crayon for Mom to see. "A crayon. Found it in the drawer."

"How silly of me. I saw that in your hand, and thought, oh, no! My sweet girl has taken up smoking!"

I cuddle the lilacs in the crook of my arm and with my free hand I tap the red crayon in the air as if it would release an ash. We both laugh and I scoot over on the bed so that Mom can sit next to me.

I lay my head on my mother's shoulder.

"So nice to have my baby home."

"Nice to be home."

"You talk when you're ready."

I answer with a 'hmmm.'

"I'll put the lilacs in water." Mom stands, takes the bouquet and pulls down the bedspread a corner. "Crawl in here and take your nap. Of course take off your shoes."

So I did. Take off my shoes. And I fall into a deep dreamless sleep.

Many hours later I wake when Mom calls me for breakfast.

I eat an egg, a bite of toast. I drink a swallow of orange juice, and then I admit to Mom that I am not feeling that good. I go back to bed.

The next day I stumble out of my bedroom to curl onto the front room couch. On a TV tray Mom brings me Campbell's Chicken Noodle soup and triangle toast squares. I eat, but claim to have a horrible headache and head back to my bedroom. At dinner time, I hear Dad demanding in a loud whisper, "What's wrong with her?"

I fall asleep before I hear whatever excuse Mom gives.

Thursday, June 19, 1969

I stir Cheerios around a spatterware cereal bowl. I wear a pair of old flannel pajamas I found in my dresser drawer. It is ten o'clock in the morning. To block out the sunshine, I cover my eyes with one hand. Mom stands with her back to me, wooden spatula in hand, stirring chunks of apples in a two quart pan. I could have fallen asleep right there at the kitchen table, but Mom demands, "Let's talk."

Under the sweet spell of the morning sun and the bubbling smell of cinnamon and apples, we talk. We'd always danced this dance, like a slow two-step, Mom searching her rolodex-mind for the next cliché. Me? I talk around subjects. Like every high school dance, or broken romance, or bad grade, I tell my mom the slimmest edge of what is going on.

I tell Mom:

"We just outgrew each other and we needed some time apart and it is probably all for the best." I stumble in this confession and then I get specific in a very general way, and say, "Andrew found his muse." I should never have mentioned the 'muse' part. It makes Mom ask, as we wander through explanations and excuses, at least four times, "Explain that muse thing again."

Mom does give me one good suggestion, right from a *Cosmopolitan* article she'd just read. She suggests that I document this 'passage.' I would have ignored her, but she leaves the kitchen and when she returns she hands me a journal and a box of Bic pens. I get all teary and I need to head back to the bedroom. I will hide this journal under the mattress, and I will write lots of words of nothing in the journal Mom has given me.

"I won't snoop," Mom calls and I'm pleased she hadn't thought I was already writing everything down, just like the "Can This Marriage be Saved?" from *Cosmopolitan.* The only thing I read on the airplane. Didn't read the answer. The title was enough to bring on more tears.

I clutch the new journal and try to sleep.

After tossing and turning, pounding my pillow, removing the blanket, straightening the blanket, I get up from bed and I write (in my new journal):

WHY IT'S GOOD I LEFT ANDREW

1. *I'm tired of ironing seven shirts a week.*
2. *When we sit in a restaurant and we're talking, he's always looking at other women.*
3. *When we are in the middle of a good discussion, he always says, "Let me finish" and by the time he's finished I can't remember what I wanted to say.*
4. *He read a book about "open marriages" and insisted I read it. I thought I'd throw up.*
5. *He's having an affair with Magda.*
6. *I don't understand what it means to be faithful anymore.*
7. *It's both our faults and neither one of us wants to talk about it.*

WHY I SHOULDN'T LEAVE ANDREW

1. *I love him.*
2. *He's going to be a rich and famous author.*
3. *I made a vow at our wedding that this was for life.*

4. *He's my best friend.*
5. *I don't want to fail at marriage.*
6. *I don't understand what it means to be faithful anymore. And I want to understand.*

WHAT DID I EXPECT WHEN WE MOVED TO CHICAGO?

1. *Jazz.*
   We couldn't afford jazz. Truth is I was so wiped from teaching and I'm not sure when I thought we'd go hear all that jazz.
2. *Meaningful conversations.*
   Exciting, late night conversations with intellectuals at coffee houses. Andrew has late night conversations but they were at Kafka's with his writing buddies and I was only invited once.
3. *An exciting life! A grown-up life!*
   I'm not even sure I know what that means.

GOALS IF I STAY HERE AND ANDREW DOESN'T COME AND GET ME

1. *Lose ten pounds.*
2. *Not look at another man. Ever.*
3. *Read Ulysses.*
4. *Keep my journal regularly because when Andrew is rich and famous he'll want to remember all this stuff for his autobiography, and I'll have it and he won't, and he'll need to come and beg me for it (ha, ha).*
5. *Take a French class.*

And then I sleep. Like I've been cleansed. I sleep all day and I sleep all night.

The next morning, I get up with the sun! A huge bowl of oatmeal. Double dose of instant coffee. I'm jazzed! Dressed in jeans and a high school sweatshirt, I head outside to the garage. Sure enough, the lawn mower is where it is supposed to be. I push that mower. With precision! With energy! Back and forth. Our lawn is half a block long. I repeat rows where even the tiniest grass protrudes. Two hours later the lawn is perfect. The dandelions are pulled. I head back to the garage to find clippers.

Then, I hear the thrum of a Harley. Two blocks away. I stop to watch brother Freddy roar around the corner. He strides toward me with arms wide.

"I understand you dumped him!" Freddy exclaims, holding me at arms-length. I squint at my brother and would have hit him if he hadn't been holding my arms.

"I've got a couple of bankers and a couple of bikers I can introduce you to."

"You leave your sister alone!" Mom calls from the back porch. She joins us.

"Just trying to help," he says and gives Mom a hug and a smooch. "Got something cooking? I'm starving."

Freddy takes the back stairs two at a time and disappears into the kitchen.

Just at that moment, the postman walks up the walk waving a large envelope. Mom takes time to visit. She nods her head towards the house. I cringe at the thought that my whole family is now going to direct their attention at any and every available man who happens to appear.

The three of us stand on the walkway talking about the perfect weather and the lawn looking trim and how it is best to do yard work early in the day, because later it will be too hot. Postman Ted pulls a stack of mail out of his bag for Mom and then hands her the envelope. "Mighty important mail, it looks like," he says.

Mom turns the envelope to read the return address. Sees that it is my name. Puts it under her pile of mail. I'm sure she doesn't want the prospect to see the return address: large black letters read, BIRNBAUM, SKITTS AND FIELDING, LAW OFFICES.

Neither of us answers him, which prompts Postman Ted to say, "Well, guess I should be getting on."

I follow Mom into the house. She hands me the envelope. I ignore my brother sitting at the table with a jar of peanut butter and a glass of milk. I go directly to my bedroom.

I retreat to the cabbage roses and the smell of dying lilacs. I put the envelope under my pillow and remove my sweaty clothes. I hide under the sheet, the wool blanket, the down comforter. I wake to hear Freddy's motorcycle rumble out the drive. I return to another dream of Andrew.

Two hours pass. No longer can I ignore the envelope. I sit cross-legged on the bed. I close my eyes and try to calm my heart. Through tears I make out that there will be a ninety day waiting period. It states clearly that there is no property to split.

Paper-clipped to the divorce papers is an envelope with *Sarah* written in Andrew's skinny, slanty handwriting. I run my fingers over my name as if I might touch Andrew's hand. The return address is the lawyer's office. It appears, the lawyer guy must have said, "This is your chance. If you wish.

You might want to write a personal note. Helps them sign quickly." Don't even know the guy and I hate him. And Andrew.

Sarah,

I'm asking you to read every word of this letter and give it the kind of attention we used to give each other. I hope you know I'm writing this with good intent—as a way of honoring our time together. Reading this will be the last thing I ever ask you to do. I think I deserve that. (Remember how we used to really listen to each other?) In the end you just turned off. I remember once looking over at you in the middle of our discussing my thesis and you just weren't there. It was the way your eyes didn't blink. You'd quit listening. That hurt. We were such a team. Sarah, I remember telling everyone how you listened with your eyes. You made me feel special just listening to me and then somewhere, somehow, you drifted away. So here are my last words to you:

First, I think it's important to say, I think we should at least remain friends. Magda liked you a lot the night she met you at Kafka's and I know she'd prefer we were all friends. But, I don't know if that will ever be possible because of that Hemingway note you left in that God awful empty apartment (what did you do with my stuff? Like my slide rule and my Dad's Esso cap and the first edition of 'On the Road'?). I can't even imagine why you'd want that stuff. And it's just not the personal stuff being gone. Think of my coming back to that empty apartment, everything gone. Nothing there except your note. You really know how to hurt a guy. Do you know what it's like for a writer to be told, "You'll be no Hemingway?"

You never gave me a chance to answer, so I think you should consider the following:

It's not my fault I didn't get into the Iowa Writers program. You were the one who didn't put enough postage on the application and we missed the deadline.

Here's the big one—there wasn't anything going on between Magda and me when you accused me of spending so much time at Kafka's. I was working on my novel. You lost faith in me. I felt it. Do you know what it's like to be questioned about every minute? About every rejection slip? About every grade? About every night I had an extra beer or two?

You never, ever offered constructive criticism. My God, you read everything I wrote. You typed everything I wrote. Never once did you challenge me. We used to be such intellectual equals and then somewhere along the way, you slipped away. I felt so isolated and lonely. What did you expect when someone like Magda came along who was really interested in my work, in my thoughts, in my struggles? I know saying that about Magda will hurt you, but we've nothing more to lose, and maybe the truth will help you in your future life.

We need to go our separate ways. You'll be a better person for it. You'll get strong again. I know I am. Divorce wasn't what I pictured, but I can't think of how we ever could have considered anything else after you lost faith in me. Faith is everything. I never doubted how important you were to me.

Andrew

P.S. I'd appreciate it if you'd at least return my baby book. What could you possibly want with it?

I can't believe he's written this. I think he was practicing being a writer. And God, what if the lawyer read it. Bet he did. Now, I'm really glad I threw out that baby book.

CHAPTER THIRTY-NINE

GABE GOES HOME

June 20, 1969

The divorce papers and Andrew's letter causes a sadness I've never felt before—like my body is covered in glue and my mind can barely think it is so slow and weepy.

To escape, I listen to Grandma Millie's last tape. Why someone else's struggles and misery ease my soul, I don't know, but it does. I listen to Grandma Millie and then I read Gabe's journal.

The reports from Medical Lake stated that Gabe is getting better. They insisted he keep a journal. Supposedly it was to keep a record of his progress. Let me tell you, there were days it didn't feel like progress. And then there were beautiful full sentences. You have Gabe's journal. I know it ends abruptly. I'm ready to tell you the whole story. So, read all of what you have, but for now, turn to those pages where you can see his progress. Start with the page that states: I dream dreams.

I dream dreams of flying over the orchard, burrowing through the wheat fields. I smell apples in my dreams, late September Winesaps, with a tart plumpness ready for the cider mill. I wake with the taste of cider on my tongue and if I keep my eyes half-closed, I see naked bodies colliding, dancing, shimmering in a harvest dance. Strange, the male figures have scythes. Scythes slicing through grain, lopping off stalk heads as large as corn cobs. And in the middle of the wheat fields dances Angelica. In a white cotton night dress. And now, barely awake, I try to slide back into the dream to see if Angelica has noticed me. How could she not? I so notice her.

An amazing day! I slip out of one of my dreams, and I find I am no longer strapped to the bed and the tube attached to the cart with the pump is gone. Perhaps they will no longer force down me mashed foods and poisonous drugs.

Doctors in white coats visit me. I am careful not to let the doctors see any of my words. I hide my journal. One doctor is totally fooled and that doctor has arranged a pass for me to work in the vegetable garden. I love hiding words in the large cabbage leaves, tucking words in the narrow carrot holes. I fear however, that words will ooze out when the blisters on my hands pop. Words will slither onto the cold white cement floor when my skin peels. The pain helps camouflage my hands, gone soft and putty white.

The to-be-fooled doctor said one day:

"You realize Gabe, I don't expect your stay here with us to last much longer. What would you think of a trial visit to your family for a few days? See how it goes. Maybe we can think about you living back at home. How would you feel about that?"

I remember my throat tightening. My mouth going dry. Words flew out the back of my head. Words flew out and over me like sparrows circling. My stash of words circled Dr. Sensor's head. When I blinked I could hear my eyelids slam.

Then just weeks later: "Gabe, what do you think? It's time. You've done well lately. We won't rush you. Perhaps in two weeks. June is a good time to go home. Time to spend time with your brother and sister. Time to share your journal. Everything says you are getting well and that you are a very smart boy."

This was not the first time this to-be-fooled doctor had called me a smart boy. Or a big boy. Or just boy. But the free-wheeling words stitch my lips shut, leaving me only with a whistling hole. What would the doctor say if I whistled? What if I whistled like the train that blows its long lonesome song every night.

I stare at him and I know the doctor can see the backs of my eyes where the words are stored in groups of five. Words bound with bailing wire. Why doesn't the doctor say anything? Know anything? The wire uncontrolled would circle his feet. Cut off fingers and toes. Slice the sun like an apple. And with no wire to hold them, the words will regroup in the walls or along the window ledge or under the crack of the metal door. Certainly the doctor is smart enough to know uncontrolled words will topple the building. Like the Tower of Babel.

They'd all die.

I squint and suck air through my lips. I try to suck in the words. The doctor has quit speaking. He must have noticed the words streaming around the room.

"I mean it, Gabe, if you could just put your mind to it you could be home. Buck up. We don't want to give you any more water treatments. You've noticed we've even allowed you silverware. Nice, huh? If things go well, perhaps you won't have to come back at all."

The conversation seems to have ended.

Then the doctor extends a letter and says, "I've read it, of course. From your mother. We want no big surprises, now do we? You need to know your mother loves you and I would imagine it was very hard for her to tell you this news."

The doctor extends the letter. I wait. What a stupid doctor to not know I can't touch the words until he moves three steps back. Finally, Dr. Sensor drops the letter on the white metal stand between us. He nods and slams the white metal door. I touch the white envelope and peel out the white paper from inside. A fine black line slivers across the white paper and the words unravel and skip off the paper like a stone on water. Every word says divorce divorce divorce. A new life. Time heals. Things change. The words fly, crashing against the white metal walls. I suck the words through my whistle hole. Bundle them. In fives. Gather them. De-code them. I must get better. I must go home. I hold my body still and sort words: father silence time home divorce new love.

I'm going home. Tomorrow. Mom will come to get me, but I could get myself home now that I have a reason. And strength.

I went to Medical Lake to pick up Gabe. He cried on the train. He held my hand the whole way. He slept when he got home. Oscar and Sally were leery at first. But now that Gabe was home it seemed to me that a certain normalcy was setting in. Except that Luke was not there, life seemed to be returning to normal. It didn't.

CHAPTER FORTY

MAKING HEADWAY

Monday, June 23, 1969

Mom knocks on my bedroom door.

"Sarah. Get dressed. We have an appointment in one hour."

She drives me to the Southill Medical Clinic. At exactly nine-fifty-nine Mom opens the door on my side of the car and I walk down the familiar walk to the entrance of the clinic. I know enough to go directly to Dr. Snippet's office. I haven't been to his office since I was ten when Mom and Dad insisted I needed a little *pick-me-up.* For three months I went twice a week to the doctor's office to play with assorted dolls until spring vacation when we drove to Disneyland and I came home the envy of everyone in my class and I had no more problems with self-esteem and my sessions with Dr. Snippet ended.

Standing in his office, Dr. Snippet holds out a hand and says, "Welcome, welcome." I remember immediately how he says everything twice. "My, my, you've grown."

What did he expect after a decade?

Finally our fifty-minute hour ends, (the short hour was confusing when I was ten, but today it is a relief). I had told Dr. Snippet all of my dreams. He listened and then he stood and walked me to the door and said, "Tell your mother, tell her from me, you need some rest."

By the time I got back to the car, I am furious. Furious at Mom for making the appointment without asking, furious with Dr. Snippet for not giving me anything that had any weight or meaning, furious with the glorious sunshine when I am so furious! I slam the door of the car.

"That must have been one good session! That's the first real emotion I've seen since you got home! Well, unless sleep isn't an emotion. Well, and your tears. But it's nice to slam a door!"

"Mom, stop! Of course sleep isn't an emotion. Why are you treating me like I'm ten years old? I need to do something! Now! Get out of the house! Something! Anything! I think I'll go see Grandma Millie. At least she'll understand!"

"Good. Glad you are going to see Grandma Millie. Rockwood Clinic is only a few blocks away."

I turn to look at Mom, my anger exploding, "What? Grandma is sick and you didn't tell me?"

Mom lets out the clutch of the car and enters traffic headed up Grand Avenue. She shifts gears and says, "I didn't think you were quite up for the news of Mom needing to be taken care of."

"I can't believe this! You never said a word! She's *my* grandmother!"

"Sarah, hush. The emotion is nice, but bring it down a notch. If you haven't noticed, she is *my* mother! Besides, exactly when was I supposed to tell you? If you haven't noticed you've been sleeping fourteen hour days…except when you did that cooking thing."

"Oh, Mom, I'm sorry," I rummage for a Kleenex in my purse.

"Don't get all weepy, now. Grandma is going to want to see you in good spirits. You might want to go easy on your personal plight. She's only been there three days. She took a bit of a tumble in the bathtub. She's fine, now, but she needs some help.

And then we turn off of Grand Avenue and Mom, exclaims, "Oh, my, just look at St. John's Cathedral! So beautiful in the sunshine. Not to be critical, and I'm not, but that would have been a nice place for a wedding."

Mom near slows to a stop and points to the towers above us. "So beautiful, on such a glorious day! Now, don't frown, I'm sure your wedding was beautiful. Not that it took, but things happen. All the time. Things happen." Mom keeps up the dialogue. "Not your fault, I'm sure." She pats my hand and I try to tune her out and for the moment I hate that cathedral. It is not beautiful. It's menacing. Its spires pierce the sky. It doesn't matter that our chapel was all Roman brick and cement block with an idiot of a pretend minister. Truth is, I know it doesn't matter where one gets married. It matters how you do or don't keep that marriage together and I didn't.

A block later we park in front of a large fake Tudor open-beamed building. We sit for a minute under the maple tree in the shade. Silently. Together. For a minute I close my eyes. If there is comfort, it is in the shared silence.

"It's a lovely care facility." She squeezes my hand and with a laugh says, "A nice place for a wedding, it you didn't want a cathedral!" As if she had read my mind.

We get out of the car and walk up the path, I take her arm and I say, "Sorry, I'm a bit self-absorbed lately."

"Indeed. But there are days we all need a little self-absorption."

"Life's hard, Mom."

"Yep, life's hard, and that's when you know that one foot in front of the other will bring you out of the shade into the sun and then, sure as shootin', you go back into the shade again."

I lace my fingers through Mom's bumpy arthritic hand and give it a tender squeeze. "Your clichés are sometimes just what I need."

She laughs a little laugh. "Well, I should hope so!"

We check in at the front desk. Mom says, "I'll wait for you here. Give you some time with Grandma. But, take my *Cosmopolitan.* Sometimes Mom's at physical therapy or if she's sleeping, you might let her sleep."

I take the *Cosmopolitan.* I tap my purse and know that my journal and pen are there should I just not be able to handle the large breasted woman on the cover of the magazine.

I walk down a long quiet hall until I come to room 409. From the door I can see a wisp of a woman curled dead center in the bed. It's hard to believe it is my grandmother. Grandma Millie has turned from a woman with the use of a cane to an invalid in a bed. She doesn't look 'temporary.' She looks awful.

Everything in the room is white: the cotton-candy-ness of Grandma's hair, the taut sheets, the bed rails, and the scrim over the windows; the shimmer of sunlight, the plastic food tray, and the remains of mashed potatoes. At least she isn't connected to some kind of machine. She sleeps and I write in my journal:

How did she get so old?

I stare out the window. If there had been room in that bed, I would have crawled in with her.

"Sarah? Sarah, is that you?" Grandma Millie lifts her hand in greeting. I hold her fleshless hand and lean to kiss her soft, downy cheek. She smells of baby talc and sour lemons.

I help Grandma Millie scoot back against the pillows. I fluff them, and close her bed jacket.

"Why didn't you wake me?"

"You were sleeping. I know how awful it is to be wakened from a sound sleep."

"So your mother says. But at least you're here. I wondered why you hadn't come sooner, but your mother said you were sleeping off a divorce."

"Mom said that?"

"Your mother does say interesting things. I told her, to let you sleep as much as you needed, that you'd get tired of sleep soon enough, but then she told me she made an appointment with a psychiatrist and had given you a journal. That part of your mother is just like me. Feeling bad? Do something. I'm glad she finally got me on your list of things to do."

"Honest, it wasn't like that."

"Don't you honest me. I know what it's like to lose a great love. Andrew might have been a bit young, but even I could see you were ga-ga over him. Trust me. You'll never forget. It will always hurt. But life goes on!" Grandma Millie sits up straighter. "What is that thing you are wearing?"

"A mini-skirt."

"Well, that's good. Maybe catch you another man."

"I'm not even divorced yet."

"That is the one mistake I made. I should have got me another man, but with three kids it makes a woman a little less want-able. Now you've done that part right. No kids with that idiot of yours."

"Grandma! He's not an idiot. He's at the University of Chicago, for Christ sake."

"No swearing in this hospital, my sweet. And smart doesn't mean someone's not dumb. He didn't keep you. He can't be that smart. And what have you got in your hand?"

"My journal."

"Read me something!"

"Grandma, maybe not quite yet. It still kind of hurts."

"That's the best time to read. So read! My eyes are tired, I can't read anymore. The television is brainless. Read me your journal."

"It's just thoughts."

"What else? Read!"

I open the book and I read:

I was only twelve, but I remember this particular episode of The Dating Game. *The contestants, a real normal, crew-cut guy with a name like Gerry Schmitling sat on the other side of a screen from a brunette named April with a huge beehive hair-do. She had just answered the question with the very same words my mother would have answered had she been a contestant, "Yes, of course I think there is a particular someone for every person." I was riveted watching this woman giggle, blush, twist her hands, repeat, "... special someone..." The audience, including me, knew she thought this guy was seconds away from becoming her prince charming and she hadn't even seen him.*

At least Mom thinks you have to see the guy, probably and preferably across a crowded room. Why I never doubted my mother about the subject of men and marriage, I've never figured out.

My brother Freddy does not believe my mother's belief about special someones. He's had a slew of special someones. The woman my mother thought was the 'right one,' the one my brother never got around to marrying, lived over on Division Street. Melody played the French horn, studied anthropology in college, and went to graduate school. She wrote to my brother while he was stationed in Forszheim, Germany, where he drank huge quantities of beer and saved up his money for a Harley. The day I went for coffee at the Crescent, I ran into Melody at the shoe department. She told me she lives in a lesbian commune in Idaho.

A lifetime with a brother should have made me smarter about men. It didn't. When you have a mother reading romance novels as serious guides to life and a brother who didn't realize his girlfriend liked girls best, your expectations about your future partner get screwed up. Stupid me. I never stopped wanting a prince charming.

Andrew and I saw Zeffirelli's Romeo and Juliet. I cried so hard I got the hiccups. Andrew and I saw the movie in October. That spring Andrew found his muse and it wasn't me.

I want to ask Andrew, "What do you do with your dreams?" Every night he slips into my sleep and takes over. I wake looking for him. It's horrible.

When I mention my dreams to Freddy, he says, "Get over it. You are so much better off without him. It's obvious he didn't appreciate you. The minute he graduates and doesn't need tuition he'll tell you he's made a mistake. You weren't quite the one. The good thing is he let you know early. You could have spent another year paying his way."

I look up, half expecting Grandma to be asleep. "You want me to keep reading?"

"Why, yes, this is very interesting. Wish someone had told me to write a journal."

I continue:

Does Henny Youngman say, "My Wife, Take Her" or does he say "Take Her, She's My Wife" or does he say, "Take My Wife?" I don't remember, but I do remember it was a joke and I never thought it was funny.

Cosmopolitan magazine (Mom has them in a stack in the closet, saying she doesn't throw them out until they are read, cover to cover). So when I can't sleep, when I don't want Andrew in my dreams, I've taken to reading them. And here's what I've learned, "One out of every four marriages ends in divorce; there are three women for every available man. After the age of thirty your chances of remarrying are equal to the chances of being killed in an airplane accident. After the age of forty your chances of remarrying are equal to the chances of being struck by lightning.

Once I saw a young couple run through a shower of rice as they headed for their car beside St. John's Episcopal Cathedral up on Grand Avenue. I was shopping at the IGA. I wore a pair of short shorts and I was skinny. As the groom helped his bride into the waiting limousine, he turned and saw me watching and gave me a long, slow once over. So much for faithfulness.

I dreamt Andrew bought a house next door. He moved in boxes and suitcases and new appliances and new furniture and then he carried Magda over the threshold and waved to me and called, "Thank you for understanding!"

I said, "Oh, sure, It was nothing," and walked back to my parents' house where the door was locked and, looking in the window, I could see the house was empty.

Mom told me how sorry she was that it appears things didn't work out with Andrew. She said she and Dad are both sorry, and she wondered if it was her fault. I can't see how our separation and divorce could possibly have anything to do with them and said so, but she said she's always tried to be a model and how their marriage was meant to be a model and it has been a model although, here she giggled, and said in a whisper while Dad watched Monday Night Sports, "I've often wondered what would have happened if I had accepted that dance with Jorge Jorgensen." This is a story I've heard since I started dating. Jorge Jorgenson was a famous accordion player who, when Mom was a teenager, asked her to dance at an Elks Club dance. With a sigh, Mom said she was true to her date and said no to the invitation. She always ended this story by asking, "Now isn't that a silly story?" I think she thinks it is a sad story and in her voice is the question that maybe Jorge Jorgenson was the one meant for her and now she'll never know.

Home alone, I see everything in twos. Cars have two headlights. A house has a front and a back door. A sprinkler is either off or on. It is either day or night. Old Lady Wilson is a widow which meant that she was once married. The bed is either occupied or empty. And it's always a double bed.

Back to my bank of dreams: they are full of the smell of the lemon-ness of Andrew's aftershave, the clatter of his car coming down Fifty-Third Street, Andrew's laughter, library shelves weighted with books by Andrew. I wake sad. It gets so that I want to sleep just to be with him. I dream the phone rings, pick up the receiver, and I can't hear his voice but I know it's him.

I've stopped telling Mom about these dreams. "Too much!" she exclaims. And then when I find just one more word to say about one more dream, she reminds me to put one foot in front of the other. Lately, those instructions not only seem exactly what I should do, but the only thing I can do.

When I look up from reading, Grandma sleeps with her mouth open. I sit for a minute in the silence of the room and then I stand to say goodbye. I lean over the rail of her bed and whisper, "See you tomorrow."

Grandma Millie's eyes open, "I heard every word. You're going to be just fine. With work, we always are."

CHAPTER FORTY-ONE

FRONT PAGE SECRET

Sunday, June 29, 1969

The next day I visit Grandma Millie and I bring the recorder. This time I will be there to capture her words. She wants so much that I hear these last remembrances. I didn't know then, but this recording was her last. Her words were broken. Disconnected. Frightening. And she didn't live long enough to explain why.

I recorded and she spoke...

June 13, maybe July 13, the date was a bad omen. Maybe it was August. I'm so fuzzy. Maybe your mother will remember. But here is what I remember.

I brought Gabe home on the train.

I shouldn't have.

I got him a job at Hennessey's. Secrets were not kept.

I remember this: Each day I packed a lunch bucket filled with his favorite foods: butter biscuits, fresh sliced ham, chocolate cake, apples from the tree.

But there were no words. It was as if I could feel his anger. Touch his anger. The distance he kept from me, from the twins, was like a cold, icy wall.

Each night I prayed.

I tried to tuck him in at night.

I would be there for him.

And then the worst. The very worst.

I prayed for strength.

Unbearable sadness.

The Gaitsberg Daily covered the most ordinary news: the grange, the Governor's proposal for a dam on the Coulee River, Clara Bow's latest movie, voting of elected officials, 4-H prize winners, ladies pouring tea—news to inform, news to appease, news to ignore – except one day. Worse than the black bordered paper for Milton Wiseman.

The same black border.

I hated Abe Wiseman. Begged. Demanded. Don't write about Gabe. He's a child.

Abe slammed his office door to stop the entire printing room from hearing me scream.

Alone, I learned, or maybe I already knew, but couldn't face why all these years his paper had ignored every major event of my life—why he had somehow forgotten my wedding announcement and then the birth announcements of my children.

Abe glared at me. "You are not the only one facing horrific heartbreak. If not for you I'd have my son. You are the cause of his death in stinking France. You are the reason he lies in a cold coffin in Flanders Field. Now get out of my office. This story will not be ignored! You have wreaked havoc wherever you go! Luke's death is news. News I will not ignore!

Grandma began to cry. I waited and waited. She seemed as if she would cry forever. She could barely speak. "All for now. Tomorrow. Come tomorrow."

I kissed her forehead and watched her fall into a deep sleep. I waited a few minutes hoping she would continue. Eventually, I packed the recorder in my purse. I was on pins and nails, as Grandma Millie would have said, had she known. I knew that she had almost told her secret.

CHAPTER FORTY-TWO

GABE'S GONE

Wednesday, July 2, 1969

"Sweetheart, wake-up." Mom pushes a strand of hair behind my ear. "Wake up, honey. I have some bad news."

"Grandma! Is Grandma okay?"

"It isn't Grandma. It's your Uncle Gabe."

I almost said, thank goodness, but held my tongue. "What?" I asked.

"He passed away. Last night."

"Tell Me. When did you see him last?"

"You know we go every month."

"Still?"

"Your grandma would never miss a visit. It's been hard. The last visit, he didn't recognize your grandma. It was hard on her. But thank goodness, the doctor said he passed peacefully."

What a strange thing to say. I barely think of my uncle, but the word "peaceful" is not a word I would have used to describe Uncle Gabe.

I remember our visits to Medical Lake. I remembered being scared. Until I finished high school and left for the University of Washington, every last Sunday of the month, after church, we'd climb in the yellow Pontiac and drive the sixteen miles to the hospital. Dad drove. Mom packed a basket with hard candies, toothpaste, old Readers' Digests. Grandma Millie brought anise cookies. Freddy and I had to figure what to give up—an old comic book, a pack of Bazooka gum, old crayons, a half used Big Five—something, anything, just so everyone brought a gift.

On the way up Sunset Hill, Grandma Millie would assure us her beautiful boy, as she always spoke of Gabe, lived for our gifts. I thought it was hard to tell. He never said thank you. He never even spoke. He never smiled. He never touched those gifts while we were in the room. Uncle Gabe never spoke once in all those years, at least he never spoke when I was in the room.

From the first visit, the routine was always the same. We'd check in at the front desk and then we would wait in The Sun Room. The sun in that room was thick with dust motes as pervasive as an invading army. Wheelchairs with curved and crumpled people were rolled in front of the windows and in front of the television. The "wheelies" sat there in the sun as if they might absorb the heat. They sat there as if waiting to get sucked up to somewhere else, because they certainly didn't seem to be aware of where they were. They dozed and drooled, and every once in a while they'd start to yell or sob. Then a nurse would roll them away.

For a long time Uncle Gabe didn't need a wheelchair. He'd shuffle down the hall in paper slippers, a nurse, not touching him, but walking with him, like he was a dog at obedience school. His pajamas and robe were so worn they looked like fairy clothes. As far as I was concerned, he was a strange man and his left hand stood out like a fin at his side, shaking. He'd sit with the five of us in a circle. Grandma would hold Gabe's hand, and the tremors would stop. Mom and Dad, it seemed to me, smiled too much and talked too much. After a while, Freddy and I would be excused to go wait in the car.

Once I asked Mom, "Does he ever talk?" Mom answered that maybe he did when he was alone with Grandma. And that's when I learned that after we were excused, Grandma would walk Uncle Gabe back to his room and Mom and Dad would sit in that spooky, silent Sun Room and wait for Grandma to return. Mom said when Grandma came back she'd always say, "Well, that was nice. He's doing fine. Getting better."

Now he was dead and I had no feelings. How do you feel something for someone who never knew you were there?

"I know you planned on visiting Grandma today. But, it might be better if you didn't tell her. Let me be the one."

CHAPTER FORTY-THREE

ANOTHER PASSING

July 3, 1969

Perhaps it is the death of her Dear Boy. Or perhaps it is just her time. Mom, Dad and I visit Grandma Millie at the clinic, and it is as if she has already slipped away. She chews her food, accepts the smallest spoonful's with our help, but the nurse tells us that Grandma doesn't swallow the food. After we leave she takes the food from her mouth, wraps it in Kleenex, and drops it in the waste basket.

The next day we arrive and Grandma Millie has a saline drip.

That afternoon, when I come alone to visit, I arrive as they adjust an oxygen mask and the nurse gently taps Grandma's back because she has a deep, racking cough.

While she sleeps, I write in my journal. I so want her to ask me to read or if there is a miracle, to ask me to turn on the recorder. She doesn't.

What I notice most is how small she's become, like a baby robin. Eyelids bruised, translucent. Hair wispy like snow in wind. She sleeps in another world. And sometimes in her sleep, her lungs vibrate like gravel rolling. Blood crusts her gums, appears at the corner of her mouth. Her hands are rumpled with veins like blue rivers. Her skin is pale, creased, as if with a touch it would fall off her bones.

If other patients cry or moan too loudly, I close the door, fearing the sounds might frighten her. Medical staff comes and goes. I can barely watch as they take her blood pressure. She grimaces in pain. She pleads, "Please don't. Please."

I give up the idea that Grandma Millie will ever again allow me to ask questions. It isn't going to happen. Grandma now mistakes me for her old childhood friend, Claire, or she thinks I am Mom.

It hurts to see my once strong grandma crumbling. I think of her as the glue in our family. Grandma Millie is the person who pulled from the piano "Oh Holy Night" and then beat out 'Bill Bailey Won't You Please Come Home." She taught me about how to wear blusher and she taught me the joy of red nail polish. She scrutinized every person I dated. She could pound a nail in a single hammer swing. She read a book a week and did the New York Times Crossword puzzle in ink. On Sunday.

Now Grandma Millie barely breathes.

The next day, all of us wait. Two at a time we visit Grandma Millie. We hold her hand. We massage her feet. We read aloud not knowing if she hears. Her doctor says, "Don't know. Perhaps a few hours. At the most a few days." And then, while Freddy and I are with her, Grandma pulls in a breath, holds it, and doesn't breathe again.

That night I can't sleep and remembrances of Grandma Millie flood my mind: lumpy bags of potatoes from Grandma Millie's root cellar, the aerosol/urine/bleach smell of Uncle Gabe's room; the bending heads of tulips and daffodils in Grandma's garden, the taste of Thanksgiving mincemeat pies, the rip of Band-Aids being torn away followed by soft kisses, the mumble of goodnight prayers, the slickness of red nail polish, the burnt starched smell of pressed lace handkerchiefs. When morning comes, I end my restless sleep and surface to the feel of white crisp sheets and the hard awareness that Grandma Millie is dead.

CHAPTER FORTY-FOUR

MY MOTHER'S KITCHEN

July 6, 1969

The graveside service for both Grandma Millie and Uncle Gabe are combined into one gathering. Neighbors come to say their goodbyes. Everyone brings potluck to Mom's house, sharing their favorite dishes and their remembrances of Grandma Millie. No one speaks of Uncle Gabe. No one knew him.

Freddy and I sit on the back porch nursing beers and not saying much.

"Sweet brother, I'm going to go sneak into my bedroom. It's too hard being nice any longer. All I feel is sad."

"You got it," he says. He reaches for a hug and plants a kiss on the top of my head. Amazing how much I love him.

In my bedroom I collapse to the murmur of the last few neighbors saying their goodbyes. I fall into a deep, deep sleep. In my dreams I fly, I swoop. Joyous dreams. All through the dreams, Grandma Millie's hand holds mine. We fly above the earth. Laughing. In the morning I wake, full of power and joy. I can't be sad for one more minute. I dress. Humming. Happy. Energy like I've already had the richest, blackest coffee.

I walk into the kitchen and everything is bright—the white eyelet curtains, the white-flecked Formica and chrome table, the chairs duck-taped to keep the Naugahyde from splitting further, the Mix-Master with its black dial and black rotating plate, the Mickey Mouse clock. On the counter, under the white enamel cupboards, gleams a toaster whose sides flip open–—a relic from the Gaitsberg farm. On the white window sill above the sink sit three African violets surrounded by "things" Mom has collected over the years: a one-inch Porky Pig, an Indian-head penny, a miniature Avon perfume bottle, a flat skipping rock, a Christmas Santa made from pipe cleaners, a miniature King Jame's Bible readable with a magnifying glass, and three of our baby teeth. All of these treasures, once accepted, are never removed. The Avon bottle is fifteen years old. The Porky Pig has been there since before I can remember.

"Mom, can I borrow the car?"

"Why, Sweetie, you're very much awake!"

"How about the keys?"

"Keys are in the saucer above the sink, where they always are. But before you go, how about some coffee? A little something?" Mom reaches for the Folgers.

"Thanks! Later! But I'd like to borrow some money, and as soon as the divorce is final, and I've found another teaching job, I promise, promise I will pay you back."

"How much do you need?"

"How about twenty dollars."

Mom smiles. I can see she is so pleased with my energy; she'd probably have given me much more money.

From the extra sugar bowl she pulls a twenty dollar bill, places the money in my hand, and hugs my fingers. "You look like a woman on a mission!"

Mom hears my hesitation. She's so smart. So intuitive. She says, "Surprise me!"

And I will.

I drive up the hill to Rosauers. I go directly to the magazine rack. I pick out the August issue of *Gourmet.* With the magazine open, I walk up and down aisles. I buy all the things I know will not be in Mom's kitchen and I buy everything I have not indulged in, in the last year: balsamic vinegar, gorgonzola cheese, miniature gherkins, bib lettuce, bok choy, fresh chives, Italian tomatoes, and chick-peas. At the bakery I choose three chocolate éclairs. I have two dollars left over!

Back home. I run up the back steps and call, "I'm home!"

Mom is at the table paging through a *Reader's Digest.*

I open the grocery bags and identify each item for Mom as if she has never seen groceries before. I flash the *Gourmet* magazine pictures at her. I spread all the ingredients over the table. I open and shut drawers to remember where Mom keeps ingredients, mixing bowls, serving plates.

Once our eyes meet and small furrows corrugate my mother's forehead. I should have taken better notice. I don't. I can't. I'm a Dervish. I bang open drawers. I scrub measuring cups and whisks and knives that are already clean. I turn on the radio. I flip past the station with Easy-Listening and find bright, snappy Chick Corea blasting *Girl from Ipanema.* I turn up the volume.

At one point Mom stands as if she might leave the kitchen and comes to stand by me at the sink. I tell her, "Sit! I'm cooking! I'm making Florentine Ragu with Sweet Gherkins and Gorgonzola; I'm going to serve it on the good china turkey platter. It will be a magnificent meal! And tomorrow! Tomorrow I will cook Beef Wellington for Tuesday dinner with double whipped mashed potatoes and bok choy simmered in raspberry vinegar and shallots. And Wednesday? Well, Wednesday will also be magnificent!"

Mom squints her eyes and the furrow between them deepens.

That first 'Sarah dinner' Dad compliments me on the interesting meal. He doesn't clean his plate.

The next day the Beef Wellington isn't served until six-thirty. Dinner is always at five o'clock. I'm surprised when Dad gets out the Christmas wine from under the sink.

The third day I drive to the Northside Mall. I use my charge-card. I have no idea if Andrew has stopped it. At the book store I buy three new cookbooks. The card works!

That night I introduce my parents to hollandaise inside artichokes (the first batch curdles, so I have to throw it out and start over with another six eggs and of course Mom protests and pleads for the starving children in China). The entree is Simplicato Vencenzia Pork Loin with Radichio salad. Maybe it is a little too unusual. Dad doesn't talk much. Mom hardly says a word. I can hear their false teeth moving around.

On the fourth day I don't consider for one minute Mom's suggestion that we have hotdogs and potato salad and cherry pie. Instead, I skin fresh tomatoes and make an Iranian lamb dish with the tiniest of fiery green peppers. Mom pushes the food around her plate. Dad helps me freeze the left-overs.

By the fifth day, I let up a bit. I let Mom slice tomatoes then she sits and watches me while I cook Beef Bourguignon. Mom rubs the space between her eyes. That night the freezer has no more room. Dad munches Tums as he watches *The Hit Parade.*

That's how things went until the sixth day, July 12th. I wake to find four birthday presents at the end of my bed. I have totally forgotten my birthday. The ritual of birthday presents at the end of the bed is one of my earliest memories.

I brush away tears, and unwrap one present (all that is allowed, the other presents must then be brought to the breakfast table so the family can watch). The first present is Avon Raspberry Summer Soap.

When I come to the kitchen, the waffle iron is already plugged in and the button glows red. Mom stands taller. Dad is already mowing the lawn.

"May I help?" I ask.

Mom answers, "It's your birthday. Sit!" She serves waffles with strawberry freezer jam. Folgers Coffee and orange juice from concentrate. Dad joins us and I open the three other presents: my own car keys to their car and a twenty dollar gift certificate for the Crescent. The final gift is a book. A book entitled, "Starting Over."

Mom makes two more batches of waffles. When I offer to help with dishes, she reminds me it is my birthday.

Mom stands between the sink and the work counter and suggests if I want to be helpful, I could use my new set of keys and run up to Rosauers and buy two cans of Carnation canned milk.

When I return Mom remembers she needs Crisco.

"On your way, you might want to take a little drive. Manito Garden. Smell the roses! Take your time." she calls as I walk down the back steps.

Freddy comes to help celebrate my birthday dinner. We have fried chicken, mashed potatoes and gravy, canned peas. Fresh applesauce. A fancy cake from a box. Chocolate. Twenty three candles. Coolwhip.

The next morning, Mom is up before I'm out of bed. She makes Quaker Oats for breakfast with brown sugar and raisins. Dad, unexplainably, has "errands" and announces he will be gone for a while. Then I notice the worry bump is gone from between my mother's eyes.

"Sit!"

I sit.

"Talk!"

And so we talk. I tell her most everything. It is the first real talk I ever remember being totally honest (well, almost totally). I mention that there was someone who had attracted me, but it was harmless. I lied. But Mom is my mother!

Mom cries. We both cry.

Then Mom says, "I think it's time you learned about what happened in our family. Gabe's gone. Grandma's gone. I promised Mom I would keep the family secret, her secret, until after she could no longer be hurt by it. Tomorrow, take the car. Drive down to Gaitsberg. Go to the Court House. Go to the Records Room. It's time you learned about my father, your grandfather, Grandpa Lane. And, Uncle Gabe."

CHAPTER FORTY-FIVE

HOW DID WHAT HAPPEN, HAPPEN?

Monday, July 14, 1969

I take from my journal the photo I have carried with me the past year—the photo of Grandma Millie on the front stoop. It brings to mind wind-whipped wheat fields, the dry snap of grasshoppers, lonesome cowboy songs: Grandma gazes toward a distant space. The twins cling to her. Gabe sits on the porch rail. Distant. Alone.

Grandma Millie told me of her fear when she was a child that their family might end in the poorhouse. I study her. Can I see her fear? Fear of the poorhouse? Fear of the neighbor lady's daughter? Or does she gaze at something as pure and simple as the orchard at harvest? I can almost feel the hot wind, smell the dry soil, and taste the smell of tart fall apples. On the back of the photo is written: *1927 – The last picture Luke took. Before he was gone.* Why didn't she know her marriage was in danger? Why didn't I fear what might happen to my marriage? Does every woman have that thing, that person that she should fear? For me, should I not have feared Magda? For Grandma Millie, Angelica? Why were we blind?

I grab the car keys and ease the car out of the driveway. I'm anxious and excited. Today I'm determined to find the answer to the family secret. I slide on to I-90 west. Destination: Gaitsberg, Washington.

The map of Washington spreads over the front seat. I've marked the route to Gaitsberg: a small black dot on a thin black road, ten miles off the freeway. An hour from Spokane.

Out the window, I pass skeletal pines shading pale, brittle grass. The highway curves around wheat fields and I pass a grain silo. On the right, a sign reads, *Where Everyone's Your Neighbor. Gaitsberg. County Seat. Population 2,015.* Time to turn.

In town, Main Street is lined with limestone and red brick buildings. I angle park in the shade of a big-leaf oak. I roll down the window to catch a soft breeze. I absorb the contrast of Gaitsberg with Chicago. I absorb the silence. I think of Chicago—all activity and movement and hustle and commotion. Here, the air feels brittle, dry, and empty; like the sky, like the fields, like the pine forests, like distant farm houses, like empty store fronts.

Parked in the shade, sunlight slipping through large leaves, I watch the deep shadows and elusive light and think of how my marriage slipped away. Andrew too tired. Andrew too busy. Andrew home late. Andrew home not at all. And then I think of how I broke my vows. How Andrew broke his vows. How I was just as unfaithful as he. Maybe more. We became a marriage of lies, of silences, of deceits, of loneliness.

Next to where I park, I watch the window of Montgomery Ward. A clerk arranges a bolt of sun-flower splattered cotton around a headless mannequin. At the corner, under a Gametes Gas sign, five men deep in conversation look up to check my car. They soon grow disinterested, cup their hands to light cigarettes then throw the matchsticks into the oil-soaked dirt. For an instant I think there should be a conflagration! A blazing fire! Something. Anything.

Nothing.

Then a lone shopper pushes a stroller up to the Montgomery Ward door. She stops. She coos soft words. She lifts from the carriage her stiff legged baby. She makes him laugh. She hugs him tight then hangs him on her hip. I think: she has a husband, a child, a life.

I wonder if the slow, silent, simplicity of Gaitsberg is a façade? I wonder if it is all pretend. Do these easy-going people hide secrets? Are they unfaithful to someone? To something? What would happen if I rolled down the window and yelled, "Hypocrites!"? I won't of course. I've been brought up to not expect answers, shade meanings, use words lightly. To never demand the brittle clarity of truth.

It's time.

I grab my purse and unstick the back of my legs from the vinyl of the car seat. I pull the crinkled back of my skirt to hang free. I lock the car and with a determined, sure stride, I cross the street and walk up the wide cobblestone path to a redbrick, two-story mock-Tudor building. On my right, the dry grass hugs a carved stone with the words: Gaitsberg County Courthouse, 1902.

Next to the wide courthouse steps, three children play on the disk of a flat, wooden, merry-go-round. They push. They run beside the turning disk. They yell with fearful joy and jump on for the ride.

At the entrance of the building, the wide, curved expanse of a two-foot wide railing shows off concrete lions. The lions appear to guard over the grassy rectangles on either side of the steps. Inside one rectangle two men play chess at a picnic table. In the other rectangle, a blind woman sits on a wooden bench and knits a red sweater. The tiniest of baby sweaters.

Inside the high-ceilinged cavernous entry way, the information clerk directs me down a dim lit hall lined with photos of furrowed fields, horse-drawn harrows, men gathered beside grain elevators, children clustered on school steps. Silhouetted at the end of the hall is a door with a frosted glass window stenciled with the word: RECORDS.

The door pushes open and hisses softly behind me and I am surrounded with the smell of old leather, printer's ink, aged paper. Overhead dust blooms on the edge of fluorescent egg-crate lights. Maroon leather-bound ledgers line sagging shelves. Hand-printed cards at the end of each aisle indicate decades. I walk slowly. I don't want to rush. I let my fingers bump over the spines of leather books.

Someone somewhere snaps gum. The small sound echoes.

"Hello? Is there someone here?" a voice calls and a teenage girl in white peddle-pushers and a navy tee shirt appears. The words: GAITSBERG GATORS fills her chest. She walks down the aisle. One arm holds a pile of papers. She pulls in a bubble of pink gum.

"Wow!" she says. "You scared me! Sometimes I'm alone in here for hours."

The girl looks around to see if anyone else is there and whispers, "You're not supposed to be this far back, but you are, and no one ever checks on me, so what can I do for you?" Her plastic name tag reads: Cindy Loop. Her pigtails are tied with yarn to match her peddle-pushers, and her lipstick is the color of Bazooka Bubble Gum—a study in surreal sweetness.

I find myself liking the girl for how cute and daffy she appears.

"I need to find…" I say and the girl interrupts. She wiggles a finger and points, "Let me tell you where everything is and then you can be on your own. Over there, the ledgers are from 1878 to 1900." She turns, "There, 1900 to 1934. After 1934, things get to be a mess because the county didn't have enough money to buy ledgers and they just stuffed stuff in boxes. It's those boxes I sort. Sort into folders. Then, I file them. That's my job. From 1955 they put everything on fiche, so that's all up-to-date, and there you are!"

"Good," I point toward the wall with the ledgers from the first of the century. "I think I'm where I need to be."

"But…" she says like she's a talking wind-up toy with a serious script, "……if you want newspapers and maps, those are in the basement." She raises her eyebrows as if to ask if I understand. "I'm here to get you what you want. But just for the summer."

"Well..."

"And..." She nods to a slanted desk behind her, "...we have procedures. On top of the desk is a form and a bell, and should I be busy, and you can't see me, you just ring that bell."

She smiles and continues speaking as if she's headed for the end of her lecture, "But, you have to fill out a form. I'm not sure why, but those are the rules. Crazy, but that's how it is." She walks in front of me to the information desk and hands me a form. "I'm working over there," she points to a corner blocked with rows of metal files. This time she wiggles her fingers to indicate she is leaving and calls over her shoulder, "Let me know when you're ready."

On the form I write my name and Mom and Dad's address. I make up a license plate number. I am not going to walk all the way down the hall, out in that hot sun, to the front street to get the license number. In the next space I write *Marriage Certificates*. In another space I write, *1915*. I lay the form next to the spindle and I tap the bell.

"Be right there!" Cindy's voice bounces off the pressed-tin ceiling.

I listen to the slap of file folders, the snap of Cindy's gum, and the slow-moving fan above the information desk. Minutes later Cindy's back. She takes the form I've filled out and waves it in the air. She calls, "Wait here! 'Twill take me just one minute."

Around the desk I study the wall full of historic photographs: Mayors and Fourth of July parades and the Snowfall of '98 and the grand opening of Hennessey's Feed Store. Across the bottom of the last photograph, of men gathered in front of the feed store, is written in white ink, GRANGE FELLOWSHIP, GAITSBERG, WASHINGTON, 1928. A dozen men face the camera, hat-wearing men. Bags of feed slump at their feet, brimmed hats cast deep shadows across their faces. I study the men: bearded, mustached, caught with eyes closed, hands stuffed inside bib fronts, a hand holding a pipe. Short, tall, slouched, sartorial. Could one of these men be Grandpa Lane?

"Here you go!" Cindy says and staggers toward me under the weight of four volumes. She nods toward a slanted desk underneath the high rounded windows. Cindy lets the books slide onto the desk.

"In early times, each year had two volumes. I brought you two years, since they were there and if you're like me, once you get started you just want to keep on reading! Right? So, you'll find all kinds of interesting stuff about marriages and births and deaths and land transactions and then, just every once in a while you'll find something real juicy, like the guy who stole cattle and they hung him." She smiles. She waits.

I return the smile and say, "Thanks. I appreciate all your help."

When Cindy realizes I'm not going to tell her anything more, she picks up a bundle of files and heads back down the aisle. "Holler if you need more years."

I run my hands over the nubbly leather surface of the first volume of 1915. Perhaps in one of these books are answers. Perhaps I will break through the silence that surrounds a grandfather who was more secret than person, more anger than love, more mysterious than real.

Thinking of this mystery in my life, I remember another time I made an effort to break through the silence. I was fourteen. My boyfriend, Ronald Miller, seemed to be not much of a boyfriend any more. I was going to just ask him outright, "Are you or are you not my boyfriend?" And then that very day he broke an arm playing football and the time to ask flew away.

It made me more determined than ever to ask Grandma Millie about the secret husband. Did she give up on him? Did she miss the time to ask him what would have kept him at home? With three kids? Tomorrow I'm going to ask her two things: what would you have done different and how could you have kept him from running away?"

The next day was Thanksgiving. At our house, Thanksgiving is a long slow day. I waited and waited and then right before it was time for everyone to bring the dinner to the dining table, I waited outside the bathroom door and when Grandma Millie appeared, I blurted out, "What happened to Grandpa Lane?"

Grandma blinked her eyes, like she was trying to remember, but before she could say anything, she made this horrid choking sound, and everyone came running, and pounded her back until out came one of the hoar-hound drops she always was sucking on and I was shooed away and Grandma Millie was placed in the Barcalounger and all the kids were told to let her be and help set the table.

I never got up enough nerve to ask again.

The memory fills me with sadness. I can still feel the silence that surrounded that Thanksgiving dinner. Not that anyone didn't speak. They did. It was a conversation with so much work in it that it felt like silence.

The Records Room feels like it is full of secrets. I open the first volume. The pages are brittle and crackly. Sepia colored ink reveals long forgotten disputes, diminutions, and celebrations. Some pages have never been opened, and the ink lets loose its grip with a gentle pop.

JANUARY 4, 1915: WILLIAM TRUE AND ELIZABETH ANNE TRUE, MARRIED BY THE REVEREND EDWIN WORDS, WITNESSED BY HENRIETTA WILLIAMS AND LESTER GOODS.

JANUARY 6, 1915: GARY RANDOLPH MILLINOUX OF MILLINOUX GROCERIES, BANKRUPT IN THE COURT OF JUDGE JOHN JONES.

JANUARY 10, 1915: EVERETT DOUGLAS, III, CONVICTED OF THE DEATH OF LILLY BETH OWEN JONES BY A JURY OF HIS PEERS, SENTENCED TO DEATH BY HANGING IN THE PENITENTIARY AT WALLA WALLA, WASHINGTON.

I continue to read. Palmer script. Scribbles. Gallant flourishes. Illegible scrawls. Studied circles. Swooping capital letters. *X*s. Thumbprints.

Cindy returns. "Want to share a coke?" she asks all bright and chipper. "Not that we're supposed to have liquids in here, but I can see how careful you are. I'm careful. There's something holy about this stuff. Don't you think?"

"Holy?"

Cindy giggles. "What I mean is more than just special. I study the signatures. I almost think I can tell what kind of person, just by how that person signs their name. Like there." Cindy points to a County Deputy's signature for a land transaction. "Look. Look at how slanty and mean that signature is. I'd bet he didn't want to sell that land. Maybe it was his granddad's land and he signs it all angry like, and now he doesn't own it anymore."

"Amazing. Do you spend a lot of time doing that?"

"No, no. I just think I'm walking around with a lot of ghosts in here and I love to think about them being real people with real lives. So how about that Coke?"

"No, thanks."

"Anything else I can do for you?"

"I'm doing okay. Doing fine."

"Okeydokey. I'm here when you need me."

In the second volume I find the entries 1915. MARRIAGES. There are only a few pages, as if the number of marriages that year were few. Perhaps the women had seen their men off to war. It almost feels too easy, because only a few pages later, I find a copy of the marriage certificate for Mildred Sarah Birnham and Luke Jacob Lane.

It is and it is not what I expected. I imagined Grandpa Lane's handwriting crude and shaky. Full of uncertainty. I imagined Grandma Millie's writing strong and bold. Pleased with her new identity.

I continue to read:

SEPTEMBER 26, 1914

OFFICIATING: JUDGE CLARENCE TOOMBS

HUSBAND'S FULL NAME: LUKE JACOB LANE

BIRTHDATE: JANUARY 24, 1893

WIFE'S FULL NAME: MILLICENT SARAH BIRNHAM
BIRTHDATE: AUGUST 19, 1897
WITNESSED BY: CLAIRE SANDBORN and THEODORE SANDBORN

Judge Toomb's signature is shaky—a slivered line. The nib of the pen must have caught because ink dots the edge of the page and puddles in the spine of the book.

Luke Lane's signature cuts into the paper—sure, swift—as if he hurries to finish, to take on his new life and his new wife.

Grandma Millie's signature is firm, flowing, elaborate as if she is pleased in her writing, sure of what she is doing.

I find Cindy kneeling on the floor, back in the corner, sorting journals. Well, she's reading journals. I ask her if she can find me ledgers or whatever she might have between 1930 and 1940. "Give me a sec," she says. "That'll be a load. I'll take a couple trips."

She returns with four volumes and six accordion folders.

"Here you go! But they're a bit of a mess." Cindy giggles and adds, "...you can sort them if you want. Can't pay you, but here..." she slides them onto my desk. "I'll be back. Let me know if you find something totally cool!"

Left alone, I gently open the first book. The newsprint is fragile and discolored, as if the county no longer could afford the heavy, rich vellum of earlier years. When I come to the possible dates when Luke Lane might have left Grandma "for the neighbor lady," I hold my breath. I tip the ledger to the window to catch the light. Turn pages. Nothing.

In the third volume, six pages in, I hit the mark. 1931. This time, Luke Lane's signature is clear and heavy, as if the letters are weighted with guilt and blame. But it crosses my mind, that maybe they are precise and clear because he now feels he has chosen the right woman.

I study the other signature: Angelica Marie Sandborn. Above the name, I hold my hand as if I hold a pen and I trace Angelica Marie Sandborn and it is in the tracing I imagine Angelica's fear. Angelica's name, barely a wisp of letters. Tentative. Her name seems to float above the paper as if she didn't want to write her signature. As if a mistake had been made. As if, were she able, she would reach out and carefully, carefully pull the fine line of ink up, off the paper, and remove it and herself from a marriage that should never have happened.

"You doin' okay?"

Cindy's voice jars me to attention. Pulls me away from a dream. I close the book.

"Yes, thanks." I don't control the curt cut of my words.

Cindy looks over the open ledger I'd studied earlier. She inches closer. She points to the lilies surrounding the ornate letters on Grandma Millie's wedding certificate. "They are beautiful aren't they, these old wedding certificates?" Cindy sighs. "The new ones, they aren't anywhere near as beautiful. And then away I go again, wondering what happened. Did they have lots of kids? How long did they live? Did they have grandkids?"

I step back and see the earnestness in Cindy's eyes—eyes wide with the care of her questions.

Cindy's voice increases in enthusiasm, "The best part is that, when I take a break, over lunch or sometimes at night, I make up stuff about how marriages turned out. Happy stuff. Thank goodness the divorce papers are all in Spokane. Like divorces weren't allowed here! Can you imagine that? So, I get to look at the best papers. The happy papers. Like, right there. Millicent Sarah. Isn't that a beautiful name?" she asks.

"My grandmother."

"Wow! Your grandmother? That's something! Right there. And your grandfather, a Luke? Mildred and Luke! Bet they were a fine pair." She looks up, all smiles, "Tell me your name again. I saw it on the form, and I forget."

"Sarah."

"That's right! Sarah. Like your grandma! This is so exciting!" Her enthusiasm spills around the dry, dusty room. She snaps her gum and grins, "She still alive?"

"I just lost her. Just."

"Oh, that's so sad. But you got to see her? To know to come here and look her up?"

I don't want to share my grandmother's silence. The secrets my family has kept.

"Yes," I answer. "But, Cindy, I'd love to have a little time alone. Would that be okay?"

"Oh, sure. I know how it is. People like to have quiet time."

I reopen the closed ledger. Land sales, Business licenses. A single arrest for drunkenness. Then in the middle of 1932, I find a page marked DEATHS. I can't believe the names, the dates, the three of them:

The first name: ANGELICA MARIE (SANDBORN) LANE, JUNE 19, 1932

The second name: BABY LANE, JUNE 19, 1932

The third name: LUKE JACOB LANE, JUNE 20 1932.

The air is heavy. I can't breathe. I hear the ominous sound of the slowly twisting fan. I try to think of anything, everything, but those three names.

"You okay?" Cindy asks.

I jump. I hadn't heard Cindy come up behind me. I shake my head, "yes."

"You sure? You look like you could use that Coke."

I place my arm on the book's page so Cindy can't see what I've discovered.

"Looks like you found something!"

Desperate to be alone, desperate to have more information, desperate not to talk to Cindy, I ask, "You said there were newspapers here in the building. I need some copies of the Gaitsberg newspaper."

"Coming right up! They're in the basement. You can't go down there to get them. I can! What do you need?"

My heart races. If I ask her for the days I want, I fear Cindy will read them. She'll read them and demand we discuss whatever she finds. I ask, "June and July, 1932. Is that possible?"

"Well, sure, but, that's a lot of newspapers."

"What if you bring two weeks at a time?"

"Great! I can carry that many. Be right back!"

Cindy returns with her arms full. "You're in luck! Wasn't that much. The newspapers were pretty skinny then. Not much happens in June. Just like now. June and July are slow, slow, slow." Cindy lays the papers in front of me.

"Thanks."

"Except, wait till you read what happened. A big, big deal! There was a murder! Can you imagine? Here in Gaitsberg? Probably the only murder in our history! After you find the stuff you're looking for, look for the murder! Not hard to find…big headlines. I wanted to stop and read it, but when I've a customer, like you, I'd get in trouble if I took time to read. Later. When you're done, leave it right on top and I'll read it going back down the stairs, I can't get in trouble for that."

"Thank you, Cindy. Thanks a lot."

"I know you'll want to read the wedding stuff first, cause that's why you're here. And the wedding descriptions are always great—cake size, punch flavor, who caught the bouquet, who cried. People around here do love weddings!"

"Thanks, Cindy."

A tentative couple in farm clothes stands at the door. I point, "I think you have more customers."

"Oh, yeah! Got it!" Cindy says and waves and then calls to the couple, "Be right with you!"

On Monday, June 20, 1932, a small announcement at the bottom of the front page of *The Gaitsberg Daily* is weighted with a black rimmed border:

> We regret to inform our readers that Angelica Marie (Sandborn) Lane, longtime resident of our fair city, died today in childbirth. Her infant daughter lived long enough to be baptized by the Reverend Aldus Anderson. Baby Lane was baptized, Marie Louise Lane.
>
> Dr. Swanzy explained that after a very difficult delivery, Mrs. Lane passed over peacefully, with her child in her arms. Services will be held this Saturday at Mt. Zion Lutheran Church.

My hands shake as I unfold each day's paper.

And then I find what I didn't know I had been looking for: Tuesday, June 21, 1932. I open another black bordered newspaper.

The headline reads: GLAD I DID IT. LUKE LANE SHOT DEAD. There is a photograph of three coffins. There are also photos of the dead: Luke Lane and Angelica Marie (Sandborn) Lane. There is no photo of the baby, Marie Louise Lane. At the bottom of the article is a picture of my Uncle Gabe. He is seventeen years old. Handcuffed. Held by two men. He is the murderer: Gabriel Luke Lane.

Gabe, the uncle I've only seen as a silent, white haired man in a sanitarium, in the photograph is a gangly boy in overalls, with thick eyebrows, the only part of him that seems to carry any weight. He glares at the camera. On either side of him are two men in three piece suits with badges on their lapels.

Then I study the other two photographs of Luke and Angelica.

Luke Lane is handsome. The photo from the attic. I study him: he wears a fedora tilted at a jaunty angle; his face is a contrast of darks and light: white teeth, heavy eyebrows, piercing eyes, deep creases around a wide smile. He looks like a Wild-West version of Humphrey Bogart.

Angelica Marie appears hardly more than a child. The photo is of her high-school graduation. She is all in white. Her hair is pulled back from her face, gathered behind an ivory comb. Curls rest on her shoulders where they barely touch a strand of tiny pearls. Her dress is cross-stitched and pleated. Her hands hold a shock of lilies.

Under the headline, I read:

Gabriel Lane has been arrested for the shooting of his father, Luke Jacob Lane, at the Sandborn homestead. The only witness to the murder was Theodore Sandborn. He is in seclusion, unable to speak of the death of his daughter and his only grandchild. His attorney, Matthew Headly, said he spoke for Theodore Sandborn when he said, "May Luke roast in hell."

The Lane boy, seventeen years old, turned himself in to Sheriff Stephen Bova, at the County Court House. Gabriel Lane announced to the Sheriff, showing no remorse and no emotion, "I shot my dad. He's dead. I'm glad he's dead." Sheriff Bova stated that after making the announcement, Gabe Lane, home on a visit from Medical Lake Hospital for the Insane, was being held in custody at the county jail.

Gabe's mother, Millicent Sarah Lane (nee Bernham) states that her son has been severely ill this past year and had been committed to Medical Lake. "I visit him as often as I can," Mrs. Lane stated. Mrs. Lane said that this was the first home visit Gabriel was allowed since his commitment a year ago.

"Gabriel Lane was always a strange child," commented Gabe's English teacher, Miss Stephanie Fortnight. She believes that Gabe was devastated by the divorce of his parents and the marriage of his father to his neighbor, Miss Angelica Sandborn.

Dr. Swanzy declared that Luke Lane died instantly. This unfortunate death came the day after the tragic childbirth death of Luke Lane's wife, Angelica Marie (Sandborn) Lane, and their infant daughter. Husband, wife, and child will be buried this Saturday. Services will be held at Mt. Zion Lutheran Church.

At the direction of Judge Clarence Toombs, Gabriel Lane will be returned to the Medical Lake Sanitarium to be held under strict observation. He has not spoken since his confession. He will be restrained and placed in isolation.

We are terribly saddened by this tragedy. We ask the citizens of Gaitsberg to remember in your prayers Angelica, her dear child and Angelica's father, Theodore Sandborn.

I am not surprised that no one is asked to pray for Gabriel Lane.

I fold the papers. I arrange them in the order they were handed to me. I close my eyes and think of the uncle we visited from the time I can remember. At the gate, the guard would take all of our names and when he asked who we were visiting, Grandma Millie would answer, "Gabriel Luke Lane." She'd say his name in a proud, clear voice, like he was very, very important. When they visited, Grandma would hold Gabriel's large, farmer's hands gone soft and pink. His nails were trimmed short. His hair was downy and if the sun hit it just right, it made him look like he had a halo. Finally, my mother would say, "Let's let Grandma have her time alone."

Of those trips what I remembered most was Grandma Millie telling her silent son that she loved him. No matter what, she loved him.

I finish stacking the newspapers. I open the book to look one last time at my Grandmother's marriage certificate.

"You doin' okay?" Cindy asks.

"Yes, thanks."

Cindy's unfazed. She looks over my shoulder and says. "No question, that's one of the prettiest wedding announcements ever." Cindy and I stand next to each other. The embossed lilies on the certificate are caught in ribbons of lilac and gold. The sunlight from the tall arched windows lies on the page like a blessing. The warmth of the page touches my hand.

I ask, "Tell me, if you were to ascribe an emotion to my grandmother's signature, what would you say?"

"Ascribe?"

"Make up stuff. Like you do. What comes to mind?"

Cindy bends over the page. She squints her eyes. "This is hard. I've only ever done this for myself."

"Pretend you don't know it's my grandmother. What word would you use to describe her?"

"She was young, wasn't she?"

"Yes, she was young."

"Well, she makes real clear, strong letters." Cindy screws her eyes and closes them and then her words pop out, "I'd say *hope*. I'd say her name is full of hope. Want to know why?"

I nod.

"Because look at how round the o's are. And her t's are real straight. And the M on Millicent is a really big deal. No hesitation. She just writes it right out like she knows what she's doing. She might have been young, but you can tell she was strong! And I bet she had a big wedding! Did she? Did you find it?"

"Yes," I say, "It was a beautiful wedding. I'm sure she had a beautiful dress."

"I love helping people find their memories," Cindy says. "Like for you. Weren't you surprised at how you can find stuff?"

"Yes," I say and then I do something totally out of character, I give Cindy's bony little shoulders a hug. "You do a good job."

"Oops! That couple is waiting for the plat of their land! I'll be back!"

I leave before Cindy returns. My footsteps echo as I walk down the empty hall, toward the bright, warm sunshine. I have not learned who seduced and who was seduced. I don't know why love changed. I know very little about my grandmother's wedding. I have learned horrible things happened, more horrible than I could have imagined. I know that love can damage and love can make you strong. But, thanks to Cindy, I come away assured of one pure truth that I believe more than anything else I've ever believed: my grandmother was strong.

Maybe Grandma Millie never told me the whole story because she was so strong.

At the top of the Court House steps, the warm air embraces me and I draw in the summer smell that will, as weeks slide by, become the rich return of harvest. On my right, below the lions, the two men sit in deep concentration as one moves to check-mate. On my left, the blind woman measures the red baby sweater with the spread of her hand, nods, and places the to-be-finished sweater in her knitting bag. With satisfaction she lifts her face to the sun.

At the merry-go-round, the three children give a hardy push, their feet hit the dry, dusty earth, and they jump on. As they slow, the youngest child, a little girl in Osh-Kosh overalls, waves a pudgy hand at me and calls, "Hey lady, give us a push!"

"Sure," I answer. I place my bag beside the steps and run to the edge of the turning disk. I push. The children hang on, gleefully screaming.

"Join us!" a child yells.

I hesitate.

"Grab the bar!"

I watch the turning disk, bleached white, worn by hundreds of feet.

"Inside foot first!"

I grab a curved bar. I place my foot on the scuffed surface.

"Now your other foot!"

I jump on for the ride.

ABOUT THE AUTHOR

Photo by Douglas Yaple

Karen Lorene spends one half of her life writing (*Buying Antique Jewelry: Skipping the Mistakes*; *Building a Business, Building a Life*; *ABeCeDarian*; *Dancing With Bear*; and now, *Tilling Time/Telling Time*). The other half of her life she maintains Facèré Jewelry Art Gallery in Seattle, Washington. The in-between hours are focused on her husband, Don, and a rescue puppy, Sam. They live happily together in a houseboat community on Lake Union. Oh, and her cat just jumped on her lap to remind her not to forget to mention her. Helga. All together.

And the photos? They are a mix of real and borrowed relatives. Identify them as you will.

Made in the USA
Charleston, SC
21 November 2014